THE
CROWN HOLDER

- A DARK SEASON -

The Crown Holder (A Dark Season - Book 1)
Copyright © 2020 W.C. Little
www.thecrownholderseries.com

This is a work of fiction. Names, characters, places, brands, media, and incidents are either the product of the author's imagination or are used fictitiously.

Library of Congress Cataloging-in-Publication Data is available upon request.

ISBN: 978-1-7348319-1-7

Cover by: CTS Graphic Designs

THE
CROWN HOLDER

- A DARK SEASON -

W.C. LITTLE

- THE CAROLINGIAN DYNASTY -

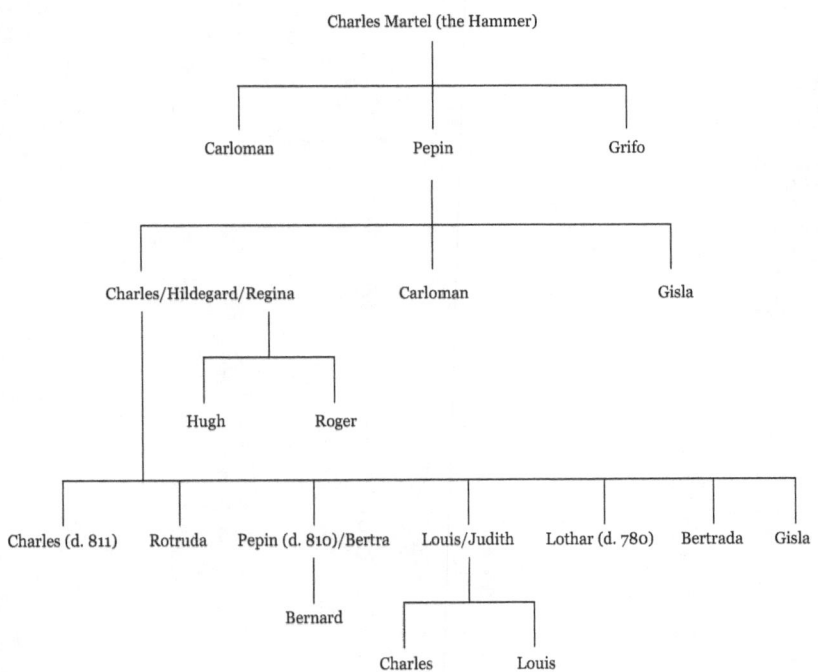

Author's Note: This Carolingian family tree has been modified to accommodate the story's plot. Some historical characters have been removed and, in some cases, fictional characters inserted. For instance, Louis had four known sons and only Charles was born by Judith. Also, only two of Charlemagne's wives are illustrated (and only 7 of at least 9 children by Hildegard are shown).

I

- A DARK SEASON -

Three hooded cloaks made their way along the back side of a patchwork fence that separated the freedom of deep snow and thick woods from the enclosure of dark, iced mud. They scurried along the fence line, hunched over like laboring beasts. Their feet punched through the snow with each step. The cloaks that covered their bodies and heads were worn and tattered; they were protection from the burning cold rather than for secrecy. It was the last few hours of winter darkness, when the nights lasted twice as long as the days. Farmers and slaves would be up and making their way to the barn before too long. They could slow down when their task was complete, but for now, the opportunity was brief and uncertain.

The three made their way past the fence and along the barn's high wall, which had planks nailed along the bottom section to cover cracks and holes. The barn was twice as high and large as any other structure in the small clearing of huts and hovels that counted as a village along the outskirts of the empire. The barn belonged to the community and no single person, placing its value beyond estimation. The wooden latch on the side door had to be wrenched free from its place, which caused the doves resting on the rafters inside to flee to the safety of the night. The three robes froze, listening to their surroundings. They hoped to learn whether the flight of the birds had any ripple effect on the quiet night. Once inside, the three removed their hoods. Silver mist from exertion and sighs announced their satisfaction that the most difficult part of their task had been accomplished without disruption.

Gudula maneuvered though the void inside the barn, feeling around with her hands. She relied on the limited moonlight that cut its way through the open flap atop the front of the barn. Gudula found an oil lamp on a large grinding stone far from the hay and stocks of wood piled along the opposite wall. She removed a small nest of crushed thistledown from a satchel she carried under her cloak and laid it down on the stone. Gudula swiftly scraped her flint on a steel pad over the dried twigs until she had a flame. The lamp was then set alight within the span of a few breaths. She maneuvered around the front of the barn and found another lamp that she took back to the stone and lit off the first.

The portion of the barn became awash in dull golden light. The three women were pleased with what they saw. The space teemed with life. The silence and serenity outside the barn was replaced by motion and sound within. Stirring animals were frightened by the unwanted visitors and filled tight spaces to create a safe distance. Sheep ruled the population as they moved in mass huddles at every motion from the women.

Katku and Pavla huddled with Gudula around the light as

Katku placed her cloth bag on the table next to the lamps. The lamplight illuminated their appearance. Katku and Gudula looked like decrepit old men. Their faces were worn by years of labor and hard living. Their teeth had long left their mouths, and each sucked on their top lips out of habit. They were short and could have been mistaken for dwarfs that the people of these parts of the endless woods believed existed. Their heads were shaved to stubble as well. Katku had a skinned socket in place of a left eye. The lord of her village much farther away to the north had put a burnt blade to her years earlier. He said it was payment for staring too fondly at young men. Despite her appearance, on her face was a look of delight that spread to the other two.

Pavla stood out from the other two. She was young, tall, and had auburn hair that shown like red fire in the lamplight. She was at the age of marriage and appeared out of place, yet her eagerness at being with the others was obvious. She had studied the other women's movements as intently as any apprentice.

Katku and Gudula's missing hair was intended as a warning for others to not approach them. They were shaved bald with every full moon. It was a common treatment for women who didn't meet expectations in a world of unknown rules and harsh penalties. Local priests had deemed them unholy as rumors of witchcraft and pagan rituals were common in the remote hills close to the western edge of the Lech River. The two had managed to evade the more severe consequences of the church's justice to date. The events of that evening would mortally change their luck, if they were found. The risk had grown inconsequential, however. There were signs all around them. Signs that screamed in a cavern of silence. Signs that brought worry and uncertainty at a time when there were few explanations. Answers had to be uncovered, and there were precious few both chosen and entrusted to find them.

The church in Rome pressed the old Merovingians to bring the crucifix to Alemannia. It was an uneasy change for the people to accept, more so for the people far from the cities and towns, in those remote places, the blessings of trade and the order of the church could not be seen or felt. In Alemannia's dark forests, there were trees, water, and animals. That is what the people knew and saw. It was simple. They worshipped what brought them life. A distant language about a faraway god would do nothing to tame the pains of empty stomachs or keep their children from dying. Some in Alemannia listened and took hold of the new ways. Some pretended to for fear of their lives. Others stayed silent and invisible as best as they could.

These three women chose to stay silent, although their acts at times kept them visible. Pavla was quickly becoming an outcast younger sister from a minor noble family. She had managed to avoid marriage and kept to the forests rather than heed the calls to sabbath service. Her older brother's distant affection and influence had so far kept the priests and their razors at bay. In her village, Gudula was the only midwife who miraculously hadn't lost a child at birth. She was seen by those that mattered as a necessity rather than a problem. Katku placed a curse on her parish priest with her one good eye. She had done so once before to great effectiveness. That knowledge put the priest she scorned in more fear of the deities of the forest than of his own god.

Katku opened a fur-covered pouch and removed a series of

steel blades small enough for fragile hands to safely wield. She caressed each one and kissed them gently on the edge before setting them back down. She then pulled out two copper bowls. Her bowls were tarnished by time and wear, yet she looked upon them fondly as if they were made of gold. She sang quietly to herself and moved around Pavla to place a bowl on each side of the blades.

Gudula had her own satchel, which she sat on the ground. She loosened the drawstrings and scooped the contents with her hands. She held a human head and gently placed it between the lamps. It was no simple skull. The top had strands of hair that would have touched shoulders. The hair looked like wet red thread in the light. Its gray skin was tight, as if the tissue underneath had been eaten away. There were no eyes. They withered and oozed away under the eyelids, leaving a shine on the skin below as though the head was crying. The nose appeared to have dissolved and caved in on itself. The upper lip seemed to have shrunk and was cleft such that the white and brown teeth were exposed. For its grim appearance, the face almost looked like it was smiling.

Gudula warned Pavla of the skull before they came to the place. She did not want to frighten the girl with the head's presence but comforted her on the necessity of bringing it along. "She was my master who taught me all that I know. I hope that, one day, you will love me so much to bring me with you on strange and wonderful nights like this."

Everything was in place. It was time to say what needed to be said.

Gudula looked to her sisters. "I am not blind," she said. "I have seen this coming from far away in time. There is no stock, no harvest for the children because the men with their armored horses and golden towers hoard them when troubled times come upon us . . . and times are troubled. We have seen wars before. They are as natural as the snow. This, we see and feel, is different. We are at the dawn, before new wars of unseen horror fall on us. The coming slaughter is now only a whisper in our ears. It is only whether we choose to listen. That is what may save us from the piles of bodies that will be left unburied and unburned, roaming the hills in anguish between this world and the next. We must listen. Here. Tonight."

Gudula sprinkled flakes into Katku's bowls and continued softly. "The time is at hand. People are frightened and the priests have no words that bring comfort. They say pray to their god. They order us to pray with their holy prince of Rome, who wishes to straddle all the world and piss and shit in our mouths. A prince intent on spreading a single tongue we don't understand, in praise of a single god we do not know. This shall be our time, when we show our people the price of wearing the sheep's fleece. The people must throw off the shackles of the stone church and return to the forests. It is this way. It has always been this way and always will be. That is why they come to us, searching for answers that look them in the face. I fear we will grow drunk on the tears of the feeble."

Katku rubbed her stubbled head as if to clean it of dust. "Our cattle lay in the snow," Katku added. "The owls seek prey in the sunlight. The mountains tremble and boulders roll. All is upside down. Before the last hunter's moon came full, we saw a fire in the sky that fell to earth and lit up the night as bright as day. The place where it kissed the land was burned and dead. Thick trees were laid sideways as neatly as autumn wheat. Powerful gods are at work."

Pavla was eager to join in. "Yes. We saw it as well. It came from the eastern skies. They say that is where the true wars will come from. Not only wars of flesh, but wars of the soul. The eastern gods are our gods in all but name. They are angered by the priests and their bleeding god. The eastern armies will be the blade used by the gods to punish us all."

The three women calmly stepped from the table and took off their robes, letting them fall to their ankles. The nakedness of Gudula and Katku showed their age. Gray skin and black veins draped over bones that were brittle and curved by time. Pavla's milky white and smooth skin betrayed her youth. She broke from the other two and walked into the center pen that kept the village animals warm from the cold and safe from the wolves. Goats, cattle, and sheep, grown and small mixed together.

This was a night meant for sheep. Grown sheep had been newly sheared for the winter looms, showing that their summer fat had waned. Autumn lambs still clung close to their mothers. The sheep mass moved with every shuffle from Pavla left to right. Pavla moved as nimbly as a child. She dove at the back hooves of a lamb and clinched a leg. It bleated and squirmed and struggled to escape her grasp. Pavla rose, covered in filth yet smiling widely. She pulled the lamb tight to her chest like a newborn babe. She sang to ease the bleating that would not help it that night. Pavla brought the lamb's head close to her heart and approached Katku. Pavla opened her mouth and held out her tongue. Katku gently slid the edge of a small knife down the center of Pavla's tongue, which dripped black blood on the head of the lamb. Pavla swiftly repeated a whispered prayer as blood began to form at the corners of her mouth.

All the gentleness that Katku used on Pavla was not given to the lamb. Katku placed her soiled knife between Pavla's breasts and the neck of the lamb and ripped it violently back toward her. The lamb let out one last sad bleat and fell limp. Gudula had positioned herself on the ground with two bowls in hand, looking to catch the glistening cascade of blood. Gudula kept repeating her own prayer in a low whisper. Katku reached for Pavla and gently kissed her bleeding mouth. Katku pulled back, caressing Pavla's face, and then put her hands to the lamb's neck to wet her fingers with blood that she ran across her forehead.

Katku hung the lamb upside down and Pavla squeezed its limp body of every drop of red life within it. The bowls filled and brimmed with steam. When the stream of blood turned to drops, Katku gently placed the carcass on the table and kissed it.

Pavla then went to her knees and smiled up to Gudula, who caressed her cheeks. "Have faith," Gudula said. "You will do well, flower. This is your first step into a new world." The words were to put Pavla at ease about the struggle to come. The girl laid flat on the dirt and hay as she nervously wiped her chest and caved stomach. Gudula straddled her waist and slowly held Pavla's arms to the ground by her wrists. Katku took the bowls of blood in each hand and positioned herself over Pavla's head. She began to sing a soft song with the beautiful voice of a child. Pavla closed her eyes and opened her mouth. Katku began to pour the blood into Pavla's mouth, slowly at first, then steadily enough to overflow Pavla's lips.

"Swallow. Swallow fast."

Pavla gulped and the red tide receded only to rise with more blood. More gulps and more extolling to swallow the cooling blood. When both bowls were empty, Katku dropped them and closed her legs on Pavla's ears. She pinched Pavla's nose and held her jaw shut with conjured strength. Pavla's eyes bulged in response. She squirmed and writhed but could not free herself or find air. Gudula bellowed with the voice of a lord.

"Accept it! Accept it all!"

The struggling waned and the brightness of Pavla's eyes went pale. Katku loosened her legs and Gudula sat up from Pavla's chest. The ceremony was fraught with danger. Hold too little and the symbols would prove false. Hold too long and Pavla would die with no message. They would wait with anticipation. Pavla finally blinked and the other women knew to reset their grasp. Pavla's stomach caved in deeply, and with all her body's force, she sprayed out the blood fed to her under sacred song, splattering all three. The older women let go of their sister, who convulsed and gasped for life. She did not rise. She would not rise until the signs had been read. Katku nodded to Gudula, and Gudula began to trace the blotches of upheaved blood on Pavla's heaving chest, connecting the puddles with swirling lines and symbols. Katku cocked her head to the side and whispered to herself as Gudula traced on the girl's skin. It was done.

Gudula began her divination. "I see . . . I see the black eagle of Frankia. Its proud head has turned into two. Two heads for one crown."

Katku twisted her head and attempted to divine the signs herself. "One head is Charles, the other his son."

"No! The old prince is gone. He is no more." Katku cringed in astonishment at what she herself could not read.

Gudula continued. "The old prince reached for the sun. He climbed high out of a desire to live in the heavens with the moon and the stars. His head has been severed, yet the other does not hold the crown."

Katku had become as frustrated as a noble woman who paid old seers for their sight only to be mired in riddles. "But who? Who are the two eagle heads?"

Gudula could only shake her head. She continued to study what was written in black. "It does not say." She focused again for more. "Rivals shall sprout from the corpse of Charles like spring shoots. The eagle will grow more heads and they will tangle themselves in war and deceit. They will not understand the true crown they covet, the thorned crown of their bleeding god. They shall be punished for their vanity, yet they who suffer most will be the woman who minds the fields and the man who marches in rank. Frankia will drown in blood."

Katku stepped back. She had begun to understand Gudula's prophecy. Gudula nodded and smiled as Katku and Pavla listened on. "The spawn of the Hammer has cursed us with their Roman pride and insults to the ancient gods." Gudula then reached for the others' hands and continued. "We shall tell all who will listen and yearn for truth in place of fear. Tell them to leave their cities and return to the forests they once roamed. They must return to the sheltering arms of Walcar's gods. I have seen it. A new season is upon us. It is the season for rivals who delight in the death of Charles. A dark season for those who lust for his thorned crown!"

* * *

Yoannis woke from the scene in the barn. It was a foreign land. Some nameless place in the north, far removed from the warm sands and sea of Alexandria. His great inhale was evidence that the dream was a fight each time. It was a struggle that grew more intense in his mind night after night. While he wouldn't admit it aloud, a part of Yoannis wanted to stay longer, to learn more, but he feared that the empty path between the vision world and the real one would trap him for eternity.

The wretched dream had him wake in a pool of his own sour sweat. Reality returned as he looked around his dark and simple quarters. Peter came through the doorless entryway, holding a clay oil lamp. It was confirmation that the vision was over.

"Are you well, Father Yoannis? I heard you cry out again."

Yoannis gave a quick nod and suddenly realized he had yet to exhale the great gulp of air that brought him back awake. "Yes, Peter. I am fine." He sat up in his small cot and reached for the brass water bowl perched at his side. He rubbed water violently over his eyes, letting it drip down his chin. "They have names now. It is like I can feel their emotions and stories. Their fears and hopes. They seem to feel a sense of joy and anticipation, although their world is falling into an abyss. Like the black monks who are eager for Armageddon. So very far from monks, though."

The dreams of the last few days were unlike those he had experienced before; the recent dreams made him feel as if he was wrapped in a sack of sleep and thrown in the sea. Freeing himself from the cloth of his confinement would only be rewarded by drowning as he swam for the surface. That was how helpless it felt to wake from his nightmares.

"Should we pray?" Peter asked.

"Pray? It hasn't worked yet. We prayed before, yet the vision has only grown worse. More powerful. Clearer."

"Let me fetch my papers and I can record your thoughts. We must be quick, before the vision fades." Although twice his age, Peter was Yoannis's scribe and servant. He left the lamp for his own quarters and quickly returned.

"Witches are a northern thing. Pagan women that both heal and kill, controlling life in place of God." Yoannis shook his head in confusion. "They are meant to scare children and women. They do not frighten me, though. That is not what they want. I believe they mean to guide me because I have claim over what others covet."

"You are the bishop of Alexandria, Father Yoannis, and should have no fear of any cursed pagan. God rests his divine touch on your shoulder. In your dream, did they take a calf again?" Peter asked.

Yoannis ignored the question. "There was a third woman this time. I have not seen her before. She was young and excited. She was . . . How do I describe it? Their . . . muse. She was naked and painted in the blood of a lamb."

"Sweet Jesus!" Peter crossed himself and pulled a stool over to a small square table against the far brown wall. He sat down and began to write frantically.

"This time they spoke of Charles the Frank, that he has died.

The lead witch spoke of a black eagle with two heads. Charles's standard is the black eagle. The rest was babble to me, a riddle I cannot understand."

Peter paused and raised his head. "Little divinity in that. The emperor is quite old." Yoannis gave his servant a frown that sent Peter's head back down to his paper. "Did they once again mention the crown by chance?"

"Yes! I nearly forgot! What did she say? Charles's rivals will seek the crown of thorns. Yet I do not understand why. The women seemed to think he possessed it."

Both men stared at each other for a brief moment, then stood up. Yoannis immediately grabbed a lamp and quickly followed Peter out of the room, through the maze of dark chambers, and into the silent night. They crossed the wide sand path that separated the living quarters from the rest of the church. On the right wall of the side entrance to the church was a torch that growled with strong flames. To the left of the simple wooden door was a massive guard in a full-length black cloak. The guard grabbed the hilt of his sword in reaction to the approaching men. Few churches required sword-carrying guards; this church, however, was ancient and core to the Coptic faith. Some souls treasured what lay within. As the torch illuminated the silhouettes, the guard bowed his head and went to one knee. The metal latch to the door echoed through the night air when Peter lifted it free. Yoannis grabbed the torch and nodded to the guard.

The principal area of the church was the alter room where the Coptic priests gave holy communion and doled out blessings. The void behind the alter was taken up by various pedestals and empty shelves. They held many of the church's relics, which the

faithful from throughout the Mediterranean had come to venerate for centuries.

There was a simple set of downward-leading stairs at the
center of the back wall. Narrow steps, as deep as a man was tall,
had been carved out of the stone floor. Yoannis didn't know the
story of the room that held the church's precious relics, but he
had always felt as if it was the oldest part of the building, perhaps going back to before the time of Christ and the Romans.

Yoannis reached inside his robe and pulled out an iron cross
that had its bottom plank shaped in the fashion of a key. He
stepped down the stairs and out of Peter's sight. Only when the
lock snapped open did Peter follow Yoannis below. The fire from
Yoannis's torch was forbidden inside the reliquary room, but
Yoannis was the bishop of Alexandria and as such held the same
rank as the pope of the church of Rome.

"Fetch the pale of water from up top, Peter, just to be safe."
Yoannis held the torch high and scanned the cramped room. It
was four walls of red sandstone, simply and poor. He held the
only key and no one was allowed to enter without the bishop
being present. He had been involved in moving the relics to the
alter area each morning for the last six years. Nothing appeared
out of place.

Yoannis approached a large dulled silver reliquary that sat in
a carved cubby hole in the back wall. It was covered in a blanket
of dust. Unlike most other relics in the possession of the Copts,
this one was not brought out for the faithful to seek or pray to.
It remained hidden from man and immune to time and touch.

Yoannis handed the torch to Peter and carefully removed
the heavy case from its home. He lifted the pitched lid and

motioned for Peter to bring the torch closer. The men saw, lying gently on a pillow of faded silk, the crown of thorns that had so famously adorned Jesus's head. Peter smiled and crossed himself. Yoannis sighed and scratched the back of his head. It was undoubtedly the original crown or at least the one Yoannis had looked upon countless times since he had been made bishop years earlier. It was beautiful in its raw simplicity. The crown might have been unremarkable to average eyes when compared to souvenirs sold to pilgrims in Jerusalem. Yoannis, however, knew where the ends twisted, where thorns had been lost to time or plucked off out of greed.

"Thanks be to Christ," Yoannis said. "It has not been touched."

Peter spoke in Yoannis's ear even though the men were alone. "If men, powerful men, will come for the crown, then perhaps we should hide it. Give it to Pope Leo? We Copts are sheep that cannot fend off the Muslim wolves that circle us this very moment. Send it off to the pope perhaps?" Peter crossed himself again, in fear of future times of trouble.

Yoannis kept his voice strong, hoping to invigorate Peter. "I would rather we put the crown to flames before we hand the crown to Rome. Rome is a den of debauchery. Vain men who lust for gold and care little for our Savior. I do not care for the desires of the princes of Europe. The scrolls tell us that the crown has powers. It will give the holder absolute power and authority over Christians and pagans alike. We cannot give the crown to those who seek personal gain."

"Then what do we do, master?" Peter asked.

"It is not for us to take action to see these visions of mine come to truth or to prevent their happening. That is not the way of the Copts. We serve God and protect what has been charged to us. It has been this way from the beginning. Have faith. Besides, these dreams may mean something different. For all I know, they may have nothing to do with our Savior's crown of thorns."

Yoannis gently returned the lid and placed the heavy silver box back in its resting place. He said a silent prayer then rose and dusted himself off. He looked around the room, relieved that the famed relic of Christ remained where it belonged and had belonged for centuries. Yet the young bishop of Alexander was vexed by his dreams. He was not a superstitious man, but the intensity and clarity of his dreams were powerful portends that his faith and the fate of his church may be in danger.

"Come, Peter."

"What are we to do now, master?"

"The sun will be up soon," Yoannis said. "You may do your chores or whatever you wish. I am returning to bed for now."

"How can you sleep after all of this, father?"

"I have a feeling the women of the northern forests are not done speaking their mind."

II

- AACHEN -

It was late January of the year 814 in Aachen, the capital city of Frankia. Frankia was the most powerful kingdom in Europe since the fall of Rome hundreds of years earlier. Frankia's borders stretched from the far western shores of Breton to the ice-covered lands of the Danes in the north, down into Saracen Spain in the south, pressing ever eastward to the rising sun and forest tribes beyond the Elbe River. While Aachen was the political heart of the Holy Roman Empire, it was no Rome. It had no strategic importance or geographic advantage to its rulers or people. It lay three days west of the mighty Rhine River and twice as far northeast of Paris, a city of far greater economic significance to the empire.

Aachen was ancient. People had flocked to its hills and valleys for centuries, even before the coming of the Romans. The lands that would eventually evolve into the city of Aachen were originally sought out for a special purpose, one of religion and mystery. Nestled at the foot of one of its larger hills was a tear in the earth's surface from which heated sulfur springs brimmed.

The ancient Gauls that occupied the area before Rome conquered the land held the caves and their dark steaming pools in reverence. It churned hot water from deep within the earth into humid red and yellow caves; they were portals for a people who did not differentiate between the spiritual and natural worlds. The caves were a physical connection to their gods.

When Rome defeated the Gauls and took their lands, the town became a destination for health and relaxation. The Romans believed that the sulfur pools held medicinal properties, and so they swarmed in from larger cities to take advantage of the natural gift. The Franks would follow the Roman lead, eventually changing the city from a secondary home for the privileged and elite to a permanent place for Frankia's aristocracy.

The structures of Aachen told a silent story as well. There was much more to the buildings than the cracked and crumbling Roman roofs and walls that marked the older parts of the city from the new. Their foundations were the earthen ceremonial mounds and priest lodges of the old nature gods. Those structures had been swept clean of their wood and replaced by the marble and limestone structures of the Latin deities known throughout the Mediterranean world. The Romans' actions were intentional; they appreciated the power of any god that could bring them health and fortune.

A blend of surviving local tribes and Latin influence gave birth to the Franks' own language and culture. The stones of many Roman buildings were often repurposed for Christian works to ensure the old ways would be forgotten yet still benefit from the fruits of better minds and stronger backs. In other instances, the inhabitants would not destroy the monuments of their Roman predecessors, preferring instead to add stone and expand boundaries as a symbol that, with the coming of Christ, the Franks had evolved. In time, however, it was apparent to all who visited Aachen that the changes and additions of the Franks brought nothing new and only added to the old Roman mystique.

The sky over Aachen on the evening of January 25, 814, was clear and bathed in moonlight. The air was frigid and silent. Wind did not stir through the hill passes and into the valley of the city. It was a panoramic scene drenched in blue, gray, and white. The star-filled sky was touched by plumes of steam and hearth smoke that enhanced the sense of serenity. The only noise came from the occasional snow mass falling to the earth from tall pines and the echo of barking dogs off in the distance.

The incredible winter storm the week earlier had finally exhausted itself, leaving a blanket of white that covered the valley in which the city rested. There was no movement in the streets, inns, or taverns. The focal point of power for all of Europe would normally buzz with administrators and clergymen moving about at all hours of the day. Telltale signs of urban life, paths of countless footprints and snaking cart tracks of mud and white slush, were nowhere to be seen. Aachen had the signs of an abandoned city. It was a silent omen of difficult days.

On this night, the only semblance of life in the old part of the city was found at the enormous palace complex along the foot of the crescent hills. The palace's fine quarry stones glowed orange in the dim night, lit by a hundred torches along its many-walled exterior. The torches caught the shadows of servants and slaves moving silently between the doors of its buildings. Great braziers burned on both sides of the gigantic bronze double doors of the main entrance, giving the wolf head door knockers the appearance of life and sparks in their eyes. Farther above, in the multiple steeples and ranging parapets that marked the tops and corners of the buildings, the dull light from below reflected off ornate copper tiles.

The palace had little sculpture or decoration. Images of icons or earlier references to older religious themes had been removed by edict of the church in Rome. Nature themes of eggs, pinecones, and pomegranates, which symbolized life and rebirth, were permitted to remain.

Beyond the grand doors to the palace, an animal theme dominated the art and architecture that adorned the interior. Boars, bears, and stags cast in bronze and carved in marble added substance to cavernous spaces. Grand tapestries of rural life and depictions of past battles broke up the monotone stone walls and trapped warmth and sound. Many masterpieces of Italy were placed liberally throughout the rooms. The grand foyer that marked the entrance to the greeting hall in the distance held a multi-tiered lantern chandelier that required its own staff. It was raised and lowered from massive chains by a team of slaves. Below the chandelier, a life-sized elephant cast in hollow bronze and swaying its trunk violently stood on a dais. It was an attention-grabber for those unfamiliar with the palace and its history.

Years earlier, the caliph of Baghdad, Harun al-Rashid, delivered an elephant to the Aachen palace as a token of good-will and peace with the formidable Franks. The beast was the wonder of the city and became a source of national pride. The elephant was named Hannibal after the Carthaginian general who reigned terror on Italy with his own herd a thousand years earlier. Hannibal was kept in a partially enclosed stall along the far west side of the palace. He was fed fruits, grasses, and vegetables from the bounty of the surrounding fields. Not surprisingly, he was cared for better than the eastern slaves who tended to him. Hannibal's fame would extend only a few years, however, as the great beast was unable to fully adapt to the climate and nutrition of northern Europe. His mark on the Frankish people would not go unheralded, as the heartbroken royal family had the massive statue struck in his memory.

Past the foyer was a narrow corridor decorated in ornate dark brown paneling that gave way to a cross section that divided the chambers to the left and right between family and guest. The family living chambers were to the left and took up two floors with endless doors that also accommodated key administrators, personal servants, and, of course, concubines. The emperor's personal living quarters took up the entire back end of the wing, with the residents around him growing in importance based on their proximity to his rooms.

On that night, the main activity in the wing focused on the emperor's quarters, where servants and church-men moved quietly from room to room. Faint sounds of clopping shoes, creaking doors, and wooden tableware shifting from one table to another carried in the air. The emperor's sleeping chambers resided behind thick wooden double doors that remained partially open so servants and staff could enter and leave with limited disturbance inside. Stations were set up along the walls of the chambers. Wooden tables were active with huddled servants and monks working away. There was a sustenance station with fresh water, steaming broth, and porridge. A nursing station was equipped with ground herbs and medicines along with fresh linens. There was also a prayer station where priests knelt over hymn books and scrolls, whispering prayers and songs.

The handmaids and servants in the chambers moved with caution from their workplaces toward the dais, where the emperor's great bed was situated. As they made their way to the elevated bed, they navigated through heaps of lying dogs as well as groups of administrators and courtier onlookers. The water and medicine they brought with them were handed to attending physicians who staved off closer contact.

In the back corner of the chamber, a massive fireplace roared from glowing new logs. Wooden lattice windows remained closed, although a gentle winter breeze running through the corridors outside could be heard blowing when the room sat in silence. In the opposite back corner, a small choir of boys in brown wool robes stood in the shadows, softly singing angelic hymns. They were awash in burnt incense. Flanking the choir were decorative wooden stands holding selections of ancient armor polished to a silver shine. A breastplate was adorned with the crucifix centered upon a fierce gorgon's head. Also among the armor was a Roman centurion helmet with its unmistakable sideways red palm. Unlike the fine steel, the palm made of hair was heavily frayed and had faded from the passage of time.

The focal point of the room was the grand bed of the emperor, perfectly made and untouched but for the pale white and bearded head that protruded from under fine cream-colored sheets. The only sign that life existed within the bed was the steady rising and falling of the surface, timed perfectly by a soft wheezing sound and nasal clicks. The pitiful head belonged to the worn and withered body of Charles, son of Pepin and grandson of Charles the Hammer. He was the protector of the church of Rome and the most powerful man in Europe since the time of the great Caesars. A man of universal fame who was loved and adored by Frankia. He was despised and feared by all others. The world knew him as Charlemagne—Charles the Great.

In the middle of the room, against a spartan stone wall and above the bed of the emperor, was draped a single tapestry. The tapestry almost reached the corners of the walls and represented the work that would have taken a handful of nuns a century to weave. It was a battle scene full of symbolism that only a nobleman's eye could appreciate. The tapestry wasn't a scene of victory but unquestionably Charles's worst defeat. There was nothing complicated about the artwork. There were no fortresses or serene forests in the background, as was typical of the tapestry style of the Franks. There were only two forces on each side, with no banners or symbols to differentiate the two. The left was the standing army of the Franks, adorned in its fine layers of steel with axes and swords raised high, waiting for the slaughter to come. To the right was the charging forces of the Saracens of Córdoba, holding their lances straight ahead, ready to plunge them through shield and mail and into the flesh inside. All the faces were grimaced in anger, screwed and distorted by their lust for death. There was no earth below. No rocks or grass, only a bridge of heroes in pieces, floating in a puddle of blood. There could be no mistaking the scene. It was Roncevaux. It would always be Roncevaux that called the emperor back to the realm of human folly.

The tapestry was a gift from Alcuin, the chief advisor and friend to the emperor. It was given to mark the twentieth year of Charles's reign. Alcuin believed Charles needed a constant reminder of the awful consequences of pride.

Charles did not know what to think of the tapestry when it was first hung in the palace dining hall years earlier. He stared at it for hours, walking back and forth, judging the beauty of the detail and questioning the symbolism. He couldn't understand why his most trusted counselor would invoke the worst day of his reign. It wasn't until Alcuin came from behind the gazing emperor and whispered the Latin words that explained it all. *Memento mori*. Remember, thou art mortal.

Alcuin had taught his friend the lesson long ago, which at the time had not found its way into the young king's heart and mind. Those were the words a slave once whispered in the emperor's ear as he rode in triumph through Rome to the cheers of its citizens. That emperor paid no heed and paid the penalty. Twenty-three stab wounds were the price of pride.

Alcuin had grown worried not only of his master and friend's unchecked hubris, but also of the unsubtle fascination with his own divinity. It was Rome that Alcuin silently blamed. It began to surface years before Charles's anointment by Pope Leo III as Holy Roman Emperor and all the ceremony of Rome that accompanied it. The sin spawned into absurdity through the years thereafter.

Rome's sacred vaults became a treasury for services to be rendered by the new champion of the faith. The arrows that pierced Saint Sebastian were awarded when Charles expelled the cardinals of the late Pope Adrian, who had Leo beaten mercilessly in punishment for charges of heresy. Leo came weeping to the court in Aachen like a child, and Charles took him into his arms.

Leo knew he had a special friend. Teeth taken from the skull of Saint Peter paid for Charles's ouster of the Byzantines from the papal sate of Romagne. More bones, teeth, and hair of other saints would follow. The robe of Christ was the final relic the emperor received from Rome but not the last one Charles coveted. The robe was consideration for opening the lands of the Slavs and Avars to papal missionaries who then traveled with confidence that they could spread the word of God without the fear of harm. Every relic was wrapped in flattery and praise, proclaiming the king of the Franks as God's Augustus. In time, Charles's collection of relics rivaled Rome's. How could the owner not think himself divine?

For Charles, Aachen was a unique place of mystery with a sense of the supernatural, as if the air itself breathed differently. In some ways, it did. Behind the imperial palace, carved into the side of the forest-covered hill, was the source of Aachen's mystery: the "cauldron." It was the famed hot sulfur springs of the empire. During the cold, dry days of winter, the cave-like entry to the cauldron would bleed steam and cover the surrounding trees like a blanket of fog. Old songs of Frankia spoke of the ancient people who performed pagan rites inside the cauldron. At times, and if urgency for divine providence warranted it, these rites would involve human sacrifice. Regardless of the lore of the cauldron and its mysterious springs, it was a place of serenity and reflection for Charles. He loved its rejuvenating waters, embraced the ease and calmness of its dark, misting pools, and felt a sense of connectedness to the area's ancient history and its importance to the land of Frankia. Paris might have been a focal point for prior rulers, but the confident warrior kept his seat of power in the place that spoke more to the idea of Frankia.

Charles had reigned over Frankia for forty-six years, taking the kingdom of his grandfather, the valley between the Rhine and Rhône Rivers, and doubling its domain into an empire. Charles changed the definition of what a monarch could be. He was an unbreakable warrior, a protector of his people, and a symbol of virtue and wisdom that hadn't been seen in centuries. His people flocked to touch his passing hand; his enemies capitulated at his planted feet. Now at the age of seventy-two, his earthly legend forged in eternity, Charles had completed his work and was ready to die.

The physician Sicho routinely checked the emperor's signs. He knew his patient better than he knew himself. Signs of breathing, temperature, and pulse were cataloged by an attending monk. There was no urgency in Sicho's actions, however; he had been studying Charles's condition for three days. The short priest-turned-doctor kept his head hung low and rubbed his neck, occasionally whispering to Alcuin while ignoring all others in the room. While the physician came and went from the bed-chamber every few minutes, Alcuin stood constant watch, thumbing his rosary and turning the pages of the well-worn prayer book Charles had gifted him decades earlier. In addition to Alcuin, a group of well-dressed men was monitoring the scene several respectful paces from the bed. They huddled around tables that held thick round candles burned down to different lengths. They watched all the movement of the room, paying little attention to the emperor's condition. At any given time, the group numbered around eight as they came and left the chamber. The member at the center of the group—Theoderic, Charles's chancellor and tool through which he executed his administrative authority—never left. The other principal member of the group was Einhard, the Irish cleric who often clashed with Alcuin and sided with Theoderic on matters of church and governance; many times, the two concepts were one and the same. While technically a man of the church, Einhard shunned the monk's robe Alcuin continued to wear and instead preferred to dress himself in the pomp found more frequently in the churches of Italy.

Charles was keenly aware of his mortality and, in a series of well-planned edicts, installed his three sons by his long-deceased wife Hildegard as equal rulers of the Frankish empire; it was a self-orchestrated succession plan while Charles was still at the height of his rule. The sons would rule equally, dividing the empire into subkingdoms and sharing in the overall wealth and defense of the realm. It was the same succession Charles was born into. With his brother Carloman in the east, Charles ruled western Frankia until he grew tired of mediocrity and let his ambition rule his senses. He ended the co-rulership after only a few years by the simplest means available to him: Charles had Carloman killed by a poisoning that was said to mimic the sweating plague. Everyone knew yet no one murmured at the true cause of the younger brother's death.

One would assume that the recent deaths of two of Charles's three grown sons would streamline succession for the next generation of Carolingian rulers. Not so. Alcuin nestled in close to

Theoderic's ear, staring at the floor. "Has the red kite sent off to Louis returned yet?" Alcuin asked.

Alcuin was like Charles in many ways. They had many of the same physical attributes to the point that they were often referred to as brothers. Both were a head taller than most other men. They were once considered to have strong builds before their advanced age brought on brittle bones and failing muscles. Despite their balding crowns, they wore their hair to their necks and kept trim beards. Alcuin was no Frank, however. Like Einhard, he was a deacon and scholar from the islands to the west of the mainland. Alcuin was a Northumbrian.

He first met Charles more than fifty years earlier, when the young cleric dazzled Charles's father, Pepin, with his knowledge of classical literature and mastery of the gospels. So impressive was this holy man of seemingly unlimited knowledge and wisdom that Charles convinced Alcuin to stay on at Aachen as chief scholar to the court and counselor on all matters related to the church. It was a topic that was central to Charles's quest for control and domination of the continent. Charles's admiration for Alcuin was so great that he trusted the man with the education and mentorship of his children and grandchildren, hoping to fill them with Alcuin's refined mind. He was to be a contemporary Aristotle to future Alexanders.

Theoderic did not take his gaze from Charles as he whispered in response to Alcuin's question. "We sent three red kites and still await the return of all of them. We were unsure of Louis's location, as the army has been on the move throughout Lombardy. Our last report a week ago suggested that he was leaving Pavia, having reduced the city to rubble. His work there is seemingly complete. He will probably leave Oliver to finish the bloody business. Even though he would most likely shun crossing the Alps this time of year, I thought it a more prudent action to send three and cover all possible options. The road from Lyon seems most likely."

It was not chance that Theoderic chose the words "prudent" and "possible" in the same breath. Theoderic's gift was identifying and eliminating contingencies. If Charles was ever a slave to his emotions or eager to wager on strategic or political alliances, Theoderic would preach patience and reasoning. He was methodical and dedicated to his role and value to the emperor.

Theoderic's appearance and mannerisms matched his persona. There was nothing out of sorts or individualized about him. "I calculate," Theoderic said, "that Louis will have received word in three, no more than four days."

Theoderic was a man of below-average height and hefty frame. He wore a leather skullcap that hid what little hair he had. He was clean-shaven most times, but given the events of the last few days, he had grown in a stubble beard, gray and white, putting his age somewhere in the late fifties. Perhaps the most notable feature of Theoderic was his eyes. They gave the appearance of utter exhaustion. His eyelids drooped along the corners and the bags beneath sagged under the weight of the dark blood within them. He was simple and neat in his appearance, shunning exotic fabrics of the east or color of any kind, preferring instead to dress himself in brown or gray tunics. The only symbol of his authority was the gold necklace across his shoulders and the embossed gold ring he wore on his right middle finger. Gifts from Charles in appreciation of the years of loyal service.

After a minute of silence and keeping with the theme of his last response to Alcuin, Theoderic continued. "I would be grateful if you could help me manage Regina. She is the most difficult of all our emperor's women. She is constantly tugging at my arm, asking for guidance on what she should be doing with her boys at this point. Giving such advice is not my strong suit or my station, as you are more than aware. There is still an empire to manage, and I must not be drawn by the passions of a mourning woman."

Theoderic was a Christian by birth and routine, but at his heart, he was a Stoic. He was a disciple of the writings of Marcus Aurelius some six hundred years earlier. He wasn't the type of man to let his emotions control his decisions, which might have been why Charles chose him for the role of chancellor.

Alcuin looked at Theoderic as the shorter man stared ahead, pulling his head back ever so slightly to study Theoderic's facial response to what he would say next. "Mourning woman?" Alcuin asked. "Our lord emperor lives still, Theo. Such talk is unseemly."

Theoderic, rather than arguing what he saw as the inevitable and preferring to not get off path, simply refocused his intent. "Yes of course. I meant no ill-respect. However, Regina can be difficult to reason with, and I fear I have little time to sit with her and explain the current nature of things. We have important delegates and emissaries not more than a hundred paces from where we stand, eager to know what goes on in this room. I must have the freedom to perform my functions. That was Charles's charge to me. I need your help in this. It is what you are good at."

Alcuin was taken off guard, shifting his eyebrows to a scowl and then turning his gaze back to the bed. "I suppose I shall take that as an attempt at flattery. Yes, I will sit with her, assuming I can find her sober and get through to her. Something about her Aquitanian blood makes it a challenge. She is entitled and prideful."

Theoderic agreed with a single nod. Alcuin had a simple tin cup in his hand. It had a splash of red wine remaining. He peered into the cup's contents. That was the third cup that he could recall. The wine and stress were not agreeing with his age, and he wondered how much longer he would be able to remain absent from his chambers. Alcuin sloshed it around gently as he pivoted the conversation.

"How do you intend to handle the mediation between Bernard and Louis?" Alcuin asked. "They are the faces of two armies tasked to do the empire's business. I wager that only a few days separate the two camps and there is no love between them. There will be a reckoning over enemy spoils and lands when the fighting is over. Do you know Charles's position well enough to deliberate on the matter?"

Theoderic huffed quickly, dropping his head as he talked. "Yes, I know his mind, but it is not his judgment that worries me. It is his authority or, better said, my lack of authority that prevents me from taking action. Will warriors heed the words of a chancellor? Charles wanted—wants—Bernard to have Lombardy, and it only makes sense. Bernard is the king of Italy. Handing him Lombardy only seems fitting, although I do realize that consolidates incredible power in his favor. True, Louis is bringing the Lombards to heel by throwing his own men and coin at the problem, but it cannot be said that Bernard has not earned what Louis won by annihilating the threat of the Avars farther east. When the armies of Bernard scraped up against Louis and General Oliver's troops in the nether regions of the Avarii, it almost meant civil war. Oliver is unquestionably Louis's man, but he and Bernard owe fealty to Charles above Louis. Yet I cannot see Oliver or Louis excepting my deliberation as law. Not while our emperor lies in this dreadful state. With Charles, the hatred every lord holds to the other, even those of his own blood, is dwarfed by their fear of Charles's justice."

Lumping Louis in with Bernard and his own man Oliver interested Alcuin. "And what of Louis? He is co-emperor and not some common duke. Would he permit Lombardy to go to Bernard?" Alcuin asked.

"I think both you and I know the answer to that. Charles needs to wake and put this matter to rest before civil war erupts."

Alcuin could sense that some support was in order and leaned in a little closer to Theoderic. "You speak the truth. It was and still is Charles's authority that the lords fear. You can call the Twelve Peers to action to enforce his words through your mouth in a moment's notice."

Theoderic smiled sheepishly. "Yes, but Bernard has trouble with his ears and Louis enjoys provocation. You and I also know that makes it impossible to gauge Louis's opinion on disputes involving Bernard. His hatred and fear of Bernard blind his reason at times. He would never say that out loud, but we both know that the power and influence Bernard has among the nobles who followed his father. That still concerns Louis deeply, and that power only grows with each battle the boy wins. Remember, old friend, Italy wanted Charles's first son, Pepin, to rule even though our Lord God took him away. Italy wants to see it through, combining all of the old Roman provinces under Bernard's sword." Theoderic let out a sigh. "Giving my opinion on the dispute makes any meeting with the Twelve Peers a fool's errand."

"That may all be so," Alcuin said, "but without a pact in place, Bernard and Louis will certainly be at war by the spring thaw. Two rams looking to knock heads for control of the herd. If there are no territories or compromise that will suit Bernard, our buffer between Frankia and the tribes of the east will be nothing more than a wall made of leaves. I fear the Saracens, too. They are sitting in silence, waiting for opportunities among our southern marches regardless of this treaty in place. All our might sits at the foot of the Alps while our enemies sharpen their swords, staring at each other. Bernard and Louis at war will be all the reason the Saracens and forest barbarians need to unleash their animals on our people again."

It was clear to Theoderic that the low murmur of conversations coming from the other men in the nearby group had come to a halt. The ears of the palace wanted to pry in on the discussion with the two men closest to Charles's mind. Alcuin and Theoderic's own conversation began with whispers and elevated into a casual tone and volume, each man forgetting that their master lay before them, focusing more on the seriousness of immediate responsibilities that governance required. Both the origin and the answer to their predicament lay in front of them, lifting his chest and slowly exhaling with a persistent wheeze. Alcuin bent forward slightly, looking down at his feet as he gently shook each leg, shifting side to side to get his blood flowing again. He realized he had been standing there for hours.

Returning to his whisper, Theoderic responded, "I know the risks, Alcuin, and how this might play out. That is why I asked Seguin of Vasconia to mobilize his forces along the Pyrenees Mountains to move into the southern border area. Eric of Friuli will mind the lands of the Avars and Slavs should Bernard descend upon Louis and Oliver in Lombardy. There was no time to wait on deliberations of all the Peers when just one chancellor will do for now. Order and observance of Frankia's authority will be kept at all costs. These are truly desperate times to come."

"Was that wise?" Alcuin asked. "Louis will undoubtedly learn of this ploy in short order. Calling on Friuli, you give Bernard support in areas he himself is duty-bound to protect. It could be seen as a consent to move against Louis and Oliver."

"Ploy? This is no ploy, Alcuin. It is a necessary measure dictated by a complicated situation. I have consulted with the few Peers within the palace and made the decision. This is the way of Charles's rule. Frankia has given its provinces wide range to govern themselves. It gives us freedom to forge paths elsewhere. When problems arise, the territories touched by misfortune must pay for that freedom. It is the way Charles chose to govern. It is what we are to do, and I continue to pledge myself as loyal to Louis the co-emperor as I do to his father." Theoderic changed his tone; he became less aggressive, replacing his seriousness with a hint of sarcasm. "Now, if you would see to Regina so that I am not harassed the moment I leave this chamber, I would be grateful." Theoderic pinched the bridge of his nose, rubbing each side with his eyes closed, feeling the slight regret for his words. "I am sorry. I am going to try resting for a few hours before preparing for my meetings tomorrow morning. If

Sicho notices any change in our master's condition, please have a servant wake me. I think some rest will do you good as well, my friend."

Alcuin bowed his head to Theoderic in acknowledgment of his suggestion. Alcuin rubbed the top of his head and looked down at the ground, deep in a world of thought. Theoderic left the room and Alcuin nodded to the small choir, showing his approval and silent insistence that they continue on course. Charles would want the comfort of the soothing songs. After scanning the room, he too left in Theoderic's tracks, heading down the opposite end of the dark hall to his own quarters and solitude. The tests and riddles that were to follow would have to wait for a few moments of precious rest.

III

- A PIG NAMED ARGOS -

To the left of the emperor's chamber was the only other room in the palace with grand wooden double doors. It was referred to among courtiers as the queen's quarters, but it was not meant for a single queen—or only queens. In Charles's world, consorts mattered, too. Massive torch sconces were lit on each side of the outer double doors. A simple wooden crucifix sat on the ledge of the stone beam above the doorway. The inside walls of the room were also lined with smaller sconces that were usually well-maintained to keep burning oil from dripping onto the floor. The small pools of oil directly below told that the sconces had been neglected as of late. The candles were intended to flood the grand room with light when the high windows along the opposite wall failed. It was the height of winter, and the short days meant the room would rely on candlelight almost nonstop throughout the day.

Just as the emperor's chamber was closed to women, the areas within the queen's quarters were closed to all men except priests, personal servants, and Charles himself. All the emperor's women were holed up in their chamber, eagerly waiting for information on Charles and the opportunity to sit with him, if only for a few moments. Their concerns and desires would have to wait until further notice; the business of the empire would take precedence, as always. The common women servants that normally serviced the queen's quarters were not permitted past the doorway. Food and drink would be left on the hallway tables directly outside. Soiled towels and linens were piled up outside on watchmen stools placed to either side of the doors. They were silently taken away to be replaced by fresh and folded ones brought over from the kitchen far away. Only those slaves personal to the wives and consorts were permitted to remain. Their lives were directly tied to their mistresses. Most would rather take their own lives than betray the trusted whispers that whirled all around them.

The interior of the chamber was twice the size of the emperor's and rightfully so. It held six small beds that could only comfortably fit a single person. Six small beds for six women that sometimes shared and, other times, fought for Charles's favor and affection. There were three beds on the side of the emperor's shared wall. The other three were on the far side wall. Two of the beds on the far wall had cribs that were pressed against the beds' wooden frames. The cribs hadn't been used in years, although there had been no interest in removing them from the room.

Whereas the furnishings of the emperor's quarters were generally spartan and devoid of life, the queen's chamber was flooded with shape and color. That was the choice of Hildegard, the most revered of Charles's wives and consorts. Although

Hildegard had died more than two decades earlier, her word and wishes were still as respected as Charles's within the palace. It was said that she had earned the informal designation as "head wife" for bearing him his first three sons who would be the basis for Charles's plans of succession. With the role of head wife came many informal privileges, one of which was the right to control the decorations of many parts of the palace, including the queen's quarters. Charles gave no objection to her assumed authority, trusting in Hildegard's judgment to make choices that remained consistent with an image he would approve of, even if certain rooms were off limits to the inspection of priests and other noblemen.

Years after her death, Charles forbade his later wives and consorts from altering what Hildegard had decorated. He wanted her touch to stand as a tribute to her memory. As long as they remained in place, the old emperor kept her alive in his heart. The women in his life who lived under Hildegard's shadow knew that it was pointless to challenge her authority. The risk was the loss of Charles's affection, and that was not worth the effort. The beloved Hildegard still ruled from beyond the grave, which was a part of life her successors learned to accept.

The windowless portions of the walls in the queen's quarters were draped in tapestries such that the lifeless stone walls could not be seen. The tapestries were alive with stories centered around the infant Jesus. He kissed a lamb and taught in the temples. The tapestries also depicted nature scenes of adoring animals that emphasized fertility and motherhood. White lilies and ferns dominated the border images, as did pears and pomegranates. Prominent on the main tapestry over the line of beds was a life-sized depiction of the Virgin Mary with her head bowed in humility. She wore a garland of red roses destined to become her son's crown of thorns.

The stone floor was softened by red and yellow rushes that combined with the black of the war eagle to represent the royal colors of Frankia. The spaces between the high windows were delineated by bronze and marble sculptures of women and children, certainly gifts from Rome itself or past trophies taken from Italian territories. For all of Frankia's might, it had no skilled artisans that could recreate the human figure or show the emotion of the soul through colorless eyes. The art of masters had to be imported. Wooden chests lined the walls underneath the window ledges, and hooks on tall wooden posts held precious dresses that were too fragile and valuable for folding away. In bowls were dried flowers and herbs that lightened the air.

Several small children in sleeping gowns played quietly with tired slaves sitting on the floor. There was a large iron cage positioned in a corner. It was taller than any man and held several wooden perches for finches of every color of the rainbow. The children loved to climb on the bars, frightening the poor birds before being removed by their nurses.

The queen's chamber was connected to the emperor's living quarters by a thick wooden door situated in the center of the shared wall. Peering through the crack of the door that was previously shut were two women. Their bodies were close, as one was stacked on top of the other. Regina was the woman peeking above the other. She was dressed in a floor-length linen gown of light blue. The neck and sleeves were rimmed in fine brown fur. Her long black hair was pulled back. She was tall and unblemished with deep rose lips. Her face was pained from what her eyes witnessed. It was not a natural look for her.

Moschia was the woman squatting below her. She was brown and leathery, dressed in a long black wool robe that blanketed the floor. Her hair color was a mystery due to the tightly wrapped headscarf that covered everything but the features of her face. She had a wrinkle-riddled complexion and purple blotched hands that held the door from closing shut. Moschia appeared closer to the grave than the emperor in the other room. They whispered to keep their intrusion unnoticed.

Regina murmured, "My uncle talks with Einhard, but why? I swear that man is more demon than priest. Someone should check below his cap for the mark of the beast." Regina was the eighth of nine women who had called the queen's quarters home since Charles ascended to the throne of the Franks forty-six years earlier. She was a lady of Aquitaine, and her uncle, Wilfred, was the duke of Aquitaine. Wilfred was unquestionably the wealthiest man in the empire who wasn't from the Carolingian family.

Moschia replied, "Your uncle is the wisest man in that room that is not lying down. He controls the Twelve Peers. He has survived rebellions and attempts on his life. There is purpose in everything he does. You know your interests are foremost in his thoughts." Regina had her doubts about her uncle's interests and even more about her own.

"I pray that you are right," Regina whispered. "The fate of my sons, the youngest princes of the empire, depend upon it."

Sitting at a finely carved round ebony table off in the rear corner of the room were three middle-aged women. One had her back turned from the door to the emperor's quarters. Her mind was not in the room, but rather somewhere else as her hands worked a puzzle on the table. She arranged the pieces in a certain order, then froze, studying the product for a moment before shifting them around again. Her name was Madelgard, the fourth wife of Charles. She wore a green dress with a tunic top and a yellow long-sleeve undershirt. The edges of her tunic were delicately embroidered with elaborate gold thread.

After a moment of calculation, she slouched back in her simple black chair, twisting a chalice of wine clockwise in her hands as she continued to stare at the puzzle laid out before her. She wore ornate gold earrings that accentuated her long, slender neck. Her wavy brown hair hung down. It was not long; it barely touched her covered shoulders. Madelgard was clearly past her prime years of fertility, but she still gave the impression of self-confidence and comfort in her own beauty. She looked over at the other two women sitting at the table. They didn't return the gaze but instead looked down at the table with worry on their faces.

"What does it mean?" Gersvind asked Madelgard. She was the youngest of the three at the table. Like Regina, Gersvind was a consort of Charles. Being a consort meant she had no official recognition as a royal wife, but that hardly mattered in terms of Charles's affections or the standing of her children among all his offspring. Gersvind wore a long dark blue dress that passed for black even in the glowing yellow light of the quarters. Her blonde hair was bound in an egg-white bonnet that did nothing to hide her youth compared to the other two.

"Stay silent!" Liudgard said. She was something of a mentor and older sister to Gersvind and was often vocal in performing her role. She was neither ugly nor attractive, yet she clearly did not command the attention of men the way the other women at the table did. Liudgard wore a dull black linen dress that covered her body all the way to the top of her neck. A small golden cross was centered on a short neck chain. Like Madelgard, she too wore her hair short, though her blonde hair seemed to fall limp from her head rather than carry the fullness and health of Madelgard's. It was parted down the center and looped around her ears. Liudgard's choice of a black dress was not for Charles, but rather Linus, her teenage son by Charles. Linus died six months earlier from the pox that struck many in the capital. She wanted her appearance to reflect her humility and subservience to God.

Liudgard occasionally shifted her eyes for seconds at a time, trading stares between both doors as if she was looking or waiting for someone to enter the room. She had a look of both excitement and fear. She then leaned over the center of the table with a whisper. "You need to put those things away, Madelgard! If one of the priests comes in the room and sees you . . . with bones in the palace, you will be bound by the wrists and your head shorn. They will send you off to a convent in the night, and you will never see the palace or your daughters again. It is ungodly." She sat back in her chair, content with speaking her mind yet wondering if it was best to leave the table to avoid the accusations that could easily spill over onto her for saying nothing of Madelgard's behavior.

"I love you like a sister," Liudgard said continued pressing Madelgard, "but you risk all for false sight. Charles will not protect you and your bones."

Madelgard brushed off the warnings and had no fear on her

face. She kept her back to the doors because she cared little for who came through them. Madelgard was a baroness from the province of Thuringia and had successfully managed the hall whispers and peering eyes for almost twenty years. Madelgard had hoped to assume the unofficial role of head wife after the death of Hildegard, but she could never pry loose the dead woman's grip on the palace and Charles's deepest affections.

"I am as much a child of God as any of you," Madelgard said, "but the priests tell us to abide this moment and God will provide. I need answers now that cannot be waited on. My girls need to know what the days ahead hold. They are of age, but Charles told no one his plans for their marriage. If anyone is likely bound to a convent, I fear it may be them rather than myself."

Liudgard shook her head in disagreement. "The convent is not a prison, Madelgard. They will be looked after and serve God."

Madelgard smirked. "Just because you are content with your lot in life now that your son is gone does not mean that others need to share your misery." Those words hurt Liudgard, not because they were untrue but rather because Madelgard brought her son into the insult. He was sacred to her, and had he lived, he would be in any discussion of succession to Charles's throne. Now Linus was in Aachen's cold ground and Liudgard had been relegated to a role further in the pack of Charles's women.

Liudgard said, "You can be so hateful, Maddie. May God have pity on you." Liudgard left the table and went to a window to keep her tears personal.

Gersvind remained and Madelgard knew she had an interested observer to whom she could express her thoughts. "These were my grandmother's bones," Madelgard said. "She read them for my family long ago. They worked for Regina, although she is not likely to admit it. The bones told her that the pains she carried early in her term would give way to twins and it was so."

"What are they?" Gersvind asked. "Are they chicken bones?"

Madelgard laughed. "No. They are the hand bones of an old witch that once secretly served my grandmother. She told me that the priests cut off the witch's hand for cursing a lord and flicking pig's blood on his fine robes. That is why I boil the bones in pig's blood. It gives them their red color."

The heretical nature of what Madelgard detailed didn't deter Gersvind's curiosity. "I just thought that was yoke paint."

There was sudden movement in the only bed that remained unmade in the chamber. A woman's hand unwrapped itself from the bundle of white sheets. A disheveled head then followed. It was Adallind, the last of the nine wives and consorts Charles had formally acknowledged. She was almost sixty years his junior. She lifted her weary head from the bed with the strength of her arms, turning sideways toward the direction of the table's conversation. Her long blonde hair and face were unkept as if she had been lying in her bed for days.

Adallind was wearing her white sleeping gown and was generally unconcerned by her company within the chamber. The laces of her gown were fully loosened such that one shoulder was bare, unveiling a supple breast that Charles's older women had lost with time and children. Her skin was tight and smooth with no evidence of disease or infection that would compromise her proximity to perfection.

"Where is Rosalind?" Adallind asked. "I must have her fetch Sicho or his apprentice. I need him to mix me something. I cannot go back to sleep." Heads turned in Adallind's direction, but no one bothered to respond to her command. Adallind was in truth a child and often ignored. The women collectively thought she was excitable and had an intelligence that matched her youth.

Regina became convinced that there was nothing of worth coming from the emperor's chamber. The situation remained as it had been for hours. She whispered into her servant Moschia's ear and returned to the ebony table with the other two. Her face was one of controlled worry. Her words were fast and broken. "What do you think she will do to us?" Regina asked the room. "Throw us to the streets like beggars? Judith has never shown me kindness since I have known her. What about our children? Surely Charles planned for this moment and has told his advisors to give our children land and titles so that we will have the means to remain comfortable. Will I have to plead to my uncle to take me in?"

Madelgard began to fill her cup with more wine. "The worst situation? Judith has Louis send you to be the wife of some barbarian in the east. Louis won't let her do anything to your sons. They are as fine a currency as your uncle's gold coins."

Regina did not react well to the answer. Her eyes widened and her mouth opened slightly. Adallind resurfaced to take in the conversation. "What? My sons are coins?" Regina asked.

Madelgard continued with her thoughts, talking to Adallind but keeping her gaze on Regina. "Surely you saw this coming, Addie. For both you and Regina. Charles was seventy-two when he took you to his bed. Your father's advisors visit you regularly. Have they not planned things out for you? I realize you were never his wife, but that in itself has not mattered in Frankia. Your status should be as protected as mine, though you have not borne him any children." Regina huffed at Madelgard's words; a smirk came on her face as she chimed in.

"Protected?" Regina responded. "That may be a bit much. Things will never be the same for any of us. We must beg the chancellor and priests for as many favors as we can before Judith casts judgment and hope for the best."

"True," Liudgard followed the discussion from a distance, "but it is Louis that we must seek out in the end, not his wife. He is the only one of Charles's sons by Hildegard that remains to succeed him. With the deaths of Pepin and Charles the Younger, his anointment as emperor should now be unquestioned."

Madelgard countered. "He is weak, though. He never was Charles's favorite and he needs to keep us at ease or our families and their men will not be so desiring to support him. Charles has left Frankia between Scylla and Charybdis. Wars with the Saracens, Saxons, and Lombards. Lightning invasions from the Northmen. We have more power than we may yet be perceived to have. Louis only needs to know that our happiness and safety is the key to keeping Frankia's territories in battle formation."

"We do not need to peddle ourselves to the slave auctioneers," Regina said as her lips quivered. "We do not need to look upon ourselves as coin or objects for sale to the highest bidder, do we? Madelgard is right. There is not a single one of us in this room that does not have family that has given men and gold to the armies of the empire."

Regina hadn't struggled with her confidence since coming to Aachen six years earlier, but the pressure of recent events changed her for the worse. She had thought nothing of her role as consort rather than wife. Even when Charles took Adallind to his bed as his newest prize, she responded to the new girl with smiles and friendship. Regina knew that her status was no mark on her, but rather one on her uncle. Charles made a point of letting his criticism of others play out through his actions rather than his words. Relegating Regina was his way of telling Wilfred that the powerful old duke stood too close to the throne. All of a sudden, Regina felt the fool. She realized that her time would have been better spent worrying about her boys, Hugh and Roger. She now wondered if it was wise to leave them in Aachen with Judith, the she-wolf prowling the halls.

Liudgard approached the table, feeling a rise in solidarity and shaking off Madelgard's prior insult. Liudgard spoke to Regina. "I agree, but it would also be wise for us to bind our fortunes together. We stand more of a chance if we unite against Louis and Judith. I think we should demand our children be granted lands at the least. Since all of us but Regina have only daughters, they can be used as dowries so we can marry them off to noble families."

Regina chuckled, pulling her hair back, running it through her fingers with her hands. "I do not intend to approach Louis or his bitch wife in some battle formation. I look to my uncle and other alliances. My sons will not be denied what I have paid for. I will continue to press Theoderic for answers as well as my uncle. Besides, I am sure that there will be a meeting of the Twelve Peers now that all of the lords of the empire have been called to

Aachen. I will see to it that my boys are on their lips as they talk amongst themselves."

Madelgard sighed into her cup. "Judith certainly has the mind for showing a stern hand and most likely bigger balls than her husband. Her people are the strongest force within the eastern realm of the empire. She has been a predator this whole time, waiting patiently in the bushes for the inevitable to happen. She grows hungrier as the days go on and our emperor's breath grows more faint."

Adallind shot up from the bed, her hair swinging in front of her face from the force. It covered her like a golden fleece. She raised her voice in a high, crackling tone. "My lord still lives and pray he is not listening in on your plotting babble. He will toss you to the floor like old worn clothes!" As with most everything else, no one paid Adallind much mind. All but one person in the room knew that Charles would not wake.

* * *

There was a little-used path that serviced Aachen from the west. The first structure along the roadway was half a day's walk outside the fringe of the city. It was the remnants of an old church that had been built centuries earlier. The church was made of the same white stone that was used to build many of Aachen's public buildings since the time of the Merovingians. The old church was small and simple. Its rectangular perimeter might have held fifty parishioners at best. The clay steeple roof and some parts of the upper section of the walls fell away long ago. Only one of the two crosses on each end of the shorter sides remained. The other had fallen to the ground decades earlier. It was moved to the overgrown cemetery behind the building. Someone from the past decided to use the cross as a sign to mark the church's cemetery. The cross was buttressed to stand upright by smaller stones placed on its sides. Several other fallen stones from the church were also reused to mark boundaries on the ground and its twenty or so raised mounds. The cross and the upright stones were frequently dug out from the settled snow as a reminder to the few who passed through the area. The area was to be kept sacred, immune from crossing or planting.

Black moss and lichen filled in many of the building's cracks and loosened mortar while fir saplings would try to eke out an existence in some of the more porous gaps. The missing roof had been replaced by slanting thatch and pitch, layered high to counter the area's heavy snowfalls and endless soggy days. To the north of the church were the signs of a dormant garden with raised earth rows and equidistant-placed sticks to assist growing vines. Between the garden and the church wall was a large broken cart with its back wheels off the axle. They were propped up against the front left wheel. The ground below the cart was dark mud that was iced over. In a few months, the surrounding snow would give way to shoots that would produce a dozen shades of green. For now, the ground in the area below the cart would remain black, yet it still had a purpose. It was home to a dozen or so chickens and roosters that patrolled inside the area, giving movement and noise to an otherwise lifeless scene.

Emerging from the woods along the back of the church was a wretched old man covered from neck to toe in a heavy wool robe. The only hair on his head blossomed from his ears. The bottom of the man's robe was faded lighter than the rest, crusted with blots of mud the same color as the path. Gregan wore simple sandals despite the extreme chill, displaying feet darker and grimier than the cloth around his ankles. The old man was carrying on a lively conversation, although no other person was present. A series of grunts from the enormous black and white striped pig named Argos, who followed a few steps behind, revealed that the old fellow was suffering from inside voices or was cold to human interaction. A horsehair necklace with a hand-sized wooden cross marked Gregan as a holy man.

As Gregan and his companion approached the front of the old church, Argos's grunts became higher-pitched and more frequent. Gregan interpreted the pig's reaction as the animal sensing that something about the old church was amiss. After looking back at Argos and mouthing a few words, Gregan approached the entryway of the old church with caution. Gregan placed a hand on the wall and peered through the cracked door. He announced his presence.

"Who is there? There's no coin here or anything of value. I am a man of God and welcome you to eat with us if you are hungry. What is your business?" Gregan asked.

When there was silence, the old monk showed his agitation. He could feel someone inside. Argos confirmed his suspicion. The silence was like an aggression and Argos continued to grunt and sniff the foreign air brought by the stranger.

Gregan screamed, "Fuck off!"

A laugh came from inside along with the sound of shoes scraping across the stone floor. "It is Einhard, Gregan. I am alone. Do not hit me with your stick or put your pig on me."

Gregan responded, "Pigs are peaceful when fed, not the same

as a boar. Your people are from the country. You should know better. Besides, Argos has the heart of an angel." Gregan pushed the door open with his foot. The slow creaking revealed another holy man of similar height and age yet drastically different in appearance. "Shit-eating sons of whores, it is you."

"Good day, Gregan. Your language is still a bit of a disappointment."

"Einhard." Gregan was as disappointed by the confirmation as Einhard was by the disgraced monk's language. "Why are you here? Is there news of Charles?" Apprehension came over Gregan's face. He was not prepared for Charles's passing. Word of the emperor's illness came from pelt merchants who left from the city several days earlier, taking the less-traveled road to Rouen.

Einhard sighed. "No. He remains asleep. He is not alone, though. Sicho and Alcuin watch over him with prayers."

Gregan nodded and closed his eyes, lifting his head up toward the sky. He whispered a short prayer for Charles, then said, "I have been nowhere near your shiny cathedral. In fact, I have not entered the old part of the city for some time. Since autumn. When I do, I go straight to the palace kitchen and back out. My normal affairs. I have caused no trouble within the city." Gregan would often bring Charles's cooks fresh truffles to make a soup that his old friend and master enjoyed. Gregan would bring Argos with him. Charles's young children and grandchildren enjoyed riding on the back of the massive pig like a small pony.

Einhard was a peculiar-looking man. He had a long face that was clean shaven. His eyebrows were overgrown and sprouted wild hairs that covered his sight. The top of his head was mostly devoid of hair and appeared to come to a point at the crown of his skull. He did have curled gray hair around his temples and the back of his upper neck. Einhard had rings on more fingers than not. He also wore a cross; it was a jewel-encrusted pendant held by a thick gold rope chain. Einhard wore a white linen robe, covered by a heavy purple and gold-lined shawl that extended to his brown leather boots. Gregan noticed Einhard's boots first, in particular that they were unblemished. The boots suggested that Einhard hadn't walked the long distance from the city, which wasn't very surprising.

"How did you arrive, Einhard?" Gregan asked. "I do not see a cart or any cart tracks."

Einhard smiled with a light, happy answer. "I rode on a mule and tied it up just around the bend. I knew that if you saw my cart or a mule you would stay in the woods until I left." He looked down at Gregan's filthy feet and grunted. "Nevertheless, here I am." Einhard walked across the doorway, minding his steps to make sure he settled on firm earth and not mud that would spill over his boots. He looked out into the field in front of him and continued. "Do you know why I am here, Gregan?"

"Looking for girls not riddled with the rotten fire crotches of the city?" Gregan replied. Einhard squealed in discomfort, which caught Argos's attention. Gregan scratched behind the pig's ear, which brought a low satisfying grunt. Gregan continued. "There are no girls anywhere near here. I do not know why you are here. Certainly not out of concern for my well-being. I believe you are more than willing to announce your purpose either way."

Einhard looked at Gregan with a fake smile. "You jest. You

enjoy mocking me and the laws of our Lord God. You are a vulgar little man."

"You were about to state your purpose, Einhard."

"Very well. Your sermons must end, Gregan. You have gone too far. Preaching to—screaming at—the people in the church for the market workers, saying that our Savior told you the Saracens have come to punish Frankia for its pride. It is troubling. Beyond troubling. Blasphemy, Gregan." Gregan chuckled in satisfaction that his rousing had caught the right person's attention. Einhard continued his condemnation, "You once stood outside the cathedral mass and threatened to excommunicate the archbishop for immorality and unchecked hubris. It is . . . intolerable." Gregan gave a shrug. "Your visions, too, Gregan. They cannot be an issue for the funeral mass or anything related to Louis's return to the city."

Gregan reached into a pocket and pulled out a dirt-covered root that he fed to Argos, resulting in another grunt of satisfaction. Gregan was enjoying the anguish that his actions were causing Einhard. He listened patiently, hoping to hear more.

After a series of additional accusations, Einhard found a stump for a seat. He worked dirt from his fingernails as he waited for Gregan's reaction. "Your archbishop likes to be tickled by boys," Gregan said. "I have that on good account. As for my visions, they are God's way of showing his word to me. I am but his earthly tongue. Do you not believe they are true?"

"I did not say that," Einhard replied.

Gregan laughed. "You will not say that, because you would be in opposition to Charles and he would jerk your leash tight."

Einhard had a look of revulsion on his face. "Charles protects you still."

Gregan shifted the conversation. The covenant between Charles and Gregan was personal to the two men and not Einhard. "I have not had any visions of importance for some time. The ones these days show me fine places in the woods for truffles."

"I do not care for truffles, Gregan," Einhard said. "Stop the blasphemy. You go too far and step on the robes of holy men much better than you."

"It is no blasphemy to preach God's word from vision. Even that fool Bishop Otto will agree."

For his unassuming and simple appearance, Gregan was well-versed in church governance, having been groomed for administrative positions in a monastery at a young age. His reference to blasphemy rather than heresy was intentional. Einhard had no interest in technical minutiae. He came to Gregan with an agenda and was intent on delivering it.

"You must be reined in, Gregan. I have no official authority over you as you are no longer at the bosom of Mother Church, yet that does not mean there are no other ways of controlling your behavior if necessary."

Gregan chuckled again, this time less sure of how to respond. "You would kill an old monk? I have more likely than not seen my last winter."

"We live in troubled times. Words kill more than steel. A man who claims his words come from God?" Einhard held up a hand to Gregan. "And do not respond with the name 'Charles.' Do not use his name to protect your actions. He has not woken.

It has been five days, and his breath grows more faint each morning. The love we bear for our emperor is forever true. However, he is but a man and not immune to God's call home. When that happens, Gregan, you will have lost your only benefactor. To whom will you turn after you have been whipped through the streets? When the fire of your words has burned the wrong hand?"

Gregan reached under a thick cloth tarp that covered the cart near his home. He pulled out a small bucket containing feed for his chickens. This was not the first time he had been chastised for his unorthodox behavior. It wasn't even the first time that it was Einhard who did the chastising. This time felt different, however. Einhard had a certain calmness and confidence in his threats. Gregan flung seeds on the patch of dark snow and mud as the chickens scurried out from inside the church. Gregan whispered, "God provides. I abide."

Einhard shook his head with a grin, shifting his weight onto his toes. "Charles controls Rome, Gregan. However, your patron Bernard shall be controlled by the church. The cloak that protects you is days if not hours from turning to dust."

"You were not always a bad man, Einhard. When did you turn your back on God? I have known you for as long as I can remember. I was one of the first ones you met when you came from Ireland. You knew no one and I treated you like a little brother. We fished in the creeks. We chased girls. When did I lose your love?"

"I never turned my back on God, Gregan," Einhard replied. "I opened my eyes to the church Charles created here, not the one in Rome." Gregan emptied the bucket by throwing the remaining contents out less than gracefully, announcing that the conversation was becoming cumbersome.

Gregan sighed and said, "You mentioned that you had things you wanted to say. I assume the usual threats were not part of the reason for coming, so speak whatever else you have on your mind and go. I have much work to do."

Einhard pursed his lips and shrugged, happy to oblige the request. He wanted to insult the poor monk who supposedly had so much to do. All Einhard saw around him was a leaking and rotten thatched roof, a white field with overgrown and dilapidated carts and refuse. Einhard saw idle hands as far as he could tell. He held his tongue and moved to the point of his journey far from the city walls. "Do not come to the funeral mass, Gregan. Your presence will not be wanted."

"By whom? Charles, your emperor?" Gregan asked.

"By me. By the church. The chancellor. Anyone and everyone who matters." Einhard was calm with his retort.

Gregan gritted his teeth and said, "Other than your emperor, you fucking squirt of duck shit?" Gregan knew that, in past instances, his reference to Charles's favor would override threats from all others.

Einhard was prepared for the insult, which was a long time coming, based on prior conversations. "Which emperor are you referring to, Gregan?" Einhard asked. "I must profess that I do not know why Charles loves you so much. It seems to be one of the great mysteries of our time. The most powerful man in the world shows uncompromised affection and caring to a discarded and disgraced monk, making him seemingly untouchable to all others. Why is that, Gregan? Why do you continue to have his favor, even at the end? Is there some great secret that you hold over the man that couldn't simply be remedied by your death?"

Gregan responded, "Charles has also been touched by God. I have known that since the beginning. I will be there for his mass. Tomorrow. Next year. The day of the resurrection. I swore it to him, and I will see it through."

Einhard laughed and said, "You mean your vision down in the cauldron all those years ago? That time when we were boys and you proclaimed Charles the successor to the kingdom of the crown of thorns? You talk in riddles and babble like some pagan wizard." Einhard was done prodding for answers that would never come to him straight away. He took several frustrated steps toward the path that brought him to the church, pulling up his white robe from the wet and black earth. "If you show to the funeral, you will be stripped of your clothes, beaten, and have shit thrown at you as children run you outside the old walls. This funeral will not be about you or your visions. It is about an image. An image of the emperor's making that is now his son's. It was the pope who made Charles emperor of all Christian lands, but Charles made his eldest living son the new emperor. The mass will be an awe-inspiring display of where the true power resides, Gregan."

"Do you have any further good tidings, Einhard?" Gregan asked.

"Yes, I do, now that you mention it." Einhard's voice turned deep. "Do not think that your closeness to Bernard goes unnoticed by more than just me. The palace has eyes."

Gregan responded, "At least one evil eye, indeed. Bernard is a godly man, a young man of passions and vice, but he is good and pure of heart in his service to God. I have watched him grow from a boy. He knows the love his father bore for me and I for him. It is true that I have openly supported Bernard, for what little good a shoeless monk brings to his cause. I have my reasons. If Bernard calls for my counsel, I will be ready."

"Bernard is dangerous to himself and everyone whom he touches. He whispers treason and is close to cutting his own throat. If you have any wits, you would be weary. Mind Louis, Gregan—he is your emperor as much as Charles."

Gregan proudly lifted his chin. "I bear no ill will toward Louis. I never have and you know that to be true."

Einhard said, "Yet you do not love him like you loved Pepin."

Gregan shook his head. "Pepin was mine to care for. Louis was yours. I now care for Pepin's son. I owe it to the father and the grandfather."

"And look where that thinking has got you," Einhard said as he looked around Gregan's humble possessions again. "God keep you, Gregan." Einhard shook his head and walked away without another word.

IV

- UNDER THE DUKE'S TABLE -

The snow swirled in all directions onto the main port of the city of Marklo, the new capital of the Frankish province of Saxony. The snow was not delicate; these flakes could be felt striking the face. Strong winds whipped the northern sea into a frenzy, sending white-capped waves cresting into a crescendo. The sea off the coast of Saxony was rough year-round; this time of year, it was violent. Smaller skiffs and fishing boats that hadn't been dragged high onto the safe stone and shell shores to the west of the docks took on too much water to stay afloat and were in different stages of sinking below the surface. There was a music that rose above the low roar of the wind. Hollow buoys knocked against hulls and hulls thumped against docks. Rigging not stowed away hummed high notes that screeched louder and higher with the growing gusts. Masts and stowed sails were caked in a layer of snow where gulls once safely perched the season before. It was hard to envision how any life could survive in the Marklo winter sea or sky.

There was life along the docks. Sentries stood guard at the

top of glazed wooden ramps that connected the docks to land
above. Two soldiers were assigned to each of the three ramps.
They were wrapped in dark furs on top of more furs so that
they resembled bears standing upright, crusted in ice and snow.
Their spears had been propped up against the tables meant for
cleaning fish. Hands had to be buried inside the fur to keep
them from turning black. These were not hard men of the Saxon
elite army. These were the palace soldiers stationed in order to
set an example. They broke minor rules in performance of their
duties. Unkempt armor or barracks not inspection-ready were
the most common reasons for being assigned to the docks. Late
for duty meant the whip for the first offense. Ears were clipped
for multiple violations. Sleeping while on sentry could mean
death. For these soldiers, their punishment was to stand and
nothing more. There was no real threat of attack in the heart of
the winter, so attention to protocol could be waived by sympathetic captains who might have been in their same boots at one
time. In any event, there was no need for vigilance; the enemy
was already there.

The ships of Northmen littered the long docks and shoreline.
They were discernible from all others. Their oar banks ran from
bow to stern. Shallow hulls were out of sorts with the rough and
deep conditions of the North Sea, yet their sailors seemed to
move them effortlessly through the water in all seasons. Their
wide bodies came to curled points at the bow and stern. Most
bows of the Northmen ships were capped by massive wooden
carvings of mystical beasts drenched in lively colors with fierce
eyes, sharp teeth, and wagging tongues. The Northmen said the
beasts were embodiments of their gods, which drove fear into

their enemies. What the Northmen hadn't realized was that, to foreigners, the depictions of their carved gods were only fables. The southerners feared the flesh and blood that came from the ships' bellies, not their bows; screaming berserkers with hate in their eyes and steel in their hands was not imagined.

It was easy to tell the ships of the noble Northmen from the rest. They were twice the size and had fiercer, larger carvings. On this gray afternoon, the ships of the nobles had been dragged ashore, safe from the grip of the pounding waves. The smaller ships had to be tightly moored together in clusters, as there weren't enough slips in all of Marklo to accommodate Saxony's guests. One noble ship closest to the central ramp was alive with noise while all others were silent. The sounds from the ship were buffered by a patchwork of walrus and seal hides stitched together and hung over the mast to transform the interior of the hull into a massive tent.

The thick hides muffled the noise within, but the sounds of pleasure and laughter were unmistakable to the guards nearby. There were the clear moans and shrieks of a woman and men delighting in their own little world under the canopy. The guards closest to the ship traded stares and chuckles. Their mouths were bundled behind their tightly drawn hoods, and it wasn't worth exposing their hands to the cold just to pull open their hoods to talk.

After a while, the noise inside the animal-skin tent came to a halt. The guards expressed their disappointment with shrugs. Moments later, a Northman flung open one of the flaps of the tent and walked around the stern of the ship, out of sight of the guards. His long dark hair and beard blended in with his coat such that it was impossible to tell where hair gave way to fur. A second man exited the tent and opened his shaggy robe only wide enough to piss over the side without getting his fur unnecessarily wet. He yelled out something in his mangled tongue to no one in particular. A woman poked her head through the slit and laughed, her long blonde hair covering her face. Her foreign words were too soft to hear even if the guards understood her. She slipped through the slit and hugged the man from the back, caressing his chest and moving her hands down toward his crotch as he kept pissing. The man began to yell and laugh as her hands approached. He fidgeted to be free of her touch.

The woman was unclothed from head to toe. Her body simmered in steam that died quickly in the wind. The guards switched between staring at each other and watching the woman move. The woman could see the guards' eyes were on her, and she wanted them to see more. She didn't reenter the tent, nor did she reach for covering despite the onlookers or the burning cold. The woman gently pulled the man's face around as he closed his robe. The Northman was tall compared to the woman. She reached up to kiss him. The entire side of her milk-white body was exposed to the guards. Her wavy blonde hair reached to the small of her back. The other man reemerged from behind the tent and turned the woman around by her arm for a kiss of his own. She kept her eyes on the guards the entire time, then decided to step off the hull and onto the smooth stones. She walked on her toes, balancing herself as she picked the larger stones to make her way to the pulsing water's edge. She looked back at the guards seductively and slowly waded backward into the freezing water, facing the guards the entire time. She waded thigh-deep, then squatted until she was submerged below her navel. She put one hand down between her legs and flushed the water inside her, cleaning herself from her business with the Northmen. Her left hand caressed her small breasts as she bit her lower lip with a guilty smile.

The guards' eyes bulged in extreme curiosity at this creature that was clearly something more than a woman. After a few seconds, she emerged and headed toward the ramp. The guards were unsure of how to react to the approaching woman. They instinctively grabbed their spears in haste and resumed their stiff positions. Both Northmen hopped off the boat and fell in behind the woman, showing her deference. Their bodies were almost as tightly bundled as the guards whom they watched for a reaction.

The woman was beautiful despite her dark, charcoal-painted eyes and blue lips. The Saxon guards could see the quivering of her jaw, yet she showed no fear or concern of the cold. She approached the guard to her left and gently pulled apart the sides of his fur hood, which was closed in tight to cover his flesh. She wanted to see the man's face and warm her hands on his cheeks.

The woman spoke softly, turning her head to the Northmen behind her. "I am your jarl, but I am also their lady. Besides, they will not talk. It would be their own undoing. I am sure I have fucked them both at one time or the other."

The guard innocently showed his yellow teeth in a playful grin.

The pissing Northman spoke. "What good is your threat, Magdeh? They do not understand a word."

"They understand. Words or no words." In truth, she didn't care if the guards spread stories of her nakedness throughout the city. She pulled the sides of the guard's hood back over his cheeks to cover his face. She kept her guilty smile the entire time and walked through the crunchy snow up toward the stone buildings nearby. "It may be best if you give me your cloak, Torsten. My husband the duke may not approve of my appearance."

Fires from hearths and chimneys scattered across Marklo. Its shores marked the boundary of Frankia and the turbulent gray seas that connected the empire to the frightening and desolate land of the Northmen. Far from the coast, to the south of the city, the braziers and great bonfires surrounding the palace hall churned out a dozen billows of dark-gray smoke that lifted into the lighter haze above and blended in with the canopy sky. The high number of fires and unseasonably active port suggested that significant matters of state were at hand.

The white scene of the Marklo landscape seemed inconsistent with the buzz of activity within its palace halls. The air inside the palace was heavy and hot, fueled by raging fireplaces that looked timid in the vast and high room. The floors of the palace's grand hall were impassable. Every seat along rows of tables was occupied with bodies and hands in high motion like the waves of the port. Hordes of slaves and staff scurried around like ants. The noise levels of the hall matched the temperature, bordering on the uncomfortable and extreme. There was an unending base of common chatter from hundreds of mouths. It was accentuated by peaks of high laughter.

Roaming packs of dogs patrolled the hall unwatched. They scavenged for scraps dropped to the floor or fed to them by bored men from their tables. They growled and fought each other, often knocking down slaves as they weaved between taller legs to avoid each other or take their prizes to the hay beds kept in a far corner opposite the wall of raging fireplaces. A fallen slave would create a cheer from the revelers and a kick from his overseer.

A group of musicians fingered string instruments and smacked on skin-covered drums in the corner opposite the main fireplace along the eastern wall. While they moved about and swayed to the tunes they played, it was impossible to hear their tunes from more than a few paces away. Their music was completely drowned out by the action of the room. They played nonetheless to avoid being beaten, much like the slaves.

Ten rows of benches were spaced parallel to the shorter walls of the rectangular hall; each seat was tight to its neighbor. Ten was a sacred number in Saxon culture. It was a sign of perfection and finality. Along the wall opposite the grand fireplace was the dais, which was elevated, twice as high as was customary for halls across Frankia. The high dais wasn't a concept particular to Saxony. Those with feeble bodies required help to climb the dais or used one of the few wooden poles erected along the sides to pull themselves up. It was Emperor Charles's infrequent visits to the palace over the course of the past three decades that many suspected was the cause of the great dais. At times he brought his own throne to set himself apart from those others in attendance.

Like the dais, the great table that sat upon it was more pronounced than those in the ten rows below. It was thick oak with legs as wide as a man's neck. It was said that the table was strong the enough to support a division of Saxon warriors, and the duke often wondered if the dais below would one day crater from the weight of the table and those seated around it. It wasn't only the size or weight of the great table that made it different from the other ten.

Along the front and sides, the great table had a series of wooden panels that acted as a skirt, shielding the activities that took place below the top from curious eyes. When great feasts were held and the imperial family was absent, underneath the top, women slaves were rumored to make their way along the line of Saxon lords, servicing them while they feasted and drank. Men slaves were active underneath as well. The young Saxon paladins with more bravado than sense would often quip in private that the men slaves only came out when the Carolingians came to court. The reality was that the men slaves were always there. Their less scandalous task was to retrieve overflowing piss pots, which would be thrown out back or given to the city's poor, who wanted the feeling afforded by the strong and partially diluted palace wine without having to pay for it.

The paneled skirt of the table was intricately carved with patterns along its borders and scenes of great Saxon battles, many of the enemies looking remarkably similar in their armor and weapons to Frankish troops. It also had scenes of mighty Saxon warriors slaying fantastic monsters of the sea, ferocious serpentine creatures with arms and legs, none of which any Saxon man could honestly claim to have seen. Most Saxon nobles didn't believe in the fanciful stories of dragons and the sort; those fantasies were spun by the old-timers for consumption by children and simpletons. To Saxons, the smile of a Frankish lord was much more frightening than any scaled beast. In many of the scenes, there was some innocent Saxon woman clinging to the hope that one of her people's heroes would save her from certain death, rape, or both.

Oddly enough, the panel at the center of the table was different than the others. Not just because of its message, but also because of its lighter color and apparent newness in comparison to the others, which had gashes and were heavily caked in wax from years of care. The center panel told the story of Christ the Judge sitting on his throne during the end times. Many Saxons coated in wool and linen ascended to heaven. Those dressed in armor were hurled helplessly downward to hell, where they were ripped apart and eaten by demonic figures. In a Frankish empire where Christ was at the forefront, the center panel was the lone Christian symbol in the Saxon palace hall. It was obvious to all whose hand was at work in its placement. It was an appeasement to Charles and nothing more. The Danes who passed by would look at it, point, and grunt to themselves in their own language. It was an embarrassment the Saxons chose to ignore.

Seated at the center chair of the great table was Germanicus, the duke of Saxony. He was given the venerable name of Arminius by his father Dagobert at birth. The choice of the name Arminius was intended as a direct provocation to Charles's rule over the Saxons. It was the original Arminius who, eight hundred years earlier, led the Germanic people of Saxony, Frisia, and even the northern parts of the province of Austrasia, where Aachen was located, and utterly annihilated three entire Roman legions led by Varus, one of Augustus Caesar's finest generals.

The young Saxon prince Arminius was later conferred the name Germanicus by Charles when he was held as a hostage in the emperor's court. As with most portions of daily life, Charles's word was law, so when he bestowed the name on the only son of the departed Dagobert, the last king of Saxony, it remained, and the name of Arminius was forgotten by all.

The story told at court was that Charles changed the young man's name to Germanicus because, as a youth, he bore an uncanny resemblance to that of the marble statue of Germanicus that sat within the Aachen palace dining hall. The truth, however, was that Charles was the type of ruler who met threats with greater force and a thick layer of irony. If the original Arminius had an anti-hero, it was Germanicus. Germanicus was the famed general of Rome who revenged the slaughtered legions of Varus by leading campaigns throughout the old Germanic tribes with the simple goal of revenge and eradication. He did so with brutal efficiency, and it was said that Germanicus's only regret was that he did not personally take the life of Arminius, who died by his own hand when it became clear that all hope of freedom from Rome had been lost.

Germanicus's seat upon the great dais was in truth no chair. It was unmistakably a throne and as grand as the table it coupled with. The arms were carved like waves that rolled and rose from the elbow and broke over the wrists to the hands. The legs were as wide as a man's fist and grabbed the stone floor with beast claws. The back of the chair was carved in intricate circular weaves that culminated at a pair of swords that crossed each other with a serpent's head in the center. Spiraled columns on both sides were capped with more fanged serpent heads that had red jewel eyes. A fir garland decorated with strips of white silk wrapped around its crown and sagged like a rope bridge in between. It was a work of beauty and skill that stood apart from all other items of the palace hall.

The chair of Germanicus's wife, Magdeh, was to his right. It was wrapped in garland as well and was also heavily carved with engravings of animals and fruit. It had no swords or angry heads. As for its height, her chair was little different than the others along the great table. The chair's fashion was very much intentional, as was most of Germanicus's decisions. Unlike Germanicus's chair, Magdeh's remained empty and the food placed in the bowls before it was left cold and untouched. Germanicus would take her wine goblet when his was not filled as quickly as he expected. Magdeh was late to attend the day's events. She was preoccupied with other matters, and Germanicus initially had little care for her presence either way.

Germanicus was a man far past his prime, but he was still caring enough of his appearance to keep his servants busy tending to him each morning. Germanicus's dark-gray hair was well off his shoulders and his beard was cut short but allowed to spread over most of his face to cover pockmarks that remained sensitive to the touch. Germanicus was closer to forty years than thirty, which meant he stayed away from the front lines of battle.

As usual, Germanicus sat with a pitcher-sized cup brimming with strong wine in his right hand. Many of his people preferred ale, like those of the islands to the west and the forests to the east. Strong wine from the south was one of the few details of Frankish life he had grown accustomed to not living without. If his right hand was consistently occupied with wine, the same could be said for his left ear, which was leaned over farther than his trunk to catch each precise word from Manric, the captain of

his elite paladins. Manric's words varied from an update of delin-
quent taxes to border disputes. Manric emulated Germanicus's
appearance and mannerisms in many ways, yet there was an
aura of confidence and superiority about Germanicus that could
not be replicated.

Germanicus's cup hand gave the impression of an invisible
boundary, one that kept him from acknowledging anything farther to his right, including his beautiful wife Magdeh. Magdeh
eventually arrived long after the food had been removed. She
wasn't present when the three northern jarls came to present Germanicus with the ivory tusks of walruses and paws of
the white bears that roamed the moonless nights of the north.
Germanicus was as indifferent to her absence as he was to the
gifts that were bestowed upon him. His concern for her presence began to shift when her brother's snide comments about
her absence began to border on insulting.

Magdeh had to be brought to the great hall by Erard,
Germanicus's head servant. Magdeh walked to her seat, unfazed
by her husband's glare. She was radiant. Her long blonde hair
was wrapped high with curled strands that were permitted to
fall on the sides of her face and back. The dark blue silk of her
dress was trimmed with a plush gray seal-skin and a neckline
that dropped the gray hide dangerously close to her cleavage.
She was thankful for the heat of the dining hall, for it made her
appearance not seem so wildly out of sort with her surroundings. She looked like her people in her features yet dressed like
some of the provocative ladies of the south. Germanicus noticed
that, too. There was no strand of Saxony in her.

Magdeh lightly combed some strands of hair with her fingers, more so when she was deep in conversation with whoever sat to her right. At this particular feast, it was her older brother, Clotho, who had the honor. Clotho was a giant of a man, taller than anyone else on the dais by over a head. If anyone simply looked like he deserved to sit in the center chair, it was Clotho. He slammed his heavy hand on the grand table repetitively with each completed line of twisted Saxon. The thick table would thump with each strike, although his strength was not enough to move the goblets and bowls like weaker wood. For a man of such renowned savagery, Clotho was, in Germanicus's estimation, as gullible as a child. It bothered Germanicus that he had to come to terms with a man whose intelligence he couldn't respect.

Clotho didn't have the bright eyes and golden hair of his younger sister, but he did have her well-defined facial features: sharp cheekbones and chin fashioned a tight face. Although Clotho's body was covered by a dark-brown fur cloak that ran from his neck, his massive arms were exposed as he pressed his hands over the table, not respecting the personal space of his sister or Germanicus's captain to his right. Each move of his fingers around a cup or knife resulted in the excitement of corresponding tendons that pressed tight against his skin like a plucked string of a harp. These were arms forged from hard years on the oars of longships and the swinging of a war ax.

Despite his massive size, Clotho's demeanor was exceptionally congenial for the festivities, and he smiled compulsively at his little sister and bellowed a baritone laughter that carried to the rafters above the deafening noise of the crowd. Clotho's visit to Saxony was more business than personal. Not only was it the second anniversary of his sister's marriage to Germanicus, but it was also the due date of Saxony's payment to the Kingdom of Daneland. As part of the peace treaty between Saxony and the Danes, Charles influenced Clotho and Magdeh's recently deceased father, Arlo, to accept an annual payment from the Saxon treasury of two hundred pounds of silver. The silver was consideration for the Danes taking their Viking raids outside the boundaries of Saxony and greater Frankia. To make the arrangement digestible to Germanicus and mend neighborly wounds, Charles asked that Magdeh be betrothed to Germanicus.

Despite the indescribable beauty of Magdeh and the relative unimportance of two hundred pounds of silver tribute, the arrangement didn't sit well with Germanicus or his mother, who had her son's ear from afar. The underlying relationship between Germanicus and Charles was precarious. Saxony had been a long-sought-after prize of Frankia since the rule of Charles's grandfather, Charles Martel. Frankia wanted Saxony not only for its land or people, which were both plenty, but for its natural barrier. Limiting the Northmen's access to the southern seas and buffering Frankia from the north made subjugating Saxony a simple decision for the Franks.

The Saxons, however, were not as receptive as other territories throughout the continent and did not kindly accept the wishes of the masters in Aachen. Saxons were a rebellious people dating back to the incursions by the Romans. Their assimilation would prove to be much more difficult by their persistent rejection of Christianity. Eventually, after countless years of violence with their neighbors, the Saxons were finally brought to their knees by Charles's father, Pepin the Great, and his radical priests from Rome.

Early in Germanicus's reign as the duke of Saxony, he made a name for himself, not in defense of his lands against the scourge of the Northmen but instead as the aggressor against the sister territories of Frankia. Germanicus took the fight to the barbarian tribes that inhabited the forest and coastal areas to the east. He did much of the work Charles failed to do himself. He was successful in his campaigns and grew in confidence as a leader to be feared. In Germanicus's mind, his actions on behalf of the empire were due recognition. When that acknowledgment didn't come, Germanicus plotted to have Charles kidnapped and then renounce his Frankia's claim over Saxony as consideration for the king's release. Germanicus's bravado was too bold, however. He let his passions and dominance over lesser peoples blind him to the reality that was Frankia's superiority in numbers, wealth, and sophistication.

When Germanicus's plot was revealed, Charles reacted with understandable brutality that would make his predecessors proud. Charles laid waste to several major cities throughout lower Saxony, enslaving every last survivor. When Charles laid siege to the old Saxon capital of Eresburg, he refused to accept Germanicus's eventual surrender unless Germanicus agreed to publicly give him the kiss of peace. Charles could have killed Germanicus and no one would have thought it unjustified. Interestingly enough, while the Saxon people were punished, the Saxon ruler was not. Instead, quite the opposite occurred. Germanicus was made a member of the Twelve Peers, which advised Charles on the most sensitive of governmental matters.

What revolted Germanicus even more than the annual public humiliation he was made to endure by presenting Clotho with the peace payment was the presence of his wife. She was perfect in every visible way, and that oddly made him despise the crown of Frankia even more. It was Charles, after all, that put her on him. Had the marriage been an arrangement of his own design, perhaps his opinion of Magdeh would have been different. But that wasn't how it was. Each morning, the first thing he would see was the human personification of his humiliation in all its beauty and perfection.

On that winter evening, every man from the tables below would at one time or another lock their eyes on Magdeh while she sat next to him. He couldn't help but feel that she was the focus of the dining hall, not him. Charles wasn't a bastard; he was a cruel and tactfully deviant bastard. Germanicus knew that Charles loved playing games of the mind with his lessers, and in Germanicus's case, he had played the game masterfully. For all his rage, Germanicus knew that this was not yet the time and certainly not the place to once again gamble his head and the future of Saxony. Instead, he would bite his lip, smile, and play the role of Charles's most beloved sycophant.

Germanicus looked up to the entry door to his great hall and nodded for his palace guards to enter. Four soldiers bearing the green cloaks of Saxony walked gingerly toward Germanicus's place at the center of the dais. Each soldier used his inner hand to carry a wood and iron chest that held the silver payment to Clotho. As the soldiers neared Germanicus, he stood, raising his hands above his head as a signal for the boisterous crowd to settle and allow him to speak. Germanicus needed the hammering of the pikes against the stone floor to fully engage the drunken hall, which eventually grew silent. The soldiers reached the floor of the dais and set the chest gently down, then opened the lid so Clotho could inspect its contents from his chair. He gave a nod of satisfaction and returned to his seat.

Germanicus addressed the room. "Friends! I welcome you to my palace. It has been many moons since I have seen most of you and I thank our Christ and Savior for your health."

Germanicus crossed himself, as did all the other Saxons along the dais. Slowly, the majority of those Saxons sitting at the tables below him did the same. It happened like an uncomfortable and choppy wave. It was not an instinctive move but something that was reactionary to the action of their lord. Germanicus was no Christian, and just as likely, there were no Christians in the crowd. This was spectacle, however. Germanicus would act his part for the emperor to the south in the event there were eyes that would find the scene worthy of whispers. Aachen expected Saxony to bend the knee to Christ and Germanicus begrudgingly played the part.

Germanicus continued. "In appreciation of Saxony's solemn truce with Jarl Clotho and as a token of our labor for eternal peace with the proud people of the north, I present you, Clotho, my brother by marriage and sacred bond, with the payment of silver. May you receive this payment and prosper under the light of God Almighty."

The hall erupted into applause as drinks rose in sync, spilling their contents. Cheers of "Germanicus!" followed.

As the applause subsided, Clotho's man, Rehgar, stood from the great table several seats down from Germanicus. He used his hands against the back of his chair to steady his wobbly, drunk legs. His Saxon was heavy with a northern accent. He took his time to turn his thoughts into foreign words for the crowd's consumption. "It is a generous gift, most certainly. However, taking a bride such as Magdeh must be worth all the silver of Saxony. Do you not agree, Lord Germanicus?" The Northman contingent of the hall responded with a strong cheer where the Saxons of the crowd sat silent or murmured an uneasy chuckle.

Germanicus was mildly annoyed with the foolish man's impudence, but he was already in a passive mindset, eager to simply get the farce over with so he could return to the business of governance. Germanicus raised his goblet in a toast of acknowledgment, thinking the speeches of the day were now over. Anything to move the Northmen one step closer to their ships and away from Saxony, at least until the following year's spectacle.

One of Germanicus's youngest captains, Algo, seated immediately below the dais and directly in front of Germanicus and Magdeh, didn't except the jab as harmless banter. Algo, a young beardless man in his late teens, light-haired and blue-eyed, slammed his cup on the table, sending its contents into the air. He stood fast and proud with an accusatory finger. The noise of the hall quickly receded to a dull murmur. "Sir, your words would cost your head if you lived under the laws of Saxony. What you speak is insulting, cheaply branding the honor of our Lady Magdeh as some chattel fit for trade. She is no chest of coins to be passed along. I assume your barbarian tongue has only misspoken the kinder words in your mind." Algo was clearly intoxicated as well; Germanicus could tell from the way his sweat had moistened the young man's forehead and the hair around his ears. Yet there was something about his unexpected defense of Magdeh that caught Germanicus's attention.

Germanicus let his outward expression give the appearance that he too was vexed by the Dane's words when in reality they didn't bother him. He knew that his wife was in fact nothing more than currency that he did not bargain for. In truth, he wouldn't give a milkless goat for her, much less a few sacks of silver. Germanicus's true concern was for Algo's behavior and why, in particular, he chose to stand up for Magdeh when veiled insults had been openly thrown Germanicus's way since Clotho arrived many days earlier. With no information and no basis other than what his eyes told him, Germanicus knew at that moment that Algo cared for Magdeh and that perhaps there was something more that required vetting. Germanicus shot a look at Magdeh, who took herself back by the sudden outburst, holding her breath with eyes opened wide. Germanicus was studying her response and flipping back to Algo, waiting for the two to make eye contact. Germanicus wasn't angry or jealous. He started spinning the situation in his head. How could he parlay this perfect and unexpected gift in a way to create a pretextual action against the Northmen and, ultimately, harm Charles, the true focus of all his hatred?

Rehgar took the chastisement for what it was, gripping his cup like a vice and carefully processing his thoughts into Frankish before speaking his mind to ensure their maximum angered expression. Clotho had experienced his share of ale-induced verbal spats and sought to walk the situation back from the ledge. Clotho leaned over to Rehgar, who sat two seats away, and grabbed his warrior's forearm with enough strength to refocus the young man's attention and give him time to call up unaccustomed words of apology.

Clotho stood and spoke to the room, "Captain Algo, I beg you to please sit. Rehgar meant nothing by his words. You are right. He is a savage in Saxony and knows little of your language and less of its customs. He has known Magdeh since before they both could walk and has nothing but brotherly love for your lady. Perhaps our cold and—how do you say it?—rough customs can be taken in ways we do not intend. My apologies to you, Germanicus, my brother. Please forgive my man's manners."

Germanicus took his eyes from Algo as he continued to rack his brain, giving a smile and subtle nod to Clotho and acceptance of the apology. With Germanicus's nod of acceptance and clear de-escalation of what could have quickly gotten out of hand, the volume of the hall began to slowly rise until, in a matter of seconds, it seemed as though the whole incident had been forgotten.

Clotho sat back down in his seat, leaned into sister and whispered into her ear. Again, Germanicus paid the peripheral activity no mind, instead keeping his focus on Algo.

Algo stared down into his cup for several breaths, collecting his clouded thoughts and reflecting on whether his actions were out of line. Rather than look to his lord for some acknowledgment of approval or, worse, his guilt, Algo put his gaze on Magdeh, who intentionally did not return the favor.

Germanicus could tell that, for Algo, Clotho's words of reconciliation were not enough. Algo had a strong affection for Magdeh. He might have been her lover.

Germanicus cracked a simple smile. He had his moment of vision, all thanks to Algo, the love-struck fool. That was it. Love and the foolish things men would do as its slave. Germanicus wouldn't lift a finger for Magdeh, even if it meant loosening the noose around her neck. Other men would, however. Men ruled by love and the fantasy of owning a woman's heart. Those dreamers would fight for Magdeh, even if he would not. The skillful tactician and master manipulator was well on his way to turning another drunken day in the dining hall to his political advantage. He had his bait. Now he looked for his prey.

V

- UNTO YOU, PEACE -

Alcuin leaned in close to Theoderic and said, "I noticed that Prince Kasim was roaming the corridors earlier. I do not like that he is given free rein of the palace, regardless of the truce. He seemed in search of someone or something that alluded him. What is his temperature? What does he know about this . . . situation? I must admit, I make myself scarce when I hear his Saracen accent in the halls."

Theoderic smiled in reaction to Alcuin's honesty and uneasiness. It was unusual for Alcuin to take off his mask as the unbreakable counselor and religious advisor to Charles, even to a colleague he had known as long as Theoderic. In these trying days, however, Theoderic could identify with Alcuin's feelings, as the recent stress was wearing on everyone in the palace. "No more than what any tavern keeper knows at this point," Theoderic said. "I believe he is more worried about the status of his master's gift and the pact it was meant to consecrate. Our relationship with the Saracens to the south is precarious at best. I am sure the prince believes that if the pact remains in place

at the . . . transition, it will likely hold, at least for the time being. The relic is strangely what Charles coveted most during the
negotiation of terms. Not lands or gold. He wanted the crown
of thorns. The Saracens claimed to have it. Shockingly simple,
I suppose."

The two men had their share of differences over the years,
sometimes with awful reactions to each other. Theoderic typically petitioned for practicality and deferred to the secular needs
of the empire whenever there were hard choices to be made.
Although Alcuin was no zealot, his principles centered around
care for the church and executing the mission of God while not
falling prey to the tantalizing wishes of the pope and his use of
relics as rewards. In many ways, the two men naturally canceled
each other out, and perhaps that was part of a plan that Charles
kept to himself. Their edges dulled over the years, though. Each
seemed willing to meet the other in the middle because, at the
end of the day, they both had a mutual affection for Charles.
Charles was the embodiment of both church and crown, and it
took decades for the two men to come to that simple conclusion.

The sun had yet to rise above the hills in the east. Even when
it did climb, there would be little evidence it had done so. The
cloudless skies just days ago seemed like a distant memory as
the gray lid that dominated the sky for most of the winter had
returned. Alcuin and Theoderic left the corridors of the palace
that teemed with life. The two men walked side by side along the
expansive and well-attended water gardens that were situated
behind the back end of the palace. The gardens were below the
imperial apartments, but the palace windows were shuttered
tight to stave off the cold. It might have appeared like an odd

choice of walking paths, given the current weather, but the men knew the active palace well and felt assured they would not be disturbed outside. Besides, the palace gardens were the place where both men routinely met with Charles when critical matters needed vetting. The soothing sounds of the flowing water and the beauty of the well-manicured shrubs remained immune from the winter cold. Charles found that the tranquility of the water gardens opened his mind to clearer thought. For both Alcuin and Theoderic, having the other man as a surrogate for Charles seemed natural and welcoming.

The bronze statues of stags and wolves that decorated the main entry of the palace were replicated in the gardens but in pale marble that only added to the feeling of lifelessness throughout the vast space. There were also statues of Charles situated at the entry and the center of the gardens. One statue in the center was set upon a large mosaic of Charles's coat of arms. The unmistakable black eagle of the floor stared at visitors just as it did at countless enemies moments before their death. With its red beak pointed to the left and wings expanded, it appeared to be swooping on its prey, ready for the kill.

One of the statues of Charles represented a youthful emperor wearing the skin of a lion and bearing a club, his body tense with motion. The symbolism was apparent to the nobles and learned foreigners who visited the gardens, assuming they were well-versed in the classics. The skin and club were the unmistakable attributes of Herakles, famous for his deeds as the son of Zeus. The decision to carve Charles's face onto the body of the Greek hero was no accident. Having performed the labors imposed upon him, Herakles was a human given the gift of immortality at his death. Clearly, Charles was projecting his own ascendency through art, even if it was blatant blasphemy in the eyes of Mother Church. No one had labored more in the name of Christianity since the days of Constantine. Through the statue, Charles was telling his guests that he labored for church and was deserving of divinity. It was outrageous symbolism that screamed in its marble silence. There was no one willing to charge Charles with the sin of pride, particularly given the power he wielded in support of the pope.

The water fountains within the gardens were the only element of nature that appeared alive at the time. All else was still and silent. They had movement and steam. Other places around the perimeter of the palace appeared desolate, smothered by the winter snows. It was the water that made the gardens special. It gushed through channels, spilling over the edges in corners, melting the snow and ice to reveal the brown earth below. The water was diverted by pipes from the hot springs of the cauldron several hundred paces up the hillside. The thick clay pipes that were cleverly hidden by shrubs and earthworks kept the water warm and running at a strong pace despite the freezing winter temperatures. The sound of rushing water and the faint chirps of birds perched in the leafless trees were the only sounds. Steaming water welled up from orange and yellow tile pools, then further meandered through a series of minor waterfalls throughout the garden complex. The ghostly steam from the water, combined with the white blanket that covered everything that was left untouched, created an eerie scene that blended well with the gray skies overhead.

Alcuin carried a silver-crowned walking staff that he nimbly twirled in his fingers rather than used for support. For an old priest, a man as old as his master, he was weathering the cold temperatures well, even if his lurching steps suggested otherwise. Theoderic's hands could not be seen. Each hand was buried in the sleeve of the opposite arm. The coat he wore was the shaggy hide of a black bear, which accentuated the pale whiskers growing in places normally kept free from growth. The coat was massive on the diminutive man and would have brought a jape or two from Alcuin under different circumstances. Alcuin wore a thick wool robe that covered him from head to foot. It was nothing more than a thicker version of his daily clothing.

The echoing from the hard hide of their shoes scraping on the slate stones along the path broke up the white noise of the bellowing water flow. Theoderic walked slowly over to a simple wooden table, where a brazier was left burning. Despite the bear fur that engulfed him, Theoderic still craved warmth. Alcuin, who was walking at his side, let Theoderic lead the way toward the table and brazier. He seemed less bothered by the temperature despite being lightly clothed for the environment. On the table was a reading glass along with various papers that were spread about in no particular order. It was a makeshift office for Theoderic as he made every attempt to hide from the chaos that passed around his own study. There was a constant stream of messengers and clerks handing off papers and books that eventually wore the old man into submission.

Theoderic had served the Carolingian family for his entire life but had recently grown weary in the last few years, much like Alcuin. More and more, he tactfully handed off many of his duties to members of the Twelve Peers. In recent years, he had become more of a secretary to Charles, as the Peers gladly took up the power he so readily gave away. By handing off his duties, Theoderic felt that this was surely the last years of service due his old master. The potential of Charles passing would speed his movement to a quiet retirement south along the Mediterranean.

The only obstacle to a life of relaxation was Theoderic's relationship with Louis. The two developed a close bond as Louis gained in authority within the palace and assumed many of Charles's responsibilities that were taught to him by Theoderic. While Theoderic did feel a semblance of duty to the new co-emperor, he was also not shy about making his wishes known that his service to the crown would hopefully end while Charles still reigned. For the longest time, Theoderic and all of Charles's court felt like Charles would rule forever. Reality had come crashing down in only the matter of a week.

Alcuin cracked a smile as he picked up the reading glass, inspecting it and recalling the gift that Charles had given Theoderic two or three years ago. Charles had given Alcuin a similar gift the prior Christmas. Alcuin quipped, "One old blind man passing along a tool of sight to another." Alcuin sighed as he peered through the glass, aiming it at the weak sun hidden behind the thick gray clouds. He then laid it down gently on some papers, making sure not to scratch the valuable gift. "Let us keep to our prayers and hope our friend and master finds his strength. I have never known his kind before. His power is unmatched in all of Christendom."

Theoderic straightened his tunic underneath the heavy fur coat as he took to the bench. He stretched his back and neck to prepare his tired old body for the few moments of work that could not be put off any longer. Theoderic stared off in a trance at the fire burning, spitting, and cracking in the brazier. He hoped a servant was close by to fuel the fire with fresh logs in case his work lasted longer than anticipated.

"Of course," Theoderic responded. "However, I am sure you can appreciate, Alcuin, that I must be in a position to act. It is in the empire's best interest that I prepare for all contingencies. It's what Charles would expect and what we knew was inevitable."

A group of four monks walking the path bowed respectfully but with clear trepidation to the two icons as they passed. Men such as Alcuin and Theoderic were off limits to contact to all but a select few. Their very breaths involved the most sensitive workings of the empire.

"I will handle Prince Kasim," Theoderic said to Alcuin. "He comes to these gardens for his morning and evening prayers. I can soothe his concerns as best as any. He is still a young man in terms of politics, and his religion corrupts his temperament at times. We must assist him in his quest for patience."

Alcuin crossed himself in relief of Theoderic's words. Dealings with the Saracens were always a delicate exercise, as the cultural differences often made compromise over the most benign matters difficult. It was a matter more suited to Theoderic than Alcuin. Religion was always at the heart of Alcuin's thoughts and his bias against the Muslim prince was close to the surface.

Kasim was cultured and learned in the politics of Europe, having been educated by his travels. He had a deep understanding of Western ways. To Theoderic, the man seemed to have a sensibility that other ambassadors of the caliphate and his own emirate had not. Most were zealots that seemed to clash with Charles's court. Theoderic felt a touch of gratitude that Prince Kasim had been stationed in Aachen to implement the peace terms, even more so now that a change to Frankish rule seemed imminent.

As the men continued their conversation, Kada, a young Dane who was one of Alcuin's assistants, approached at a brisk pace. Although there was no one other than Theoderic present, the young man felt the need to whisper in Alcuin's ear. "No improvement, master," Kada said. "Sicho believes his breath continues to slow." Kada stared patiently at the ground as he waited for instructions; he knew his update was not one well-received and he felt nervous even though he was blameless for the message he delivered.

A sense of sorrow took over Alcuin's face. He patted young Kada on the shoulder in appreciation. "Thank you, Kada. Another report in two hours. I will be in my study."

Alcuin wondered what Charles would think if he in fact awoke from his slumber and saw the world operating around him. Would he be content with the peace and serenity of those at his bedside? Would he be pleased to hear the soft songs of the monks who had stayed in his room throughout the ordeal? Would he be disappointed at the quaintness of the room and the limited attention being paid to him? Alcuin felt it was impossible to know for sure. This situation was new territory for every living soul in the empire. Kingdoms were not suited for fifty years of stability. Perhaps Frankia was meant to suffer for its good fortune and the softness it had developed in knowing only one sovereign for so long.

The Charles Alcuin had met almost sixty years earlier no longer existed. That young man, fascinated with knowledge and eager to make his own myths, had morphed into something beyond the scope of a mortals. People often commented that he was Constantine reborn. The champion of Christ, unbeatable on the field of battle. He was loved and worshiped by his devoted soldiers, whom he considered his own brothers and sons. He knew their names. He knew their mother's names. Charles would sit around the army campfires and laugh without care for the violence that awaited him the next day. Young men from the corners of the kingdom flocked to him in pilgrimage, hoping to cast their lot with something close to the immortality bequeathed upon saints. They loved him, and he loved them. It was an unbreakable bond, even at the point of lances twenty thousand strong.

The growth, prosperity, and pride Charles brought to the people of Frankia wasn't limited by invisible borders. As a devoted defender of the faith, he became the champion of Rome and its leader. Every victory he claimed was in the name of Christ as he walked the papacy back from its centuries of decay and struggle for relevance. Charles was undoubtedly the sword hand of the pope, who in turn goaded the warrior king with heavenly flattery. Flattery, built one honor upon another, became part of Charles's persona. He began to believe in his own divine narrative.

In 800, Pope Leo III crowned Charles the first Holy Roman Emperor in over five hundred years. Even before the anointment, Leo became concerned that he had made a mistake—that he had no further gifts within his authority to entice Charles to do the church's bidding. It worried him that titles and praise could do little more to motivate Charles further in a quest for souls and church land. Pope Leo and his cardinals showed their gratitude through physical gifts and by connecting Charles with the trinity itself. Rome's vast vaults of holy relics became the bank from which Charles was compensated for his victories, and Charles loved it. His ability to hold heaven in his hands produced an indescribable meaning for the man. Collecting relics went from being a curiosity to an obsession as his possessions mounted and his relationship with Rome grew stronger.

His devotion to his relics eventually manifested itself in the modifications he made to the palace. The quarters opposite the chambers occupied by his wives and consorts were reserved solely for Hildegard as the head wife. It was the place where she prayed and performed her needlework, a sanctuary from her sister wives and the court in general. It was Hildegard whom Charles openly loved above all others. She bore Charles nine children, including Louis and the recently deceased Charles and Pepin. Her passing weighed heavily on the man. He would forgo his own quarters, preferring instead to hole up in her room for days on end while the kingdom sailed rudderless. It was only through the soothing and patient words of Alcuin that Charles would eventually emerge from his mourning and the draw of Hildegard's quarters.

Hildegard loved and admired the life and struggles of Opportuna of Montreuil, who was a childhood friend of Hildegard and had been canonized upon her death. Opportuna became her personal patron saint. Charles focused much of his early relic-collecting on items related to the young saint and showered them on Hildegard the way many smitten men gave their loves minor trinkets of endearment. Charles gave

Hildegard Opportuna's abbess crozier and several of her bones, which were said to cure various illnesses. It was Alcuin who suggested that Charles harness his passions for both Hildegard and relic-hunting by converting her chambers to a massive reliquary that housed the holy relics of Opportuna and others collected in his wife's honor.

As Charles's enthusiasm for relics grew, so did the importance of the objects he sought. His passion took him from minor saints of local prominence to those at the core of Christianity and ultimately to Christ himself. As time went on and the pain of Hildegard's death pierced Charles's heart less, Charles expanded her old living quarters to house all his relics, with those directly attributable to Christ himself as the centerpiece. Like other facets of Charles's life, he consumed himself with the transformation of the living quarters. The room that once housed his wife's bed now held relics that rivaled those in the Vatican. It helped with his grief, providing a sense of purpose that ironically could not be filled with being an emperor alone. It became a solemn place for the emperor where he found himself praying and meditating in contemplation of his life's purpose. He often forewent the trip to his gilded chapel on the other side of the palace in preference for the room that brought him closest to his beloved Hildegard.

It was the destruction of the Muslim scourge in northern Spain that generated Charles's his most prized possession: the robe of Christ. It was the very robe woven by the hands of the Virgin Mary and worn by the Savior at his judgment by Pilate. The robe was stripped from Christ's body before he was flogged by his Roman torturers and set upon the cross.

Charles did not need much coaxing to stem the northerly movement of the Muslims, who were now in retreat yet still dangerously close to Frankia's southern marchland of Gascony. Nonetheless, when Pope Leo III called on the holy warriors of Christendom to repel the Abbasid Caliphate from the lands of Europe, Charles answered the call. The robe was gifted to him by Leo two years after his infamous visit to Rome, where the pope shocked the world through his unsolicited coronation of Charles as Holy Roman Emperor. The robe was presented to Charles at a private ceremony deep in the catacombs beneath Rome, where saints and martyrs filled the maze-like tombs with their mortal remains. The spectacle was intentional. Pope Leo told Charles that the cloth had been the source of prior miracles in that, when the time came, the robe of Christ would herald his ascendancy to the realm of the apostles. By draping his own body in the cloth, Charles created a connection between himself and the divine. Charles took the cloth back to Aachen, secure in knowing he was chosen above all others.

Theoderic found Prince Kasim deep in the confines of the water gardens. The walkways where the men stood were freshly scraped clean by palace staff and dried by thick wool blankets. There was a separate area of stone flooring where the snow was removed. It was the size of a palace bedroom. The large area had been specifically prepared as an accommodation to the prince. The prince knew the palace well from his prior visits and often sought out the corner nook of the gardens for its high shrub walls and tranquility. In his mind, there was no one to intrude on his daily prayers other than the statues of Charles with their cold stares. The pad had been prepared at Theoderic's direction; it was something of a harmless trap aimed at confusing Kasim.

One of Theoderic's many gifts was his understanding of the people who came and went from the palace. He knew their drink and flesh preferences, keeping his knowledge discrete. More times than not, the information was provided to him by the many eyes and ears that worked throughout the palace and beyond. Kasim was difficult to read. Theoderic's eyes and ears could find no credible vices in the man. Theoderic didn't believe the man was without corruption; more likely, he was just more skilled at hiding whatever he didn't want seen. Theoderic believed that every man had a dark side, even if it wasn't one founded in cruelty or depravity. Theoderic could only conclude that the young man's slavish devotion to his god was what helped him hide his sins.

Kasim carried himself with dignity, a clear sign of his nobility and a refined upbringing. He was friendly and patient, which made him an ideal emissary. His every move seemed intentional and thought out with care as if he found perfection in little achievements. Theoderic guessed that Kasim was in his early thirties. His hair and beard were still jet-black and oiled with no trace of gray. His hair was only visible in the palace when he was in the presence of royalty. Otherwise, he wore a simple headscarf that crossed directly above his eyebrows and came down halfway over his ears. His beard was neatly trimmed and short to proudly display angular and handsome facial features. His skin was consistent with dark bronze, which made the white of his eyes engaging. He was confidently handsome, and he knew it. Kasim was layered in several long tunics of orange and yellow. The fabrics were made of fine linen and silk. To Theoderic, he appeared comfortable in his dress despite the frigid temperature.

Kasim was studying the stone floor on which he stood, trying hard to remember the precise direction of Mecca. Despite being devoid of leaves, the high and thick shrub walls closed in on the nook, making it difficult for Kasim to orientate himself. His last visit to the palace had been in the summer a year and a half before, when the morning sun shone clear between the hills of Aachen. The haze of the morning clouds kept the sun's rays hidden behind a dull gray screen. Kasim was a slave to consistency and order. Unsatisfied with his guess, he shifted his rug ever so slightly in the uncooperative sun.

Theoderic stood a respectful distance behind Kasim, purposely shuffling his feet on the stone path as he waited. He wanted to remind the prince of his presence, given the younger man's preoccupation with a ritual the older Christian man didn't care to understand. Kasim paid Theoderic no mind. He had his priorities. Mildly satisfied that he had found the spot where the sun would rise, Kasim gently unfurled his rug and sat shoeless on his haunches. He placed his hands on his thighs and came to the realization that Theoderic would remain there with little care that his very presence was a capital affront in the prince's homeland. Kasim turned his head only far enough to the left to pick up the blurred form of Theoderic.

When Theoderic realized he had the prince's attention, he stood a little taller and held his right hand to his chest. "How do you say it, Prince Kasim? *As salāmu 'alaykum*?"

Kasim smiled to himself and closed his eyes. He didn't know

whether to feel offended or honored by the chief administrator's attempt at Islamic civility. He was an emissary and thought it best to assume the latter. "That is well done, chancellor . . . And unto you, peace, my friend."

The air was silent for a few long seconds. Theoderic was uncertain whether it was advisable to push the prince to communicate during his moment of prayer. In truth, he didn't care that he would offend a Muslim, but he did care about offending the cousin of the man with one of the largest armies in the known world.

"So, Master Theoderic, tell me truly: how fares your emperor? I pray for his quick recovery. My cousin would be most distressed should the Great Lord Charles . . . fail to recover."

Theoderic giggled sheepishly to himself. "I would think your emir cousin would rejoice. Perhaps not openly. Charles is responsible for more Muslim deaths than the pox."

Kasim always had a bit of disdain for Theoderic's presumptions. An unveiled insult made it difficult to contain his displeasure. He saw Theoderic as a pure politician rather than as a servant of the emperor. Kasim chose his words carefully. "Peace is a fragile thing, Master Theoderic, and even more so when one of the strong threads that holds the bond has been frayed." Kasim rose from his rug and Theoderic frowned.

"I think I understand your eastern logic. We have a saying that is similar to that: it's better to dance with the devil you know." His grin exasperated the statement, and Kasim found himself struggling to hold off a strong rebuttal.

Kasim responded, "My cousin respects Charles. He is a worthy adversary and cares for his people. Men who wield power with honor and shield those they are sworn to protect are to be respected, lord chancellor."

Theoderic scanned the garden grounds casually to confirm the two men were indeed alone before he responded. "Do recall, Prince Kasim, that the peace declaration that was put to paper included Louis's signature as well. My Lord Charles is a cautious man. We call him Janus in private." Theoderic held up his hand in jest to fend off some witty response. He knew Kasim would pick up on the Latin reference. "Sacrilege, I know, but the man truly sees both forward and backward. He prepared me for this type of . . . contingency for some time. It is, after all, the nature of things, do you not agree? The peace is binding either way."

Kasim looked beyond Theoderic to the back wall of the palace, searching for someone or something to garner his attention. The sun began to peer through the clouds, and the meager warmth felt good on his back. "Do you think Bernard cares for paper oaths? And what of your pope, who has seen our warships all along the port cities of his peninsula, drifting closer and closer with each passing moon? Surely he has Bernard's ear. Our emissaries to Rome tell us your pope is quite taken with Bernard and sees him as a pious young man, perhaps a more zealous champion of your faith than his father, Pepin, had been. To the contrary, lord chancellor, the peace seems dangerously fraught with contingencies."

Theoderic pursed his lips and gulped in air. He knew he was dealing with an intelligent man. Theoderic smiled at the prince, showing his bottom yellow teeth that turned brown at their base. "There are no contingencies, Prince Kasim. Bernard is still a welp, unskilled in the art of kingship . . . although he does have a rare skill for extreme and effective violence. A valuable trait in these uncertain times, I am sad to say. Regardless, his father's claim to the throne passed to Louis. It is unusual in some customs, but that is the Frankish way. The barons and dukes accepted the installment of Louis and so the nobility of the empire have no cause to object."

The prince interrupted Theoderic; the phrase "no cause" had caught his attention. "They say Louis is no Charles except when it comes to taxing his nobles for the cost of separating pagans from their heads." Kasim's words were intentionally provocative. He wanted to see how wide Theoderic could smile. "It is the grandson, with the backing of his father's people and old friends in Italy, that invokes the better image of an emperor rather than the last remaining son of Hildegard. Is this not true, my friend?" Kasim asked.

Theoderic was no fool when it came to the nuances of politics. He knew that he was being goaded to anger. He also knew that the best way to counter an adversary feigning concern was to flip the fear using the same logic against him. "Prince Kasim . . ." He paused, lining up the keys to his argument. "Suppose you are correct and there is a power struggle should our Lord Charles pass into the hands of our Heavenly Father and another make a claim to the throne or there is otherwise a period of internal unrest—you pick the names of would-be sovereigns however you see fit. It does not change the fact that Frankia faces constant rebellion in Saxony, incursions of these . . . northern animals, not to mention the ever-present menace of the hordes on horsemen from the east. They cripple our trade and threaten our allies who buffer our borders. Where is the wisdom in reigniting a war with your cousin, Hakam, the Emirate of Córdoba? He is a formidable adversary. It seems clear your emir could instead take advantage of our precarious situation and sow more aggression farther into Europe and toward the heart of Frankia herself." Theoderic chuckled with a tinge of fake nervousness, suggesting his rationale was so obvious. "No, Prince Kasim, it is Frankia that stands the most to lose if this peace does not hold. I fear you presume too much of our strength."

The prince laughed aloud, carrying his voice above the rush of water. He tended to his prayer rug, rolling it with gentle hands. "If my cousin was so confident in his position, then why would he offer your emperor the relic as an incentive to peace? Do you know how much we have labored to possess it?"

"The crown of thorns?" Theoderic asked. "You mean that . . . tale in a gilded box? Come now, Prince. You offend me with such a weak position. Relics are a value to only zealots and common people," Theoderic said in amusement. Kasim was surprised that Theoderic would openly voice his opinion that was clearly in contrast of Charles's own beliefs. Theoderic continued, "For all I know, for all anyone knows, the crown of thorns was crafted by some old weaver in Syria five years ago. Its delivery has no bearing on the terms between our two masters. It will make for a good story, nothing more."

"A story perhaps, Theoderic, but one of Charles's own making. It is no secret, even as far as the palace of Baghdad, that Charles has become obsessed with his own divinity. He is the one who insisted on the crown as consideration for the peace. He is the one that sent scores of your monks and scholars to plunder through Muslim treasuries and libraries in search of proof the relic was true. Its value is whatever Charles priced it at, and that was his price for peace. So, for my cousin, the crown of thorns has limitless value."

Kasim began to gather the rest of the simple belongings he brought with him, wrapping his Quran gently in red cloth with the utmost care. He would not find any peace on this morning, and while it pained him to shirk his obligations to God, he knew that the situation was excusable. Kasim continued his words unfazed by the work of his hands. "Hakam took delivery of the relic quite seriously. He took me from my duties in Byzantium to see its safe delivery from Alexandria. My cousin struck a bargain, and he intends to honor it, Theo. Peace is all that matters."

"Very well, Kasim!" Theoderic said somewhat enthusiastically, enjoying a mental spar with someone worthy of intellectual respect. He reached out a frail hand from inside his shaggy coat to shake Kasim's hand, willing to put the issue to rest. In Theoderic's heart, he didn't believe the Muslim's words. They were not looking for peace and never thought of themselves as weak. "Would you be so kind as to join me at dinner this evening, Prince? There is a savory fish stew from the kitchen today."

"I thank you, but no. I must be ready for the arrival of the crown. I was to join the caravan that brings the crown of thorns north, but upon receiving the news of the emperor's unfortunate state, I came directly from Paris. I am still a little saddle sore, truth be told. The crown travels north from Lyon, I have learned, under heavier yet slower guard. That was yesterday, which would place its arrival late tomorrow night."

"Ah. I understand. Your people have a sense for the dramatic. It would be a miraculous scene if my lord wakes in time to see the fine soldiers of the Córdoba Emirate cross through our gates with the one symbol he cherishes above all others. It would blend nicely with the legend that seems to have sprung from the earth around him."

"All blessings to Allah, I hope that it is so." The two men left the gardens through the back entrance to the main hall of the palace complex. One of the faceless palace guards, cloaked in his ornate battle furs and savoring the warmth that radiated from within, opened the door.

VI

- I HOPE YOU DIE -

Germanicus stood on one of the long docks of Marklo's main port. The port was on the western side of the mouth of the mighty Elbe, where the river opened up and gave way to the North Sea. He had come at his harbor master's urging. The port needed to be inspected for Viking damage and necessary repairs before the spring brought calmer conditions and vessels from around the empire and beyond. Normally, the administrative task would fall on Saxony's lord admiral, Almund, but he had left by land months earlier on diplomatic duty. Even Saxon men more accustomed to water than earth had to respect the winter seas if they had interest in seeing the summer. Germanicus took on the task himself rather than leave it to a subordinate. It gave him a reason to leave the confines of the palace. It wasn't just an excuse to avoid his wife and the leeches of the court. It also gave him a sense of purpose when most all other aspects of governance slowed for the season.

The port and the waters of the bay had been overrun by Clotho's ships for almost two full fortnights. They had treated his port with disdain and disrespect, the way drunken soldiers would raid a captured tavern. They looted Germanicus's barges and storage huts of valuable salt, fine horsehair ropes, and lead cleats. There was no respect for their host, and Germanicus didn't care that his guests were unaccustomed to the societal rules of the mainland. Clotho would have feigned an apology and said it was expected for northern guests to take items from their hosts as mementos of their journey. This wasn't taking a little carved horse for a son or some glass trinket for a wife, however. This was a mass looting that would set back his fishermen and traders who eked out an existence and would come to the palace for recompense. More than that, it was a matter of decency and respect for a powerful neighbor that had already handed over enough silver to equal the raiding of a dozen monasteries.

It was the most brutal time of the winter, and most sea trade had come to a halt several months earlier, yet Germanicus was quick to complain to his captains that the Northmen had over-stayed their welcome with their ships that clogged the lifeline of his capital city. Germanicus was witnessing the one scene that gave him a minor feeling of relief. He wanted to smile in satisfaction, yet there was nothing to be happy about. The last group of Clotho's longships had left the docks and joined the long zigzagging line that disappeared into the dark-gray horizon to the north.

The weeklong snow had stopped falling and the winds died down to a tolerable gust. Germanicus couldn't help but feel as though the Northmen brought the abominable weather with them and that now that they had left, the last weeks of winter were sure to follow. Germanicus looked down at his leather boots, which were heavily bound in thick greased cloths to insulate from the cold and water. The small waves of the high tide slapped without rhythm against the posts and planks, splashing water along the surface ice onto his feet. The raging sound of the northern wind had subsided, but the groans and creaks of the wooden wharves that gave way to the power of the sea made Germanicus cringe in annoyance.

The shoreline along the port bay was riddled with barnacle-crusted beams of scuttled ships that the sea had coughed up from its depths over the last few weeks. Ropes and planks from parts of the older and little-used dock system were now farther on shore than the remnants of the ruts created by the Northmen's beached longboats. Other flotsam made its way to land as well. Waterlogged hides from trade boats littered the high water-line where the dark stones turned to white. To Germanicus, the hides looked like dead bodies that had dotted the crescent coast. He assumed that several of them were actually the remains of humans and was glad the northern winds would carry away any stench that would prove him right. "If they are Northmen, all the better."

Germanicus knew that if his port was unable to fully withstand the persistent churning of the winter sea so deep in the bay, the waves farther out in the open sea would wreak havoc on sailors indiscriminately, or at least that was what he wished on the northern scourge. If Clotho was visited by mortal misfortune on his return voyage home, many of Germanicus's problems would flutter away like the swirling seafoam all around him. He could renounce his savage wife for one. That or have her killed; either way would suit Germanicus fine. It was a wish he had little chance of seeing played out. There were no better seamen in all the world than the Northmen. Hate them as much as he did, it was a well-settled fact.

The winds that fought the last few longboats had brought his ears the laughter and songs of the Northmen as they rowed into the open sea. They didn't sound like men facing the potential of death. For all his disdain, Germanicus did respect the Northmen's mastery of the sea. He knew they almost preferred the challenge of troubled waters far from the sight of land, the way a paladin preferred a violent and enraged stallion on the cusp of battle. The harness of unpredictable power seemed cathartic to such men, and Germanicus had a shred of understanding as to what that meant. Still, he said a prayer to no one particular god, wishing Clotho's death.

He whispered the last line of his prayer. "I hope you die." Germanicus turned around to head to his captains waiting impatiently on the firm ground farther up the ramp. They knew this was a moment their lord preferred to keep to himself. It was like that with Germanicus. There were few men within his palace and ranks of captains that he trusted with his true thoughts. He always thought his father would have been that person, a man he could sit with to plot and scheme his way back to significance. That opportunity was taken from him long ago.

Germanicus's captains began to gather around him. Two foot soldiers grabbed their spears for their return through the city's sleepy market to the palace. One of the foot soldiers stopped, which captured the attention of the rest. "Lord, ahead." He pointed to the western horizon, where the shoreline gave way to the short cliffs and stone walls above that protected the city.

Germanicus tried to follow the line from the soldier's gloved finger, squinting at the fuzzy specs somewhere in the distance. "What? What is it?" The lord called with frustration, not with the young man but out of spite for his own failing eyes.

"There, my lord. A rider in red with a yellow banner. He is there, skimming along the cliff. A herald from Aachen, my lord."

"Ah! A kite. Our emperor. How fortunate! One steaming pile of shit is swept away only to have another dropped on our heads. I can only assume the pimp wants confirmation we have paid his whore now that she has left our bed." Germanicus sighed with frustration and looked to the ground. "I suppose this means I will not be joining you lads for a game of morris this evening. Fortune pisses on me once again." The men stayed put. Germanicus wasn't willing to cater to the herald by lessening his journey one step. As the red kite came close enough to hear, he decided to take any edge off and prepare his men for the uncomfortable chastising he intended to thrust upon the messenger.

"Perhaps our emperor has asked for me to come fondle his old balls for him? My rough northern hands would feel nice on his pink scrotum, don't you think, Manric?"

The younger captains were tickled that their normally serious master could engage in campfire humor. They all chuckled in appreciation, and the older Manric wanted to encourage it further. "If so, send me in your stead, great lord. When I get his pants around his ankles, I will geld the bastard and bring his boys back to you. A new trinket for your collection."

"Charming, Manric," Germanicus responded. "Chivalry to the south would frown on such acts."

"Who the hell is chivalry?" Manric asked.

"Excellent question." Saxony was still wild in Aachen's eyes, and its people had not adopted many of the customs of the more cosmopolitan southerners, the new idea of chivalry and its honor code being one of them. That suited Germanicus just fine.

Germanicus was already bored with the banter. His genuine curiosity refocused his attention on the oncoming herald. Germanicus hadn't been involved in any plotting against the emperor as of late, and he was honoring his demeaning pledge to the Northmen. He felt like he should have a sense of guilt over some misdeed at the worst. If it was suspicion of plotting or treason, Charles would have sent one of the Peers whom Germanicus trusted to bid him to Aachen for questioning on the matter.

More likely than not, the visit was reconnaissance. The red kite was probably there to give some insignificant instruction when in reality he was looking for signs of discord among Saxon and Northman, which would suggest the annual meetings to re-affirm their truce terms were failing. That probability bothered Germanicus more than the thought of treason accusations. He would be beyond annoyed if his master Charles had sent a spy to make sure he had honored his commitments of the peace with the Northmen. That was it. He was to be treated like an unruly child. "Let us see what our most noble emperor has for us this day, lads."

Germanicus slammed open the intricately carved double doors of the private dining hall located next to his living quarters.

One servant was cleaning the square stone floors with rags sopping out of a wooden bucket. Remnants of the Northmen's visit were to be eradicated. That meant cleaning even the most minor trace of fish sauce that had seeped into the tight crevasses between stones that dog tongues had failed to find. Another servant was lighting lamps and torches within the room in preparation of the duke's return, illuminating giant wooden beams that hung high overhead and held an assortment of shields and banners of various tribes and people the Saxons had conquered in the twenty-eight years since he assumed the dukedom from his father, Dagobert.

Obscurely positioned in a back corner of the colorful array of banners was a tattered blue pendant with gold diamonds arrayed throughout. Centered on the banner was a silver griffin, longnecked and proud. It was a rarely used banner of Frankia and represented a cavalry squadron based in the borderlands of the cursed forests of Bavaria. The banner was not taken during any war, but rather a territorial skirmish that arose twenty years earlier when Charles's first son and namesake mistakenly attacked Germanicus's troops.

Germanicus had crossed into a disputed border area that separated Saxon lands from Bavarian lands. Under Frankish laws, he had the right to do so. He was conducting maneuvers and inspecting troops in eastern Saxony when he received word of Bavarian outlaw bands plundering Saxon border towns and villages that were lightly garrisoned. Germanicus made the decision to give chase and extinguish the bands as an example to would-be opportunists. Bavaria at the time was under the authority of the younger Charles, who happened to be in the region as well and performed many of the same functions. Saxon scouts ran into Frankish scouts. Insults turned into brawls that gave way to pitched battle. Germanicus had little fear of the repercussions of taking the field against the empire. Saxony was ripe with sedition. His older cousin Widukind was waging his own war against the emperor's troops in the lands to the south. In the end, the young Charles would cede the field to Germanicus and only lose a fraction of his cavalry-men in a chaotic fight he clearly lost.

Germanicus's men recovered the banner of Charles the Younger, which had been left trampled in the mud. It was taken home to the Saxon capital and left unwashed. The symbolism would ring throughout both Saxony and Frankia. Even a trained dog would still bite the master's shin if his tail was stepped on. Charles the father would do nothing despite his son's insistence that the subject be made an example of. It was a lesson of humility for the son who would one day be emperor. Sometimes rights and wrongs well taught never came full circle to produce their fruit. Charles the Younger would die years later in a field far from Saxon or Bavarian lands.

Germanicus shouted orders to no one in particular. "Food and wine. Why are there no new logs on the fire? And bring the red kite to me. In here." Germanicus removed his long fur and leather coat as he walked toward the center of the room, deciding to throw it on a table rather than hang it on the rack himself. The coat hit the table and slid to the ground. A servant hiding in the shadows moved quickly to grab it. Germanicus crumbled into a long bench positioned against the tapestry-lined wall of the hall, waiting for another servant to remove his high, soggy boots. As he sat back and breathed deeply, the double doors opened again, this time much less violently. Germanicus lifted his head in mild curiosity. Two palace guards in green tunics came hastily into the room with the messenger from Aachen. Germanicus had changed his mind at the port. He didn't want to withstand the veiled insults of the red kite outside in the seaside cold. He preferred to make the boy stew and wait in the performance of his duties. Besides, Germanicus preferred to take unpleasant tidings by comforting himself with wine and warmth.

The guard at the front of the pack spoke up upon entering the room. "Great lord, the herald says he has word from Theoderic."

Germanicus grunted with amusement while lying on his back, trying to guess at what sort of information warranted a message from the chancellor. "Everyone, speak in Frankish," Germanicus said. "We will have no fodder for mistrust here today." Germanicus summoned the herald forward with a wave of his hand as a male servant took to wrestling his boots. "Say what you have come to deliver, boy. My men know all my thoughts and I know theirs. We keep . . ." Germanicus paused midsentence. Having lost patience with the servant unsuccessfully tending to his boots, Germanicus stopped to deliver a swift backhanded slap to the top of the older man's bald head. The smack of skin on skin gave the mild impression of a horse-whip. This was Germanicus's form of silent speech, which caused the servant to scurry off silently. "We keep no secrets here. Out with it, boy."

The red kite moved between the guards and bowed deeply. "Chancellor Theoderic is sending word to the Twelve Peers as well as the dukes and barons throughout the empire that our great lord and father, Emperor Charlemagne, has fallen into a deep sleeping sickness and has not awakened despite all prayers and the attention of physicians. After consulting with Einhard and Bishop Otto, the chancellor intends to exercise extreme caution. The bishop is to administer last rites if Emperor Charlemagne's condition does not improve."

Germanicus leaned forward, placing his elbows on his knees. He began to flick at dried cheese and meats placed on the nearby stool. He appeared unmoved. "When did you leave Aachen?"

The red kite responded, "Three days this sundown, my lord."

"Fast. It is a wonder that you can walk. What else?" Germanicus asked the ked kite.

"The chancellor has asked that each Peer and ranking member of the nobility come to Aachen immediately upon notification unless good explanation can be given in his stead. The palace is to be made available to all noblemen." The herald stumbled. "M-m-m-minimum convoys, Lord Germanicus. Imperial troop deployment has been tripled along the main Frankish roadways to ensure traveler safety. The chancellor wishes—has requested limited numbers of staff and attendants so the palace can comfortably accommodate each nobleman's needs."

"Where is Louis? Is he not in Lombardy?" Germanicus asked.

"I have no sanctioned message regarding Emperor Louis, my lord."

Germanicus exploded on the red kite. "No sanctioned message? I did not ask for a sanctioned message! I asked of the location of the co-emperor! What of Louis's whereabouts, you fucking little prick?"

The herald stood with his mouth wide open and tried

focusing on the wall in front of him rather than insulting the duke and Peer with direct eye contact. "It is my understanding that Emperor Louis's last communication to the palace originated from Lombardy some eight days prior. His whereabouts at the time was in the plains south of the Alps."

"What else?" Germanicus asked.

"That is all, my lord." The herald dreaded prolonging his stay, yet he had his orders. "A reply message, my lord? Something to carry back to the chancellor? Or are you to leave for Aachen immediately?" He braced as if he was about to be struck.

"I have not decided. There is much to see to beforehand. I will call for you shortly." The boy bowed in relief. He had heard of men in the lands of the far north who beat heralds for sheer amusement, despite their protected status. "See that this boy is fed. No wine, though. He needs to stay sober for his travels. He will need a fresh mount as well."

The herald took his first breath in moments, then made an abrupt turn on his heels, which was mimicked by the accompanying guards. They then left through the double door. Germanicus nodded to his junior captain, who remained. "Fetch Manric, and both of you come back." Germanicus lifted his bare left foot and massaged his sole. Alone to ponder the information, he wondered deeply about the situation he had envisioned a hundred times in the past.

In every other instance, he laughed off the news of Charles's death. Charles was supposedly at the gates of his heaven three years earlier but somehow managed to hang on, to Germanicus's extreme disappointment. In Germanicus's dreams of Charles's death, he checked the vast stores of gold and silver in his treasury. He called on his vast army as well as the rabid dogs of the north to strike a different alliance that would cast off Saxony's bond to Frankia. He foresaw summoning back his people who had left their homeland in search of new beginnings in Friesland and farther to the islands of Britannia, forced out by Frankia's land-hungry nobles who had less than subtly pushed their borders east at the expense of Germanicus's towns and villages.

Germanicus was no fool. He learned much from the failed scheming of his elder cousin Widukind, who led his own rebellion years earlier when Germanicus lacked the power to control his own nobles. Charles would see that even the most well-planned attacks against imperial forces would be stamped out, regardless of the cost. Germanicus's own scrape with Charles the Younger was different. It was arguably unprovoked and not intended as an act of insurrection.

Widukind burned churches and pissed on black eagle banners. His was a war of passion rather than strategy. Widukind would be brought to heel, but not before he was forced to stand in witness of four thousand Saxon men, women, and children beheaded in the fields of Verden. If Charles would slaughter thousands of Saxons as punishment for symbolic dissidence toward the empire and its Christian god, then a direct confrontation against the full might of Frankia could mean eradication of all of Saxony, especially with Louis as the sole sovereign.

Germanicus knew Louis would expect a possible Saxon rebellion. He might even want one as a basis for arousing Frankish pride in their lone emperor. The continent was dysfunctional and fractured so long as there was no single cause to cement bonds. Frankia had Saracens to the south. Avars and Slavs amassed in the forests to the east. The Danish threat from the north was more apparent to Germanicus than anyone. Yet there would be great risk in calling vassal territories to rally to Saxony's banner. Was he ready? Could the silver-hungry Clotho be a reliable ally? The Danes of the north were unpredictable and just as likely to attack Saxons as Franks at sea or in the open field. He had seen their savagery firsthand in battle and now in his own city. Germanicus knew he was looking for assurances in a complicated world that had suddenly become more uncertain.

No. The plan would be to sit and wait. Nothing could be gained by hasty maneuvering. Widukind had once acted hastily, and his legacy suffered for it. It was Widukind who would be remembered at Saxon campfires for kissing the bishop's crozier and the emperor's feet. Some fates were much worse than death. Germanicus would take a different approach. He thought it wiser to allow Frankia's cracks to naturally form and look for allies who frowned when he frowned. While Germanicus would openly admit that Louis was intelligent and learned, he would secretly profess that the son was not his father. Germanicus believed that if Louis was led unattended into the deep water of Frankia's volatile politics, he would most certainly drown.

Germanicus stared up at Charles the Younger's diamond banner when two captains came into the hall and awaited orders. Was there a place for more Frankish banners or was the beam meant to secure his own noose? "We will not take the first fruit that has fallen from the tree, lads." He spoke as if his men had been working on the puzzle with him all along. They did their best to not look confused and draw their master's ire.

"No. We will go to Aachen and listen rather than talk. We will attend their mass. They love to kneel and stand, stand and kneel. We will let the barons and dukes of the empire blather and puff up their importance. Let us see if the pot is ready for rabbits or if it needs more time to boil." The captains nodded as if they understood their master's mind.

Germanicus left the room shoeless and undid the jerkin buttons beneath his throat, choosing to walk along the stone floor over the rushes wherever possible. The ice-cold floor was a welcome reminder that he was alive. He entered his living quarters, hoping to catch a moment of rest; the logistics of hosting the unpredictable Northmen for two fortnights had translated into little sleep. He walked to his neatly made bed; fine white sheets made by eastern hands called to him. He spoke to the partially open door on the other side of the room. It was the door to his wife's living quarters. "Maggie?" He only called once, and not very loudly. He had half-hope for no response. Germanicus pulled the undershirt over his head, revealing the physique of a man that didn't match his confident voice. He was malnourished despite having the luxuries of meat and cheese always within his reach. Skin now hung limp on his chest in place of carved muscle. His best days were behind him, yet he felt as though the next few months could change the words of his song, which had yet to be written. As he turned over the sheets and placed one knee in the bed, the door across the room crept open, revealing his wife.

She was wrapped in a bedsheet and nothing else. Her long

blonde hair was disheveled, but it made her all the more appealing to the eyes. "Yes, my king?" It was an obvious insult the duke chose to ignore.

"Charles is dying or dead already. I am summoned to Aachen."

"The master whistles," Magdeh said, "and the dog comes to heel."

Germanicus looked at her with a slight annoyance; she was stepping up her insults more quickly than normal. "Careful, woman. Your behavior in the dining hall still stings. You are already close to a beating." Magdeh giggled, but it was a serious warning.

Germanicus continued, "Theoderic sent the summons. Charles breathes. He does not wake. The Twelve Peers. All dukes and major barons have been hailed."

"So it is a clerk who scratches on paper that whistles for a king?" Magdeh asked. "This would not do where I come from. I do not understand Frankish ways."

Germanicus sat up and looked to the table next to the bed. He chose wine over food. "Yes, I know. Your brother would make the chancellor's herald eat shit or ram a hot iron up his ass. Maybe both. And then he would send him back to Aachen, humiliated and half-dead. A boy that carries no blade. And what is gained? It is no mystery why your people still live in huts and have never kept a single plot of earth they have taken."

Magdeh smiled. "Careful, king. You are close to a beating."

Germanicus grunted. She had wit if not tact. "Regardless, we are heading south tomorrow morning. Make whatever preparations you need. Assume we will be there for a full moon, if not longer. Bring only one slave."

Magdeh took a single step into Germanicus's room. "Me? I am to go as well? I do not like that place. It has strange spirits. Besides, that beast Judith wishes me dead. I do not wish to be in her presence. Take Hetha or your admiral's whore if you want someone in your bed." Despite her protests, Magdeh kept her voice calm. In truth, she wanted to go; she simply didn't want Germanicus to know the trip would give her pleasure.

"Did you not enjoy yourself the last time we traveled there?" Germanicus asked. "I seem to remember you in all smiles at the sight of the palace's wealth. It is a noble gathering anyway. Your absence would not give the proper impression. Besides, your brother would want a Northman present. It would make him feel a head taller than he already is."

When she realized Germanicus wasn't interested in taking her bait, she simply turned back into her room.

"And, Maggie," Germanicus said. Magdeh paused without turning around. Germanicus wanted to return the favor of a sharp insult. "Do not bring any of your fine silks or eastern dresses you have become so captivated with since we married. All dark skins and furs. Paint your eyes black like some animal. I want you to look as savage as the day we met. When the Peers meet and the time is right to show Saxony's love of the empire, I want to have proof of my fidelity. I want the court to see in flesh what low I have stooped to in order to preserve the peace of the empire."

Magdeh felt his piercing arrows. For all her hard upbringing and pride in who she was and where she came from, she could never match Germanicus's cruelty. He had a gift for it, most evident from the night of their wedding. After uneventfully consummating the marriage, Germanicus left his quarters without dressing. His captains had taken over the abutting mistresses' quarters and filled it with drink and whores. They laughed at the naked Germanicus boldly entering the room. Magdeh knew just enough of the Saxon language to pick out the insults, mostly from Germanicus.

Magdeh came into the union with the best of intentions. She was sixteen when they were wed. She saw herself as the wife of one of the most prominent men in the most important empire in all the world. She would live in a grand stone palace, wear dazzling jewels, and birth the future rulers of Saxony and perhaps all of the north. The marriage was her father and brother's decision, in response to overtures from Charles. Up until the day of her Christian ceremony, which was a farce to all in attendance, she welcomed it each night she lay down for bed. Northern girls believed in tales of love, too.

Day after day, the weight of the foreign city of Marklo added to her misery. She had no friends. The whispers of court followed her. Germanicus stayed distant and only visited her quarters when consumed by wine and anger. It was a hostile existence that she regretted. Magdeh considered taking on dark-skinned lovers from the lands that she had never seen far to the south. Her vengeance would be to produce an heir that all would see was not of Germanicus's blood. She never acted on her plot, realizing that her husband would never let such a child see the light of day.

Instead, she sought out old northern women who lived in the outer settlements of the city for concoctions to permanently cleanse her womb. She could still recall the putrid taste of the black syrup. Liquid death tasted like sweet musk. The desperate move almost took her life, yet she saw it through for no other reason than to not give Germanicus the pleasure of her death.

Knowing that Germanicus would produce no line through her, Magdeh moved her plot to the next step. She decided to make him a cuckold, to publicly tarnish his name and image as a virulent man worthy of ruling Saxony. Yet no matter how many men she openly slept with, regardless of rank or appearance, it never mended her wounds or reached his heart. He was indifferent at best and encouraging at worst. That hurt her deeper than a thousand insults. Her existence was trivialized. Her marriage was a sham in every sense and would remain so long as one of them remained alive.

Germanicus didn't acquire his talent for degradation from his father. Dagobert could be a cruel ruler and a demanding father. These were not unusual traits among Frankish or Saxon nobles. Dagobert died young, leaving Germanicus rudderless to rule a complex land caught between its pagan past and Frankish future. Dagobert was absent from most of Germanicus's childhood. He traveled back and forth to Aachen as he saw to Saxony's assimilation into the empire. The rest of Dagobert's time was spent in clandestine meetings with tribes unwilling to bend their knee to Charles.

Germanicus's true tutor on matters of cruelty and rule was his mother, Thygrid. Thygrid was hard and shrewd. She was a woman who had to fight for her legitimacy as regent and fend off Dagobert's distant relatives. She served in her official capacity as regent for seven years while Germanicus was elevated from the status of an Aachen hostage to a member of the capital's court. It was a court that attempted to influence his mind and turn him against his own people.

Thygrid was jaded from her time as regent. Matters related to Aachen's church elite were of particular concern. Mother and son adopted a policy of smiling and nodding to the priests while they pressed their thumbs behind their backs. Germanicus couldn't let his Aachen advisors know she had such significant influence over his mind, so he made a common point to claim her mad or bewitched after Sunday masses in Charles's new cathedral. She knew her son's mind, however, and didn't object to claims of his slander when they reached her chambers in Eresburg.

Germanicus knew that he now needed his mother's counsel. The situation growing around him was enormous, yet his plan for achieving what his father and reckless cousin could never obtain was to do nothing. It was bold in its simplicity. It was a plan he believed only his mother could understand.

Eresburg was not along the road from Marklo to Aachen. It was a day's diversion to the east, which meant that Germanicus would have to move quickly if he wanted to meet with Thygrid and still make it to the empire's capital in respectable time. Theoderic's request to travel lightly was fortuitous. If Germanicus pressed the horses and touched on Magdeh's obstinance as an excuse, his detour to his mother in Eresburg could go unnoticed.

Eresburg was the old capital of Saxony. Germanicus had fond memories of the city and its palace. Most involved his father. The ancient city was central to the Saxon way of life and religion, and Charlemagne would not permit its continued influence. Charles didn't burn down the city, but he did have the focus of Saxon government relocated to Marklo. It was one of the first major decisions of his early reign, and it worked masterfully. The decision served multiple purposes. It would relegate the heart of dissidence and the launching point of every Saxon plot as immaterial. It also pressed the political center of Saxony north, close to the threat of the Northmen.

The city of Eresburg was still more than an hour away, but Germanicus could see palace soldiers up ahead in their heavy green cloaks. There were only two of them. It was a pathetic escort, far from where anyone could see the semblance of ceremony otherwise due the ruler of all Saxony. To Germanicus, that seemed like something his mother would do. He loved her and she him. Yet she was hard on him the way a father was supposed to be. Germanicus assumed the inglorious welcome was an intentional jab to let him know she objected to his behavior without having to say a word.

His wife was flagrant with her insults, which, for Germanicus, made them easy to deflect. Thygrid's insults were indirect and tacit, and that vexed him deeply. In the end, Germanicus only truly cared for his mother's opinion of him and his rule; all others, even his wife's, were of no concern.

Germanicus wanted to impose his anger on the guards, who seemed less than enthusiastic about waiting for him in the cold. Germanicus slowed to a trot and began with his interrogation. "Why do you greet the duke of Saxony so far from the outlying villages and why just the two of you? Did you lose some paltry wager with your captain, you sons of pig-fucking whores?"

Both guards greeted Germanicus and bowed as deeply as

they could without falling from their saddles. Neither seemed shocked or concerned by the outrageous insult, as if it was to be expected. "My Lord Germanicus." The elder of the two guards took control for both. "We do not come from the city, my great lord. We were with your mother. The Lady Thygrid is in the woods' edge, west of Kalvarienburg."

Germanicus responded, "It is a little early for spring jaunts through the countryside. Steeds snap legs trotting through unmarked trails covered by the snow. She is too old besides. A fall from horseback and that would be the end of her days."

The older of the two guards spoke. "Your mother is standing witness over a livery of seisen ceremony, great lord. She asked us to wait for you here on the chance you might come through Eresburg on your way to Aachen."

"So she knows of Charles?" Germanicus asked.

The younger guard said, "Yes, great lord. She knows of his sleeping sickness."

Germanicus nodded, then continued with his questioning. "A seisen ceremony? Why? Has she no other matters of importance to tend to? Surely if she knows of Charles and my possible arrival, why tend to old ceremonies when Frankia uses monks and scrolls for such a trivial exchange? We follow Frankish law now, for better or worse."

The older guard simply frowned. He knew the reason and he knew Germanicus knew the reason; no response was necessary. Germanicus knew his mother preferred the old ways. The ways that would keep the idea of Saxony alive a day longer. She was adamant about such matters, even if it riled the court in Aachen.

"If you must proceed to Aachen with haste," the older guard

continued, "your mother has asked that you please make the most of your time and join her on the return to the city from the ceremony."

Germanicus looked at his small travel band and picked his closest captain, Manric, to join him and commanded the rest to proceed forward to the city. While there was no threat of attack within his own kingdom, Germanicus knew it was best to leave as many of his guards as possible with his wife and the train to stave off Magdeh's remarks before they began.

Germanicus, Manric, and Thygrid's two guards rode towards Kalvarienburg, up to a break in the patches of forest; it appeared to have been cleared years ago in preparation for farming that never occurred. They followed the same tracks the two guards had made to intercept Germanicus.

There was a group of seven men in plain clothes, along with Thygrid and four other soldiers from the palace guards. Thygrid was the only woman, but that was to be expected. No one remained on their mounts, and all were circled around a single boy no older than ten. The boy had been stripped of his heavy clothes and stood shivering in the cold wind. No one paid Germanicus's arrival any attention, least of all his mother.

Normally, Germanicus would take this as an insult and rebuke the men for their insolence the same way he greeted his mother's two guards, but these were Thygrid's people, and they were presently doing their lady's bidding. He would remain silent and log the insult in the back of his mind for consideration at his next argument with his mother. Germanicus did not think to partake in the situation that he came upon but instead decided to remain on his mount and watch a ceremony he might likely never see again. He pulled a small block of tough cheese from his saddle-bag and took his time carving off a piece into his mouth, then tossed Manric the remaining portion. This gathering could prove mildly entertaining in an otherwise unremarkable journey to Eresburg.

Thygrid stood in mud an ankle deep. She wore the green cape of her palace guards and was otherwise naked from any adornment that gave her the appearance of nobility. The end of her cape was frayed in fresh mud and dampened by snow. The entire circle chose to stand in the wet and ice-crusted depression rather than on the higher patches of clean snow and brown grass all around them. Thygrid acknowledged her son's presence with a quick nod and continued speaking her lines, which had been interrupted by Germanicus's arrival.

Thygrid spoke, "Aachen would brand us all outlaws and heretics by this ceremony. Some things we do are to remind us of who we are not, not rather than who we are. I call upon your sacred honor as Saxons to speak nothing to a Frank of what you witness this day on pain of your own death." Thygrid stood silent and scanned the circle to solicit nods from each man. Her eyes shown as proudly as those of any prince. "Who speaks for this boy?" Thygrid asked the crowd.

An elderly man wrapped in a fine fur riding cloak stepped forward into the circle surrounding the boy. "I do, Lady Thygrid."

"Name him, name yourself, and state his relation to you."

"This boy is Corbusson, aged ten. He is the son of Corbus. Corbus is a vassal paladin to me, the baron of Hastfala."

"Is this boy your relation?" Thygrid asked.

The baron of Hastfala answered, "This boy has no blood or marriage tie with my family, Lady Thygrid."

Thygrid continued, "Other than our laws that require Corbus as vassal paladin to answer to your banner for a call to war, is it your solemn word by the base of the Irminsul that the paladin Corbus is not in your debt?"

"Corbus is not in my debt, my lady." The baron of Hastfala replied. "That is my solemn word by the base of the Irminsul."

Thygrid nodded and scanned the circle. Her black and gray hair was bound high, signifying her widow status. The beauty of her youth could still be seen through the lines on her face.

"And who owns this branch?" Thygrid raised a fir branch, freshly broken from its tree and still holding its winter needles. The branch was almost as thick as her wrist, and Thygrid struggled to hold it above her head without shaking.

A second man stepped into the circle to the left of the boy. He was perhaps a little older than the first, yet his stomach was much more bulbous, and he stood shorter. "The branch is mine, Lady Thygrid. I am Landwin, the baron of Flutwide. I snapped the branch from a great fir tree that grows on my lands before we began the ride of my boundaries."

Thygrid's seriousness melted away as she looked down at the small boy, barefoot and standing on top of his own tunic. His trunk was bare and he wore soiled tan breeches. Thygrid smiled at the boy and spoke to him softly to calm his nerves. "Corbusson, my child."

"My mother calls me Corby."

"Of course." Thygrid gently cupped his face and calmly spoke, "Corby, do you know why you are here?" The boy nodded nervously. "Did you ride with Baron Landwin?" He nodded again. "Good! Now, Corby, what I now ask you to do is very important. Can you tell this livery circle where Baron Landwin took you? You must speak loudly and describe the four points Baron Landwin announced to you. Do you remember them?"

Corby took a moment to recall the lines in his mind and then answered with a nod more excited than the last.

"Good. Take your time, sweet child."

The boy gulped and looked to Baron Witimer for permission to speak, which was given with a nod. "Baron Landwin took me to the old stones called the Three Sisters before the sun rose. The three great stones that stand as tall as a man. He rubbed the stones with the branch."

"Good. Where did you ride from there?" Thygrid asked.

Corby answered, "We rode over hills toward the rising of the sun, to the Diemel River, where two streams from each side feed into it. He dipped the branch along the water's edge."

Thygrid nodded. "Good! Then where did you go?"

"We rode north with the flow of the river for a long time, until the sun was overhead, to the small bridge that they called the 'fishkill'. The water is shallow there. The baron dipped the branch in the water again."

"Well done, Corby. Did you then ride to this place?" Thygrid raised her hands and looked around.

"Yes, my lady," Corby responded. "Baron Landwin touched the branch to the piled stones that mark the path right over there."

"Well done indeed." She rubbed his head with her gloved hand in appreciation, which drew a nervous smile. "That was the most difficult part. You have done well." Thygrid stepped back into the circle and her seriousness returned. "Barons. The boundary has been marked. Complete the ceremony."

Both barons nodded in unison. Baron Landwin moved to Thygrid and, with a bow, took the fir branch she had held by her side. He then stood in front of Baron Witimer, reached down with his right hand, and scooped up a handful of black mud.

"I, Landwin, baron of Flutwide, rightful and undisputed owner of the lands marked by sacred boundary this day, having received acceptable consideration, do hereby grant and deliver seisen of these lands unto you, Witimer, baron of Hastfala, and you heirs, to hold and enjoy its harvest bounty from this day forward."

Baron Witimer held out both hands, and Baron Landwin placed the mud in one hand and the branch in the other. Both men bowed to each other in acknowledgment of the act.

A third and younger man entered the center of the circle. He wore the same gold colors as Baron Witimer and bore a resemblance. Germanicus assumed the man was the baron's son, as was the custom in these livery ceremonies. The young man took off his gloves and picked out two small handfuls of mud from Baron's Witimer's hands. He wiped the mud over Corby's cheeks and forehead. When the young man finished, he took the stick from Baron Witimer and then slowly moved behind the boy.

Baron Witimer then spoke in a deep and loud voice. "Corbusson, son of Corbus, you are charged to remember this day for as long as you live and may you live long. The livery of seisen and the possession of the land acknowledged by you, from Baron Landwin to me, Baron Witimer."

Baron Witimer and the man behind Corby looked to Thygrid for her approval. With her nod, the man with the branch grunted and swung the stick swiftly across Corby's back, breaking it to pieces and sending the boy to the mud. The circle of men then quickly descended on Corby as the two barons moved away and watched on with no emotion. The circle of men punched and kicked the squirming boy, who did his best to not cry or shout in pain. The men knew the routine. You beat the boy to the edge of unconsciousness, but no further. Thirty years from now, a child witness rendered dumb from fists and feet wouldn't remember the day the marked land of Baron Landwin was transferred to Baron Witimer.

The striking stopped once Corby lacked the ability to defend himself. He lay on his stomach, submerged in the mud, too weak to remove himself from its freezing embrace. With the beating complete, the deed was done. The young man who swung the branch tossed a small bag of coins into the mud next to Corby. The bag was quickly picked up by another man who must have been a relative of the beaten child. Two men draped the boy in a thick fur blanket and scooped him from the mud. He was laid over the back of a horse while the young man who picked up the coins studied Corby's drooping head for life.

Thygrid gave a proud and satisfied look to her only son. "Come, Arminius. Ride with me to the palace. We will talk of minor matters along the path. Then we will sit down like mother and son and you can tell me of your plans for Aachen."

VII

- THE ARRIVAL OF THE RED KITE -

The imperial highway out of the territory of Provence began at the port city of Marseille and cut north through the forested heart of Burgundy. It followed along the track of the winding Rhône, hugging the shoreline of the river for long stretches and crossing at certain junctions where the trees were thin and the river's banks narrow. As with much of daily life, the roads and bridges that made up the highway were the product of Roman engineering. They were undeniably reliable. Many of the original stone paths and cement bridge pylons remained in place, worn smooth over the years yet as durable as the day they were set in place. The centuries-old presumption was that if it was good for the Romans, it was good for Frankia.

Marseille was the busiest port in the empire. With the Spanish lands south of the marches firmly under emirate control and the duchies of Italy to the east constantly fighting with their Lombard cousins, Marseille was the sensible focal point for the empire's Mediterranean trade. The stretch of highway out of the city was one of the most traveled arteries of the empire, passing through Lyon before splitting off in multiple directions into the heart of Frankia. For many travelers, the highway system gave a false sense of protection and relief. Arriving in Marseille by sea was undeniably a treacherous undertaking. The coast and shipping lanes were infested with Berber pirates looking for potential slaves and patrolled by wayward Saracen warships that cared little for water borders or truces.

The perception was that the soldiers of the empire kept the peace in the port and on the highway. Along the highway system, the old Merovingian rulers created stations that were erected no farther apart than a half-day's travel and monitored by mounted patrols that would routinely travel between the bases. The stations were like small stone defense towers with living quarters and stables that collectively signified the authority of the crown and the importance of the road system. Some of the stations with greater strategic importance flourished into small villages and markets.

Under Charles the Hammer's rule, highway soldiers were given authority to impose justice on sight in order to ensure peace and promote trade, regardless of the crime. Beatings and amputations were the most common punishment, but execution was often preferable if, in a foot soldier's discretion, the circumstances warranted it. The simple rationale was that severe and swift punishment would deter crime. The reality, however, was much different. While the soldiers were initially successful in ridding the port and highway of common criminals, they quickly figured out that their authority provided rare opportunities to amass wealth. In time, the soldiers learned to manage highway crime. For a tax on the proceeds paid by predators, the highway soldiers informed cutthroats of valuable cargo. For a heavier tax paid by prey, the highway soldiers would keep those same cutthroats at bay.

The soldiers also incited violence between rival bandit gangs by selling favor to the highest bidder without pulling their own blades. Smugglers paid tolls for assurances they would arrive at their destination unannounced. The crown took no interest in its soldiers' behavior. The terrors from the unmanned borders and vast hinterlands were far more concerning for the average Frank, and so long as trade still flowed from city to town relatively unaffected, magistrates and lords simply took their entitled share and looked the other way.

The highway system did provide its benefits to the empire. The same arrangement of stations used by soldiers as bases for patrol operations was also used by the crown and nobles as message posts. It was a communication system the Muslims brought from the south and implemented in their conquest of Spain. The Saracens realized the power of information timely received and used it to their advantage whenever possible. As they did with many aspects of their new neighbors, the Franks integrated the same messaging system over their Roman roads. The proud and superior Franks were multicultural copiers of rival empires, even if they didn't admit it.

Like the Muslim system they copied, the Frankish system had message-carriers that used fine, sleek stallions that came from the eastern lands and were capable of great speed and endurance with light loads. Boys and petite young men carried letters or spoken communications from one post to another, sometimes relaying their messages to other riders farther along the length of the roadway. The riders were called the "red kites" after a type of raptor found throughout the wooded portions of the empire. Like the long red wings the kites unfurled as they soared through the air, the colorful crimson capes of the riders fluttered in the wind, demonstrating the speed and endurance for which they were famous.

Franks believed it was bad luck to kill the birds or rouse them from their nests. Similarly, to molest or impede a red kite rider in the course of his duties was punishable by death, which could conveniently be carried out by the highway soldiers if they were so inclined. What would have been surprising to most Franks was the fact that many of the red kites, particularly those that were stationed at the routes to and from Aachen, were not themselves Franks. Most foreign emissaries and members of the trade elite preferred riders who came from their own lands and could be counted on to deliver reliable news from abroad, many times amounting to thinly veiled espionage.

* * *

There weren't many places Kasim traveled within the palace, so despite the countless doors and halls that seemed identical, he made his way through the corridors with purpose, carrying himself in something less than a rushed gait. While there were plenty of foreigners within the palace, there were few guests that Kasim had much in common with. Most mornings and nights, he would take his meals in his room, preferring to chew slowly and write quickly. Much of the food didn't agree with his palate; it was heavy with meat and grease. Kasim swore that half of all meals included swine, and it occurred to him on more than one occasion that members of the clergy must have had some influence in the kitchen.

As the envoy of the Córdoba Emirate and given his relationship as cousin to the emir, Kasim was given honored status. The respect afforded to him was tempered, however. Einhard and most other members of the church who lived or worked within the palace thought the accommodations to Kasim were disrespectful to the empire and more so to the faith. He was the enemy brought to the hearth. A new Judas brought to the supper table. Kasim had assuredly witnessed and perhaps participated in the deaths of countless Christians. That was not forgivable to Einhard, who wanted the foreigner removed from the palace altogether if not conveniently murdered on his travels back to his own lands. To alleviate internal unrest after his first year at court, Theoderic had Kasim's quarters moved to the far end of the palace's private wing. The consummate politician explained to the Muslim envoy that it was his intent to give his eastern guest the best view of the sun setting over the burning forests. Kasim only smiled and nodded with understanding.

Most envoys arrived in Aachen with an entourage. They came to the capital with their own clerks, concubines, and clerics. Horse-pulled carts unloaded exotic furniture and multiple trunks of clothes and personal trinkets at the steps of the palace in obvious attempts to show off their nation's wealth and significance on the world stage. The Abbasid caliph, Harun al-Rashid, would send his emissaries with gifts of flattery intended to purchase Charles's favor. The caliph once sent Charles a giant gilded water clock that later adorned a corner of the dining hall. Years earlier, Niketas, the older brother of Irene, the empress of Constantinople, arrived with six peacocks, which he presented to Charles as a birthday gift from his sister. Despite the cheers and awe expressed by those in attendance, members of Charlemagne's closest advisors scoffed at Irene's gift; they considered it beneath the expectations of an empire that wanted to claim its significance in a Frankish-dominated world. Charles saw most emissaries for what they were: flatterers and sycophants. Yet the emperor kept his disdain private and accepted all gifts with humble smiles and thanks. It was not lost on Kasim that the emperor's mannerisms were like those he himself had been taught back home.

Kasim arrived in Aachen without pomp. He brought no shiny gifts meant to charm the emperor. He knew his host would see through any cheap attempt to buy influence. His cousin's army was held ready by a shaky truce. It was the only validation he needed to remind his host of his nation's importance. Kasim's possessions fit into two saddlebags. Robes, tunics, and a Quran were all he brought with him. He kept no entourage. Kasim's only companion on his visit to Aachen was Basalt. His given name was Bazan ibn Khaldun. Bazan's first commander, Tariq ibn Ziyad, the famed general of the emir's Gibraltar division, gave him the name Basalt years earlier.

The name Basalt was earned in battle. Tariq watched in awe as the giant stood atop the basalt rocks on the base of the Pyrenees Mountains. Wave after wave of Gascon pikemen fell on Basalt's division as it attempted to reach the safety of the mountains. Basalt answered the assault. He swung his double shamshirs in a frenzy, splintering the pikes like brittle sticks and saving the lives of many Muslim warriors. Basalt was the grandson of the famed Grandoyne, the Muslim hero from the Battle of Roncevaux, where Charlemagne was repelled from Spain and lost his greatest warrior and friend, Roland. Even the Frankish version of the song draped Grandoyne in great esteem. The song credited Grandoyne with the death of several Frankish Peers and nobles before he himself fell to the blade of Roland.

While he didn't have legendary battles or kills to his name like his grandfather, Basalt was formidable and feared. He was blessed with his grandfather's famous size and grim appearance. He covered his whole massive body in robes of black and the deepest navy blue. Only his piercing white eyes and the whiskers of his long black beard confirmed the draped hulk was indeed a man and not some creature of nightmares. What little of his face that could be seen was decorated with scars that were a warning to the Christians that the man would not die with ease.

The furnishings in Kasim's quarters were spartan. There was a cot, a table with two chairs, and several colorful Persian rugs that brought traces of red and green to a brown and black world. The rugs were not Kasim's, but rather items regifted from Charles. Caliph Harun of Bagdad had them sent to the emperor, and Charles thought the young Kasim would find humor in walking atop the fine threads weaved by the rival caliphate.

Basalt required no accommodations. He used one of the rugs as his bed and a leather satchel for a headrest. With the winter cold, he would occasionally use the other rug as a blanket for warmth. He slept in front of the door to the room as a security measure, like a watchdog eager to protect his master. His great shamshirs were kept in the corner, concealed in wrapped cloth. It was forbidden for anyone to carry weapons in the palace except for the palace guards. If anyone had no need of steel within the dark palace corridors, it was Basalt.

As Kasim turned down the second-floor hallway of the residential wing, he saw Basalt standing firm at the door of their quarters, his legs spread wide before his dark cloak, which blended in with the hall's dim lighting. Basalt was preoccupied as Kasim approached. Someone or something behind Basalt had captured the giant's attention. Basalt was forever loyal and respectful. Whatever was fluttering behind him would not prevent the man from facing his master and avoiding showing his back. Kasim didn't relent in his pace toward his guard. Despite the disturbance that preoccupied the vigilant servant, Kasim had no hesitation. If there was anyone Kasim trusted implicitly in this world, it was his rock. They had spent many hard times together. They encountered hostilities more times than he could count. Basalt never gave his master reason to question his loyalty. As Kasim got closer, the sight and sound became clear. It was the crimson cape that gave away the identity of the person Basalt had blocked.

It was a boy, a red kite. Kasim assumed the actions of the hysterical boy were an attempt to get his attention. Basalt was holding the kite close, using his powerful right arm to hold the boy behind his back. Basalt was not wearing his khimar, or headscarf, and Kasim assumed his companion had been roused from within the room, as he preferred to keep his appearance as guarded as possible around people who would only stare and whisper. The noise the boy was making was one of pain, and it only seemed to increase as Kasim approached. He was on one knee as Basalt held his twisted wrist in the air. Kasim and

Basalt kept to their native tongue to ensure their conversation remained private.

"What is this? Why is there havoc in the hall, Basalt?" Kasim asked.

Basalt grumbled his response. "He will not say much of his purpose, master. He says he has an unwritten message that he refuses to deliver to anyone but you."

Both men were calm, as if the squirming boy did not exist. Kasim could hear the creaking of doors opening around him and knew palace guards would soon be close by, ever suspicious of their Muslim guests.

"And you are hurting him for this?" Kasim asked.

"Yes, master," Basalt said. "He must have some cunning to have made it to the quarters unmolested. I will not risk it."

"Let him go, Basalt. He is clearly harmless. Look at him," Kasim exclaimed. "He is a child. He cannot even grow hair on his face."

Basalt looked to the side and retracted his hand. The boy fell to the floor, curled in a ball as he cradled his wrist. His cries turned to a soft whimper. Kasim stood above the boy and spoke in Frankish as smoothly as the rough language would allow. "I am the emissary of Córdoba, boy. What is it that you have for me?"

The boy was unresponsive, and Kasim's concern for the inquiring eyes of other rooms forced him to action.

"Be still, boy. You are in no danger. My man will take you in my room and see to your hand." Kasim nodded and Basalt effortlessly scooped up the shaggy-haired boy under the armpits and carried him into the room. Basalt sat the red kite in one of the chairs and inspected his left wrist. The boy shirked at his touch, more from fear of the giant than his actual force.

Basalt shrugged and spoke in Arabic. "He has the bones of an old woman. If anything is broken, I cannot say."

Kasim squatted to look in the boy's eyes. He had studied the boy's appearance and manner since Basalt released his wrist. Kasim was a master of observation and could deduce many things from what remained unsaid. Hidden by hair on the boy's left ear was a series of piercings that began at his lobe and worked up the ridge. His hair was kept long, and Kasim assumed he meant to conceal the holes that had closed in but left telltale scars. Kasim believed the young man was a Saxon by birth. Kasim had spent several summers in the Saxon capital of Marklo as part of his emissary duties, traveling by sea to visit the camps of the rebel leader, Widukind, the cousin of Germanicus, the duke of Saxony. Kasim was charged by his cousin, the emir, to do his best to form a loose alliance with Widukind. It was al-Hakam's intent to strengthen the emirate by fostering as much discontent among Frankia's territories as possible. Saxony was ripe for support.

Traveling the Saxon camps, Kasim noticed the use of young boys for administrative duties among the army ranks. The Saxon men of fighting age were simply unavailable, being sent to the front lines of resistance. In their place were the boys of Saxony who had yet to pass the pagan rites of manhood, which in part meant the transfer of decorative earrings from the left ear to the right ear. Whatever the reason, Kasim believed this boy had been plucked from Saxony before undergoing his religious rituals. It was important for Kasim to build trust, and a typical way of doing that was to breed sympathy and camaraderie.

"My friend here is strong, as you have seen," Kasim said. "Sometimes he does not know how he can hurt others. He meant you no harm . . . and I . . . I do not mean you any harm." Kasim's words were gentle and smooth as if he were trying to calm a startled horse. "Basalt, bring our young friend some water."

"Ale," the kite sniffed. "I would like some ale if you please. I am in great pain from my travel. I rode two mounts to their death."

The boy was unaware of Muslim custom regarding the fermentation of grain and grape, and Kasim simply brushed away the proper, deeper response. He noticed the Saxon accent in the boy's speech.

"I'm sorry, my friend. I have only water." The boy gave a short nod. Kasim continued, "The risks you have taken to see through your task is very telling of your courage. I am not surprised, though. I count the men of Saxony among the bravest men I have ever met. Did you know that I have eaten at the table of Widukind on more than one occasion? He was a most impressive man."

The boy paid no attention to the comment and nodded again in agreement as he took the water from Basalt.

"What must make it difficult for you is to risk your life as a kite for a land that would rather slaughter your families and tear down your gods than lift you up to their level."

The boy looked at Kasim with a sharp skepticism. He felt that the foreigner had examined his thoughts somehow, yet he was too much in agreement to question the man's intent.

The boy whimpered, "Yes."

"I know how you feel," Kasim said.

Kasim led the boy along with several more comments to suggest that, despite their disparity in appearance, they were more alike than different. After a while, Kasim got the boy to laugh, and it was then that he knew he could press the rider for more information he might not want to give or might not even know he had.

There were a dozen scenarios running through Kasim's mind. A Saxon boy riding as a Frankish kite taking on the delivery of a Muslim message. It was all unusual and made it difficult for Kasim to guess with any certainty as to the boy's purpose. He had an uncomfortable suspicion that his interaction with the boy wasn't going to add clarity.

Basalt handed the boy a wet cloth, thinking he would want to clean away the layer of grime on his face and hands. The boy looked at Basalt with uncertainty about what he should do with the rag. Unsure, he set it aside with a weak smile. A small muffin of bread followed the cloth, and the boy eagerly grabbed it with his good hand before considering what was given to him. He wondered if the bread was filthy or polluted by Saracen hands. Perhaps the bread was poisoned. His suspicions were quickly doused by Kasim's calming voice.

"It is very good," Kasim smiled and said, "even though it is from a Frankish kitchen."

The boy shifted his eyes between the muffin and Basalt's gaze before he finally giggled and took a deep bite.

Kasim spoke softly. "Now tell me, my red kite, why have you sought me out? What message do you have for me?"

The questions reminded the boy that his task was difficult,

at least in his own eyes. He was given a specific message, but he understood nothing of its meaning, and that worried him. He shook his head as he responded, "I was told to say certain words to you and only you." He glanced quickly over to the trunk of Basalt, who remained close by.

Kasim grinned. "This man is in my service, my kite, and would rather die than betray me. Tell me, my friend, and have no fear for what you say. You sit with friends."

The boy had never met a Saracen before the events that brought him to the palace, but the look in Kasim's face and the calmness of his voice caused him to nod his head in acceptance of the master's words.

"The Saracen kite said . . . Samson's hair has been shorn"—the boy spoke the rest with hesitation, as it made no sense to him—"by a shepherd."

Kasim watched the boy's lips, waiting for more that never came.

"What do you mean a 'Saracen' kite?" Kasim asked. "Who sent you?"

"I was at my post, and a rider came from the south. He wasn't a Frankish red kite. He wore robes like yours beneath his cape, but not as fine." The boy was more focused on his muffin than his words, which Kasim took as a good sign.

The kite continued, "He slouched in his mount as he approached the station. The stable master noticed he was wounded and took him to the barn."

"Good, good. What else, my brave kite?" Kasim patted his knee in appreciation.

The boy responded, "That was all . . . lord." Kasim's puzzled frown frightened the boy. Kasim wondered if something had been lost in translation. "Y-You must understand. The Saracen kite was wounded when he arrived at my station. H-He almost fell from his mount. He could barely speak, and his accent was heavy." The boy paused in consideration of what he would say next. "He told me that if I brought you this news, I would receive this, a hundred times over!" The boy reached into the letter satchel under his cape and pulled out a coin. He showed it to Kasim and Basalt. His hand trembled, yet he presented it without fear.

Kasim took the coin and studied it. It was a dirham, a silver coin minted in Córdoba. The boy had completed the unusual task as best as he could and now had the courage to ask for his reward. If the message the boy delivered was cryptic and confusing, the specific words he used regarding his compensation were not, nor did Kasim think it was mere coincidence. The presentation of an emirate dirham under the pledge of compensation in an amount a hundred times its worth was a phrase relied on by Córdoban kites operating under the specific direction of the emir.

If a Córdoban kite died in the performance of his duties for the emir, his family was awarded a hundred silver coins in compensation for his service. Many young men took on the occupation for this assurance alone. But mentioning it to a foreign messenger was odd to Kasim. He knew it was a hidden message. He had never received a message like it before, but he identified the style of the delivery. It was an order to kill the kite, and Kasim looked at his guard in search of confirmation that he understood the same. Basalt gave the slightest of nods, and Kasim knew there was more to the message that had yet to be discovered. He smiled at the boy to hold his confidence that the foreigners were his friends.

"Are you sure there was nothing else said, my brave kite? Please take your time. Drink more water. We can send for ale, if it would ease your mind."

The boy smiled at that suggestion. "Yes! Ale will do over water every time . . . lord."

"Good! Good! Basalt, fetch our friend a flask of ale to quench his thirst. I will stay with him and we will work on his mystery a little more."

Basalt quietly left the room. He was unsure of how to find ale and made for the kitchen. He figured the kitchen workers' fear of him would work in his favor. Basalt returned and the boy seized the flask, tipping it up as drops trickled from the corners of his mouth.

"Coin, lord. Perhaps you can send your man for my coin, too?" The boy smiled widely. He felt as though he had run his course and succeeded in his charge. Kasim patted him on his knee again.

"No worries, young friend." Kasim thought to act on the boy's greed and walked over to his cot. He moved the cot from the wall and dug his fingers between a series of dark wooden floorboard planks. With a grunt and a creak, he pried a plank open. Kasim reached in and grabbed a huge leather pouch that took two hands to remove. The boy watched every move, rising slightly out of his chair to peer over Kasim's shoulder. He licked his lips in anticipation. Kasim set the bag on the table with a *thud*. The sound of coins clinking together was unmistakable, and the boy's face brightened.

"You see, I am prepared to pay your rightful fee, but before I do, we must go back to your time with the Saracen kite." Kasim took the other seat. "Drink. Let us talk, my friend. Close your eyes and go back in your mind to the arrival of the Saracen kite."

Kasim let the boy inspect the contents of the bag and ask whatever questions came into his mind. Kasim wanted the boy to be free of worry and not focus on the pattern of questions. As the boy stacked the coins into small towers of even height, Kasim came to the determination that, despite the red kite's belief that he was taking on the work of a Saracen kite, the man was instead operating in a hastily designed disguise. The Muslim he described was not large, yet he was not as small as a typical kite, either. He had a dark complexion and wore a khimar and turban; Kasim felt that there was nothing unusual about that. Several other items seemed out of sort to Kasim. Above his leggings, the Muslim wore thick leather padded breeches that stopped above the boot. The Muslim's cape was unusual as well. While it was red like those of all other kites, both foreign and Frankish, the bottom of his was trimmed in gold. Kasim believed the boy was no kite but rather a cavalryman who had shed his scale mail in the hope that he could ride quickly along Frankia's highway without fear of questioning.

Kasim didn't ask Basalt how the boy's life ended or what had been done with the body. The guilt of taking the life of an innocent would haunt him, he was sure of that. His dreams were already haunted by three ghosts, and he wasn't sure how he could fit another nightmare into his sleep. His only instruction to Basalt was that he did it with mercy and quickly so the boy wouldn't know his life was at an end. The rest could be left unsaid, as he and Basalt were of the same mind. The unspoken message was clear from the red kite had become clear. If Kasim was correct and the rider who brought the message was a Muslim cavalryman, it meant that the rider was most likely one of the guards that accompanied Naji on his journey to the capital. This was perhaps the worst possible scenario Kasim could imagine. The crown of thorns was in peril.

Kasim and Basalt were in full stride atop their mounts as they headed south along the highway toward Lyon. It was dawn. They had ridden through the first four stations and switched out horses for a second time after the third tower. After more than a full day of riding, Kasim could no longer feel his legs. They originally rode on Arabian steeds but had to switch out for local horses as their preferred breed was rare this far from the city. The sight of Basalt on a Frankish destrier seemed to better suit his size, yet he was sure his faithful servant would prefer a horse of Arabic blood.

Kasim used the most of his ride, thinking of what awaited him down the road and how he would react. While the task that had apparently been disrupted was not his fault, he did feel a heavy sense of disappointment and obligation to set things right. After all, Kasim was responsible for recruiting Naji. He learned from the Saxon kite that their destination was most likely the fourth post out of Lyon, which meant that he had less than half a day of hard riding before he arrived. Using his skills at recalling small details to arrive at hard conclusions, Kasim felt that it was more likely than not that the Muslim rider had not traveled too far since being wounded. Kasim asked the boy many questions about the Muslim rider's wound and horse. He asked about the location of his wound and the pattern of the bloodstain. He asked about the rider's horse. Was the horse's neck foamed from sweat? The boy had answered freely, and then he died.

VIII

- THE RAZOR OF ZARAGOZA -

Naji was a son of the Berber tribes of North Africa. He was known for his trustworthiness and ruthlessness in service to the old emir, Abd al-Rahman. Naji left his military obligations of the Córdoba Emirate more than two decades earlier and now served al-Hakam, the new emir, in other ways. He earned his reputation as a young commander, not by taking the heads of European infidels but instead by putting down wave after wave of Muslim rebellions in the border lands in the north of Spain.

Naji was best known for his brutality toward the people of Zaragoza, a border city that had changed hands to the Franks on more than one occasion. His soldiers had killed so many men during the siege of the city that the imam from the neighboring town of Tudela walked into his camp one night, prostrated at Naji's feet, and begged him to take no more Muslim lives. Naji was young and cold. He thirsted for blood in honor of his master, so when he surprisingly gave his word out of deference to the courageous old imam, he did so grudgingly. His cruelty, however, remained unfazed by his pledge. To satiate his brutality toward the men of Zaragoza and punish the rebels, he bound all those he captured attempting to flee the siege and shaved off their hair and beards with dull razors that left them mutilated and far from the sacred image of the Prophet.

To the Muslims of Córdoba, a shaved head was sacrilegious; it was a way to debase the faithful to the level of the infidel— *haram* or forbidden in the eyes of Allah. Many men preferred death rather than defying the will of the Prophet yet Naji did not honor their request. Naji would earn the famous label of the Razor of Zaragoza across the emirate.

In time, Naji's brutality caught up with him. He was trapped in a ploy by men from Zaragoza who held revenge in their hearts. He was lured from his troops camped outside Toledo by another imam that begged for a parlay. This time it was Naji who was subjected to the humiliation of being shaved and scarred by those he had once treated with brutality. The retribution devastated the warrior. Unable to look his master in the eyes, Naji left the army in disgrace and traveled back to his homeland in North Africa. Wandering the dry wastelands of Magreb, he reflected on his life and the fate he brought upon himself. Naji vowed to never brandish a blade in anger again, and to seal his covenant with Allah, he swore to not cut his hair or beard again.

Although Naji would stay true to his covenant, he eventually found other ways to express his loyalty to Emir Rahman's son, Hisham, and later his grandson, the current emir, al-Hakam. Hisham called the Berber back from Africa to be the emirate administrator of Mediterranean trade. A true servant and son of the emirate was a valuable commodity. Naji set up base in

Barcelona and took to his new life, searching for purpose. It was in Barcelona where the old warrior first crossed paths with Kasim.

Kasim saw signs of concern at the Frankish station on the horizon. The first thing he noticed was the flag that had been hoisted above the tower portion of the station. It was a black flag, and that meant that the soldiers who monitored the roads were to be on alert for hostile activity. This was the fourth station before entering the city of Lyon in central Burgundy and the first one that flew the black flag.

Kasim hoped the warning would not be used as a predicate for violence against him or Naji's men. He knew Naji and his small caravan would be unwelcomed at best. There were many horses tied off at posts outside the stone tower and several more untied and wandering around the roadside, feeding on tufts of brown winter grass. Although he was still far away, Kasim could tell that the untethered horses were smaller than those along the posts, and he knew them to be Arabian breeds. He also noticed that there were no men in sight, despite the many horses.

Highway stations were under the control of imperial troops, and disorder like that on display was generally not tolerated. Kasim pointed ahead to the scene, and Basalt responded by putting his heels to his horse. Kasim and Basalt didn't slow as they approached the posts along the front of the tower. The untethered horses fled at their approach, and those tied to the posts scrambled in fear of the thundering hooves. Kasim used the force of his sudden halt to propel himself out of his saddle, landing into an immediate stride toward the door. He learned much more as he approached. Men were propped up along the southern grass and mud along the backside of the stone tower. They were wounded Muslims and exhausted from their pain. Kasim took a passing inventory of their agonized faces.

There were five men sitting along the back of the tower. Two other men tended to them. Kasim had no doubt that the men were cavalrymen of the Navarre regiment, known more for their role as escorts for the emirate family and high-ranking imams than their prowess in battle. It was their particular clothing that marked them for Kasim. They had the distinctive crimson long-sleeve tunics and leggings. The joints of the arms and legs were tied off with black cloth. Their waists were marked by thick leather belts that tethered their thin scimitars and daggers. Their fine and embroidered red capes were also trimmed in gold, just like the Saxon kite had described. Some wore their elaborate steel chest and back plates over dark orange overshirts. These were the men of Naji's caravan and, at that moment, shear panic and dread poured over Kasim.

Kasim thought the men were pathetic, despite their impressive appearance. Years away from war made the regiment soft— a troop of glorified bodyguards. Whoever brought violence to the horsemen must have thought little of their threat. Kasim didn't need to study their faces and look for men he might know. He was looking for the one man the Saxon kite called Samson. Kasim believed Samson was most likely a self-proclaimed pseudonym for Naji.

Naji would have been an easy man to spot. Kasim yanked open the station entrance door with such violence that it took the wooden planks off the top hinge and scraped the floor before coming to a sudden stop three-quarters of the way open. The hatched windows of the station were clasped shut, and only a few candles burned from wall mounts. Kasim stood in the doorway, scanning the darkened interior, waiting for his eyes to adjust to the black shapes moving within.

Sitting on a stool with a straight back against a wooden stud post in the middle of the room was Naji. His arms were limp along his sides and dried blood caked his forehead. Kasim noticed three other cavalrymen who lay motionless and unattended on the floor. He didn't know if they still lived.

Kasim exhaled and said, "Aziz Hakim Naji."

Naji responded, "I expected you some time ago." Naji opened the left breast of his cloth tunic to inspect the area for damage. He grimaced in his effort.

"I came as fast as I could," Kasim said. "You did not make it easy for me to figure out the riddle that was sent with the kite. I see you kept your hair, though. Not so much like Samson, I would say."

A short, bald highway soldier moved from the darkness and into the space between Naji and Kasim. "Frankish," the little soldier screamed. "In this kingdom, in this station, you speak Frankish! You know this is the law that gives you privilege in these lands!" He rested his right palm on the hilt of his sword. His agitation was evident.

Naji couldn't hold back his frustration. He blurted back in his best Frankish, "If you and your men went to look for those who assaulted us, you would not have to be troubled by our rambling tongue."

"And leave your men here unattended? Ha!"

Kasim entered the argument and said, "You speak of laws,

yet you make no attempt to respect my rank. That, captain, is also a law of the highway."

The Frankish captain grimaced with a smug expression. Foreign officers operating under direction of their sovereigns were afforded the same privileges on the highway system as their Frankish counterparts. If Kasim suggested the Frankish captain look for the offenders, it was his duty to do so. The truce with Córdoba extended those rights over Kasim, yet Kasim knew the Frankish captain was reticent to give even minimal assistance. Most of Naji's wounded men were left outside, which was a major affront to Muslim customs regarding guests in distress.

Kasim followed with more chastisement of the Frankish captain. "This man," he said, pointing to Naji, "is a personal representative of the emir of Córdoba. I am the emir's cousin and emissary to Aachen. I travel under seal of Charlemagne to be kept unmolested. Protected with your own life, if need be." The captain scoffed at the notion. "To refuse us is to refuse your emperor, captain."

The captain studied Kasim's dress and guessed there was some truth to his claims, yet the uneasy peace with Córdoba was raw among many Franks and could cloud even a sensible soldier's judgment. The captain spat at Kasim's feet and raised his chin in a symbol of defiance. He was prepared to test his unwanted guest despite all signs urging him to do otherwise.

Kasim looked down at the floor and smiled. He wanted to belittle the man with taunts of decency and self-respect. He was even prepared for the possibility of violence, yet he knew the greater matter that brought him to this point governed all.

Kasim pushed the troublesome Frank from his thoughts and turned to Naji, choosing to ignore what he couldn't control.

Kasim disregarded the captain's demand and chose to speak in his native tongue to ensure that what was said would remain known to only those he trusted. If the captain was comfortable disregarding the laws of the empire that were designed to protect him and his men, Kasim would return the insult.

"What happened, Naji?" Kasim asked. "Where is the reliquary? What of the crown?"

Naji responded, "These people are no better than animals. You show them a wound . . . all they want to do is shove a hot iron into it and smear it with pig grease. Did their ancestors learn nothing from pillaging Africa and Asia? These men could have been saved."

Kasim and Naji were familiar with each other, yet there was no bond between opposites. It had been six or seven years since he last saw Naji at the port city of Cadiz. It was the place where Naji held informal negotiations with the pirate leaders of his tribal people. Naji picked the city because he knew his people would not join in talks far from their main base in Morocco. Al-Hakam knew his general had no skill with words, but he implicitly trusted the general to fulfill his obligations to his master. It was a good decision. The Berbers had always felt distrusted by the Arab majority and so the decision to place negotiations in the hands of one of their own was critical to ensuring that the shipping trade with the rest of the Mediterranean remained open.

If Saracens were indeed exotic-looking to Franks, then Naji must have appeared wholly unnatural. It wasn't his abnormal height and lanky frame that caught their attention. What was out of sorts was his hair and beard; the symbols of his prior transgressions. Naji collected not only Frankish stares but also the curiosity of Muslims. Kasim knew Naji's story, how the old general's degrading acts against fellow Muslims brought down his pride. Yet he also knew the laws of Islam. Men were to wear their hair and beards in the image of the Prophet. Hair between the ears and neck. Beards were to be full and well-kept. Naji had moved beyond the norm of what Kasim knew to be appropriate.

His beard came down to a point at his chest, but it wasn't thick and full. It was stringy and patched in some areas due to the dull blades of his punishment. There were thin strands of white along both sides of his mouth. In truth, Kasim found that Naji's beard was no longer than those of most Berber men. What truly differentiated Naji from all other Muslims, and anyone that Kasim had ever seen, was the length and style of his hair. It was so long that if it could flow unbound, it could touch the ground. It didn't flow straight or curl. It appeared as if he had only a few dozen strands that looked more like ropes springing from the scalp.

Rather than care for his wounds, Naji tended to his hair. He looped it in his lap to prevent it from touching the dirt floor of the station. The thick strands looked like a dark rainbow, as if its color told a story. They were charcoal black at the tips, transitioning to a salty mix before blending into a solid gray as it grew from his head. Looking at Naji and knowing the experiences of his past, Kasim thought Naji's hair was a testament to a painful life; he had seen tragedy and felt a guilt few others had ever experienced. If he had to, Kasim would guess the hair was a reminder or covenant the man had made with himself.

Naji spoke as he tended to his hair. "We were attacked by Frankish men, about twenty or more, halfway from the station to the south. A few of our men lay behind murdered. We had no choice but to leave them." Naji shook his head in disappointment at himself for leaving fellow Muslim brothers dead and unattended to. "They were waiting for us in the trees." Through his teeth, Naji spoke with a grimaced tone. He kept his eyes closed in a painful squint as he recalled the event.

"The reliquary, Naji."

"They wore ragged clothes, Kasim. No colors or symbols of Frankia or some province. They deliberately took on the look of highway robbers, but their swords were well-crafted and new. The bolts from their crossbows made the sharp noise of a Byzantine model, not the toys from around here."

Kasim grew anxious and agitated. He wanted to skip through details that could be put off for the moment. Kasim leaned in to break Naji's trance. "Naji, answer me." Kasim's voice exuded desperation. He said the next sentence slowly and with deliberation. "Tell me you still have the case."

Naji refocused himself into Kasim's eyes. "Of course not. Do you think that I would send for you if I did?"

"Son of a whore!"

"That is unnecessary, Kasim."

An old man shuffled in from a back room, carrying a small bucket and rag. He motioned to Naji that he wanted to tend to his wounds, assuming the foreigner spoke no Frankish. Naji winced in pain at the man prodding the gash on his forehead with the cleaning rag. Naji cursed and clinched as if he wanted to strike the Frank. The old man cowered backward at the threat and stepped away from the rag and bucket. He knew Naji's words were a curse to him, even though the language was a mystery. Naji dispensed the old man with a sideways glare and wave of his hand.

"I tell you, Kasim, these men didn't demand gold or our weapons. As it were, they said nothing at all. They went directly to the cart where the reliquary was held and fled as quickly as they set upon us. They took the larger cart filled with coin and goods that we used to mask our presence as traders. Their leader— I believe him to be their leader—he was young and deliberate with his actions and words. His Frankish wasn't the broken kind of some mud hut villager. He was a large man, though still smaller than your man Basalt. He was no common cutthroat . . . but he bore the scar of a throat that had been cut."

Kasim looked away from Naji and mumbled to himself as if he were adding numbers in his head. "Why didn't you . . . Do you not know what this means? Of course you do not. You were instructed to guard and not ponder the task. Just guard it. From Alexandria to Aachen." Kasim's fear quickly morphed into anger. "With your life! Which you did not do!"

Naji remained calm and cracked a condescending smile. "Careful, Kasim. You go too far."

Kasim realized that the aged warrior still had pride despite having stripped himself of rank and honors. Kasim looked to the floor and nodded in agreement. He did not believe Naji was at fault, yet he was the only person he could impose his frustration on. Kasim scanned the room. The dull darkness and smell of death were beginning to pierce his sinuses and temples, both of which sought the fresh cool air outside.

Naji took the break in the tension to tend to his wounds. He wet the rag left on the lip of the bucket and dabbed at his forehead as Kasim exited through the broken door.

Basalt was outside, tending to his brothers who lay along the wall. He was not comfortable with words and left the inquiry of Naji to his master. It was for the best. Had Basalt been inside the station, the Frankish captain's life might have been at risk.

Kasim was staring south along the road, looking and wondering where the assailants were at that moment. He knew that asking Naji would be a waste of time. Whoever took the case wouldn't likely travel in the direction they had fled. More likely, the true course would only be taken once the thieves were safely out of sight. Besides, Kasim was well aware that the Frankish laws that permitted him privileges to travel unobstructed were limited to the roadway itself. His rank as an emissary of the emirate would only spur common Franks to violence if he traveled through the southern wilderness, where his people were held with the same disdain as the devil himself.

Kasim walked to where horses were posted near the water trough. There was no sense in remaining. Naji exited the station shortly after and squinted to protect his eyes from the bright afternoon sun. Naji stopped to wrap his hair around his waist and stuffed the end into the fold of his tunic. He sensed that Kasim's disappointment was eating at him.

Naji said, "Do you not believe this is all part of some Ionian theater? Elaborate words and motions. Nothing real."

Kasim just shook his head, preferring to keep his eyes on his hands which worked the straps of his saddle.

"What do you mean?" Kasim's voice carried his frustration.

"All of this scheming. For what? Some trinket? I have attended more peace negotiations than most all men who walk this earth. Nations do not bind their understanding on fanciful ornaments. They exchange daughters. They deliver prosperous lands and chests of coins. This?" Naji shook his head. "I followed orders like a soldier, defraying my own thoughts. I just do not understand."

A feeling of disappointment came over Kasim. For all Naji's accomplishments, even if infamous and wildly unsettling, he expected more from him. "This is what the Franks demanded for peace. It matters little what you think, Naji."

"I think of gold," Naji said. "Gold makes kings, boy. It buys ships. It purchases armies. Why sue for peace and demand the symbol of some fanciful tale over gold?"

Kasim raised an eyebrow at being referred to as a boy; it was a minor insult that might have been more of a poor choice of words than a direct jab. "Gold? It's a useless metal. It cannot be sharpened. It cannot withstand a war hammer. It has value only because men say it does."

Naji sensed that the educated boy from the highest of families was attempting to show his superiority. "And twisted limbs of a thorn bush, do they have more value? I tell you we are on a fool's errand!"

"Yes!" Kasim shouted. "Much those twisted limbs have much more value!"

Naji retorted, "Nonsense!"

"If a king will happily march his armies into slaughter, if he risks all to connect himself to his god in the eyes of his people, then the answer is yes," Kasim said. "Your own inability to understand the importance of your task has placed our peace in jeopardy."

Naji chuckled. "Ah, and then there is that inconvenient matter. What if this was just a ploy to undermine the peace?"

Kasim's natural inclination was to challenge every comment from Naji, but the point had merit. Who would covet the crown of thorns except for an equal zealot or someone bent on chaos? It was an afterthought now that the Franks' prize had been lost, yet Kasim felt compelled to examine the aftermath of the heist. The reliquary had been placed in a case built specifically for this trip. Emir al-Hakam wanted the reliquary to have a chest fit for its status as a revered symbol of Christianity. It was the emir's intent to bathe the reliquary in an air of legitimacy that Charles would acknowledge and appreciate.

The chest was massive. It sat atop a flat-bedded cart and was anchored by black leather straps. The case was built from the hard, red oaks brought to Valencia from central Spain. The steel casing of its borders was crafted by the emir's finest smiths to be made impenetrable as well as beautiful. It was etched with the symbols of Frankia. The black eagle and fleur-de-lis were prominently displayed on all sides. The generous use of thick wood and metal meant the weight required two hackneys for the long trip north. The latch was a size and weight that required two hands to operate. Yet when Kasim walked up to the lone cart huddled among the Córdoba palfreys, the latch and door of the case looked like thin wire of a wicker basket that had been trounced under bulls' hooves. Kasim inspected the wreckage and wondered what could have snapped the locked latch and curled the steel. He yanked on a loose plank that had fallen over the hole made by the thieves.

To Kasim's surprise, the case that the reliquary was placed within was still inside. The case was something of a reliquary that housed the true reliquary. The recent stewards of the crown of thorns looked upon the original reliquary as having so much history of its own that the reliquary itself warranted revered treatment. The case sat on its side and was cracked open. Kasim could tell that it was empty, but he turned it upright anyway. The interior of the case was upholstered on all sides with fine red silk. There were runs in the fabric where the points of the smaller, original reliquary had snagged the silk during the heist. Kasim was gentle with the case. He knew it was much sturdier than its age suggested, yet he wanted to give the old box the respect it deserved. The reliquary was shaped like a small building with a pitched roof. It was twice as long as it was wide and much larger than Kasim had expected.

The case told a story. Engraved in the thin silver plates that covered the box on all four sides were scenes from the crucifixion. All Muslims were familiar with the story of Jesus. He was considered a holy prophet of Allah and was to be revered by every Muslim. Kasim knew the parts of the Quran that spoke of Jesus and Mary better than most imams. A vital part of his role as an emissary assigned to Christian kingdoms was not only to understand the religion that created the divide between their people but to also promote where the two religions were in harmony.

Kasim once presented Charles with a copy of the Injii of Isa, the Muslim gospel as revealed to Jesus.

"Great Emperor, the Injii is one of the five books of the Quran. It details the gospel as told to Jesus. And Mary, the blessed Virgin, she is in here, too! She is the only named woman in the books of the Quran. The greatest of honors."

Kasim remembered the delicate hands of the emperor as he turned the gold-illuminated pages of the Injii. The words were Arabic, and Charles ran his fingers over them with reverence. Kasim spoke with soothing words.

"You are touching the name 'Miriam,' Lord Charlemagne. That is our word for Mary."

Charles's face radiated with a childlike delight, and for an instant, Kasim felt that an understanding between their two peoples was possible. It was now Kasim's turn to feel that sense of connectedness as he ran his own fingers over the reliquary images raised from the surface. The judgment by Pilate. The scene of Jesus carrying his cross to the mound. The crucifixion, with Jesus flanked by the two thieves. Mary kneeling at her son's body. He thought the images, the very box itself, were the most beautiful thing he had ever touched and felt that the way it was discarded by whoever raided the caravan was a travesty. Kasim wanted to take the case with him on his quest to recover its contents, but that wouldn't be practical. Before he left, he would see to the case's safety by handing it to one of Naji's cavalrymen for safekeeping until he could return it to its rightful owner with its contents intact.

Naji checked on his wounded cavalrymen, then turned his attention back to Kasim. Naji couldn't evade the feeling that he was a glorified pack mule in Kasim's service. It wasn't Kasim's younger age or higher rank that fostered Naji's disdain, nor was it Kasim's refined speech or the ease with which he walked within the circles of Córdoba's enemies. Kasim was a talker and Naji was a man of action. Kasim had the relationships in Alexandria, where the case came from. That was what Kasim was: a man of relationships. He was the man chosen by the emir to hand the reliquary to the king of all Franks. The eyes of princes would watch Kasim as he presented the case. When Naji stood guard over the case from Alexandria to the forests north of Lyon, no one else watched but thieves. Considering everything, however, Naji felt as if the blame would fall on him because, after all, the relic was lost while in his care.

Naji spoke, "This failure will only act to disgrace me further. I thought my life was over twenty years ago. This is much worse. I am shamed. This loss is the careless act of a child!"

Kasim said, "It is through no carelessness that you were called upon, Naji. You were the only Muslim that could complete this undertaking. That is why I asked the emir to let me use you for this task."

"A task at which I have failed."

"No! Delayed? Yes. You are a Berber. You are a great general. No other could cross from Africa with the assurance of safe passage other than you. No one could stand against the stares of the Abbasids in Alexandria better than you. You also have a great knowledge of the southern realm of the Franks."

"Yet that has not done me, or my emir, any good, has it?" Naji raised his hands to the sides of his neck, moving his head from side to side. The pain from his wounds was quickly becoming an afterthought.

Kasim spoke, "Have courage in your faith. It is the will of

Allah that you and I have come to this place. At this time. To seek out the man who has taken our peace!"

The men wasted no time preparing themselves to leave the roadside station. Kasim knew there would be opportunities on their travels to question Naji further about the run-in with the bandits in the hope of gleaning some information that might be in the dark spaces of his mind. He needed something. Kasim told Basalt that they would travel light, just the three of them. The remaining Muslim men would be sent along the roadway, back to Lyon, where Muslim merchants were known to visit. Traveling with more than three men would only bring unnecessary suspicion.

Basalt imposed his will on the station captain and his men. The little man's objections lasted one insult and were answered with a backhand that rendered him unconscious; the other soldiers fell in line. Basalt collected water flasks and dried beef to last a few days. Fresh and fed horses were chosen.

Kasim bridled his new horse in thought. He wasn't exactly sure where to go in a world that was hostile toward him. He had traveled portions of Frankia before, but those were measured movements, with royal escorts and the seal of Charles to ensure safe passage. Part of Kasim wanted to return to Aachen, but that would announce that the crown had been lost, and the relic was the only reason he had left the safety of the capital. He also had a strong suspicion that Aachen was the one place where the relic was not headed. Whoever hired the thieves was willing to risk all. The possibilities should be limited. Bandits applied their trade for gold and silver, and such an assault would require a fortune for their theft. Charles's health had muddied the waters.

The desperate would come out from their lairs, but not from hiding. It was impossible to guess with any certainty.

"Where will we go, Kasim? Aachen? Rome? Many find it clever to hide themselves in crowds. I know no better place for hiding from Muslims than the holy cities in the empire."

"Either Aachen or Rome would be a fine place to hide if that was the thief's intent—to hide from the emirate and wait. We will go back to Marseille."

The word "Marseille" struck Naji like another fist to the jaw. "Is that wise? Why would we go to the city that has one of the largest garrisons in the empire? Rome is a merchant city. Marseille is a military port. It will be swarming with Franks. The thieves would be walking into the wolves' den. You must have some idea where the crown is headed."

"To Louis, you mean? Why? He is emperor already and has little need to advance his own cause. Bernard? Perhaps. They say he is a holy man and covets the connection with Christ as much as his grandfather. Then there is the pope. He may want the crown to auction off between the two. There are many more possibilities, more than there are stars in the sky."

Naji said, "Yet none of the names you mention thus far are in Marseille."

"Yes. We go to Marseille to search for one who surely knows more than I. There is a Jewish merchant there who may be able to help. He knows the roads of the empire like no other. We have little time. Daylight burns."

Naji wanted to say more. He wanted to protest his thoughts for shunning Marseille. He wanted to announce the reason for his rekindled anxiety about returning to the city where he landed ashore. The truth was that returning to the port from which Naji arrived suddenly frightened him more than the Franks that surrounded him in all directions. He worried that word of his actions in Alexandria had followed in the ships that sailed after him.

IX

- THE SON OF ROLAND -

The first thing Oliver saw was a brown cloud billowing up from beyond the hillcrests. It was not the smoke of a fire. Fire smoke billows black and reaches quickly for the high realms of the sky. The cloud spreading from beyond the hills seeped more outward than upward, drifting to the south with the wind. It dissolved like blood polluting a bucket of water, thinning its color as it floated away. In time, the cloud became a tan haze that replaced the light blue sky. A dark line then began to form on the ridge of the hills far to the east.

Oliver looked on from his saddle with no emotion. His wavy brown hair sprouted from under the sides and back of a silver helm that hid his father's good looks. His eyes shifted from inside the carved-out lion's eyes to watch the black line of the ridge grow in length.

Oliver could feel Draca, the dragon, tense his muscles with each hollow snort. Draca did not neigh. He grunted and snorted. He stomped and scraped the hard earth with his front hooves; it was the way the animal spoke to his master. Draca's anxious protests were not enough. He had more to convey. He shifted to each side and reared backward on his haunches as if he were about to pounce forward. He wanted the flesh cage that circled him to disappear and watch with horror at the power he possessed.

Oliver didn't tighten his legs on Draca, preferring instead to let the mount express his eagerness. The force and size of the dark warhorse pushed back the pikemen cushioned all around. Draca was an angry beast that delighted in the prospect of battle. Oliver knew his friend had a sense for war, and he loved him for it. Some horses knew battle was upon them when they were brushed with care and draped with their heavy coats of mail. Draca seemed to sense it earlier. He could smell the sweat of anxiety in the air and hear it in the distant horn blasts. Creatures like Draca were a rare gift from God, and Oliver dreaded the future day of a battle without him.

His impatience noted, Oliver bent over, uttering soft words to focus the steed's attention away from the little men huddled around him and instead to the scene developing ahead. He gently scratched Draca's dark brown neck with a gloved left hand and combed his black mane with his fingers. Draca responded with convulsing flesh that flexed and relaxed with the slightest of touches. Oliver understood his friend more perhaps than he knew any man.

More times than not, Oliver needed no reins to guide Draca through turmoil. There was never a movement backward. They moved forward as one body with a single mind. Muscle and steel merged together in a terrible dance that brought quick and certain death. The weight of a father's heavy fame seemed a manageable burden when he sat on Draca's back. Oliver was the only son of the famed paladin Roland and named for his father's closest comrade.

Oliver wondered with curiosity rather than fear as to when the dark growth that overtook the hilltop would wane. Several calm breaths turned to many and still it spread until the brown crown of the hills was fully lined in black. From this distance, he knew that the black mass would begin to advance much faster than it appeared. As he scanned the countless ranks of his own soldiers, who stretched in filed lines as far as he could see in either direction, he wondered if his men understood what awaited them.

Many of Oliver's men were young and knew little of battle. Even the older ones had likely only seen skirmishes here and there. He was certain that few of his men had experienced a situation like the one that was moments away from unfolding before them. It was typical behavior. The young ones fidgeted where they stood, standing on their toes to get a clear look over the harder veterans lined in front of them. When they weren't staring ahead, the younger men glanced from side to side, looking for strength in the faces on either flank.

Radwig made his way to Oliver's side as the sea of Franks gave way to a familiar face. He was beyond late. Radwig's journey to his master was not an easy one, and Oliver found it fitting punishment. Radwig flailed and stumbled with each step, relying on the soldiers in the ranks to keep him from falling. For a moment, the troops were amused by the drunk man instead of focusing on the death that headed for them.

The ground was moving under Radwig, and he hoped it would cease when he reached his destrier, which was waiting close to Oliver. It wasn't the first time Oliver watched Radwig struggle with his drink before battle. It had become an unwelcome tradition. In the end, Radwig's behavior was a minor inconvenience in that Oliver's man had never failed him.

Radwig labored in getting his left boot in the saddle stirrup and had even more difficulty pulling himself up onto the horse. Two soldiers had to place their pikes on the ground and push the portly man upright. It wasn't that Radwig was short as much as his mount was enormous. Despite the destrier's size, it had to be separated from Draca by a buffer of several columns of men. Draca seemed to save some of his most intense fits of violence for other horses. When paired directly next to each other moments earlier, Draca slammed his head into the other horse's neck and tried biting off its left ear.

Radwig finally found his seat. He steadied himself to control vomit from spewing forward. He burped air instead of wine, and that pleased him. Radwig gave Oliver a respectful nod to let him know he was sound now that he sat where he felt most comfortable in the world.

"Cavalry charges are evil things, Lord Oliver. They question a man's conviction like nothing else."

Radwig scanned the valley and hills off in the distance, from where the black line had formed and the brown cloud spread. He had to squint until his eyes were almost shut; age had taken the details of sight. He noticed that there were no natural impediments that would slow down the oncoming cavalry; it only confirmed his statement. He fought to clear the fog in his head and wondered if the pain of sobering up was the preferable option to getting more drunk.

Radwig was a monk, which was ironic since his name meant "war counselor" in Frankish. He was not a pious, tonsured man with pink hands and frailty, but rather a hardened warrior who took the cloth as an afterthought. As a young man, Radwig had ridden with Oliver's father and stayed on with the son as his personal priest and advisor. The idea of taking on the cloth was his own. It would mean that he could protect the once-impressionable Oliver from church influence that he knew the father would want suppressed.

Oliver responded to Radwig, "I do not agree, old man. The defense of a cavalry charge can be a beautiful thing if done properly. God forgive me for saying it, but there is beauty in slaughter. These Lombards before us claim their own cavalry are rivaled by none other, save perhaps the Saracens. A bold assertion, I think. We will test that claim right here. Right now." Oliver's words were not boldly spoken for others to hear, nor did he animate himself. He spoke like an old war master watching from afar, relaxed and unconcerned with the common soldier who would bleed that day. Unlike the comfortable old generals, Oliver sat at the center of his army, with banner boys to his back, so there was no mistake as to his commitment to the cause.

Oliver continued, "Cavalries are tricks. Do you not think so, monk? Dreadful tricks, but tricks nonetheless. Like some animal that growls and hisses or shows its teeth to look fiercer than it truly is, all to mask some fear or weakness."

Radwig had a puzzled look on his face. "Lord?"

"Tell me, old friend, have you ever seen pikemen fall to a cavalry charge? True pikemen, trained to toe a line at all costs?"

Radwig closed his eyes as he ran through the images of his battle memory that reached back almost forty years. "Aye, lord. Eric of Friuli fell on the Avars in the fields of Drava when your father was a general to Charles and I was one of his pages. We were observers as part of an emissary mission to meet Princess Irene. We watched from afar, but it was still . . . very violent. I do not care to hear the screams of horses." Radwig didn't use words carelessly, so Oliver took his response to heart.

"Were Eric's men braver than the Avars on that day?"

Radwig shook his head. "I do not think it is proper for one man to question the bravery of another while watching from afar, my lord. I cannot say. It was savage, though."

"I would wager that it was the Avars who were weak of mind, because when a disciplined cavalry meets equally disciplined pikes, pikes win every time."

Radwig laughed. "Is that so?"

Oliver firmly responded, "Aye. It is so. And these motherless bastards will prove me right."

The old monk didn't know whether Oliver was referring to the Lombards or his own motherless bastards, but the point was clear. This battle, which was moments away, would be won in the will of men. The will to trust in your captain's commands to stand and hold when your eyes and instincts told you to run.

Radwig crossed himself and grunted with a slight sense of cheer. He chose his master well. Better to die by this man's side in the slaughter of heathens and traitors than live a hundred more years at peace tending to some monastery garden. Radwig knew his frontline fighting days were long from over, and that suited him fine. Over the years, his arms had shrunk while his belly grew. Yet even if Radwig would no longer stand along the front line, he was content with a few new scars.

Radwig wore his brown monk's robe with no armor. It was heavily worn with patches and faded by the sun, but it was recently washed. Oliver had ribbed his old advisor before. Even though Radwig had enough silver for a superb uniform and mail, the response was as expected. "This is the finest rag I own, lord. Besides, I believe it is best to approach Saint Peter in unsoiled humility." His wooden cross hung low from his neck by a thin leather necklace. The enormous silver broadsword at his waist hinted that this man of God was not cast from some mold; he was neither full monk nor total soldier. When Oliver once asked him why he wore no protection, his answer was philosophical and practical: "Blessings keep me on my feet, young master. They keep me nimble, as these old bones cannot hold the weight of steel like they used to. When it is my time to be called, plates of armor will not matter much."

Ironically, Oliver's father, Roland, was a testament to that truth. His fine plated armor didn't save him from Saracen steel. His son did not understand the subtlety in Radwig's answer.

Radwig's hair flowed back in white with gray wavy strips reaching below his hood. In truth, he looked more regal than his humble clothes suggested. Oliver was sure Radwig was a forgotten son of some noble family, and yet for all the familiarity between the two, he hadn't the courage to ask. Radwig's white beard shone in fine contrast against his sun and wind-burnt brown skin. His eyes told a story of more battles than all others about him. He had no use for fear, and because of that, Oliver had every use for him.

Radwig looked at Oliver with the kind of pride a father must feel. Radwig saw Roland's strength in his son's hard jaw and in his words. He'd known the man since he learned to walk and took the little boy into his care after his father fell at Roncevaux. Having no family of his own, Radwig understood how the boy felt. The two gravitated to each other to fill voids in their lives. Seeing Oliver in his father's old armor brought on a smile and fond feelings of the past. Radwig remembered how tough Roland could be on his son, but the experiences, hard words, and lessons were for a reason. Some boys responded to love and affection. Others needed a thick stick to the skull. Oliver was most certainly the latter, and the boy had grown to a man content in accepting that.

At the time, Radwig cringed, but now both he and Oliver could find humor in Roland's insults and discipline. Radwig laughed at his own difficulties with mounting his horse. He remembered little Oliver trying to mount his pony as his practice sword hung between him and the saddle, blocking the right leg from slinging itself over the pony's back. The boy would fall over and over, twisting his saddle sideways as his father shook his head in disappointment. "Sweet Jesus, boy," Roland once said. "I was born on a horse . . . and what of you? Had I known it would come to this, I would have shot you into the sheets instead of between your mother's legs."

Radwig looked to Oliver, who continued to appear unconcerned about the far-off threat that grew closer. Radwig thought, *He shows no fear even as death barrels down from the hills. Men would follow him into hell itself.* Oliver looked the part of the general his father had once been. He took pride in his appearance, especially his father's armor and helm. It was a connection to the legend, Charles's proclaimed right hand, that no one else could own. The songs of Roland told of a Saracen lance that pierced his heart, bringing death without the knowledge of whether his fellow Peers would survive. The mail and sword of Roland were legendary. The songs went into the most minute detail of the armor and sword's appearance and supposed magical properties. It was a relief to know that, with the armour, Oliver could have that part of his father.

The armor was supposed to be on display in Aachen with the palace's dark memorial to the other Peers, but Charles made an exception to encourage Oliver to serve Louis as loyally as his father had served the king. The armor that made its way to the Peers' room was Roland's replica suit from the baggage train, made perfect down to the piercings and dents. Oliver was disheartened that his father's sword, Durandal, was not recovered with the armor. He often wondered what it was like to wield the blade that Charles once carried into battle before he was gifted the famed sword Joyeuse.

The bards told of Durandal as having a tooth of Saint Peter embedded in its hilt and being consecrated with the blood of Basil of Caesarea. The songs said that Roland snapped the blade in two rather than let it fall into heathen hands. Other rumors told differently, that it was taken from the field of chaos by some faceless enemy. Although Radwig was at the battle in the mountain pass, he couldn't confirm whether Durandal was destroyed or taken and encouraged Oliver to keep hope. The loss of the sword made the armor that much more precious. Oliver would see the plate oiled and polished daily, but he refused to mend the hole that tore through the ram's head embossed in the center of the chest plate. He wanted all to notice it at first sight and know that Roland still lived through the son.

The dark cloud ahead of Oliver and Radwig began to take form. Men on horses now took shape, ranging far from north to south. Colors began to emerge from the darkness. Great flags of red and green bearing white crosses hung erect in the air, evidencing the speed of the riders. The colors marked the unmistakable presence of the Lombards, a vassal state of Frankia that chose to play a submissive role no more. The army of Desiderius, king of Lombardy, had been soundly defeated by Oliver on the plains of Pavia weeks earlier. The famed cavalry of Lombardy, led by famed General Alboin, was late to join battle with the infantry, and the result was utter disaster for Desiderius.

The Lombard cavalry, minus the recently deceased General Alboin, now came before Oliver. The force represented Lombardy's great gamble to make up for the earlier mistake. A rout of Oliver's army could rally the cities of Lombardy to unite once more. It was desperate, but there was no other option but submission. Oliver knew the Lombards would attack with the ferocity of a trapped animal, risking all to repel their Frankish masters. This would be a battle of passion, which was what the Lombards chose to bring to the field. Yet it wasn't only the sight of a fast-moving mass that would bring on the fear to Frankia's ranks; it was also the noise and, even more so, the unnatural feeling of the ground in movement.

The noise came before the earth vibrated. It was a low, dull, swelling song that started off like the rumbling of some beast. It grew in intensity as new sounds joined the chorus. Hooves slammed into hard-packed earth in a thunder that an army of drummers could not match. Then came the clanging of metal and screams to create a terrible harmony. No threats or curses were recognizable; it was only raw rage. Those new to the experience would surely tremble as they looked to their left and right for an excuse to flee. Of course, no one would run. That wasn't the Frankish way, and besides, those in doubt knew they'd more likely die from the hands of their brothers if they turned their backs.

"Prayers and piss." Radwig looked over at the boys standing back and between him and Oliver. There seemed to be abundant displays of both prayers and piss, and that made him laugh. Radwig continued, "I was piss at my first battle. A sea of piss! The commander fed me a strong backhand for drowning his boots." Radwig laughed loudly at the memory, and the boys around him glared in puzzlement. "Your father, Roland, was a prayer. Is that not amusing? Me to one day be a monk and him so very far from one."

Radwig grabbed his reins tight in preparation for his screaming sermon to follow. Part of his duties to Oliver was acting as the general's mouthpiece. Oliver commanded respect through his actions and cared little for the art of speech. Oliver believed that he could move men better through his actions. The old monk raised his sword, and a mass of heads turned its attention from the scene in front of them. He began with Deuteronomy.

Radwig stood in his saddle, punching the air with his blade and bellowed as loud as he could muster. "Be strong and of good courage. Do not fear or be afraid of them, for the lord your God,

he is the one who goes with you!" Oliver crossed himself, causing a wave of soldiers to follow.

Radwig then added in his own crude motivation in lieu of the
Old Testament. "What are these whores of Judas to us? Do they
not know that even the beasts of hell cannot withstand the chosen sons of Christ Almighty? Frankia will hold every line from
now until his return! Neither heaven nor earth hath warriors
like the men of Frankia!" Men roared in support of the vulgar
lines, thrusting their pikes and swords in the air. The sound
spread and echoed throughout the long ranks.

Oliver smiled with a mixture of pleasure and amusement.
He knew Radwig could rally the dead from their graves. "When
the archbishop hears of your blasphemy, Radwig, he will have
your balls."

Radwig held his mount steady and shrugged his shoulders in
indifference; his face betrayed a childish grin that Oliver replicated. Oliver's attitude soon changed with a single heartbeat. He
remembered the anger that disturbed him as the men formed
up before dawn. He saw the young faces who needed to be directed where to go and how to form proper lines. Up to that moment, he chose not to let it crowd his thoughts. Battle formation
was no place to show any emotion other than savagery, and savagery wasn't part of his constitution. His anger sprung from the
decision of the Twelve Peers back in Aachen and, in particular,
Wilfred, duke of Aquitaine.

Wilfred was the unofficial member who took control of the
Peers upon the death of Oliver's father. Oliver believed Wilfred
had thrown his influence and gold around in meetings and insisted that the troops, mostly his own Aquitanian men, be

directed away from Lombardy. Wilfred saw the threat of the Lombard rebellion as rather minor in comparison to the unfinished wars with the Avars farther to the east. Wilfred diverted his prime forces to buttress the armies of Bernard. Other troops were sent to the edge of Spain to add certainty to the fragile peace with the Abbasid Caliphate. Wilfred's motivation was obvious to Oliver. It was a slight to Louis and an attempt to coddle favor for his family's own ambitions toward the crown. Oliver steamed internally and could hold his frustration no longer.

"That old sheep fucker sends hard men to the east, and I am handed farm boys and drunks. I wonder how many cavalry charges Wilfred has stood against?" There was more to it, he thought. Wilfred had always stood in the shadows of Roland's deeds and preserved his resentment for the son.

"Aye. Safe to say he'd be both piss and prayers, my lord. Perhaps there's a shred of hope in all of this. What if Aquitaine simply has supreme faith in your abilities, Lord Oliver?"

Both men laughed to each other. The soldiers looked on in bewilderment, wondering how the only men on horseback could remain so calm. Radwig ripped his reins to send his steed violently sideways, catching the attention of all the men who circled Oliver. Radwig raised his arms to the heavens so the men would notice that it was the time for another reckoning. Radwig returned to the Old Testament.

"Do not fear, for I am with you! Do not be dismayed, for I am your God! I will strengthen you and help you! I will uphold you with my righteous right hand!"

Insults were more popular than scripture. Those few older soldiers who had heard the battle song of a cavalry charge before paid little attention to the monk's tame recitation of crude Latin, choosing instead to dull their fear by squeezing the last drops from leather flasks. That was the third answer to fear. Drunkenness was surprisingly tolerated among the ranks so long as the men could respond to commands. The very sight of Radwig had been Oliver's tacit approval of drinking before battle. If men couldn't hold their drink and mind their orders, they were pulled from the ranks after the fighting and afterward whipped mercilessly in front of the entire camp. Repeat insolence was dealt with by instant execution.

The older men in the ranks joked among each other, patting the shoulders of the boys at their side and telling cruel jokes to break the tension. Better to be drunk and merry if certain pain and possible death were rushing forward. Several of the older men bent over, holding themselves upright by the spears as they emptied their stomachs.

"Piss, prayers, or wine, it seems, monk."

Radwig shouted his approval. "Aye, my lord!"

"Tell more to pray, monk. From the looks of the ground all around us, there is already enough piss and wine to suck us all ankle deep in mud!"

Radwig roared again in laughter with his face shining at the heavens above.

"Good," Oliver said to himself. "The men will take comfort in his lightheartedness." Oliver was content in knowing his men would have courage, regardless of its source. Yet if the sound racing toward the Franks didn't rattle his tested men as they stood in wait, Oliver knew there was another challenge to come. It was the physical sensation that came from the rumbling mass before them, disrupting the very peace of the firm earth below their feet. It wasn't until the field began to vibrate that the Franks accepted that there would be no escape from the slaughter to come. All ranks of men, regardless of their experience, looked to the earth beneath their feet, wondering if the ground itself would crack open to swallow them. Sand among the dry winter grass began to dance and shift like water. Lines that held their position began to skew and mix in an early state of chaos.

Radwig's horse sensed the men's fear and stirred with the ranks. Radwig pulled on his reins to restore control. Draca remained unshaken, and Oliver knew he road atop royalty. Courage was not limited to man alone, and Oliver felt blessed as he smiled to himself. The world was collapsing around him when Oliver slowly unsheathed his sword. Using the broad side, he smacked the back of the young banner boy to his left, awakening him from his frightened trance; he was staring intensely at certain death coming for him. Oliver's nod to the boy was all it took for him to raise the yellow banner he had pointed to the earth. The leather-clad boy climbed on another soldier's shoulders and swung the banner with both hands by its end, hoping his effort would not go unnoticed.

The Lombard horde was now dangerously close. Captains yelled to the pikemen in the front lines to hold their formation and screamed until their lungs burned. An old commander standing in the front rank barked at no one in particular. "Make yourselves large, boys! Stand tall! Shoulder to shoulder! They are the water. You are the stone! This is but a game to test your will." Clearly Oliver's words had made their way into the soldiers' training. The old commander continued, "Horses will not plow forth, but you must toe your line! Make that wall!" What the commander did not add was that any move to turn away or give space would provide the charging horses a sense of hope and that meant certain death. He walked along the line, yanking on pikes to ensure they were held firm and at the proper angle.

Oliver and Radwig looked on silently with approval. Endless drills and repetition were important to armies. They sparked action without thought, which could be the difference between death and survival in battle. The last thing that Oliver wanted at that moment was doubt among his men. All he wanted was stubborn flesh. Horses would not charge a mass with no space and no possibility to leap over top, preferring instead to search for a way around danger. It was a belief that had been tested with horrific results over the centuries. Still, cavalry had remained an intricate component of armies on purpose. For that reason, most of the tall and large boys of Frankia shunned the pikeman position, fearful of facing cavalry head-on in the front ranks.

Radwig shifted his gaze between the stoic Oliver and the cloud that stormed close enough for him to make out beards on faces and symbols on red tunics and green shields. Even Radwig's unshakable nerve seemed suspect despite there being a half dozen ranks between him and the front lines. As he gulped in air, watching for some change in Oliver's stares, a second cloud emerge from behind Oliver's left, growing with each heartbeat. Oliver kept his gaze on the Lombards but pointed off to his left with his gloved hand and raised his voice in a heavy layer of confidence so Radwig could hear him over the rumbling earth and growing screams.

Oliver barked to Radwig, "I present to you the Bloody Hearts of Carantania. Cacatius claims his Bloody Hearts are the best cavalrymen in all of Europe, not our friends here in Lombardy. Look at them! They certainly do not pull back on their reins, do they?" Oliver smiled and pressed Draca closer to Radwig, which brought a look of concern to the warrior monk.

Oliver kept his gaze on the motion in front of him as he spoke to his old friend. "I have found the Carantanians to be a proud people, Radwig, and formidable fighters yet accepting of Frankish rule. They have been . . . influenced in recent years to come to heel. The Duchy of Bavaria is the rightful overlord of Carantania. Yet Cacatius wants his lands free from Bavaria, under his own dukedom, and this is part of the consideration to be paid. Louis has made it so. Our friend Wilfred was simply not agreeable to my calls for hardened soldiers, and Louis has made note."

Radwig looked at Oliver with extreme confusion and questioned his master. "What in God's name was all of that nonsense you were preaching, lord? Proper pike lines against a cavalry charge?"

"I maintain my argument," Oliver said with a chuckle. "There will be more chances to prove my position, old man. Whether it be rebellion ripe for slaughter or battles with Bernard's own men. No sense in risking my theory on a bunch of piss-soaked boys when we have willing souls here ready for use." Oliver sighed and continued. "I suppose whether they have the finest cavalry is fairly debatable. Yet in truth I do not need these

Carantanians to fight like the Achaeans reborn. I only need them to disrupt Desiderius's initial attack for our pikes to go to work." Oliver snuck a glance at the Carantanian cavalry swarming from around the Frankish left flank and moving headlong to a point of interception between the front of the first Lombard horses and the front line of his pikemen. He cursed through pursed lips. "Goddamned fools! I warned Cacatius to leave his red tunics and flags at home. Half of the Lombards are in red. Yellow is also the Carantanians' ancient color." He gestured with his left hand as he shook his head in disappointment.

Oliver had to scream in order for Radwig to hear him. "Our men will remain blameless for random killing, Radwig! The fault will rest with Carantania, not us! When the masses slow, have the first lines press toward the horse bellies! Soak this field!"

The first horses of the Carantanian front reached the Lombards mere paces ahead of Frankia's front lines. Neither force bothered to yield. The result was thunderous. Masses of flesh and steel propelling into each other and brought on a high screeching pitch combined with a low thunder from the impact. The dust clouds from both forces merged into a giant plume that engulfed the area far into the Frankish ranks. Bodies and arms occasionally rose above the tan clouds. Radwig crossed himself in awe at the chaotic death unfolding in the haze at the center of the contact.

Oliver had only to lean forward to alert Draca that it was time to press ahead. The beast responded and sent Franks hurling to the side as he carved a path to where the Lombards were slowed by Frankia's Carinthian allies. Radwig felt pity for those who were about to fall into an army of steel points, yet he executed his master's command all the same. "Captains! Forward!" A horn blew and Frankia's lines advanced forward.

X

- A LOVER OF OVID -

As duke of Saxony, Germanicus had the privilege of riding ahead of all others in his train into the city of Eresburg. His mother and her company of palace guards rode several lengths behind him. Magdeh would follow many more paces behind Thygrid with the extra horses and servants. Thygrid had no objection to the arrangement, as it was customary for a ruler of Saxony to set himself apart from all others when entering the walls of his cities, even at the expense of his own family. This was a minor show of pageantry that had his mother's approval. Magdeh preferred the arrangement as well. She had not spoken to her husband since they were last in the palace of Marklo. For the three nights of their travel south, Magdeh spent her evenings in her own small tent, curled up with her young Saxon slave.

Eresburg sat atop a tree-covered plateau that overlooked rolling forests on all sides and a valley to the south. The old tales said that the city mound was the grave of a great giant that once roamed the land. To Germanicus, that was as absurd as the tales of dragons. This was a city chosen by men long ago as an obvious refuge of defense, and that was all.

Eresburg was a bustling city by Saxon standards; it was an insignificant town by Frankish comparison. Like most of Saxony, it functioned under Frankish rule but did not thrive. Decades of rebellion against the masters to the south had a devastating impact on its people. Recovery was hard; the Franks were cautious of the Saxons, who fought desperately for over a century against Christian conversion. The two peoples were distrustful of one another, and nothing about the current peace suggested that those wounds would likely be mended anytime soon.

Eresburg had four smiths operating within the city at any one time. This was a means by which emissaries and traders into the region measured a city's economic health. By comparison, Marklo had around ten and Paris likely had over twenty. The city sat on the southern bank of the slow and winding Lippe River, a narrow branch of the greater Dremel. Its docks and piers were primarily vacant, as heavier merchant traffic preferred the distant Elbe as a better means of traveling the region north to south. The modest stone walls that wrapped around the elevated city were colored in an assortment of gray and black. Many parts of the wall were scorched dark by fire. Others were light gray, where new stones had been mortared awkwardly into the existing structure. Stone piles inside the wall were sources for new construction materials and free for the taking by those inhabitants who had interest in establishing new trades.

The extended lands outside the walls were engulfed by limitless farms in the rolling plains. There were few buildings in this region, where herds of livestock grazed and fed when winter snows receded. In the wintertime, when the harvests had been stored and the livestock was slaughtered and cured, many of the men of the city took to the shallow river harbors and boatyards along the shore to build and repair cargo barges and fishing boats to keep the city's people fed and to breathe life back into the region. Eresburg was symbolic of Saxony itself: hard people working hard jobs, silently content with the life that their old gods had given them.

Eresburg was the ancestral home of Germanicus's family. Men from his bloodline had ruled from within its walls for hundreds of years. Marklo might have been the newly anointed economic and political hub of the territory, but Eresburg was Saxony's true heart and ancient capital.

Despite his deep ties to the city, Germanicus preferred taking in Eresburg in small doses. Eresburg was not along the main road to Aachen. Visits were normally limited to changing out horses, restocking supplies, and perhaps grabbing a hot meal with old allies and relevant family members to get a sense of the political happenings of the empire without the filter of court prattle in the new capital in Marklo. Those types of visits were tolerable and permitted him a comfortable level of nostalgia—just enough to realize he enjoyed the chaos and diversity of life back in Marklo.

As he approached Eresburg, Germanicus looked to the clearing toward the north, where there was no smoke or sign of activity. There had been a time, when Germanicus was a young man, that the clearing caught every person's eye. Those memories had grown as faint as those of his father's face. The center of the clearing used to hold an oak tree of enormous size, a colossus among dwarfs, towering above the distant landscape of pines. It was so massive that its great branches expanded horizontally beyond the trunk and sagged to the earth under their own weight. The Saxons used the bricks from the fallen Roman buildings to support its limbs and keep them from snapping.

The giant oak tree was called the Irminsul. The Irminsul was beyond sacred to the Saxons. It was central to their gods and understanding of the world around them. No one but Saxon priests were permitted to touch it or decorate its branches with swaths of colorful cloth. Even children were not permitted to touch or climb the tree under pain of death.

Charles had come to Eresburg almost thirty years earlier as the useful hand of the pope. He didn't come for converts; he tried that once before and the people of Eresburg mocked him with nods and smiles then spat on the ground when his back was turned. The Saxons had proven stubborn despite hundreds of years of missions from Rome's holy ambassadors. For as warlike as the Saxons were, they were not overly rebellious to their church tormentors; they were instead indifferent. The strategy changed with Charles's ascension to the throne firmly secure. On that occasion three decades ago, Charles came with the intent to destroy the false Saxon idol.

The Saxons fought to protect the Irminsul, and their numbers of able-bodied men fell to a small fraction of what they once could field. When they realized that their fighting was futile, they begged and pleaded. They prostrated themselves to the Christian cross and cajoled the soldiers through the cries of their children and old women. Charles wouldn't accept their pleas. He was intent on grinding the ancient oak down to its roots.

Saxon men taken prisoner in the rebellion were ordered to destroy the tree. Yet no Saxon would take an ax to the Irminsul, not even at the threat of execution. Charles thought the Saxons would bend to his will and pick up the ax after the first hundred imprisoned warriors were beheaded. They still refused, and that was when Charles found his true wrath. Women and children were added to the execution pen. The numbers grew from the hundreds to the thousands. In the end, Eresburg was wiped clean of all men under the age of forty and women beyond breeding age, yet still the Saxons refused to strike their sacred tree. At that point, Charles changed his strategy.

The Saxons would not forget as they watched Frankish soldiers work for days with the axe, then bring the torch. Saxon women pulled out their hair and beat their chests and the men smeared their face black with earth. Before the burn came, Charles recited the only scripture that all Saxons there that day would remember to their death: "I will fill your mountains with the slain; those killed by the sword will fall on your hills and in your valleys and in all your ravines. I will make you desolate forever; your towns will not be inhabited. Then you will know that I am the Lord." It is said that the fire from the fallen tree scorched the heavens and that it was only the tears of the Saxon gods that extinguished the embers. Some pieces of the great oak were salvaged in the night and were eventually used to make the chair that Germanicus would place on display in his dining hall.

As Germanicus and his captains made their way down the winding road toward the city upon the plateau, one of the soldiers broke off from the pack, pulled up on his stallion's reins slightly, and stood in the saddle. He looked like he was staring off into the town ahead when in truth he was homing in his hearing. "Bells! Chiming at a brisk pace." It was surely an announcement regarding Charles.

There was only one small cathedral in Eresburg and two wooden churches. It was a paltry number given the size and significance of the city. The people of the city were slow to take on the requirements and formalities of Christianity, and so the nobles of Eresburg put little effort into spending valuable resources on a religion that they only feigned an interest in.

Germanicus entered the city of Eresburg like a prince returning from campaign. He wore his battle armor, freshly polished and cleaned with fine sand. He rode his stallion with his back stiff and strong, acknowledging some familiar faces in the outlying settlement and watching along the walls and towers as he climbed the winding road to the city above. Germanicus replayed scenes from his childhood as he made his way to the family palace.

The same hag who ran the fruit stand near the main water well outside the walls was still alive. Germanicus thought the old woman was at least sixty when he was just a child thirty years earlier. He and the boys of a few palace guards found loose boards in the back of the old woman's stand and were able to sneak through and steal summer fruit from the back rows. He would gorge himself on pears and grapes until he got sick. Germanicus was the wealthiest youth in all of Saxony and didn't need to steal; he just did it because it was dangerous at the time.

Down the back alley of the leatherworkers' quarters was where he met up with a young prostitute from Myrstan's whorehouse. He could not remember the girl's name anymore and could only vaguely recall her face and features. "Her name started with a D, I think," Germanicus said to himself with a reminiscent smile. Perhaps if she was more attractive he would have retained her image and name in his mind more clearly. She was his first woman, but the event was not a story made for bards to carry across the realm. He remembered how brutish he was with the patient girl, pulling up her dress from behind and bending her over a giant water barrel. It could not have lasted a half-minute, but that was all it took for Germanicus to tell her he loved her and wanted to take her away. "What a fool." He laughed to himself before the amusement on his face was wiped clean. His mind followed the timeline he always wanted to forget from the encounter. The girl was found later that summer, caught in the quiet reeds of a finger of the Diemel River. Her clothes were floating next to her body, her neck brutally opened deep and wide by some dull blade.

All his memories of Eresburg seemed to have some tragic or dark element to them. He looked over at the soldiers' barracks near the west side of the palace and remembered another en-counter with the same boys he used to drum up trouble with around the city. The boys were playing with wooden sticks in place of iron swords. One of the boys whacked Germanicus by accident, causing him to squeal and the other boys to laugh. Germanicus would have none of the embarrassment and swung his stick wildly at all three. The boys struck back at him and yanked the stick away. Forgetting their station as the sons of common soldiers, they attacked Germanicus and scuffed him up, bloodying his nose and lip. When Germanicus ran back to his living quarters in the palace, he passed by his father, Dagobert. The young Germanicus was weeping and yearned for his bed.

"What has happened?" Dagobert asked.

"Some boys beat me. It was the barracks boys. There were three of them. They teased me and—"

Dagobert slammed the papers in his hand into the scribe at his side and yanked young Germanicus by his arm. The boy tried every ploy he could think of to release himself from his father's grip. He twisted his body. He tried falling to the ground. He pleaded with his father that he would never fight again. It was those words that stopped Dagobert in his tracks. He grabbed the boy by both arms, pulling him up and close, almost nose to nose. "You will fight again. You will fight them now."

"No, I cannot, father. There are three of them."

"I will give you a choice. You will fight all three or you will fight me!"

Germanicus knew this was no game. His father was a serious man and had no time for childish things. The rage in his father's eyes held the truth. Germanicus didn't wrestle from his father any further as they left through the side doors of the palace. He was stunned by his father's words, trying to digest them all. Father and son made it to the nearby barracks. Germanicus kept his eyes on his father the whole way, waiting for some sign that his rage had broken into mild anger. It only seemed to grow. As they came around the corner of the barracks next to the sparring area, Germanicus saw the three boys and what had to be one of their fathers. Seeing Dagobert, the soldier, in his riding jerkin, fell to a knee, and the three boys slowly followed suit.

The soldier stared at the ground and said, "Great lord! I beg your forgiveness. My son has told me what happened. He has no excuse. All three will be beaten like slaves, great lord—n-now, if it pleases you."

Dagobert looked around as if his soldier had said nothing at all. He walked up to the boy being held by his father. "You beat my son? The three of you?"

"N-No, my lord. I mean, yes, my lord, but I—"

"You will fight him again," Dagobert growled at the other boys. "All three of you will fight him again. One after the other until it is done." The first boy began to shake his head. Before he could speak, Dagobert laid out the terms. "You will fight or your father dies. Right here, right in front of you. The same goes for you other two." The three boys looked at Dagobert in silent shock. "And if any of you decide to fall down or put in false effort and let my son win, your fathers lose their eyes. Do you understand me?"

The boys gave nervous nods in unison.

Dagobert then nodded to Germanicus and walked away from the cluster. "Very well. Get going."

Germanicus stared at the first boy, who had something like a smirk on his face as he waited for the noble boy to come catch his beating. That wasn't the way it went. Germanicus called on his father's rage, partly because he feared his father's fist, partly because he didn't want to see a man lose his life or eye at best. Most of all, he wanted to pass this bizarre test his father had thrust upon him, and the possibility of failing that test would have hurt worst of all.

Germanicus only recalled the beginning of his attack and how quickly the first boy's expression changed. It was all blood and fists. No skill from lessons, just anger and fear in equal parts. When it was over, after he had fought and pummeled each boy, one by one, he turned to his father. His shirt was lost, his knuckles red and swelling. His chest was heaving. He knew he had passed the test. Dagobert gave a simple grunt to the soldier and guided his son by the shoulder, back to the palace to be examined by one of the servants. Germanicus kept his eyes on the path in front of him, but he could feel his father staring down on him and smiling. That was one of his last memories of his father before he died from a festered arrow wound in battle against the Bavarians.

As Germanicus rode up to the stables, he wondered if his father was smiling down on him now. He doubted that was so, particularly in light of the farce that had just played out with Clotho and the Danes. Many of his life's decisions were based upon what his father would think, and at that very moment, he had an idea of what Dagobert might want, and it did not please him. He also wondered what his mother had in store for him. The very fact that she refused to speak on the matter while attending the livery ceremony and instead wanted to wait until they returned to the confines of the palace gave him cause for concern.

Germanicus took his time in the palace compound before entering the living quarters. He wanted to pay respects to the wife of the old stable master who taught him how to ride when his father was not around. The old man had long since died, but Germanicus always showed his appreciation by tending to his wife and making sure she was properly cared for. He had a few moments to spare anyway. He knew his mother would want the additional time to prepare her dining hall and clean herself from the long day's travel.

Germanicus's iron spurs scratched the stone and jingled with each step he took into the dining hall, echoing throughout the room. He heard her voice before he saw her. Thygrid yelled at her son. "Why do you insist on disobeying me simply for torment? My hall, my rules. No spurs, no swords." Thygrid's words seem to have no effect on her son. His eyes adjusted to the dark, and from the sound of his mother's voice, he could tell she was up in the musicians' roost, staring down at him.

Germanicus looked up at his mother. She wore a mourner's dress, and her long gray hair, hanging to each shoulder, was parted down the middle. Her ears held back her hair from covering her stern and attractive face. She was close to sixty but looked more like a woman in her forties. The uninformed might think the two were husband and wife instead of parent and child. She had cleaned and relaxed herself from the day's earlier events and taken a goblet of wine, which wasn't that unusual for her.

The sight of her perched high in the musicians' box brought a series of questions to his mind as she made her way down the wooden stairs to meet him below. Why had she never remarried? She was still somewhat young when Dagobert died, and she had always been beautiful. That, along with the modest wealth of Saxony, would certainly have attracted the finer suitors in the empire. Why was she wearing black? Was it for Charles? She bore him no love. As far back as Germanicus could remember, she had filled his head with thoughts of rebellion and overthrowing the crown. She refused all invitations to Aachen when summoned to the imperial court. She grudgingly opened the city gates to Charles's troops and the Twelve Peers when she ruled Saxony as Germanicus's high protector.

Germanicus spoke as Thygrid approached. "The word seems to have spread throughout the entire city already. If Charles died already, then surely his funeral has taken place or is perhaps today. Frankish custom seems to follow the Saxon ways, from what I can tell. That is two sundowns. Do I continue on to Aachen knowing he may already be in the ground?"

Thygrid landed lightly on the last few steps of the stairs, unable to completely control her excitement at seeing her only boy in a new light. "Of course! The Twelve Peers and nobles will be meeting, and it is said that Louis was in camp around the Alps. Your attendance is necessary."

Thygrid looked up at her son, inspecting his shoulders to make sure muscle still filled his armor and his flesh hadn't wilted away. Germanicus had indeed faded with time. He had grown weak and feeble underneath the winter jerkin and armor. She knew he would need his health now more than ever.

"My son, this will be a chance to bargain for more land. Death breeds uncertainty, even more for rulers in waiting. Louis will want to show his power through new campaigns." She pulled down his head and kissed him gently on each brow. "He will ask for your sword and our men. Be slow in your support. I do not know. Make up some excuse about the sweating sickness in Marklo or some defensive wall project. He will open his purse."

Germanicus had ideas about Louis, and they didn't involve an arrangement over troops and future campaigns.

Thygrid took her son by the hand and led him over to the

main dining table on the dais. She sat him at a random chair and took another next to it. "Tell me, how goes your marriage? Two years now?"

"I hate her," Germanicus answered.

Thygrid chuckled. "I do not recall asking you if you cared for her, my dear boy. I can assure you I hate her ten times more over. Am I to be a grandmother? I should have been one half a life ago. What about her people? Do they honor the terms?" Thygrid asked.

Germanicus disregarded the talk of children. Thygrid knew her son was only modestly interested in planting his wife when they first wed. She was beautiful, but so were the half dozen mistresses who kept him busy in the winter doldrums. If a child was on the way, Thygrid would be the first to get word through her network of eyes and ears that kept tabs on palace life in Marklo.

"Aye, they honor the terms, at least in this land. There has been many a word from sailors returning from Friesland that speak of mass slaughter at the hands of Northmen. Entire settlements of Saxons along the far western coast have been scraped from the earth."

"Well, my son, the treaty only protects Saxons on Saxon soil. You almost have to praise the barbarians for having the wit to play with words."

Germanicus chuckled at that response. Calling the Northmen barbarians. Saxony itself was no land of enlightened thought. Two hundred years after the introduction of Christianity and there were still vast pockets of people who had never seen a priest or high buildings of stone. It had been an issue of contention for both Germanicus and Charles. The lower class of

Saxony's population was promised new lands within church holdings if they converted to the cross. Many did, but in words only, not deeds. The land promises sent many Saxons west to the marshes and lowlands of Friesland to start new lives as Christians. Raids by Northmen was their reward.

Thygrid spent the next few minutes making small talk with her son, asking him about mundane matters of state and gossip regarding the nobles of Saxony. She was looking for a way to broach a different subject, one that had been haunting her for decades and too delicate to mention along their ride to the city. The death of Charles was the catalyst for discussing the matter with Germanicus, but she knew he was going to revolt from her no matter how she spun the message. After some time, she saw her opportunity to make her move. The two were sharing cold meat and nuts from a wooden plate; they both drank local wine to wash it down. Thygrid studied him up and down as she lightly fed the meat into her mouth using her fingertips.

"I see you're wearing your father's armor. The Irminsul is long dead. You need a different symbol. Where is the new suit I had made for your wedding?" Thygrid asked.

Germanicus thought nothing of the question; he was ready to move on and finish up. "The boar chest plate? It is with the baggage horse. It is not fit for long rides. It tends to rub my skin."

"I wish you would move along from this worship of your father. He was a good man, but he is gone. He has been gone for almost thirty years. You are your own man. You have a name for yourself. It is past time to step out from his shadow. You should have the Irminsul plate recast."

"Many a Saxon nobleman would object. Besides, I have

done nothing, mother. I am an unremarkable sycophant. That bitch wife is right with it. Charles calls and I come running." Germanicus took a moment to test the accuracy of a statement through his own memories. He was saddened that it was true. "My father had a dream that Eresburg, not Aachen, would be the center of all Europe. From Eresburg we can claim all the north and the islands of Britannia. Create a new, greater empire without the shackles of churches and the fear of Saracen swords. Far enough from Rome to plant our own banner of faith and what it means to be Saxon."

He tossed his dagger on the plate in frustration. "I'm closing in on half a century on this earth and I've accomplished nothing." He then took a long, hard drink from his cup. "So if I honor my father, I do so because I have no achievement of my own to stand on."

Thygrid slammed down her cup and grabbed his hand. "Nonsense! You moved to take Charles as your hostage after the war with Moravia. You wanted lands and titles as compensation for winning the war for the empire. You got what you wanted. Any other noble would have his head removed from his neck and put upon a spike."

Germanicus stared at the floor. "Meaningless titles. Being made a Peer? He bound me with gold rope, forcing that whore Magdeh on me. Now I am his mayor of the Northmen. It is all a punishment. A sick farce. That is how the old dog rules. Charles will continue to haunt me from his grave."

There was no better time to say what needed to be said. "Arminius, your father was not the man you think he was. He was a good man, but not a great man. He—"

"Yet you loved him."

Thygrid paused before answering. "I loved him as much as I could, which was not much."

Germanicus became annoyed and stood from his chair. "Why? Why would you say such things? From what I am told, he never harmed you. He never took another woman. He was a good husband to you."

Thygrid shook her head. "I . . . He was a good man and husband. It was not your father that failed me. It was me who failed him."

Germanicus's annoyance grew. "Stop talking in riddles, old woman. What does that mean?"

"I knew another man before I married your father." She paused to gauge his reaction before continuing. His face was stern and frozen with anger. She then dropped her head in shame. "Charles. It was Charles."

Germanicus barked out a laugh that reached the beams of the hall. "Charles? I do not believe you! You are repulsed by the man. It is easy to say that your prayers for his ruin are what has kept you youthful all these years."

Thygrid responded, "It is true."

"Why do you disgrace my father to shame yourself so? Almost thirty years he has been gone. You rarely speak of him and never with much affection. Now, at the most disturbing of moments, you foul his memory and label him a cuckold? There are easier ways to insult him and bring me to anger, woman!"

Thygrid sighed and said, "This has weighed deeply on me, my son. I have played this scene in my mind a thousand times. It has never been easy."

Germanics asked, "Why do this? What is to be gained? You mean to hurt me? I think no less of a man because you turn yourself to a whore for a foolish girl's pleasure. The bed of some greater man."

Thygrid cried into her hands. She looked back up at Germanicus. "Why? Because it is time for you to know who your father truly is."

Germanicus grunted in rage and slung the plate and goblets from the table. "Lie!"

"It is not a lie!"

"Why?" He asked. "Why tell me now if it is as you say?"

"Because you worshipped your father the way all boys do and there was nothing to be gained from telling the truth until now." Thygrid tried to reach out for Germanicus's hand but he yanked it away with violence. "Can't you see? Charles did not take your head after you attempted to take him hostage. When your father was a ruler, he would slaughter Saxons by the thousands without so much as a care or reason. But with you, when he brought you into his palace as a boy, he treated you like his son. Why is that?"

"That means nothing," Germanicus responded. "He treated many a barbarian and pagan with kindness."

"Charles has left the empire in shambles. Louis is a weakling. Bernard lusts for the throne but is impudent and reckless. You can now smash the shackle that has held back Saxony all these years, or . . ." She paused, focusing on the words to follow. "We can claim what is yours by right. The eldest living son of Charles."

Germanicus pulled his head down to his chest, using his

hair for grip. His face was almost purple with anger. "No," he whimpered.

"It is true. He is your father."

"How?" Germanicus asked. "When did . . . ?"

"It was at my wedding to your father. The feast the day before. Your grandfather . . . my father brought his entire court to Eresburg. He emptied the treasury and taxed his barons to poverty to pay for the celebration and gain the attention of Aachen. I was his only daughter and in that cast of fate his only chance at bringing a dukedom to Sturmi. Your . . . Dagobert was not a man of land and wealth. His people lost all in their wars with Frankia, but he did have a famous bloodline. My father was promised that if Dagobert was placated by being gifted a noble wife with vast holdings, he would be rewarded by being made a duke and given leave to join the court in Aachen. Who could refuse such an offer from Pepin, the son of Charles the Hammer?"

Germanicus could only sniffle.

"Charles was sent to my wedding as the symbol of Aachen. It was the first time I ever saw him." Thygrid stood and pointed across the room. "There. He entered the hall through those doors. He had no courtiers with him. No staff or servants. Nor did he wear some ridiculous crown. There was no need. He shone like the sun."

"Whore!"

Thygrid snapped her head back from the door and almost forty years in the past. She stared at her son with sadness. "Is that truly what you think of me?"

"You fucked another man the night before your wedding!"

Thygrid knew her son would not understand, but for that

insult, he would be punished. "How can you understand what it was like to be there at that moment? The barons I knew smelled of horseshit and were impossible to tell apart from their own servants. This man looked like an emperor from the old songs. He talked like a philosopher. Do you have any idea what it is like for the most powerful man in all the world to stare at you like you are the only thing that mattered? He was not the tallest or the most handsome man I had ever seen, and I had a hundred come for my hand. It was the way he consumed a room."

Thygrid closed her eyes, smiled, and shook her head. "His words were elegant, and his eyes were like fire. His every move was like some subtle dance. He was Caesar reborn. I swear it. Everyone wanted to touch him. To be near him. And for all those dukes and princesses, all those men of power and fame, he chose me. To touch me. This hand. It was immediately a growing scandal, and your grandfather looked on hopelessly." She caressed her right hand with the left.

"Enough!"

Thygrid continued, "I remember the moment we were together like it was yesterday." She walked toward an open shutter, clutching her shawl tightly. "We talked for a moment or two about the classics. I was shy. He was persistent. Father insisted that I take up the Frankish ways and learn to live and breathe like one of them. Dagobert was never impressed and thought it below Saxon standards. Charles, his Latin was flawless and mine was garbled like some peasant girl. He only smiled and comforted me for my effort."

Germanicus made for a side table that held a large wine jug.

It was half-empty and he shouted for a servant to bring more. He should have known that no servant would dare enter that room.

Thygrid smiled fondly and closed her eyes as she spoke. "Charles said his favorite poet was Ovid, and I knew that very moment that he wanted me. I cannot say why, but it being my wedding made him even more appealing. Who but a god could strike down his own holy sacraments? And he was every bit a god."

"You are a hateful and spiteful creature. I curse your soul!"

"Do you want to know what he said to me? Of the words that did me in?" Thygrid asked.

"Another word and by our gods I will cut out your fucking tongue myself!"

Thygrid had no fear of her son's threat. It was entirely possible he would see it through, but Thygrid had almost forty years of anguish and guilt that she had to set free. She walked to him almost sensually, as if she was Charles the seducer. Thygrid began to rub her own arms and chest, looking to warm her soul with memories long past. "Ovid's song of Ulysses and Circe. When he left Circe there alone in the cave where they were lovers for countless days, and the burning she felt for him when she watched him leave. The hopelessness of loss. It was not lust. It was not love. It burned and pained the core of Circe's soul."

Germanicus was broken as she spoke gently into his ear. There was no way to put the words back in her mouth. "Enough," he said. "I beg you."

Thygrid whispered Ovid's lines as she rounded to his back then returned back to the young Charles. "I let him take me in the garden. I wanted to feel Circe's burn, and that would be my only chance. I knew it. Up against the oak tree you used to climb as a boy. He—"

"Enough!" Germanicus turned and shoved his mother away, sending her hard against the top of the long table. She was bent over in front of him and considered trying her luck with one last insult. One last attempt to punish her son for his gullible love for his father and for shaming her as a whore, but reason got the better of her. She knew the story of Germanicus and the three barracks boys. How it shaped him as a youth. This was her moment to shape him as a man—a man in her image. Hard and driven for true greatness. She was panting hard as she rose to face him. It was eerily silent for some time.

"How can you know for sure he is my father? He had you once. A day before your husband. I could be either man's son. Perhaps both. Who knows for certain?"

"I see nothing of Dagobert in your face, my son. And your father . . . You were my only child. Not even a miscarriage in all the years we lay together. Your father was too blind with pride to see what stared him in the face." Her words were soft again. She felt a thread of guilt at having thrown the truth at Germanicus's face so harshly, but it was the truth that had been buried too long. Now it was time to see how he reacted.

"This is . . . too much. I need more wine." Germanicus grabbed his cup from the table and hoisted it in the air, not lowering it until rose-colored water came down the corners of his mouth. After several deep gulps, he took a breath and grabbed one of the chairs to steady himself. He sat and felt as though he had just finished a fight for his life. "I still do not know why you told me. Why now? What purpose does that serve other than to prove to me your cruelty?"

Thygrid came to his knees, bending down to his own level. "There was no good time. This just seems to be the best of any bad choice. What you do with it is up to you. Toss it away if you wish. We can never speak of it again if you like. Son and mother can instead trade blows aimed at your wife or complain of unruly nobles."

Germanicus interrupted, jerking his gaze toward the rafters, and sniffled. "Ha! Likely not!"

"Then use it. Use it to stoke your fires. Become angry at Dagobert. Angry at Charles. Hate me if you like. Strike me. Spit on me. If rage can lift you to greatness, then it is there for you to take!"

The meal that night was a cold one. Germanicus could either eat with his mother and the men closest to him or sulk in his quarters until they made for the long road to Aachen the next morning. He brought his men with him to his mother's hall. It wasn't unusual for him to use his men as a shield. Besides, he knew that if he kept to himself in his room, there was the chance that Magdeh would come poking around.

Among his men, several had distant family ties to Thygrid's people in Ostfalia. Hospitality was a deep part of Saxon culture such that sending his landed captains to dine elsewhere was almost taboo. He had other reasons, however. It was his hope that if others were around to make small talk, she would leave their violent conversation in the past out of fear of creating a scandal. The wife, Magdeh, was enough of a scandal to last a Saxon lifetime. In the end, as much as Thygrid wanted to harm Dagobert, she wouldn't want to bring public shame on her son.

Magdeh had an uncanny ability to read Germanicus's thoughts— so much so that he often suspected his wife was in league with her winter witches. He barely knew her, yet she was the only person other than his mother who could read his eyes and know his mind. For that deciding reason, he chose the mother's company over the wife's, which spoke volumes for his fear of being alone with Magdeh when there was no one to deflect attention toward.

Thankfully, his men were full of stories that evening and suspected nothing despite the tempest of noise he had made in the same hall earlier in the day. He kept thinking of the oak tree in the courtyard. Dagobert had wanted it to grow into the new Irminsul in the hope that his people would one day shed the preposterous Christian god and return to the old ways. Germanicus now envisioned the tree's reduction to firewood. He thought about going to the barns that evening to grab an ax and do what needed to be done. If not, it would nevertheless be his first refurbishment to the palace once his mother died.

His captains were grateful for the abundant food and decent wine. Thygrid and her younger ladies listened intently to the fascinating stories of encounters with the Northmen and their bizarre customs. Stories of sorted sex might have been sinful and beyond discussion to ladies of Frankia, but the same could not be said for their Saxon counterparts. With each forced laugh and sip of her wine cup, Thygrid would study her son's face, attempting to read his stone expression. His responses to his men's goading were simple yet nothing to give rise to suspicion.

He gave nothing away and retired early, leaving his young captains in the company of his mother's maids and talk of bold living that passed him by years earlier.

When Thygrid awoke with the rising sun the next morning, she opened the shutters of her sleeping quarters to see Germanicus and his men loading their mounts in preparation for the journey to Aachen. It was earlier than normal, but she should have expected the subtle exit. Thygrid raced through her room and out the main door, hoping to catch her son before he left. There was much left unsaid. If the chill in the stone floor of her hall was not enough to prove her desire to set things right with her son, then running shoeless through the evening snowfall in her sleeping gown certainly would. She could not bear the idea of Germanicus leaving without telling him she loved him and perhaps finding a strand of common ground to repair their relationship through the passage of time.

"Germanicus!" She stopped a few paces short as he finished strapping in his saddlebags and turned to her. Magdeh was watching from her palfrey with true curiosity. What Thygrid saw was all the response she needed. Gone was Dagobert's armor, which he had worn into the city, the armor that bore the Irminsul, the symbol his father cherished most. Germanicus had slept in his old living quarters rather than in his father's that evening and unpacked from his old storage chests the breastplate he wore as a young man when he defeated Charles's eldest legitimate son, Charles the Younger, in the battle at Westphalia twenty years earlier. The emblem in the center of the breast plate wasn't the Irminsul, which adorned Dagobert's armor. This plate bore the fork-tongued serpent of deep-wooded

Ostfalia, the symbol of his mother's ancestral land. The Irminsul was insulting to the Franks because of what it stood for: an old religion for a people who were dying the slow death of assimilation. The Ostfalian serpent was different. It was not just heretical—it was audacious. If there was any creature in all the world that was further from the lamb of Christ, it was Lucifer the serpent. Of course, Germanicus didn't believe in Jesus, so the idea of Lucifer was equally absurd. He didn't believe evil needed its own god when he saw the personification in so many Franks and Northmen.

The old armor was freshly polished, and Thygrid assumed her son had been up most of the night, taking out his fears and uncertainty with each rough scrub. Most men would have difficulty fitting into the armor of their youth. Germanicus's racked frame held it with ease. He hoped that he could fill the void with something more than flesh.

"Germanicus is gone, mother. He left last night. I do not believe he will return. When I come back from Aachen, Arminius will speak with the Lady of Eresburg."

XI

- THE BUSINESS OF LOMBARDY -

It was early afternoon in northern Italy. The sun hung bright in the cloudless sky, giving the appearance of a sweltering summer day. It was the end of January, however, and the snow-covered Alps to the north reminded all within the plain below of the true season. The sun only gave a touch of warmth when the bellowing wind from the mountains above subsided for a moment. From the view outside the great red tent, the conditions for battle foretold how the fighting would turn out before the first soldier advanced. It was perfect ground for a tactical mind and the side with the advantage of numbers and health.

It was surprising that the enemy had accepted engagement and felt no need to seek the obvious protection of the thick walls behind them. The field sloped gently down to the opponent, and the terrain was relatively flat in all directions. There was no mud either, courtesy of the dry winter conditions. Today's field favored speed and size, two qualities that Frankia had in abundance. Louis, the last living son of Charles and anointed co-emperor, knew the advantages were the gift of the Lombards' obvious desperation. His man Oliver would bring victory fast and certain.

War wasn't normally conducted in the winter, a season when most huddled in shelters with rationed food in a battle of attrition against the cold and ice that claimed stomachs and livestock. People welcomed the planting season that eventually came with the spring thaw and rain. The army of Frankia was indifferent to the seasons. It was bold in its actions and openly delighted in its superiority. Unlike most armies, Frankia's was in camp throughout the year. If not fighting, its soldiers and cavalry were in a constant state of preparation, scrubbing armor, building ports, and repairing camp defenses.

Charles's father, Pepin, installed a professional army. He took on men who volunteered and in turn were paid in silver, not forced at spear point. They were not called home for the harvest but spent the entire year in endless training, honing their speed and effectiveness. Slaves and old men tended fields back home. Newly acquired territories typically provided front-line soldiers and men for nonfighting ranks to manage supply trains and the daily needs of their domestic betters. If anything, the men of Frankia preferred winter campaigns, knowing their enemies were ill-prepared to meet their own devotion. Frankia was always prepared to do battle on its terms, which was effectively displayed before the inspection by Louis earlier that morning.

Surveying the hard-won battlefield that afternoon, Louis nodded with satisfaction at what he saw. Dead Lombards cloaked in their red and green tunics and robes far outnumbered those bodies in Frankish colors. He didn't need heralds bringing word from Oliver to tell him what the canvas before him plainly showed. When the sun rose earlier that morning, the vast and empty field before him was awash in inviting, golden rays. The tents littered the plain with dull yellows and whites. With their pitched centers, the Lombard camp looked like a sprawling forest of budding saplings. There was something beautiful about the endless columns of men and horses moving in concert within the field. There was order and thought in each movement.

When Louis stepped out of his tent six hours later, the scene had morphed into something unrecognizable. Louis now looked upon the field with a different sense of satisfaction. It was the pleasure a child felt when he stacked a tower of wooden blocks high and then violently knocked them over. Smoke plumes rose in place of the enemy's tents far off in the distance. The unmistakable smell of burnt hair and flesh lightly filled the air. The endless brown plain that lay ahead of the burning tents was now strewn with horses and humans lying motionless. His troops were the only ones moving about, careless of any further violence. Some planted their spears into dead and dying enemies out of pure anger or in answer to pleas for a merciful ending. Louis's men knew such an action was prohibited under Charles's rule; Louis was made of a more liberal temperament. He wanted his enemies to know they faced Louis, not Charles. Charles was respected for his strength and mercy. Louis wanted to be known for his uncompromising savagery. Mercy was a trait borne by kings confident and content in their rule.

Once the soldiers cleared the field, the next to foray into the blood-soaked plain were the monks from both camps. The unwritten code of battle permitted both victor and the Christian vanquished to say rites for those teetering between life and death. Brown-robed men carried their pastoral staffs into the field. They used their crosiers to balance themselves as they stepped between bodies. To Louis, they looked like children crossing streams by walking atop dry stones. The wooden staffs marked the monks as immune to violence. That was not subject to deviation. Whether Frank or Lombard, to lay hands on them meant death and eternal damnation from Rome itself.

The irony of the monks walking the littered field wasn't lost on Louis. "They are herding the poor bastards to their maker like a sheep to the slaughterhouse." The monks waded slowly and aimlessly through the fields with no design or method to their direction, which bothered Louis. Louis was a slave to symmetry and order, preferring his classical tutors from Rome and Athens over the insistent and pious Alcuin. He wanted the fields cleared quickly and efficiently. "Some of these fools are blessing the same bastards." It was time to finish the business of Lombardy, circle around the ancient Alps, and march back to Aachen.

The old Lombard rebellion his father could not quell had now been put down, and that gave the son a sense of satisfaction he rarely felt, yet he remained fixated on the monks in the field. They vexed him, and he wasn't entirely sure why. "Goddamned monks. Playing God. Who is the judge of life and death here?" Sometimes, in the hope of prolonging the inevitable, they gave the wounded water with their blessings. For the monks, there was little time to utter prayers for the dead.

The dead waited for the "vultures." Not the vultures circling the sky, preparing for their feast of flesh, which were also plenty. For the Franks, the vultures were the same foreigners within the army that prepared the soldiers for war. Once battle had been waged, the quiet vultures of camp took up their back satchels and pull carts and made for the fields. For them, the busiest part of the campaign was always the aftermath of battle. Their first and most important order after battle was to collect armor and weapons from the dead. Arrows were top objects on the list of valuables. Only certain arrows would do, however. Arrows that kept straight shafts were worth more than their weight in silver.

During Charles's campaign against the Córdoba Emirate, arrow supplies were low. The camp munitions captain instituted a competition among the vultures. The three vultures who collected the most quality arrows were given an officer's ration of wine for a month. The practice didn't last long. Charles put an end to the competition after a vulture crammed an arrow into the eye of an opponent whom he accused of stealing from his stack.

Next among the hierarchy of vulture finds was chain mail and scale mail, which was so valuable that a simple suit could eat up a foreign soldier's yearly wages. Bad luck or not, links and scales that evidenced death blows could be mended by the smiths in camp. It was common knowledge that men fought better in fine mail, and the Franks wanted to give their men every advantage possible. The next items collected were weapons of steel. Lombards weren't known for having the best swords, but embarrassing reports of Frankish blades cracking during the cavalry charge two weeks earlier meant that foreign steel had value, if for no other reason than to symbolically render Frankia's enemies as impotent.

The reports of poor steel infuriated Louis. He believed that control of the empire's metal and armaments industry had gone to unscrupulous men who were outside of court and felt immune to the reach of the emperor's hand. Louis believed that slights to the crown under his father's reign would require attention going forward. "Oliver must bring these dogs to heel. He fights like Alexander. He needs to mind his preparations like Caesar." At the least, it was better to repurpose the steel for other uses and keep it from returning to enemy hands.

Next were the shields painted with the white cross on the green background of Lombardy. If the vultures scraped the enemy wood and hides, they could perhaps use them to cover siege machines. Louis couldn't see his men using enemy shields. Franks would find it unlucky and cowardly to take up the objects that protected their enemies yet did so little to save their lives.

Louis stood alone under the entry canopy of his grand red tent. He took a deep, satisfying drink from the goblet held at his side. He then wiped his lips dry with the inside of his right forearm, which was uncovered by his intricate steel brace. Below his thick fur cloak, Louis wore armor fashioned after his father's famous Roman breastplate. It was lifelike in form, showing the creases of well-defined muscles that gave the wearer the appearance of Adonis or Apollo. Skillfully crafted into the chest was the classical story of the bearded Odysseus as he slew his wife's suitors. It was ironic that Charles had admired armor that displayed a man protecting his lone wife. Charles had more wives than generals, and he was not shy to use them as political and military bait.

Yet there was a reason why Louis chose to emulate Charles's prized ancient armor. If Charles likened himself to Herakles,

Louis knew he had to pick his own classical patron. To no one's surprise, Louis chose Odysseus at every opportunity. There was intent behind the choice. Odysseus wasn't the strongest or fastest Greek, but he was the smartest. Homer called him "*polymetis*," or "Odysseus of many minds." What Odysseus didn't possess in might he made up for with intellect and trickery. Odysseus was also a talker. He won people with words as easily as with the point of a dagger. Louis could relate.

Louis convinced the hard men of the marches of Hispania that he was their true patron and supporter. He embellished stories of Charles the Younger's love for the Saracen kings who sent him lavish gifts and fanciful emissaries to bind treaties. He told of trade routes being sealed with kisses on Arab cheeks while the bodies of Frankish sons formed walls along the neck of Spain. Louis managed to outlast his siblings, who died during risky campaigns to prove their loyalty to their father's vision. In truth, it was a political and tactical charade. Through sleight of hand and misinformation, he convinced his father he was worthy of the future title of sole emperor despite other suitors that might have had a better claim but for their lesser blood. In the end, he did what his internal adversaries could not do: he survived and went on.

While Louis wore no beard, there was no mistaking that he was Charles's son. Like his father, Louis was above average in height and fair in build. His nose was the Carolingian trademark. It was large and narrow with a hump at the ridge where most others were concave. The rest of his face was bold and handsome. He figured to keep a full head of hair like his father, even after it eventually grew gray. For all his looks, purple dyes,

and gold adornments, Louis was not Charles, and he was reminded of that to the point of nausea even before his reign as
co-emperor. It was only to be expected, however. He was an ac-
cidental sovereign.

The original honor of emperor was reserved for his
older brother, Charles the Younger, who was the first son of
Hildegard and Charles's favorite son. Charles the Younger had
been groomed for succession since birth despite the fact that
the Carolingians put little credence in inheritance. As such,
the young Charles carried himself differently than his father's
other sons. He rode with the king ahead of the army and wore
a miniature suit of plate mail like his father. He sat at Charles's
side when he handed down justice to petulant lords and honorable enemies. Wherever the elder was, the younger was surely
not far off.

As the third son of Hildegard, however, Louis was not jetti-
soned to some insignificant post in Rome. Like his older brother
Pepin, who was given Italy and lands to the east, Louis was made
a king of Frankish territories. As king and overlord of the duchies of Burgundy, Briton, and Neustria, Louis was charged with
the power to wage war on formidable foes such as the Saracens
of Córdoba. Both Louis and Pepin performed their duties faith-
fully and won many battles for their father. There was only one
throne in Aachen, however, and Louis would remain comfortably off in the distance throughout his father's reign.

The count of headless pagans and consecration of new
churches the elder sons brought to their father didn't hold the
divine currency Charles had hoped for. Pepin died of wounds
suffered in battle five years earlier, and then Charles the

Younger, the subsequent heir to the throne, followed the next year. Charles was devastated by the losses, and with his advanced age, he made quick work to install Louis as his successor and co-emperor. When crowned by his father's own hand, Louis thought his fate had come full circle and divine providence had surely worked in his favor. The nobles of Frankia were respectful to Louis at first, yet it was a tempered affection. Though Louis saw the lack of enthusiasm for his ascension as equally as treasonous as an unsheathed dagger, he held his tongue, knowing his complaints would only give credence to what could only be remedied by time.

Time, however, didn't dispel what haunted Louis. The affronts mounted, yet they remained minor and largely unnoticed to all but him. There was never an overt comment or a refusal to obey his command that Louis could point to and proclaim, "There! There is the treason that challenges my throne and haunts my mind!"

Louis saw a form of tacit dissent that others could not. Whether it was a brief and shallow bow from his dukes or the eyes of generals that focused more on his faithful friend, Oliver, he saw them all and he kept notice. He counted and he watched, measuring ally and potential enemy. He listened to whispers and employed spies. He made lists that would remain hidden until he sat on the throne alone. When the time was right, he would strike, but in a different way than his father had struck down his own brother Carloman. It would be powerful and ruthless so no one could judge him to be made of false courage.

On a fine white charger, a captain approached the covered overhang of the red imperial tent. He didn't pull back until he was on top of his emperor. He leapt from his mount in a single, graceful movement, seemingly unfazed by the weight of his cumbersome scale armor. The captain wore the deep-red cape of his rank. The helmet he hugged on his side bore the matching feathered plume. The captain stood to the side of his emperor's gaze and saluted with his empty hand.

"Where is Desiderius?" Louis asked.

The last response Louis wanted to hear was a report of an escape. The king of Lombardy had proven evasive through the years, avoiding Charles's soldiers and assassins through cunning and bribery. He finally came out of hiding at the head of the Lombard army. To catch or kill the old foe would complete the achievement that his father could not claim.

The young captain stared straight and reported, "Lord Oliver believes he has the king of the Lombards, my great lord. He lives."

Louis grunted at the captain's use of the word "believes." He thought for a moment to challenge its use, but it was most likely direct wording from Oliver, who knew the old king to be a slippery serpent. Louis accepted the comment with satisfaction and quickly glanced at the captain before turning back to the canvas of carnage before him. He vaguely remembered the young man's face. He was the son of some forgettable baron from Louis's holdings in Neustria. "And what of my cousin?"

"Oliver has him, too, great lord. Lord Oliver reports that Lothar was injured during his capture yet presently lives."

"Then hurry back to Lord Oliver and tell him to bring them to me immediately. I'll have them unharmed. Tell Oliver to have a physician see to Lothar if need be."

Louis sat at the large wooden table in the back of his tent. Smoldering braziers flanked him. Cracking hot rocks were used in place of wood to keep the tent free of choking smoke. Louis grabbed stacks of maps and inventory reports, attempting to look occupied. He wanted to give the appearance of being busy as he waited for Oliver to bring his new captives. He didn't want Desiderius to think he placed much importance in his capture. That couldn't be further from the truth.

He sat uncomfortably in his battle armor, creaking with every shift in his seat. The pinching of his skin between metal creases became unbearable so he decided to stand and peer at the large map that took up the entire length of his desk. It was painted on a thick weaved sheet and showed the lands south of the Alps.

Louis could hear the commotion of soldiers in armor approaching the tent. He kept his gaze fixed on the Alps, running his fingers across the fabric. The Alps bothered Louis. It was a protective shield that hid and sheltered many would-be subjects such as Desiderius and those rebellious lands farther to the east. What vexed him even more was the thought that his work in Lombardy was nothing more than a fool's errand. He had no business south of the Alps. The quarrels of the region should naturally fall on his nephew, Bernard, king of Italy. Yet here was Louis, fighting a war that could only strengthen a potential rival rather than his own claim. It was his father's idea to send him south while Bernard worked to extend the borders to the east. "That fucking horse's ass," Bernard said to himself. "There has to be an arrow meant for Bernard somewhere in this world."

Draped by black wool was a large crate in the far corner of his tent. It whimpered lightly from time to time, but the racket from

the approaching soldiers morphed the canvas walls of the tent
and seemed to excite whatever was covered. "Silence," Louis
said, "or I will have the girls return and play their game."

The flaps of Louis's tent flew open as a body tumbled forward. The filthy man tried leaping from the ground to look for
another flap from which to escape, but a rope around his neck
was jerked taut and the force backward took the man's feet from
underneath him. He landed on a fine wool rug with a *thud* and
deep moan. Oliver entered through the flap behind the man,
taking up the slack in the rope. He kicked the man, more as an
insult than out of anger.

Oliver said, "An additional spoil to be presented to you this
victory day, my great lord. This is Walucar. He is the son of—"

Louis cut off Oliver. "Walcar. This wretch is the only son of
Walcar. Divine king of the Slavs. You do not look like much of a
prince. Shorter than I expected from the great tales of your father. Yes, Oliver, I know who he is, but I do not fully understand
why he is here. I must say it is something of a surprise. I would
have expected you dead. Is it not a great dishonor among your
people to be taken captive? Can you understand me, Slav?"

"The Prince Walucar is an obstinate creature, great lord."
Oliver kicked Walucar in the stomach to call him to attention.

Louis laughed. "Have care, Oliver. You have planted your
foot on the ass of a god . . . as his people would put it. Besides,
his nature is not his fault. He has his father's blood in his veins.
They say the Slavs still burrow in holes for shelter in parts east
of Bavaria." Louis bent over Walucar as he writhed in pain. "If
you can understand me, then tell me true: why are you here
among the enemies of the Franks, Walucar?"

Walucar would not raise his head or acknowledge his captor. Walucar groaned and said, "Your mother was fucked by mules."

Oliver shook his head with a smirk and began to move in response. "His people apparently formed the force that was to protect breaks in the Lombard lines. I have come to believe that beaten people have a tendency to flock together. They collectively wallow in their lost cause." With a deep grunt, he gave Walucar another taste of his boot. The last kick seemed to have been severe enough to break Oliver's own foot. He tried shaking out the pain.

Louis's eyebrows rose in part surprise and part respect. No one had ever talked to him like that. Vinegar from a man who surely knew he was breaths away from the end was somewhat admirable. Walucar sat up on his knees and wheezed. With his eyes closed, he waited for the next fist or foot to come crashing across his face. Instead, Oliver straddled Walucar across his back. Then, with both hands, he grabbed the rope close behind his neck and snatched it up with all his might, sending the legs of the smaller man flailing in all directions as he tried to grip the earth below his feet. Walucar's arms swung wildly, reaching as far backward as possible to desperately grab hold of Oliver, but it was pointless. Just as the vein in his head looked to burst and his bulging eyes began to go dim, Oliver let go and Walucar fell flat and motionless.

Louis pulled a handkerchief from inside his robe as he came closer to inspect Walucar. "Merciful Christ, he smells like shit."

"He was hiding in one of the camp's latrines. We doused him with buckets of water. The dirt is from the trip over. I dragged the little bastard behind Draca to dry him off." Oliver looked down at Walucar and scratched the stubble of his chin in contemplation. "Would you like him cleaned?"

Louis gave a quick chuckle. "What for? He will be back in the earth before sunset."

Louis awkwardly knelt over top of Walucar. He looked puzzled as he studied Walucar's eyes and said, "What would your father say of you now? Not only captured, but having come to such an inglorious ending. Son of the great Walcar – king of the Slavs. Some say my father loved Walcar more than his own brother. Then Walcar betrayed my father. Thousands of Franks died. Slavs tenfold. It's a mystery to all except those two men. Walcar paid with his life and the lives of so many of his people. For what, we will never know."

The flap opened again, and two men carried a third by his armpits. It was Lothar, the last living son of Carloman and cousin to Louis. His curly-haired head flopped limply with each step. He was clean but disheveled. The two soldiers let loose his arms and he fell lifelessly to the ground beside Walucar.

"Is he dead?" Louis asked.

Oliver pursed his lips. "He was breathing when we tossed him over the horse. Check him, Faro." Faro rolled Lothar onto his back. The breast of Lothar's fine red jerkin fell open when his shoulder landed, showing a white undershirt caked in half-dried blood. Faro held one hand over Lothar's mouth and pinched his nose with the other.

Louis intervened after a few seconds with no response. "Close enough, I would say. What a bore. I was half-expecting him to be as entertaining as the Slav. Where is the king of the Lombards, Oliver?"

"Ah, yes. I will fetch him." Oliver removed himself.

Oliver was the first to enter the tent. He looked casually at Louis as he pulled back one of the tent flaps, through which a small and elderly man entered. He walked in without escort or chains. The old man Oliver accompanied wore a monk's robe. The robe sagged from his shoulders as if it were only hanging on a hook. The man took several deliberate steps into the room. There was no bow of courtesy or respect.

Louis gazed at the man with a puzzled look on his face. Louis thought that this was surely the work of a man drowning in his desperation. There was no possibility that Desiderius could be mistaken for a monk. He was not tonsured. He wore his hair in the Greek fashion. The ends of his short gray hair were purposely curled, as was his beard. The bulge of the robe's hood hid a thin and wrinkled neck. It was clear to Louis that the man was sick. Louis assumed it was the nerves and guilt of decades of fighting and hiding that had worn the man down.

"He has not given us a name. He was with a Lombard burial squad." Oliver swept away the bottom fringe of the man's robe with the toe of his foot. "One of the trackers that we set on him after Verona noticed these fine boots as he made his way through their camp. The scout then inspected his hands. They were red and the skin shifted from flesh with blisters. He is certainly no grave digger. I doubt he ever held a spade before the battle."

Louis looked down at the man's feet. Monks wore sandals even in the winter. Sometimes monks who had no fear of accusations of pride covered their feet with wool socks, but that was rare. This man had black velvet shoes untouched by wear but for the minor traces of dirt that crept over the leather soles.

Louis took two steps closer to inspect the petite man squarely in his eyes. The old man's chin trembled as if he wanted to talk but was stricken by sorrow. Louis had seen Desiderius once before at his father's traveling court. That was decades ago, but the hair and eyes were hauntingly familiar. After an awkward silence, rubbing the palms of his worn hands, the old man mustered the strength to speak. He mumbled in a low shallow voice.

Louis interrupted, "Speak up, king, and in Frankish. In this tent, you stand on Frankish soil."

"My sons?" The old man asked.

Louis took a gulp of wine to collect himself. He felt a morsel of pity for the old man immediately upon hearing his voice. The years of rumors and tales of the old king Desiderius laughing away at Charles's failures to bring him to heel didn't seem to fit the helpless creature in front of him. Louis reminded himself that this was the enemy. He had the blood of countless Franks on his hands, and if the situation was reversed, he would struggle to contain his own guts from spilling out at the cut of Desiderius's dagger.

Desiderius had run a shadow kingdom since Charles proclaimed himself king of the Lombards years earlier. Desiderius would move from city to town, avoiding capture and assassination. His palace was a caravan. Armies had to be summoned by heralds riding through villages. His people would publicly curse him and privately pray for his soul. Louis convinced himself that the man's form and manner were tricks, like some cunning animal that could pretend to be dead in the face of certain death.

"Your sons?" Louis asked. "Do you mean my hostages, old

man? Or did you forget that you willingly handed your sons over to my father like cattle years ago to keep your head on your shoulders?"

Desiderius stared off into the distance and sighed gently.

Louis felt liberal with his insults. "You know the custom well, having been in this position more than once."

"Tell me they died well."

"Died? No, king." Louis motioned with his eyes, and Oliver left Desiderius's side and walked to the corner of the tent. He had no fear that Desiderius would attack Louis. Desiderius was weaponless, and with his brittle body, he was more likely to fall before he reached Louis. Oliver didn't get the impression Desiderius was bent on violence anyway. He looked content in his fate. Oliver saw Desiderius for what he was: a tired old man finished with fighting and only looking to preserve his dignity at the end. Oliver stood beside the cube covered in black wool and waited for Louis's nod of approval. Oliver snatched off the black sheet covering the cube to a light whimper of fear from underneath.

Under the sheet was a cage of iron and wood. The cage was thigh high and perhaps large enough to hold a single man of average size. The iron bars were as wide as a thumb and close together to keep its contents from spilling out. Yet the bars could not disguise even what must have been difficult for ancient eyes to see. The mass of purple and red compressed flesh were two men. The men faced each other on their sides in a sickening embrace. They were naked and entwined as a single unit, bulging out between the iron bars in some places. The hair and beards on the two heads were long and unkempt, yet there was enough room around the eyes for Desiderius to make out the features of his sons.

Louis said, "You must think they are mistreated. Not so. That smell in your nose is the shit-covered Slav that squirms at your feet. You know him and this other corpse better than these caged animals. You kept cousin Lothar at your hearth for years."

Desiderius fell with grace to his knees. He bowed his head. His chest expanded with each deep cry.

"Your sons," Louis said, "as you like to call them, have the pan below them cleaned daily. They are fed and given water as well, although that must be done with care. Adelchis has bitten more than one monk, though they are both rather docile now. The time in the crate has not only bent their bones and made their muscles rotten. It has also curbed their foul mouths. I am afraid they cannot walk or stand."

Louis casually inspected the top lock on the crate to ensure some ironic twist of fate would not free the sons from their cage and by some miracle catch him unaware.

"They were treated with customary kindness until your failed plot on my father's life over the summer rendered their lives forfeit. The monks manage the pain and cries through different concoctions given to them with their food. Take comfort in that. They will live for so long as they or you choose. I give you my word."

"Monster!" Desiderius cried. "You are no prince. You are no Christian."

"And what are you, Desiderius? A breaker of oaths, a rogue ruler and failed usurper! An unholy trinity! You lie in bed with pagan Slavs to save your soul. You tried to assassinate my father at least four times that I am aware of. More likely than not, you have a plot cooking in the pot this very day. Simply put, you have shed the veil of nobility that would have afforded you and your sons the treatment of princes."

Louis reached under the left side of his fur cloak and presented a finely decorated short blade. It looked similar to the Roman gladius. Much longer and wider than a dagger, it had a hilt meant for a single hand. Stabbing, not slashing, was the way to wield the blade. Louis held the knife gently with both hands, presenting it to Desiderius as the old man remained on his knees.

Louis said, "Even though you have stripped yourself of all noble entitlement, I will do you this kindness. A priest will see to your rites." As if part of a ceremony, Louis placed the blade on a wooden stool near the cage. He purposely pointed the tip toward the crate to suggest that the blade could be used to slay more than one noble Lombard. There was no chance that one of the twisted arms could grab it. Louis peered into the cage and then to Oliver, and both men exited the tent together. Oliver waved the rest of the soldiers to follow.

When it came to punishment, little had changed in a thousand years of Roman rule. Hangings and public executions were the plight of the ordinary man. Nobles were afforded the dignity of dying by their own hand and outside the eyes of prying commoners. Suicide was a sin. Yet like other covenants, even the rules of God were subject to liberal interpretation when applied to the nobility.

The thick leather and cloth walls of Louis's tent worked well to retain the heat and even better to muffle the sound from outside. Where the inside was quiet and subdued, the scene outside bustled. In the course of an hour, the camp area surrounding the tent had become a sea of sound and movement. Men on horses trotted by casually and small regiments of troops move back and forth between larger groups. Monks pulled stretchers by hand, laboring away as they carried the moaning wounded from one tent or another.

The vultures were also busy unloading the armor and swords collected from the field, tossing them into large sorted heaps where apprentice armorers selected choice stock for quick refurbishment. Fires burned as well. The few women and elderly in the camp were made busy by preparing stews and boiled meats for ravished and exhausted soldiers. The storage carts of the enemy were intentionally plundered first. Louis, like his father, felt compelled to reward his men for their deadly work. He moved quickly to fill their bellies after a well-deserved day of service.

Louis spoke to Oliver after surveying the scene. "Let's go for a walk."

Oliver looked back at the closed tent flaps and then to his master. "Do you not want to see this ended well?"

"Ended well? I do not see how anything can end up well from a broken old man taking his life and those of his sons. He can have the dignity of privacy. Say farewell to his sons if he believes they are somewhere in that cage."

"Are you not—"

Louis interrupted, "No. I have no concern. Where can he run? Who would take him? But for the beating of his heart, his life is over. He will not leave that tent unless he is carried out on one of the rushes. The war, if that is what you wish to call it, is over. Our efforts are best spent looking forward to the administrative aftermath. I need to plant the seeds of sedition should Bernard be gifted this land, as I suspect." Louis paused and scanned the landscape behind his camp. "I have always found that I do my best thinking while on foot. Let's walk up the hillside a bit and look down from above. I like to see the beauty of an encampment from a distance."

Louis started to walk and noticed that Oliver was a step or two behind him, which he thought was unusual. He wondered if Oliver was silently conveying his objection to the way he had chosen to end the life of his rivals and own blood. Perhaps he just wanted to make sure the killings were done right so the matter could be put to final rest. "Keep a guard on each side of the tent, Oliver, if it will put your mind at ease."

"What of the Slav and your cousin?" Oliver asked.

"If either still lives, have them gelded in front of the men. My uncle's line will end with Lothar." Louis wished his brother Pepin's line would end, but Bernard would be more difficult to capture and cut. Louis continued, "Do not bind their mouths. I want the men to hear their shrieks."

"Open their necks afterward?" Oliver asked.

"Of course not!" Louis cried. "That would be merciful, and my cup of mercy is now dry. Once done, have the crate cleaned of Lombards and have those two squeezed inside."

"What if Lothar has already died?" Oliver asked.

Louis waved off the question. "I do not see the need to worry about such details. If one lives, the dead one can keep him company for the pitiful remainder of his worthless life."

Oliver wasn't necessarily in agreement with the punishment, including the gelding. It was all too cruel in his mind, although his opinion would not come from his lips. Rebels or not, Oliver still felt death deserved dignity whenever possible. He called on Faro to relay the orders and came back to his master. The two men walked through the back of the camp that slowly climbed up the rising land to the sloped part toward the north. It was a bit of an effort for Louis under the armor that he was unaccustomed to wearing daily. His labored breath betrayed his fitness while Oliver remained silent.

After several hundred paces up the valley, the men found a few rocks large enough to double as short stools. They took a seat and surveyed the landscape from above. Oliver brandished a leather flask he kept under his cape. He gave his emperor the courtesy of the first draw. The conversation focused on succession and the proper man to assume dominion over Lombardy. While Louis was co-emperor, he knew his father would likely vest Lombardy to the control of Bernard. It was a natural fit for the king of Italy even though it was Oliver's command that brought the rogue territory into the fold.

While Oliver himself did not harbor expectations of controlling a territory so far away from his own province in Briton, a part of him still felt some disappointment that his master would not even suggest that it should go to his family. It wasn't the territory itself that he sought. Oliver was his father's son, and the idea of rule was cumbersome to him. Oliver was a fighter, not a talker or a ruler. He lamented the idea of returning to his own lands to hear the complaints of neighbors over fences and farmers over stolen cattle. He was not young, but he still yearned for battle and all the glory that came with victory. At that moment, what he really desired was a sign of appreciation and an acknowledgment that he was necessary.

In Oliver's mind, he saw the two men as morphing away from the role of master and servant. He couldn't put a name to the relationship, but it was one where he felt a certain comfort and understanding. He knew it was his thought alone, and to utter his mind to others would mean banishment at the least. Yet Oliver knew the temperature of the men in the valley below who faced death earlier that day. Men who mattered. If given the freedom to speak honestly, each man would admit that although Louis was the face of the new empire, it was Oliver whom they trusted in. It was Oliver who gambled around the firepits and shed tears at the funerals. He was there with the men when it mattered, not tucked away, safe from steel and arrows.

As Oliver drained the last few drops from the flask, a sight in the field below caught his attention. Three men were riding from camp towards them. "Look, my lord. The kite in front carries the eagle on a yellow banner. A herald from Aachen."

Louis looked down at the earth below his feet. There were only a few reasons for a herald to come from Aachen. "I can think of nothing good in that pouch."

Oliver had a vague understanding of his master's concern. He would never bear the weight that Louis carried, but he was all too familiar with the shadow of a famous father. "Have faith in the Lord God, my emperor."

The herald dismounted his horse as it came to a halt. He twisted his steed by the reins to reach into the leather pouch at its flank. The dust-faced youth presented a bound letter to

Louis on one knee, his face to the ground. Louis stepped back and looked over to Oliver. "You read it."

Oliver paused for a moment, then took the letter from the herald, who remained on one knee.

"It bears the seal of Theoderic, but the letter is from Einhard's hand. He bids for you to return to the capital as soon as you can. Your father," Oliver said, "has taken ill and remains in a deep sleep. Einhard fears the last rites may be given before you arrive."

Louis nervously scratched the stubble of his chin. "How old is the letter?"

The kite responded, "Five days, my lord."

Louis turned from the herald and walked a few paces. He was certain he would show no emotion, but for some reason, he felt that his outward expression was a personal matter for no one else to witness. Einhard was not a man to engage in excitable overtures. If anything, he was known for his understatement. Other than his father, Einhard was also the only person who could summon Louis without fear of recourse. He was more than a friend. He was more than a teacher. He was the understanding uncle Louis never knew.

Certain parts of Louis felt relief that this segment of his life, one filled with frustration and pent-up rage, was near its end. Then the awful reality seeped into his mind. No one understood him more than his father. Not even Einhard. For all the disappointment he had caused Charles, he knew his father loved him, and though Louis wasn't the chosen one, he still felt love for his father in return. Despite losing his mother and brothers, Louis suddenly felt alone for the first time. A new era was at hand.

"I have thought about this moment for some time." Louis knew those words would catch Oliver's curiosity. He used them as a string to drag Oliver away from the red kite. When out of range, he pulled Oliver to the side and continued. "I am now the sole emperor of Frankia."

Oliver felt slightly uncomfortable and hesitated to bring up the technicality that his father might still live. "Yes, great lord."

"My concern is that if I go to Aachen, it may be perceived by others as a sign of weakness, that I require some sort of ceremony or affirmation by the Peers and church."

Oliver had trouble following and responded by searching for more. "Lord?"

"I fear that"—Louis's eyes came to a squint, shifting from one point to another as he worked out the rationale of his uneasiness in his head before it came from his mouth—"that upon my father's interment, people may expect a ceremony to continue, to pass his crown on to me, under the approval of Rome."

"Great lord, you were crowned by Emperor Charlemagne's own hand only a year ago. All the empire and the rest of the world knows this."

Louis snapped out of his daze and took Oliver eye to eye.

"You underestimate that man whore in Rome! Pope Leo! He prostituted himself and his holy favors to my father in return for Christ's blessing and title of holy roman emperor. I have shown him no love, nor has he shown me any in return. He will surely expect that I kiss his holy ass in return for his formal blessing in place of Bernard."

Oliver scoffed as if he was grazed by the insult. "And what of this?" Oliver gestured to the scene below. "It was Leo who bid

Charles to bring war down on the Lombards. It is done and done well. Has he another thirty count of silver he covets?"

Louis was pleased at his old friend's anger. He would need implicit loyalty now more than ever. He shook Oliver by his broad shoulder with a smile. "Leo desires Pagan converts to the east. Saracen heads to the south, all the way to Jerusalem, no doubt."

"Christ, is that all he wants? Put otherwise, do you need him or does he need you?" That, in fact, was the question that mattered most. Whether Oliver understood the true issue or simply stumbled upon it was immaterial.

It was most certainly Louis who needed Pope Leo III rather than the other way around, but Louis kept his opinion to himself. After all, it wasn't the pope who painted the political landscape the way it was. True, he added his own touch in the corners, but the world as it existed all around Louis was a product of his family's provocations or reactions. Louis was simply the unfortunate beneficiary.

"The memories of our nobles run short, Oliver. They see this as an auspicious time and demand more from me than they ever would have of my father. Our borders are frayed at the edges. Then there are nameless tribes of forest savages spilling in from the east for plunder, only to scurry back into their dark forests just as fast. Our armies are stretched thin, provinces are taxed to the point of open rebellion, and what complicates the situation is the need to play the role of law-bringer to false kings like the fool down below. All the while, Bernard has gained power and influence through his own victories in the lands of the Avars and Slavs. He is piling up tattered and blood-soaked banners. His boyhood fantasies have come to life."

Louis was in his emotions. He could express himself to Oliver with no concern, but now that his sole rule was at hand, he knew that opening up to the one person he confided in required some restraint. No one ever saw Charles frustrated.

Oliver responded, "Bernard is just a boy. I could stamp out his life like some insect." Oliver saw none of the dangers that Louis did. For Oliver, complicated knots weren't untied with care; they were severed in two by a swift, sharp blade. Answers came simple and were usually violent.

Louis held back the urge to offer a sarcastic response, a reminder that Bernard had equaled Oliver's victories in only a few years.

Oliver shrugged, feeling as though he had a license to continue. "You are the emperor, regardless of your father's state. Enter the city crowned and cloaked in purple. Attend his funeral and tell the Peers and nobles you are off again to lead us east to finish the war your brother started with the Avars. Dismiss Bernard and take his men. Give the nobles their theater, then leave them to spin rumors. Meanwhile, we will carve the empire into the form you choose."

Louis didn't even pretend to hear Oliver's counsel. "It's all from the weaving and spells of that whore mother of his, Thygrid. She needs her throat opened with the same blade taken to her son. I am emperor and need no one's leave to come and go as I please. To go to Aachen may just as easily be seen as a weakness."

Louis violently ran his fingers through his hair, pulling hard on the ends in frustration. He couldn't help himself. He didn't have his father's restraint; the rants came too easily. Louis looked down and saw the first train of men being led west to the coastal ports south of the Alps. It was a slave train of Lombard men fit for hard labor in far-off lands. Their lives were part of the penalty the broken kingdom would have to pay for its king's decades of poor decisions. Louis assumed the newly minted slaves were likely bound for Daneland as partial consideration for peace terms Charles had reluctantly agreed to last summer. It was another truce on shaky ground; Louis only hoped it would hold true for the time being.

"What if he dies before I reach Aachen? Goddammit, he could have died days ago." Oliver crossed himself out of habit, and Louis continued on in a prolonged exhale. "If he's laid to rest while surrounded by no one but rats chewing at scraps of his flesh, Frankia could explode into turmoil. Bernard is in the city as well. He will sow sedition."

"It seems there is no simple answer," Oliver responded. "What will you do?"

"I must assume this is my father's time. This is not the first time he has danced with the angels, but I fear it is his last. He has been obsessed with his own passing the last few years, so let us assume it is his time."

The emotions that hit him with the news seemed to have passed, and Louis was now cold and intent on plotting his options. He twisted the gold signet ring that his father had cast for the year before. It was embossed with a cross flanked by the Frankish fleur-de-lis. The symbolism wasn't lost on him. The cross, not the flower symbol of Frankish sovereignty since the reign of Clovis, was centered on the ring. This was his father's own doing. Charles kept the church relevant by eliminating each new Desiderius who scoffed at the threats from the heir of Saint Peter. Charles coveted the praises from God above all others.

A year later, the ring still felt unnatural on his hand. It was too small and pulled on his skin as he twisted it. He realized the weight was more than the gold alone. "My father is determined to make his funeral an even greater spectacle than his coronation. The man wants to carry his precious image to heaven." Louis's words began to carry a heavy air of disdain; the love between father and son had faded away.

"Is he not justified, my lord?"

"My father has kept cardinals from Rome, emissaries from the Holy Lands, and all sorts of Christian frauds at court for more than a year, stoking his own sense of importance." Louis shook his head and stewed. The reality of his inheritance was settling in. Having the sole signet ring was not freedom; it was bondage. Louis would be bound to the world Charles had created for himself. A world of mysticism and fanaticism that Louis had managed to avoid as his father grew more pious with age.

Louis stopped twisting the ring. It only made the uncomfortableness worse. Louis continued, "He has taken his priceless relics—bones and teeth—had them removed from their jeweled boxes, and brought from his chambers down to the vault of his chapel. Connecting himself to Christ . . . He would be called blasphemous if Pope Leo wasn't his pet."

Oliver shook his head. "What of the crown the Saracens hold?"

Louis rolled his eyes with contempt that had brooded within him for years. "Ah! The most holy of all relics! Did you know that he gave up all the lands in and around Zaragoza and Tortosa for it? Assuming it is even real. The man is truly blinded, but his word is absolute on this matter. I had no say in it. True peace with the Saracens will be unsettled until it arrives. He expected to have it placed on his head at his interment."

"And if that doesn't happen?" Oliver asked.

"Then the terms of the truce have not been satisfied. War with the Saracens may return."

Oliver gave Louis a sideways scowl. "But that would be for you to declare, would it not?"

"Aye," Louis said.

"With the truce still so . . . fresh, would it be wise to do so?"

"I don't know if a declaration of war has ever been wise, Oliver."

Oliver didn't like the disparaging remark, but he learned to keep his emotions at bay long ago. "Who could benefit if your father is not laid with the crown?"

"Certainly not the Saracens. Bernard the bearded child most definitely. The whore pope?"

"Then you must be off to Aachen, a place where you can control matters . . . and people."

Louis paused, took a deep breath, and finished his thought with an exaggerated exhale. "I will go. It seems the most prudent of unappetizing options."

Oliver returned the assurance Louis had given him earlier, placing his hand on his shoulder. "Take Faro and as much of my front guard as you see fit, my great lord. They are good for show, if that is what this is truly about. Christ knows they are not for shit in the field!" Louis did not bite at Oliver's attempt at levity, so the seasoned soldier pivoted quickly. "I will stay on with Mauger and Radwig to see that order is restored within Pavia's walls. We will have the streets cleared and sufficient provisions secured while you decide on governance. Our soldiers will be the law while you handle Aachen."

Louis gave Oliver a quick glance and a nod of approval, then looked down into the plain below, watching the slave train continue its rendezvous with the sun and the far-off sea. "Yes, we will ride before sundown."

"And what of Desiderius? His sons?" Oliver asked. "If he has not finished what needs to be done?"

"He is already dead. I can feel it."

"And if not? If he is intent on bartering for time?"

Louis shrugged. His mind had already made the trip to Aachen. "Desiderius has nothing that is worth his life. Kill him quickly. And the creatures in the cage. Strip and throw them in a pit with the rest of the Lombards. Do not let them have words or ceremonies. My leniency ended with the blade I left him."

"Yes, great lord. We should return to camp so your men can prepare. You will have to take the long road around the Alps. The old men say this has been the coldest winter they have ever seen. Even the well-tended passes are overrun with snow that will still be around in the height of the summer sun. You will have to travel light and use your kites and their stations to make it anywhere close to the five days it took for the message to arrive."

Louis continued to study the slave caravan. He had seen men chained and branded for bondage countless times in the past. Why it had his attention now was unknown to him. They marched in single file with minimum guards. The line now stretched with enough men to protect a sizable city, and Louis knew they were probably beaten to the point of breaking before they started off, tethered to each other by an endless rope with individual nooses for each neck.

"Yes. Time flies. I will ride hard for Aachen. See to it all, Oliver."

XII

- THE FINAL BREATH -

Sicho, the chief physician to the emperor, had his ear directly on Charles's mouth, listening for a breath. The only noise he could hear was the constant cracking and hissing of the large bedside candle that had melted down to a stub. Sicho looked up and gently surveyed Charles's chest with his fingers, trying to locate the optimum spot to detect a heartbeat. The beat had grown so faint over the last few days that it was necessary to remove the wool sheets and nightshirt Charles was wearing as a precursor to any inspection. Sicho gave a short nod toward Bishop Otto and Theoderic. His heartbeat was weak, but it was still there. Charles still lived.

Otto had administered to Charles his last rites three times since he initially fell into his deep sleep. He contemplated whether to perform a fourth. The decision to administer multiple last rites was not church-sanctioned but rather the presumed wish of Charles. One of the matters Charles struggled with in the latter years of his reign as Holy Roman Emperor was his piety in the name of Christ and fulfilling his obligations as lord and sovereign over the people of Frankia. Sometimes Charles felt that his actions as emperor weren't in line with the teaching of the gospels he learned from Alcuin and Einhard. When Charles conquered Saxony and imposed Christianity on its people, he beheaded four thousand men and women who refused the cross. His public decision was stern. In private, his burden was oftentimes unbearable. Charles's holy advisors told him it was God's will to execute those who rejected Christ. Charles had his own reservations, but he did the bishops' work anyway. Days and years passed. Guilt continued to seep into his mind, impacting his actions and behavior. He became erratic.

All the pagan blood and screams were hard to cleanse. In order to shed his guilt and perform his functions as sovereign, Charles sought absolution from God in the form of daily confession. Even if Charles had taken ill and been restricted to his bed, he would have Bishop Otto or even Einhard brought to his bedside to take his confession. His reasoning was that since so many people were taking actions in his name or on his direction each day throughout the empire, he felt obligated to seek constant forgiveness from Christ. Otto believed a final renewal of last rites was what Charles would have wanted.

Given the progressively shallow heartbeats over the last day, Sicho believed that the time had come. Charles was ready for the bishop one last time. Theoderic told one of his young clerks who was running his errands to fetch Alcuin and Einhard so they could address the royal family and say their final words and prayers. Upon receiving the notification, Alcuin had his own monks, who served as his personal staff, feverishly work to notify the mothers and offspring throughout the palace of his decision to address the entire family in Charles's private dining room across from his living quarters. He purposely gave the monks no information other than that Charles still lived, that his last rites were being performed, and that the crown expected all family members to gather at the private dining hall at sundown for further information. Alcuin feared any other detail would spark plotting and complaints. He told the monks to make their announcements and say nothing further, just to move to the next door in the long, dark corridor where the emperor's family members resided.

Alcuin stood alongside Charles's dining table, awaiting the arrival of the immediate members of Charles's family in Aachen. After short deliberation between Alcuin and Einhard, the men believed it was Alcuin, perhaps the man that knew Charles best in the world, who would address the family. Einhard realized that since Alcuin was not only the palace's spiritual advisor but also Charles's oldest and closest friend, he should assume the role as chief coordinator of the family gathering and ultimately, when the time came, the funeral. Alcuin pretended to have appreciation for Einhard's suggestion when in truth he loathed the idea. It was true that he cared deeply for Charles and his family. Some children, particularly Charles's older ones, were also students of Alcuin's and got to experience his wisdom and gentle guidance as he transitioned into a kinder man in his later years. Still, Alcuin knew that several of the women had grown difficult to deal with, and sought special treatment when it came to Charles, not necessarily out of love or adoration for the man but rather out of a sense of concern for their own well-being. Damn

Einhard, Alcuin thought to himself. He knew how to play a situation long before it arrived.

Alcuin stood tall with a gentle smile, keeping his hands clasped at his navel. He donned a deep red cloak adorned with white crosses that he sometimes wore when he and Charles were at prayer together. Alcuin nodded to each family member as they entered. He knew them all. Some he knew better than others, but he was the one person who could bridge the family man to the emperor. Some were already crying while others began to gently weep as they saw the bishop and his attending monks enter the living quarters. For the children of the family, he had bread and honey set up on a long table, along with various cured meats, fruits, and cheeses. Red wine was also made available in adequate quantities. His rationale was that if the mouths in the room were busy filling their bellies, they were less likely to interact with each other and spark unfortunate chaos. Alcuin also brought in extra benches and chairs to make the family more comfortable.

It was not unusual to have Charles's wives and consorts gather collectively. While they had their disagreements, there were equal instances when they found strength in each other. Major ceremonies and state functions often found Charles surrounded by all the children of his loins. The unwed mothers of his children were not stigmatized by unofficial bonds of marriage, nor did the church ever take any action to challenge Charles's family practices. In truth, there was no preferential treatment afforded to firstborn status or the status of a mother who bore children out of wedlock. Charles was known to love all his children and their mothers without prejudice of ceremony.

Over the years, Charles had twenty-three children by nine different mothers. Sixteen children still lived, yet only three were male heirs. Of the living children, all but the son by his deceased wife, Hildegard, were in attendance. Louis's absence was expected. He was crowned co-emperor of the empire and was in the far-off lands of Lombardy, quelling a rebellion that had gone on much too long. Word had been sent to Lombardy, however, and the expectation was that Louis was en route to the palace, traveling hard from the plains south of the Alps. Unfortunately for Louis, it did not appear that his fast stallions could outrun Charles's mortality.

Alcuin felt mild empathy for Louis. The man whom he had a hand in raising since birth would want to be there for his father's funeral. Alcuin knew that Louis was particular about his image in relation to his father, even more so because of the number of would-be emperors and empresses that were sure to sprout from Charles's passing. Nonetheless, Alcuin knew that there was nothing to be done as far as delaying the funeral to come. Frankia and the tradition of Catholic law were adamant about interring Christian souls to the earth no later than two sundowns. It was something Alcuin intended to honor.

Alcuin heard the heavy iron latch of the doors to the dining hall release in front of him. Slowly making their way through the doorway were Liudgard and the younger Gersvind, Charles's fifth wife and consort, respectively. They were short and petite with blonde hair pulled up high. They wore fine black dresses that ended in white lace around their wrists. Both women were holding the hands of girls aged around ten, yet they were almost as tall as their mothers. Two smaller girls around the age of five followed behind aimlessly, looking around the cavernous room they had yet to explore. Gersvind whispered to her eldest daughters, who took the smaller girls by the hand and walked over to thick rushes placed close yet a safe distance from the burning fireplace. Alcuin knew the room would be alive with children despite the solemn occasion and had the children's nurses move many of the dolls and wooden figures from the queen's quarters to entertain them while the adults carried on.

Alcuin often called Liudgard and Gersvind the "lost laces" when he spoke about them to Theoderic and Einhard in private. The harmless joke didn't settle as well with him as it did when he first uttered the phrase. Back then, he never considered the reality of their futures. As they gathered among other women who were more aggressive in asserting their rights among Theoderic and other nobility, it became clear that the women were truly lost. Women in the middle of Charles's pack were too old to have his physical affection and too recent to conjure up nostalgia and esteem, particularly given that there was no male heir among their children. They were destined for lives of obscurity.

While Liudgard and Gersvind were unaware of their label, they knew their place with Charles. In their roles, they found a common cause and strength in allying with each other for whatever the arrangement might be worth. At best, when Louis took control of the palace, the women could hope for humble living quarters near the palace and sympathetic treatment from Alcuin or Theoderic passing them coin from time to time. The problem, however, was evident; Alcuin and Theoderic men were not far from their own death beds. Their girls were surely marked for covenant life.

Yet despite their sad futures, Gersvind and Liudgard loved Charles and they wore their sorrow on their faces. Puffy red eyes greeted Alcuin as the women bowed to their new benefactor with humility and grace. Alcuin kept the conversation short and formal, thanking them for such steadfast care and constant prayers. Gersvind was the mother with a true talent in embroidery. She put her skills to work one last time for her old lover and friend, making Charles an embroidered shawl of fine Egyptian thread. The cloth was a deep purple, symbolizing Charles as royalty in connection with God. It had *Rex Mundi* embroidered in gold thread on its four corners. Gersvind told Alcuin she wanted Charles to be buried with the shawl, something from her hand that would travel with him to eternity in heaven. Alcuin smiled and cupped her cheek in acceptance, all the while knowing that he had no intention of honoring her request even though he found the gesture touching. Alcuin shepherded the group over to the tables of food. There would be more dire faces to come.

Shortly after Gersvind and Liudgard had settled into the room, Regina arrived. She carried herself like a queen, dignified with her straight spine and shoulders rolled back, hands clasped together at her stomach. She brought with her Charles's last two male heirs, the twins Hugh and Roger, aged five. The boys were under the care of their nurse, a plump elderly lady who had no tolerance for undisciplined behavior, more so in the current setting. She held the boys close by on arrival and kept a sharp eye, ready to twist an ear if that was what it took to capture their attention. Like Liudgard and Gersvind before her, Regina displayed signs of crying in her eyes and shallow sniffles. Her beauty was unaffected by the sorrow on her face.

"Alcuin, when might Einhard be available? I have matters of Aquitaine that I wish to discuss with him." She blinked in an attempt to hold back her emotions. Alcuin was not surprised by Regina's request for Einhard since he knew her concerns all too well. She had tried to impose herself on Theoderic immediately upon learning of Charles's illness, but the chancellor brushed her aside with little tact and let it be known that he had no patience for her cajoling. Einhard was her next target. He was Louis's closest political ally in the palace and could influence others to support claims he believed would have interested Charles.

Regina wanted her boys' future preserved with land and title commensurate with their station as princes of Frankia. They were the only living sons of Charles other than Louis; all other children in between were miraculously girls or young women, some already married off themselves. Lands near Aquitaine would be the obvious selection for Regina's sons, as those were her ancestral lands, but there were many political pieces in play at the time. Charles had become negligent in his duties to family planning over the last few years. He singularly focused on solidifying Louis's role as emperor as well as handling foreign threats and settling promises to Pope Leo III.

"Einhard is with Chancellor Theoderic, performing a similar meeting with the members of the nobility and foreign representatives who have arrived. I will pass along your request to meet him." Alcuin had wanted to plant a new idea in Regina's head as an alternative to her sons not receiving the titles and lands of her expectations. "Lady Regina, if it pleases you, I have a meeting scheduled with the bishop of Chur this evening. I would be happy to suggest bringing your sons into the monastery of Saint John at Mustair to continue their education with the intent of placing them in direct service of the archbishop's staff in Rome. It would be a high honor."

Regina responded with a short and desperate chuckle, her eyes enlarging as she finished. Her voice shifted to a mild hysteria. She was working herself into a frenzy in front of a man who had little control over matters of state alliances. "My uncle is duke of Aquitaine and a Peer. His soldiers still make up a third of the empire's armies. It would only be fitting for his nephews and the only other princes of the empire to assume rule equal to their stations, Master Alcuin. Surely the blood and sacrifices our people have made in support of the empire merit proper recognition."

Alcuin grabbed for her hands to calm her, knowing any outburst would surely excite Liudgard and Gersvind into joining the conversation. "Calm, my child. I shall pass your words on to Einhard. Has our Lord Charles ever let your boys suffer? He loved—loves—them so. All will be well."

Regina pulled her hands out from Alcuin's grasp and held her breath as she looked to the floor and studied the accuracy of his statements. He spoke the truth. Charles was very affectionate with the boys. She could recall them feeding ponies in the stables with their father and walking the grand garden to pick ripe apples and peaches, the boys gorging themselves with a bite or two before tossing the fruit to the ground in search of sweeter prey. She wondered if that affection translated into genuine care for their future.

Charles had many children with mothers just as eager to

see him prove his love and honor his promises. Had she done enough to secure that for her boys? When was the last time she showed Charles any affection or asked for his bed? To Regina's knowledge, she was the only mother whom Charles had ever taken to the hot baths of the cauldron. That display of intimacy had to be worth something. Could she have done more?

Regina nodded to Alcuin and kept her head low as she continued to the area set up for the children. She looked to the nurse and took control of her boys by touching them gently on the back of the head, guiding them over to the bread and honey. She shifted her eyes to the door, a subtle instruction to the nurse that she was temporarily dismissed. There was to be an intimate meeting with family only—as intimate as a room of twenty people could be.

After the exit of Regina's servant, there was a momentary pause when young Adallind entered abruptly with Rosalind falling rapidly behind. Adallind was all emotions. Her chest expanded and contracted while her fingers danced around the long blonde hair that hooked behind her ears. Alcuin didn't have to approach Adallind. Adallind came directly to him.

Adallind asked Alcuin, "When can I see my husband? Can he talk? Can he hear me if I talk to him? Please, Master Alcuin, tell me all is well."

Adallind was a child in age, emotion, and behavior. At the age of seventeen, she was the youngest of Charles's companions. She had lived in the palace for the last eight months, excited beyond words at her future marriage to the emperor, whom she worshipped more than loved.

Adallind wore a fine yellow linen dress with pale white trim.

The cloth made her hair shine like gold. Rosalind had suggested she conduct herself with restraint and humility when she entered the room, but the obstinate girl refused.

Rosalind kept her eyes on Adallind the entire time, unsure whether to touch her arm and offer comfort. Rosalind was lumpy and discreetly covered in brown and tan layers of cloth with no visible jewelry or other objects to accentuate her image. Rosalind might easily have been mistaken for Adallind's slave or servant when in truth she was Charles's fifth wife. Charles's marriage to Rosalind was publicly known as a political and tactical ploy. Rosalind was the daughter of Burchard, the duke of Swabia. Burchard was once a loose ally of Charles made solid through the bonds of marriage. It was Charles's uncle, Carloman, who held what was known as the Blood Court at Cannstatt seventy years earlier, where he tried and immediately executed hundreds of the ruling nobles of Swabia for suspicion of plotting treason with Burgundy and Bavaria. Rosalind's grandfather, Odis, was one of the few Swabians who survived the accusations. Odis was eventually granted the duchy. Charles, being a man of honor, awarded the continued faithfulness of the dukedom when he took on Rosalind as his wife. It was a marriage for the courtiers' viewing and nothing more, irrespective of any desires Rosalind might have had.

With Charles unavailable to her, Rosalind took up the role of the palace mother. None of the women in Charles's life considered Rosalind a threat, and as a result, she moved with freedom throughout the court, finding purpose in the job as a counselor and confessor to these women who knew the pressures of court life. Since Adallind was the newest and shiniest toy in Charles's box, Rosalind quickly attached to her, comforting the young woman as she navigated the hornet's nest of competing women. Rosalind was comforting her even more now that it seemed as though her childish dreams of courtly romance were proven to be as foolish as the love between two people with fifty years of separation could be.

Alcuin spoke to Adallind. "Calm, my child. You can see him momentarily. There will be an order set to sit by his bed. You will be the last to see our prince." He spoke the last line in the hope of convincing the young woman that there was some honor in being last.

"But . . . But I am his current wife. I . . . Even though I am not his wife in the eyes of Holy Mother Church, I am the one he loves and adores. I must—"

Alcuin reached out and grabbed Adallind gently by the shoulders in an attempt to calm her emotions before she reached hysteria. "My sweet Adallind, please be calm, if for no other reason than to show Charles your strength and courage at this difficult time. That is why he chose you—you know that." Alcuin now thought pandering would have a positive impact. How much, though, he wasn't sure. He could sense from Adallind's stare that she wanted to hear more. More of Charles's secrets and feelings about the young beauty to patch her fragile ego. Alcuin gave her what she wanted. Anything to keep order before she entered the living quarters. "For all your beauty, Charles admires your blood. Your Neustrian blood. It said your ancestors were the descendants of Clovis. He had need of you when he first gazed upon you, and he needs your royal blood now." Alcuin brushed a fallen lock of hair from her face. "Charles instructed me to take special care of his flower of Paris. You above all others." The last line brought a half-smile to the child's sobbing face.

Alcuin spoke softly. "Rosalind, would you please take Adallind over to the table and pour her a hot cup of wine? She needs your friendship now more than ever. I promise we will all have our time with the emperor in a moment." Rosalind, a true wife to the most powerful man on the earth, politely and with quiet humility and grace guided her young sister to the table with Regina.

Alcuin breathed deeply to collect himself and walked to the doorway to summon one of his assistants. He had expected Bishop Otto to return after the administration of the last rites. It was imperative that the rites be completed before Charles passed, and for all Alcuin knew, that might be happening that very minute. Alcuin asked his servant to fetch the remaining family members as fast as possible, hoping to assemble the extended family so they could enter the bedchamber as a united front. Ceremony and perception had been a pillar in building Charles's persona, and the complex structure of traditions needed to stand firm in the winds of chaos.

Alcuin needed no notice or announcement regarding the next visitor; the noise disrupted the tranquility of the gathering. The clanking of metal spurs on stone and the clinking of mail links heralded the man moments before arrival. Bernard's booming voice made his identity apparent. The grandson of Charles was having an elevated conversation with a woman whose voice was just as loud and animated. Alcuin knew that Bernard was joined by his mother, Bertra. Bertra was the widow of Pepin, Charles's second son and the king of Italy, who died fourteen years earlier.

The title was vested in Pepin's only son by Pope Leo III the following year. The title was a father's precious gift, and at times, it was more a burden than a blessing.

Any man who knew Pepin would have no trouble identifying his only son in a room full of nobles. There was a good deal of irony between Pepin and Bernard. Bernard had reached the same age as his father when he died laying siege to Venice. Like many Frankish sons, the two had never met each other. Despite the void, Bernard grew to be the replica of his father as if the hand of divine providence was at work. Pepin was a man of deep faith, a heavy drinker, and a strong believer in action over discussion. Bernard followed suit.

Bernard took on his father's features and mannerisms. He had flowing, deep black hair and beard, heavy muscles, and sharp lines. He had the look and actions of a cultured savage. Bernard was wild in his behavior yet clean and refined in appearance. It was a characteristic that drew women to his flame. That was what happened when blunt Frankish lords took lands in refined Italy. They adopted the fine clothes but kept their rough upbringing.

Bernard wanted to be the spearpoint of the empire's might, finding great joy in the way his grandfather harnessed the young man's rage and love of bloodshed, putting him on Frankia's enemies with extreme effectiveness. Like his father, Bernard left the torture of administration and nation-maintenance to men like Theoderic and Louis. Men who had ink for blood and feared the rush that came with mortal risk. Bernard was a man of candor, incapable of trickery or scheming. He met his problems and adversaries head-on, without fear or concern for consequences. Every man knew exactly where he stood with young Bernard.

Alcuin's servant ran ahead of Bernard and his mother to open the door to the dining hall. Bernard had a way of swinging doors open, disregarding tact and manners that came with privilege but were desperately needed at that moment. Bernard entered the room and continued his animated conversation with his mother without concern for the environment around him. After a moment, the two came to a pause as Bernard scanned the room. "I do not see the chancellor," he announced, looking through Alcuin as if he was not there. "Why is he not present? Is there something more pressing this time? A tax on wool or road repair in some fucking Saxon swamp?"

Alcuin cringed at Bernard's sharp tongue. Among Bernard's qualities, he was a steadfast religious man, although one would never know it from his crude and erratic behavior. Bertra gave Bernard a sharp glance, ready to twist his ear or smack his cheek. Bernard was beyond repair, she knew. The energy she would have expended attempting to influence him was better spent elsewhere.

Alcuin meekly responded, "Lord Bernard, I am sorry for any confusion. Chancellor Theoderic is currently in seclusion with members of the nobility and foreign emissaries who were here in Aachen or recently arrived. We thought it best to divide ourselves among the family gathering and all others. I will advise the chancellor that you have asked for him."

Alcuin bowed his head in submission. He felt a bit of guilt at the coldness that had developed between him and Bernard. As with Charles's children, Alcuin was a teacher to most of the older grandchildren, including Bernard. The two were once close, particularly since Bernard had no father and Charles was often away from the palace. At one point, when Bernard was around nine years old, Alcuin believed the boy was bound for the priesthood. He had such a love of the gospels and the marvelous stories of the Old Testament.

Something happened, however, when Bernard left with his mother to visit her father and family in Genoa. When Bernard returned home to Aachen, he was distant and brooding. He shunned his lessons with Alcuin and instead spent his time at the palace barracks, training with other noble boys and learning the art of the sword with the same fever he used to devote to his religious studies. Bernard spent his days and evenings hacking practice swords against oak posts, not relenting until either his hands bled or the sword broke in two.

Bernard grunted with a sense of acknowledgment as Alcuin searched his eyes for the boy he once knew and found nothing. It was Bertra's turn to speak. She had been silent for over a minute, which was painfully too long for her.

"Alcuin," she said, "it has been whispered that Louis's eldest son, Charles, is to accept Charlemagne's signet ring at the watch ceremony before the interment. Why? Who made such a decision without any thought to the significance of the act itself? That right should go to Bernard, not grandchildren who still piss their beds. Make the change!" Bertra glared at Alcuin with an iron jaw. She exhibited uncompromising determination and persistence in everything she did, having spent years championing Bernard's right to his father's claim as co-emperor.

Bertra wore a gray robe and a matching headscarf that made her appear more like an enraged nun than a doting mother. She lacked all sensuality. It was impossible to tell what Pepin would have seen in Bertra. Their marriage was, in the end, what one would expect: a match of political convenience for Charles.

Alcuin cleared his throat, more to buy time than to ensure a firm voice. "Lady Bertra, please understand that we—that is, Theoderic and myself—are taking every detail into consideration, and the issue of the signet ring is no different. The boy Charles was chosen as a surrogate in the event that his father, the Emperor Louis, does not arrive in the capital before the funeral." Alcuin paused to cross himself and gaze down at the ground. "Surely you must understand that we are . . ." Alcuin chuckled nervously under Bertra's cold stare and elaborated again. "That is, Chancellor Theoderic and I are only following prescribed custom. Emperor Louis is the anointed co-emperor. He automatically assumes the power of sole emperor upon his father's passing."

Alcuin's words only served to light a fire in Bertra. She knew what Alcuin was going to say before he opened his mouth. It was his timid and condescending voice that stirred her to raise herself right into his chest. The short woman made the taller man shrink with surprise and fear. Bernard remained silent. He carried a smirk on his face and tucked his thumbs under his black leather sword belt. He felt a sense of satisfaction and retribution when his most trusted advocate put on her performance.

"I know Louis was anointed, you blathering dog." She placed sarcastic emphasis on the word "anointed," ready to tear apart what she saw as baseless ceremony. "Tell me this, Alcuin. When the pope pressed oil on Louis's forehead and set the crown on his head, did it impart authority on him?"

Alcuin looked around, puzzled, unsure of how to answer. "My lady?"

Bertra growled back at Alcuin. "I spoke clear, you old fucking woman."

Alcuin knew the words she wanted to hear. He stared at the ground and answered. "Pope Leo did not crown Louis emperor. It was Charles's own hand that did so."

"Ah!" Bertra said, "Then how does one become a Holy Roman Emperor by being anointed by another who is neither holy nor Roman?"

"Our Lord Emperor Charles, his word is law. Even Pope Leo himself has written by bull that—"

Bertra was waiting on Alcuin's arguments. "Louis has been in Ravenna and throughout Lombardy for the better part of the last year, yet he has not stepped foot in Rome and knelt before Leo to see the ceremony through. Why is that, old master?"

Alcuin replied, "I do not presume to speak for our emperor, Lady Bertra."

Bertra walked toward the table with the sitting wives and consorts. The wives were technically her mothers-in-law, although she had nothing but disdain for all of them. Not a single one could match her uncompromised strength. "Tell me, Alcuin, how many tribes has Louis vanquished? How many slaves has he taken? How many heathen souls did he bring to Saint Peter? Does he not still flail away in Lombardy, wasting men and coin to fight the toothless old king that cannot even fend off the scheming of his own generals? Where is your warrior prince, Alcuin? And by warrior prince, I do mean Louis and not his dog, Oliver."

"Emperor Louis is laying siege to the city of—"

Bertra blew into a full rage, causing even Bernard to take a step backward as the vein in her forehead almost ripped her headscarf in two. Spit flew from her mouth. "I was told that he held games out of boredom from his endless siege of Ravenna. Meanwhile, the work of the empire, the slaughter of its enemies, falls to Bernard in the east. This one! Look upon him! You know him quite well, do you not? A man of twenty years who has ridden into the field of battle after battle like Alexander reborn, doing Charles's business, the work my husband started while his little brother Louis played with stick swords. Louis was rubbed with oil to keep his hands soft and pink while Bernard washed Avar brain and skull shards from his hair, you babbling old whore!"

Bernard got a chuckle out of that insult. He often tried to imitate his mother's creativity in the delivery of insults but never could. The other women in the room quietly left their seats and migrated farther into the corner, minding the children as they stared at each other uncomfortably. Holice, the youngest girl, began to cry, yet Bertra kept on.

"There will be a reckoning, Alcuin. While we are all here. While the Peers and other nobles are present to acknowledge and pay homage. A formal reckoning of what has been paid in blood and sweat to this empire."

Bertra was no fool. For all her antics and threats, she knew that, when the time came for Charles to depart the earth, it was the funeral and the critical days after that would set the stage for

Bernard's elevation. The ceremony, the church, and the gathering of the Twelve Peers and nobles made the perfect storm for Bernard.

Bertra, along with many others throughout the empire, never understood Charles's hesitancy in acknowledging Bernard as an heir to the empire. Charles didn't reject his grandson. In fact, Charles doted on him constantly, forming a bond of admiration and pride. The throne of Italy had been Charles's to give, and he did so freely. Yet when it came to the ultimate act of acknowledgment, sitting the young warrior in his father's empty and unclaimed seat as co-emperor, Charles mysteriously remained still. The disenchantment Bernard felt toward Alcuin as a boy must have resurfaced as a man when his many victories never translated into the formal recognition he sought. Who better to whisper in his grandfather's ear than Alcuin? Whispers that were never spoken. Perhaps that was why Bernard shunned Alcuin. He was the surrogate for the young man's contempt for his grandfather.

Alcuin rubbed his hands nervously. He scanned the room and the open door, realizing the scene had escalated unnecessarily. "Please, Lady Bertra, let us revisit the matter when Chancellor Theoderic is available and we learn more about Emperor Louis's arrival. I beg you to please keep matters civil and respectful for the time. Please consider what our Emperor Charles would want at this time. Your concerns have and will be of the utmost importance." Alcuin kept his head down as if he was seeking Bertra's blessing, and perhaps he was.

Bertra breathed deeply and straightened herself, looking back at Bernard with a nod of acknowledgment. She had said her peace for the time being, letting those of mild influence know that Bernard was an issue that would not fade away. "Revisit. Utmost importance. I have marked your words, monk, and will hold you accountable." Bertra and Bernard both scanned the room. Noticing that the children had stopped playing and the women were on the verge of weeping, mother and son decided not to participate in whatever farce Alcuin had planned.

As Bertra and Bernard left the room, the doorway was blocked by tiny Gisla, Charles's younger sister and abbess of the convent in Aachen. She had been a constant visitor to the palace during Charles's sleep, bringing her older brother richly embroidered shirts and tunics that her nuns both at home and abroad had woven for their prince. She also prepared a special broth for Charles using the truffles from the old hermit Gregan and a recipe from the long-passed cook of their father, Pepin. Gisla was the definition of humility and virtue, and her older brother adored her for it. Unconcerned with the power struggles among the family, Gisla looked like the epitome of the Virgin Mary to her great-nephew. The son and mother would have mistaken the little lady for just another nun among the palace staff if not for her habit and robe. They had embroidered lining of light purple to signify her status as a member of the royal family.

Bertra stared at Gisla and gave a nod. There was no reason to take on Gisla. She had no power, and so there was nothing to be gained. Gisla stepped to the side, giving way with her standard humility, her thoughts singularly focused on her brother's well-being. She began to address Alcuin when one of Alcuin's clerks entered through the doorway, grabbing both sides of the doorframe to balance himself. The entire chamber knew the words before they were spoken.

"Master Alcuin, Bishop Otto calls for you. Our Lord Charlemagne, sir, he has passed to join our Father in heaven."

Gisla reacted as if the words had punched her in the stomach. She wrenched over and reached her hand out for the doorframe to brace herself for the coming fall. Bernard moved swiftly to her aid, scanning the room to see which others were impacted. Alcuin's shoulders slumped as he crossed himself once again and found a wall to stare off into. A series of moans came from the gathering of women across the room.

Bertra stood stoic, waiting patiently for the moment to pass. She had no love for Charles. His slight to her son was unforgivable. Bernard was touched by the words heralding his grandfather's passing yet would wait until he was by himself before he opened up to his own feelings.

Alcuin processed the words of the clerk and what they meant to him and the empire. He had always known that the day was not long off, perhaps only minutes or hours away. He thought of life without Charles more often than he thought of the countless years they spent together. In a way, he felt troubled, not at the passing itself but at the way it had come about. To Alcuin, Charles was the most dynamic and inspiring man of the last five hundred years. Giants like Caesar and Clovis left the realm of mortals with shouts of agony and women beating their chests in the streets. Charles left in a sad winter silence. This was not befitting of a man of unchallenged status and glory. The father of the empire and the champion of the cross deserved so much more to his final chapter than wilting away like a late-summer flower. Alcuin owed the man as much.

Word needed to go out to the ends of the realm and beyond. Bells needed to be rung until cracked, and monks had to pray until their knees bled. The funeral of Charlemagne had to be a spectacle talked about for the next thousand years. "Thank you, Odo. Please summon all red kites to my chamber. Word must go out immediately to Rome, Louis's camp, and the Peers."

The day was January 28, 814, and a beautiful cloudless sunset was taking shape.

XIII

- JANUARY 29, 814 -

The sun shone radiantly in the endless blue sky. The stones of the palace and cathedral complex glisten white from the extreme brightness. The complex was unmistakably the grandest display of architecture in the capital and perhaps in the entire empire outside of Italy. Much of Frankia was built in wood, rock, and plaster. Aachen was a city of carved stone and concrete with the palace buildings as its centerpiece.

Frankish architects were fine craftsmen, but the house of the cathedral of Charles's dreams required the finest minds of Rome. Frankia's builders were men who knew how to preserve parts of the ancient city and disassemble pagan temples to raise the glory of the papacy. Charles's cathedral required minds that could combine height with complexity and beauty. Charles had no budget for his complex; the only limitation was how quickly gold and silver from conquered lands could be brought to the city, recast as coins, and placed in chests to be shipped back out for materials and labor.

Like the eternal structures of Rome and Athens, the palace and cathedral were built on the strong backs of countless slaves. From quarries to long roads, carving sites, and finally assembly, men of a hundred scattered tongues lived their short and miserable lives stacking giant blocks upon one another until the stone puzzle, topped with gilded crosses, reached the clouds.

While the cathedral was technically attached to the palace through long corridors that shuffled clerks back and forth, there was no mistaking the superiority of the house of God to its sister building. The difference was in the details. While the palace looked like boxes pushed together, the cathedral was an assortment of ornamental buildings of different shapes and elevations and assembled in their own sense of harmony.

Its main tower held a family of marble statues that were visible from the tall open windows. The Merovingians stared down at the visitors below. The tower's metal-tiled spire was thin and came to a sharp point topped with a gold crucifix that punctured the clouds. Next to the tower was the octagonal chapel called the Palatine Chapel. Its eight cleft walls morphed into a dome that held a banner of the dreaded Carolingian black eagle.

There was symbolism in the octagon as well. Alcuin had taught Charles that eight was the number of a new beginning in the Book of Genesis. The eighth day was the first day after the creation. Charles wanted all scholars who could read what was not written to understand his message: Aachen was that new beginning. Numbers of the Bible continued in the church's design. One seeking entrance to the cathedral had to climb twelve steps representing Jesus's apostles. There were also three entry doors cut from the light cedars of Lebanon. They were identical in their symbolism of the Holy Trinity.

The interior of the cathedral was as impressive as the exterior. The environment inside was a total indulgence for the senses. Hearing, sight, and smell were treated to an overwhelming feeling of soft peace and grandiosity. The walls of the hall beyond the chapel were draped with thin banners representing the provinces and territories of the empire. Each banner displayed the colors of the regions and emblems that identified the lands and their ruling families. Lions, eagles, and fleur-de-lis dominated the themes in a rainbow of colors. Doric columns forced the eyes upward to their gilded capitals, which glistened from massive circular chandeliers that hung along the spine of the building. Towering stained glass windows on the east and west sides of the main hall blended with the flame light. The rising and setting of the sun from outside flooded the spacious interior with warm blue and green hues.

The wonderous beauty to the eye was matched by the harmonies delivered to the ear. A massive assembly of bells of different shapes and sizes hung high in the main tower at the entrance and lined the windows of the corridor that connected the back of the cathedral's chapel to the rest of the palace. The daily calls to the lord's prayer used the three bells of the center tower. All sixteen bells were put into action that afternoon, starting at the apex of the sun and continuing until sundown. The bells bellowed tones that vibrated the stone floor and walls. For the funeral of Charles, a fast melody of notes, high to low, echoed throughout the city. The sounds were carried by the positioning of the building in the valley at the foot of the ridge, drawing people from the city and beyond to the source. The bells were only silenced for the term of the funeral ceremony to allow the proceedings to continue with comfort.

More sounds came from a host of monks and choir boys, each group stationed on balconies on opposite sides of the main hall. The mixture of low tones and high notes passing back and forth between the groups ensured constant angelic cover over the murmuring crowd and the scuffs of hundreds of feet plodding along the cold stone floors. Turtle doves that nested high in the rafters and column capitals did not respond well to the intense sounds. They circled in confusion, navigating their way from rafter to rafter in excitement over the noise and gathering below.

The bitter cold air that rushed through the city was no deterrent for the people any more than the ever-present blanket of snow into which the streets and walkways were carved deep until they reached the dark and wet earth below. Commoners and landed men alike migrated to the heart of the capital in the hope of seeing people of prominence in their fine clothes. Many of the faithful wanted to hear a sermon from Bishop Otto or, more likely, were just gathering among each other to recognize that the day was a moment they would tell their grandchildren about.

The city officials had commandeered slaves and held them in the nearby trading post. Their task was to haul oversized braziers from the public markets and civic areas to the cathedral. There, in some of the less congested areas, they built giant pyres that sent smoke to the heavens and brought slight comfort to the gathering faithful. People of all walks of life, both rich and poor, came to the foot of the cathedral's twelve steps and placed winter blooms of pine, trinkets, and crucifixes along the walls. They were alms of adoration, as much as simple people could afford or produce in the bitter winter.

Alcuin and Theoderic quietly left the cathedral and stood halfway down the main corridor that connected the cathedral to the palace. It was a narrow and doorless space where the two men could speak and see anyone approaching. The murmur of the gathering crowd within the cathedral mixed with the chorus. It kept their words from echoing into the palace.

Theoderic said, "None of the red kites have returned with news of the crown. We have run out of time."

Alcuin responded, "I am sure it has something to do with Kasim spiriting from the city the other evening. This is some trick, a scheme the Saracens have played to compromise the peace while we are at our weakest."

A red kite approached as Alcuin and Theoderic finished their conversation in the corridor. He came from the palace side of the walkway and was escorted by two palace guards who had to be dismissed by Theoderic with a wave of his hand. Theoderic sent the red kite to follow the reports of Kasim's travels; his face looked grim, and Theoderic feared the worst.

Theoderic motioned to the kite and said, "Speak quickly and quietly. The funeral is almost set to start." Theoderic turned back toward the cathedral entrance to make sure the three were still alone.

The kite was breathing heavily and had to take a gulp of air to speak. "The emissary Prince Kasim stopped at the fourth station north of Lyon. The station flew a black flag, so I kept my distance until it appeared safe to approach."

Alcuin was annoyed and confused. "Eh? A black flag? Was there some sort of attack?"

The kite shook his head and responded, "I spoke with the captain of the highway station. He said there had been fighting further down the road, master. A caravan of Saracens came to the station seeking aid. There were several injured and dead Saracens at the station. There were also Frankish soldiers that patrol the area. It did not appear as if the two groups had fought. I did not see any injured Franks."

"What of the Saracens? Were they soldiers?" Theoderic asked the boy.

The kite slowed; he had caught his breath. "They had queer clothes, red robes that flowed over shiny tunics, and breeches. They carried swords, but they didn't seem like soldiers. They arrived with a grand wooden carriage that looked like it had been set upon and raided."

Theoderic looked puzzled. "Why would you say that? That it had been raided?"

The red kite responded, "Master Alcuin asked me to keep an eye out for anything unusual. This cart looked special. It was large. The wood was carved and finely decorated. The door at the back had been ripped open by some beast. Thick wood was splintered, and metal was bent. The captain said that Prince Kasim came for the caravan, but then the prince looked inside the cart. He then left it without taking anything with him."

Alcuin asked the kite, "Did the captain say anything else?"

"The captain said that the emissary arrived from the north shortly after the carriage came from the south. The emissary left with two others. They headed on the same road south to Lyon. They left in great haste. They left their men, wounded and healthy alike, and the cart."

"Blessed Jesus, Theoderic, Kasim is looking to take the crown! This is treachery!"

Theoderic responded, "As much as I detest the man, it doesn't sound like he is at fault. It sounds like someone else took the crown and the prince means to get it back. We must proceed with caution and mind our wits."

Otto came down the corridor. The bishop said to Alcuin, "The family is about to be seated. We must begin shortly." The bishop saw the expressions on Alcuin and Theoderic and slowed his pace as he neared them. "Is there something wrong?"

Theoderic spoke up as Alcuin turned his head to ponder the situation. "We will be right in. Thank you, bishop."

Theoderic spoke to the red kite. "Go back to your barracks and gather five more kites or as many that remain. I will be with you after the funeral." The order was met with a bow and quick turn back toward the palace. Theoderic then grabbed Alcuin by his shoulders. He wanted to make sure his words were not spoken in vain. "Alcuin, we must go back in there and look as though nothing were amiss. Do you understand?"

"Yes, of course, I—"

"We can only hope that Kasim is making an attempt to honor the truce and deliver the crown. We can involve ourselves in the hunt as soon as the service is over. We still have some time until our emperor is interred. Hopefully the crown of thorns is nearby."

Alcuin simply nodded his head in agreement, and the two old

men took a moment to catch their breath before heading back into the cathedral.

Two dozen monks dressed in special yellow robes were matched in groups of three. They slowly marched along the corridors of the Palatine Chapel, swinging their ornate censers, which were fashioned like little churches to deliver incense of the highest quality and value. The cloves, frankincense, and myrrh brought from faraway lands purified the air of the cavernous space with sweet and musty aromas.

The usable space of the cathedral was clearly a product of some mind focused on grandiosity rather than the evolution of years of practical use. Despite its size and area, the cathedral held a surprisingly limited number of parishioners. Services were normally held for standing parishioners, but an exception had been made for Charles's funeral. An assortment of benches and chairs had been brought in from all over the palace and other fine administrative buildings. What should hold a thousand standing souls had been reorganized to seat around four hundred. The remaining space was taken up by impressive marble and bronze statues strategically placed along the sides of the walls, focusing the seating towards the center. The sculpture, along with rich tapestries and wall paintings showing various scenes from the new and old testaments, gave the parishioners a visual guide on the struggles and passions of the men of the scriptures.

Along the high walls within the octagonal area of the Palatine Chapel were semicircular nooks that were carved into the solid limestone blocks so that candlelight radiating from the back of the nooks illuminated various relics collected by Charles over the years. Kings throughout history had passions ranging from prancing stallions to precious jewels the size of fists. Charles was drawn to his religion. It was the use of relics that allowed a faith based on a man's conscience to connect him to his god. For Charles, to touch and gaze upon items sacred to his beliefs was more valuable than all the silver in Spain. On display within the nooks and situated in front of white candles were the bones of recent saints along with pieces of pottery once owned by the apostles themselves. Charles wanted to create a temporal connection between the parishioner and the divine.

To protect the relics from theft and careless hands, Charles had the nooks covered by thinly cut sheets of sanded alabaster that fit into the stone voids with precision. When the candlelight filtered through the pink alabaster, the images of the relics bloomed in a soft fuzz of light that gave the admirers a feeling of being in the presence of something sacred. At the head of the octagon were two empty nooks. One nook was still awaiting its relic while the other nook, which held the holy robe of Christ, had its alabaster removed to access its contents.

The robe had been given to Charles by Pope Leo III during his last visit to Rome. During the presentation of the robe in Rome, a blind cleric under Leo's patronage read the ancient Greek inscription from the reliquary. The cleric said that the words were engraved by Helena, the saintly mother of Constantine. Her words claimed that the robe possessed incredible powers of healing. However, if utilized at the time of death, the robe could elevate its holder directly to the status of an apostle. Charlemagne was said to have cried when the gift was presented to him. He was overwhelmed with gratitude and affection for

Leo, pledging his undying support for his papal rule and vowing
to provide him with support against the threat of the Abbasid
Caliphate, which had decimated Christian borders over the past
few decades.

At one point in the year 808, Charles became deathly sick
from an unknown illness. He was elderly, and the physicians
privately had little hope for his recovery. Theoderic considered
bringing Bishop Otto to administer the last rites. The Twelve
Peers took the power from the churchmen and met in secret
to consider using the robe of Christ to cover Charles and cure
his illness. The final vote of the Peers was to let God decide
Charles's fate. The Peers believed their emperor would gladly
have chosen to adorn the robe upon his death for the chance at
the ultimate prize of being seated with Christ's apostles. Their
belief was confirmed when Charles awoke and gave his explicit
instruction to leave the robe encased behind its alabaster wall
until he had passed.

The robe bore the markings of time. Eight hundred years
of changes between cold darkness and scorching sunlight and
fire and floods had browned the robe beyond its original light
gray. It was frayed along its edges. Several of the cloth buttons
were missing, presumably at the hands of lowly Christians who
wanted to keep a piece of divinity for themselves. Certain cuts in
the fabric were stained black and allowed to remain unrepaired,
as it was the belief that the gaps were the work of the Roman
whips. Its ragged appearance only enhanced its legitimacy as
the simple clothing of God's humble son.

There was a great debate among the priests, bishops, and
learned clerics of Aachen about how to adorn Charles with the

robe. Some said that he should wear the robe at the time of the funeral ceremony. Others believed that it was heresy to wear Christ's own clothes. Every member of the church was a student of ancient Greek, which automatically made each one an expert on the translation of Helena's inscription on the reliquary. The clerics of Rome fought over the interpretation of the reliquary's use of the verb "*calypto*." Some referred to the gospels, where it had been translated to mean "to wear." Others were adamant that the Byzantines of Constantinople would have used the verb of "to cover." It was a simple yet important detail. Charles's eternal soul would depend on the correct meaning. Monks attacked clerics. Clerics hurled insults at priests. Priests claimed to hold the final decision and sided with the translation to read "to cover."

Displayed perpendicular to the seats for the cathedral and situated in the center of the chapel was the body of Charles. After his body had been washed in goat's milk and wrapped in blessed linens, he was placed on a special wooden dais brought in from the dining hall. The elevated bed that he rested upon was propped up at an angle so the parishioners could view the emperor's remains without approaching the octagon or standing up from their seats. The bed was covered and skirted by silk of the darkest purple. Yellow banners carrying the black eagle were brought from the cavalry stables and placed on poles on each side. He was dressed in his fine red wool cape with a deep black fur collar, which ran down to his feet. The cathedral monks used tricks dating back centuries to force his hands into a prostrating prayer position at the center of his chest.

Symbols of his royal importance, such as his famous

jewel-encrusted sword Joyeuse, were displayed along his side. The robe of Christ was layered on top of his red cloak, covering the area beneath his hands and ankles. His formal gold crown, topped with crosses at the four corners, was placed flat above his slightly raised head.

Charles's two favorite hunting dogs, Artemis and Ares, were allowed to attend as well. They were the fourth generation of sibling hounds, and Charles had named them for the ancient Greek gods of the hunt. They took their place on the dais and curled up as close to their master as they could manage. They stayed with him and would not be moved, forever faithful, even in the end. It was Alcuin's idea to let Charles's dogs into the cathedral. They had been kept from his side while he was being prepared for viewing, which sent his companions into a fit of panting and whimpering outside the doors. Of all creatures in the realm, Alcuin thought that perhaps they loved Charles the most. Unconditional love should be rewarded. Their presence would vex the bishop greatly, but Alcuin held sway over all matters involving the funeral and suggested it was something the brooding old bishop would have to live with.

The monks who cared for the cathedral were put in charge of seating the parishioners. The royal family members were gathered in the private dining hall before the ceremony. Their numbers were too great to assemble in any other room of the palace, and there was never a consideration that the family would intermingle with those unrelated parishioners waiting outside in such a solemn occasion. The family was the last to enter the chapel. Members of the royal family lined the right-side rows, taking up almost all the benches and chairs.

The women in Charles's life, the wives and consorts, sat behind his children but ahead of Charles's other blood relatives.
Alcuin and Theoderic considered placing the unpredictable
wives in the back, toward the entrance, for quick escorts to open
air. Regina and Adallind had proven to be erratic and further
drama was to be avoided. In the end, the two women were allowed to remain with their sisters. All told, the children, grandchildren, nieces, nephews, and cousins of the departed emperor
numbered close to two hundred. It was a tedious ordeal for
Einhard, Alcuin, and Theoderic to manage. The decades-long
rift between Alcuin and Einhard had been put aside for the time
being without either man having to offer the other a truce. Both
men realized that attention to the ceremony over the next few
days took precedence over their petty personal animosity; they
owed it to their master and friend.

The ceremony itself was to be strictly performed in accor-
dance with church procedure. The prayer of the holy eucharist
and then the holy communion would be carried out as it had for
centuries, whether for the funeral of a pauper or a king. It was
the logistics of the event that vexed the palace men. In Charles's
plan, there was no full ordering of parishioners, which left the
three administrators in a precarious position, with second cousins and illegitimate grandnephews demanding a seat as close to
the emperor's body as possible. Alcuin knew many by name or
face, having been a tutor to so many of Charles's offspring. The
others were vetted at the instruction of Einhard through sec-
ondhand information, which was usually verified true or fake by
the group of priests in service to the crown. The confusion and
demands came even before Charles had passed. There was petty

jockeying, attempted bribes, and fake documents that had to be navigated and delicately refused. Once the plan was in place, Alcuin and Einhard agreed to temporarily ostracize themselves to the water gardens during the day. At night, they would retreat to Charles's chambers, attending to only to those legitimate complaints and requests and disregarding those from questionable lineage.

The same ordering system for the royal family also applied to the left-side rows reserved for the nobles and dignitaries, both local and foreign. The first row on the left was reserved for the Twelve Peers. The Peers were respected, hence their prominent placement. They did the empire's less glamorous governance, which wasn't meant for tapestries or songs. Some nobles, like Wilfred, were also related to Charles by marriage or other distant blood ties. Both their position as nobles and their distance from the front row made the decision to sit along the left front an easy one.

Had Kasim remained in Aachen, he would have had a seat close to the front, unless, of course, Alcuin and Einhard overruled Theoderic. As with the seating of the members in attendance, extreme care was taken to effectuate Charles's instructions even if the three planners had their own preferences. Dukes and barons littered the rows after the Peers and foreign emissaries. The remainder of the left was reserved for important church ministers and merchants of extreme wealth that paid for the privilege of attendance.

In the palace archives was a parchment that dated from Charles's earlier brush with death in 797. In the document, Charles ordained that the seating should provide for his three sons by Hildegard so that they were seated on the first row and ordered from left to right based specifically upon his choosing. Pepin was the second son of Hildegard, but in the document, Charles placed him first from the left. The parchment then placed the other two of Hildegard's sons based upon the timing of their birth. This meant Charles the Younger was to be seated second, followed by Louis. All other children from Charles's loins, whether boy or girl, born out of marriage or by official consort, were to be arranged by the order of their birth.

Bernard was aware of the parchment. It was Einhard who told him of its existence. Bernard didn't think the old monk cared about his personal interest but instead wanted to drum up drama, if for no other reason than to spite Bernard, who had treated him with disdain for his rivalry with Louis. Bernard's hope was that Alcuin and Theoderic would honor his father and the contents of the parchment and sit him in his father's seat.

That was the plan—or at least the plan if Louis was present for the funeral. Had Louis been present, Charles's simple marble throne from the palace would have been brought into the cathedral and set apart from the rowed seating. It would be reserved to Louis. Louis was co-emperor, after all, even if he wasn't anointed emperor by the pope. Bernard would have found little cause for objection.

As a compromise to the protests Alcuin and Theoderic knew were simmering around them, the men decided to leave the chairs for all three sons of Hildegard empty and instead cloak them with large banners of their family crests, thereby reserving the space and honoring the memory of two sons and the absence of the third. Bernard's father, Pepin, was represented by the

Italian white cross on a red background. The gold fleur-de-lis and diamonds on blue was the symbol of Charles the Younger. Louis's seat bore the black eagle with only a single head.

The grandchildren were seated beginning at the middle of the second row. The ordering of the children proved to be troublesome to arrange. There was the issue of whether to give deference to children based on their age or the order of their mothers. There was no right answer, and threats would come their way regardless. The only sons of Charles seated in the second row were Regina's twin boys, Hugh and Roger, aged seven. Regina wanted them in the front row since they were Charles's only living sons besides Louis. It vexed her to learn of her boys' relegation. The twin boys were seated to the left of Bernard, who took his seating with humility.

Regina had dressed the boys in matching gold tunics and breeches. Their short brown hair was precisely parted and combed. They had the manners of perfect little princes. They took their seats with grace, following the instructions of their mother to the slightest detail. It was Hugh that broke the silence. He found the grand and soldierly Bernard so impressive. Regina's boys were sheltered in the palace. Soldiers and guards kept their distance from the boys, who had little interaction with other men. Bernard didn't recall ever noticing the boys before. He knew they existed because they were a minor threat to his own claim. Hugh wanted to touch Bernard's armor, to see his reflection in Bernard's chest plate and ask him a thousand questions about the men he had killed. Bernard surprised himself with his patience and humor at the disrespect he had been shown by being seated next to his little uncles. He assumed his temperament was the result of the staggering volume of wine he had drunk at the palace barracks that morning. Bernard gave Hugh his hidden dagger as a gift. He thought such a gift would distress Regina and that gave him a touch of sinful joy.

Emma was the daughter of Bertrada, Bernard's only sibling. She sat on Bernard's right. Emma was four and had been crying since a nurse left her at her seat and pinched the little girl's ear to remind the little baroness of her manners. Emma was blonde and had perfect bronze skin. Her red eyes and elegant black dress looked as unnatural to Bernard as the dagger twisting in Hugh's hands. Bernard had never met Emma, as he had not seen his sister in years. When Emma began to whimper, Bernard looked to the ground and laughed to himself. This was a further test of his humility, yet the thick irony that came by being surrounded by children was becoming heavier.

Bernard looked over to the corridor and saw the person he had been waiting for. It was Gregan. Gregan had cleaned himself and combed what little hair remained, which gave the old monk a fresh appearance. Gregan had donned his finest wool robe and wore his leather shoes. He had snuck through the side entrance, avoiding Einhard's watchful eye. He stood nervously among taller, younger monks who were more focused on the spectacle in front of them and disregarded Gregan.

Bernard whispered to the sweet little Emma. "Do you see that monk over there? The short one in the middle?" Emma sniffled and nodded. "Bring him over here. Let him sit next to me and you sit in his lap. He has a pet pig. A huge pig named Argos!" Emma giggled and sniffled at the same time. "If you sit on the old monk's lap, I will see that he lets you ride his pig. I promise.

The monk will do what I ask. You and I are family. Your mother is my older sister."

Emma got up without fear and went over to Gregan. She grabbed Gregan's hand and pointed over to Bernard. Gregan nodded, and the little girl walked Gregan by the hand over to her empty seat. Gregan stopped the girl halfway across the front row and stared at the body of Charles. This was the first he had seen of his old friend in months. Einhard and the powers of the church were as active as bees to keep the radical little man from paying his respects as he had for years. Sadness washed over Gregan and he quickly fell to a knee and made the sign of the cross. He said a silent prayer and slowly made his way back to his feet, feeling the pain his old knees experienced from coming down on the stone floor. Einhard watched the scenario unfold from his seat and stewed in anger at not being able to intercede. He looked over to Theoderic, who gave him a puzzled look.

The older children of Charles were seated next. They filled in the seats of the second row to the left of young Roger before filling the front. Bernard's smile reappeared. As each of his thirteen aunts were seated, Bernard noticed that he was older than all but the last few women. He shook his head and chuckled to himself.

The service was set to begin. The monks had cleared the hallways and the psalms of the choirboys had come to an end. Alcuin and Theoderic remained to the side, holding their prayer books and rosaries. Bishop Otto stood off from Charles's body, looking to Alcuin for permission to start with the prayer of the holy eucharist. There was the general sound of rustling throughout the packed chapel. Then came the clopping of hard-sole shoes.

Bernard paid no mind and kept his eyes trained ahead. The clopping was joined by a spattering of more clopping, but the sounds were less heavy. The noise grew louder, and as Bernard looked out to his left, he saw his aunt Judith walking briskly toward the front. She had her two boys, young Charles and Louis, by the hand, dragging them forward. Walking a few steps behind was Judith's servant, Ogiva. The entire group was dressed in black. The boys wore fine leather jerkins and simple gold-banded circlets on their heads. The looks on the boys' faces gave the impression that they would rather be anywhere else than in the chapel at that moment.

Judith hadn't come through the private palace entrance at the front of the chapel. She came from the back, where all others had entered. At that moment, Bernard couldn't recall seeing Judith waiting with the others in the dining hall. She was usually animated enough to warrant some attention. Judith stopped at the front row and looked around without fear. She grabbed the banners covering all three seats placed as symbols for Charlemagne's absent sons and handed them to Ogiva, who promptly returned down the path she had come. Judith slung young Charles, heir to Louis, by the arm and placed him into the first chair. She then guided young Louis by his upper back and into the third chair while she would take the second. Judith looked around to take a visual inventory of any who expressed objection to her actions. The Palatine Chapel was still. Most bowed their heads in pretend prayer to avoid her gaze. She saw Bernard sitting directly behind the final seat and smiled at him smugly, reveling in his surprise and silence. Judith finally took her seat in the chair meant for the deceased Charles the

Younger, then nodded to the bishop of Aachen to commence with the prayer of the holy eucharist.

Bernard's humility had its limits, and Judith had just soared far beyond the boundary. Rage. The young man had a difficult time controlling it. He usually had the good fortune of being able to release his anger in the sparring pits or on an unfortunate whore. This was not the forum to turn his thoughts and emotions over to his fury. He cradled each of his elbows and bent over in his seat to keep himself silent. Gregan gripped his knee as tightly as he could to focus the young man and not frighten young Emma to hysteria.

Bernard had worked very hard to achieve greatness, and although he was still a youth in the eyes of the Twelve Peers and the other high nobles, there was much to risk by flying into anger and staking his claim at his grandfather's funeral. He had experienced insults and frustration at every turn along the path to assume his father's great legacy. He spent four long years of battle in service to his grandfather, eager to prove his legitimacy as the heir to Pepin and perhaps his grandfather's throne.

There were two forces at work over Bernard's soul. His mother would whisper encouragement in his ear. She groomed the fatherless boy to rule nations, not men. The other force was the powerful nobles of Italy, who were quick to offer their advice but unwilling to concede power to the territories closer to the seat of power in Aachen. They saw Bernard as potential protection against the territorial bickering that hid below the surface during Charles's reign and was sure to erupt with his passing. Bernard had much to lose, so he kept to his seat and brooded.

The prayer of the holy eucharist was unremarkable. Bishop

Otto stuck to protocol and sounded as if he had read from a prayer book, though the reality was that the elderly man had performed the prayer thousands of times in the past and wanted to move along. The bishop doused the body of Charles with holy water brought from the River Jordan and then painfully knelt to kiss the holy robe while whispering a prayer as he looked at the gilded octagonal dome above. The interlude between the eucharist and the holy communion was filled by a series of hymns from the choir of monks. Other relics from the chapel displays and Hildegard's old quarters were walked along the sides of the rows, held above the heads of the seated parishioners for their viewing.

The steel latch of the chapel doors clanked softly and most heads that were looking ahead or were bowed turned to face the sound. An armored man began to make his way through the doors. Although it had been several years, Bernard knew the man from court. It was Germanicus the Saxon. The hymns came to a conclusion as the eyes of the parishioners stayed locked on Germanicus. The space was silent but for the duke's heavy heels and random coughs. The man did not kneel or cross himself when he entered the chapel. Instead, he walked forward with his head high and helm in hand. This was a Christian ceremony where weapons were forbidden, but the monks and palace guards had no standing and even less courage to enforce the rules against the duke of Saxony. Most parishioners were shocked, but Bernard just looked on Germanicus with mild curiosity.

Germanicus wondered how many took notice of the forked-tongued serpent head on his breastplate. Outside of Saint

Peter's in Rome, the Palatine Chapel of Aachen was perhaps the worst place in Christendom one could be so brazen. Germanicus walked until he came to the front row. He looked over at Judith and the fury in her eyes and gave a subtle scoff as if he were less than impressed with who she was or where she sat among the family ranks. Germanicus's parents had wed several years before Charles married Hildegard, Louis's mother. That would make Germanicus the first born considering that the laws of Frankia didn't reject highborn bastards. For a brief moment, he considered sitting on the right side of the chapel as a way to announce his claim as an illegitimate son of Charles. If he did so, the natural seat would be the first chair of the first row, right where young Charles sat scowling and confused. The thought of tossing the little prince by his neck and whispering "hello sister" to Judith was almost worth the potential bloodshed that would certainly follow.

Discretion got the better of Germanicus. If his intuition was right and dissidence was likely on the horizon, there would be time to stake his claim. That was, after all, his plan. Sit, watch, and wait. Causing havoc to prove a point that might not even need addressing seemed unwise. He was too hardened by years of politics and subterfuge to jump at uncertain opportunities. Instead, Germanicus moved to the left and stood directly above Einhard, who was seated in the first seat of the front left row. While Germanicus was still several rows back, Einhard had turned his gaze as if he wanted to deny the Saxon's presence. It was now unavoidable. The man was literally standing on top of him. Germanicus's crotch was almost touching his shoulder. Einhard sat frozen, yet his anxiety was obvious to everyone as he exhaled in deep breaths.

Germanicus placed his right hand on the hilt of his sword and uttered to Einhard in a low voice, "Up. Get up."

No one, not even the Peers in attendance along the front row, did anything to intervene.

The two men were very familiar with each other. Germanicus had served as a Peer for over five years, yet their history went back decades. His selection as one of the Twelve Peers was one of a multitude of peace offerings Charles had made to the Saxon nobleman. Charles would prefer to win certain allies through assimilation if possible. The theory was that if Germanicus built a feeling of comradery with other princes of Frankia's realm, he was less likely to entertain homespun offers of treason. To Charles, some minds were easier to conquer than harts.

Germanicus saw past the pageantry of the position and witnessed the reality of fake authority. In Germanicus's mind, his brother Peers were sycophants who were sent to the provinces of the empire where they would siphon money and men to finance questionable causes for the glory of the crown. They were expected to project images of power and authority. Germanicus found the position mired in double talk and bureaucracy. During his time as a Peer, Germanicus witnessed firsthand the politics of rule and the suppression of the Peers. They were constantly harassed by Theoderic and Einhard, who sought to undermine their work of managing the military and economic functions of the empire.

Germanicus's official title was the Peer of the Seas, which meant that he oversaw all nonmilitary aspects of the Frankish navy. This included acts such as the appointment of admirals, the building of fleets, and the negotiation of sea trade with foreign powers. Einhard was no Peer, but as the holder of the keys to the empire's payments to Rome, he did have significant influence over matters of finance. When Germanicus wanted silver to acquire lumber for constructing vessels to replenish fleets lost to pirate attacks or gold to bribe Northmen controlling trade routes, he would face Einhard's smug and toothless smile. The condescending bureaucrat was quick to admonish the unskilled foreigner and chastise him about the complicated and intricate matters of international finance that precluded the crown from accommodating his requests at the time.

Einhard would instead tell the Saxon to visit the existing ports for route inspections and to exercise his privileges as Peer of the Seas to fleece gold from the port tax collectors. Germanicus was frustrated with the role of Peer. While not as sophisticated as those Peers closer to Frankia's bosom, he knew hypocrisy when he saw it. It made his angst grow greater with time and opened his ears to his mother's murmurs. He didn't want or ask to be a Peer. He accepted the appointment, however, as it gave him a reason to frequent Aachen and keep his ear to the walls for murmurs of how the emperor intended to handle the occasional Saxon uprising. The fact that the cleric Einhard would sit in the same row as Germanicus the Peer made the Saxon want to run his dagger through the old man's temple.

Einhard sat silent, trying to look as unmoved as possible, as if he hadn't heard Germanicus's demand. He was having a difficult time acting the part. "Up, you motherless whore."

Theoderic didn't hear the words; he was too far away. It was evident, however, that there was some animosity at hand. Theoderic motioned for the choir to sing another hymn rather than have the chapel remain open to silence. Einhard had heard enough. He knew Germanicus to be a serious man. He quickly considered the possibility of Germanicus striking him during such a hallowed occasion and wasn't entirely convinced the barbarian would hold back his hand. They had violent encounters in the past. A few years ago, Germanicus choked Einhard to the brink of unconsciousness for interrupting a private meeting of Saxon nobles in the palace gardens.

Einhard grabbed his walking cane and rosary beads and made for the area along the front right, where Alcuin and Theoderic stood. The three were often lumped together in the eyes of most members of court, so the movement seemed natural in a room with no other viable seats. Germanicus took the empty seat and nodded to Richard, the duke of Burgundy, his fellow Peer, who was sitting to his left. Richard seemed unfazed by Germanicus's antics and instead kept his concentration straight ahead. The duke of Burgundy had no love for Einhard, either.

With Germanicus seated, Alcuin gave Bishop Otto the nod for which he was waiting. The hymns came to a smooth end, and the bishop moved on to the communion. The communion of over four hundred parishioners made the service brutally long for the children and those who spent the morning celebrating the life of Charles through drink. The Palatine Chapel cleared out slowly nonetheless, as many of the minor family members and emissaries from foreign lands took advantage of the opportunity to interact with the more powerful members of court.

Many of the immediate family members and all the attending Peers remained off to the right side of the chapel, talking quietly among themselves, seeing the onlookers for what they were. Alcuin and Theoderic stood farther off to the side. Monks had silently brought in large satchels of packed snow gathered from the back-side of the cathedral. Alcuin ordered that it be brought in and used to blanket Charles when the chapel was cleared of onlookers. The chapel was relatively cold, and Charles was not much more than skin and bones by the time he passed, but the emperor had died two full days ago. Alcuin thought it was senseless to not take advantage of a winter death at the risk of sending away parishioners with stories of how odious the cathedral smelled.

Alcuin talked to Theoderic as if he was attempting to win an argument. "There is quite a bit of precedent. As you well know, the Apostle Mark wrote, 'He rose early on the first day of the week.' The first day of the week is tomorrow, Sunday. Charles wanted to honor the transformation of Christ to the divine. Therefore, it would seem appropriate to hold off his interment until tomorrow morning, despite custom. We only have to move him to the corner of the chapel. Besides, it's a private ceremony, which means little planning on our part. Oh! In addition, it has long been a custom among Bavarian kings to delay interment of the departed to dawn on the morning after the funeral rites have been performed. It is the request of Judith, and I do not wish to cross her."

Einhard scoffed. "She wishes to hold a watch. An old pagan ritual, you mean. I cannot believe such an absurd ceremony is going to be permitted. Heretical, if you ask me. I think the watch ceremony is just a harken to some forgotten barbarian rite where the people drink themselves to a state of stupor and debase themselves in front of the dead for God only knows what reason."

Theoderic chimed in with agreement. "It would not matter either way. Judith has sanctioned it so that other nobles from her Bavarian lands could see her two boys reveling in traditions more befitting their forest people. Part of me wishes I was present to look at the faces of the little princes as they hear the ether move out of a corpse's body."

Alcuin shook his head and said, "I will consider myself fortunate to be lowborn and left out of such a celebration." He found it ironic how the nobles loved to play the role of champion and revel in their own self-importance when it came to degrading their rivals and taking captives. When it came to more delicate matters of state, however, such as deciding when the emperor became too pungent to keep from the earth, they were all busy talking among themselves, leaving the hard decisions to lesser men.

XIV

- NUMQUAM ITERUM -

Germanicus mumbled a curse to himself as he carried a large square wooden plate that held several cut and arranged racks of lamb. It was fresh from the kitchen spits. The racks bled brown and pink juice that pooled on the bottom of the plate and rolled onto his fingers when his balance was unsteady. It was still hot enough to burn skin; he didn't flinch despite the pain. Germanicus followed behind Vaclen, the duke of Thuringia, who carried a tray full of silver goblets resting upside down. The servants and slaves that worked within the palace corridor did nothing to help the lords, nor did the lords demand assistance. The servants quickly moved from their path and stood with their heads declined until the lords passed. The two men walked upstairs with haste from the kitchen below and Germanicus creaked with each step. Armor wasn't meant for climbing stairs, but then again, neither was it meant as the uniform for a servant.

Germanicus was jealous of Vaclen. The Thuringian warriors wore long and thick leather coats in place of steel plate.

The wealthier lords like Vaclen wore layers of silk underneath leather to protect their bodies from sharp edges. The delicate fabric caught the blade and kept cuts at bay. It was a trick learned from the horsemen of the steppes far to the east. Despite Vaclen's insistence, Germanicus still believed it wasn't wise for fending off swords, but that was of no concern within the safety of the palace.

One elderly servant was a quarter of the way down the stairs when he noticed who was coming up. He turned so quickly to make his way back to the top that he almost lost his balance and fell to the stone floor below. Three of the palace dogs followed the trail of mutton juice that dripped to the ground. They skillfully skirted in and around Germanicus's legs, hoping to trip up a fine meal. Germanicus thought he would wait until he got to the top of the stairs and look to make sure no one was looking before he kicked the leader of the three.

Vaclen protested. "I do not understand why we cannot let the servants bring everything to the door. We can carry it in from there."

"Tradition? Church ritual? I do not know the answer," Germanicus said. "You are the church man, Vaclen. You tell me. Your people have churches much older than ours. Surely such a ritual is from the scriptures."

"Are you saying you are pagan, Germanicus?" Vaclen asked.

Germanicus responded, "I would never openly admit that I was pagan. I am just not one for church ceremony, if that's what this is. Surely we debase ourselves as servants for some secret purpose."

"If Bernard is admitted as a Peer, he will be doing this servant nonsense, which means one of us no longer has to demean ourselves. You and I came into the Twelve at the same time, so the choice would be a coin flip, I suppose."

Germanicus grunted, "You suppose wrong. I will bribe my way out of this."

"That is not very Christian of you, Germanicus," Vaclen joked.

"Arminius," Germanicus said.

"Eh?"

"Do not call me Germanicus any further. My true name is Arminius. I will answer to no other."

The comment made Vaclen chuckle and shake his head. "As you say . . . Arminius. And why the armor? Who are we in fear of within the palace doors? We cannot carry blades, so what is the threat? Absurd."

Germanicus was losing his patience with Vaclen, who suffered less under the weight of his eastern garb. "Keep silent, Vaclen. You sound like a stable boy looking to shun his chores."

Vaclen neared the open door at the end of the south-wing hallway. Ogier the Dane came from inside the corner at the same time and almost collided with Vaclen. The giant blotted the light from within. "Goddammit!" Vaclen shouted. He moved quickly to steady himself and not lose the stacked goblets. He looked up at the mass in front of him and recognized Ogier immediately. He wanted to tell the Dane he looked like some great bear standing on its back legs, but the angered expression on Ogier's face made him immediately reconsider. "My apologies, Brother Ogier." Vaclen bowed his head with reservation and courtesy, giving the doorway to Ogier to complete his own task. Lords were not conditioned to apologize, nor were they familiar with being cursed. It was different, however, among Peers. Vaclen made his way to a long, thin wooden table near the door and set down the tray of goblets.

Vaclen stroked his black beard, which came down to a point, and curled the corners of his mustaches, which grew longer than his cheek hair. He looked down and noticed for the first time that he was carrying thirteen goblets on the tray. It was that way when the servant in the kitchen handed him the tray, so he assumed it was a simple mistake. Twelve was the normal count. Twelve goblets for the Twelve Peers. It was rare that all twelve met together for unexpected meetings such as the gathering that day. Vaclen had not seen it happen in his five years as a Peer. Nevertheless, twelve chairs were set up around the room where he would place twelve goblets.

Vaclen said nothing of the thirteen goblets and went about placing a goblet on the stools positioned next to each chair. The chairs of the room were identical in every way but for the decorated upholstery on the fronts and backs. He placed the twelfth goblet at his own chair, which was adorned with a black-winged dragon set in orange. Not knowing what to do, he put the remaining goblet on the thin table along the side wall and moved back to his own chair. Germanicus had set the racks of lamb along the opposite side of the table, where three large jugs of wine had been placed and were uncorked to breathe.

Germanicus sucked the juice from his right-hand fingers and kicked one of the dogs that placed his nose on the edge of the table. The kick worked. The dog wailed from the strike to its ribs and fled out the doorway with the other two following behind.

Vaclen said, "That would get you the noose if you were a

servant. They say Charles loved his dogs more than his own children."

Germanicus responded, "I care not. His days of passing judgment are no longer a concern." Germanicus paid Vaclen no mind and made his way to his chair. Germanicus was short with Vaclen, but that was because the two were familiar with each other. They had become kindred spirits as two princes of remote territories who were both new to the peerage. They received little guidance or kindness from the others. Perhaps they gravitated toward each other because of the fact that, like in Saxony, Christianity was also more of a mystery than a true practice in Vaclen's land. The Thuringians never took up arms like the Saxons, yet Vaclen was scorned and belittled by the Peers just the same. Vaclen thought of the irony of the peerage, a supposed band of equals bound in service to the betterment of the empire. The reality was much different than in the songs.

Wilfred, the duke of Aquitaine, entered the room, then Richard shortly thereafter. Wilfred was by far the wealthiest lord of the empire who was not a Carolingian, and he had no shame in reminding anyone who did not know or had forgotten along the way. His gold cloak centered with a furious red lion was no accident. Unlike the rulers of all other territories of the empire, Wilfred minted many of his coins in gold rather than silver. It made for chaos and despair among farmers and the common man, but that was a minor inconvenience for Wilfred's self-image. Perhaps Wilfred had reminded the court of his wealth one too many times.

For all his wealth, Charles chose Wilfred to mind the Peer's chamber pots. Wilfred knew better than to protest. He crossed along the rushes of the room with a large copper pail in each hand. Wilfred hurried to his station, then got the usual comment, in this instance from Germanicus. "I hope you packed those pails with extra cloves, Wilfred. I suspect there will be an excessive amount of shit spewed today." It was a cheap and expected comment, one that was uttered at least once every few meetings.

The truth was that few Peers used the buckets for much other than lightening their bladders of wine, although there was a story that Baron Gautier, an original Peer, would squat over one of the buckets next to a Peer whose babbling or senseless debates irritated him. Wilfred remained silent in response to Germanicus and took his seat, looking forward at nothing in particular. He had deep disdain for Germanicus and, for a quick moment, wanted to show the Saxon how insults were carried out. Wilfred considered Germanicus unworthy of the role of Peer, which had been given to him as an appeasement and nothing else. He practiced restraint, however, and Germanicus would never know what was on the Aquitanian's mind.

Richard left, then reentered the room carrying another jug of wine, which he sat alongside the others. His long black and gray hair marked him as a man well past his days in the field of battle. Richard wore no armor due to a thigh wound that resulted in a noticeable limp and made it difficult for him to comfortably carry the weight of chain and plate. It was a rare concession from Charles. Instead, Richard wore a deep blue jerkin that bore the yellow stag of his ancient family. Richard didn't make for his seat like the others. Instead, he walked to the decorated back wall that held partitioned stations. His feet were deep in fur rushes that muffled the noise of his right leg, which normally scraped across the floor with each step. Richard paid no attention to the first eleven stations along the back wall. He knew all the stories of the original Twelve Peers and had looked upon them all countless times over the years. For Richard, it was the last station that was important to him.

Germanicus believed that Charles intended the back wall to be the focus of the Peer meeting room. It had Germanicus's attention every time he entered the space. The wall was cordoned off into twelve sections by oak pillars carved into eleven lances that ran from stone floor to tile ceiling. The lances were painted in yellow and black spiral stripes, the standard of the emperor's cavalry. Each section along the wall held a wide white candle placed upon a pedestal at the top center of each station. The candles illuminated displays carefully organized below. The helms, armor, swords, and shields were hung for each of the original Peers. They were arranged in a way to suggest they adorned live bodies, now frozen in battle position for all time.

There was a simple wooden plaque centered above the stations. Large words had been branded into the wood. The two Latin words required no formal education. *Numquam Iterum.* Never Again.

The displays of each station were not cleaned or polished, nor were tears or holes mended. They were kept in the original state, when last worn by the famous original Twelve Peers. Chain links remained mangled. Thick plates displayed their punctures. Crusted blood flaked onto the floor below. It was said that Charles intended the display to be both an effigy of honor and reminder of unchecked hubris, something Alcuin secretly believed the emperor himself struggled with.

The first station was an effigy to Turpin, the archbishop of Reims. Turpin was one of Charles's closest advisers. Turpin was considered an expert on the battles of the Old Testament and Charles often asked the archbishop to interpret how the Jewish leaders would react to his own tactics. Turpin knew the passages and minds of the old Jewish warriors, like Joshua and Gideon. Charles would call on Turpin the night before battles to pray with him and give sermons to the captains on the importance of righteous vengeance and executing God's divine plan.

The third station between Berenger and Gerin belonged to Gerard of Roussillon. Gerard lost all his battalion fighting the Saracens several years before Roncevaux at the Battle of Pamplona. As the only survivor, he was plagued with guilt and a sense of shame from watching his men parish while he lived. Oliver found the disgraced captain in the midst of hanging himself from the base of a bridge outside of Montpellier. What Oliver felt was not pity, but intrigue. Gerard was a captain of little prominence, yet he carried himself with pride and cared for his men who he treated like sons. Oliver asked Charles to give the captain a chance at redemption at the highest level.

The sixth and seventh stations belonged to Yvoire and Yvon, the twin brothers from Rouen. The twins deserted their family farm to heed the call of Christ and join the famous Tenth Division. The young men were massive and wielded war axes in battle. It was a familiar weapon as the twins built their impressive size by felling forests back home. In battle, the mounds of bodies piled up around the brothers who fought back to back in open combat. Word of their ferocity would find the ear of Oliver, who urged the emperor to add the brothers to the Peers.

The eighth station held the heavy plate armor of Engeler. Engeler was a Gascon paladin from Bayonne. He saw his village burned and raided three times as a young man and followed his uncle, Theutgaud, into the ranks of the Tenth. When his uncle died at the Battle of Toulouse, Engeler took on his uncle's armor and horse as his own. The young warrior became a slave to his anger and would often have to be dragged from atop lifeless enemies he hacked to pieces. Like Yvoire and Yvon, he proved his savagery in battle and was singled out by the Tenth Division's captains to perhaps join the Peers. Charles accepted the man, but only with a solemn pledge that he channel his anger for the purpose of good outside the battlefield.

Roland's station needed no explanation. Unlike the other Peers, his display had no helm or sword. Roland wore no helm into battle as he wanted all enemies to see the face of the man that brought their lives to an end. His famed sword, Durandal, was not delivered by Emir Hisham. It was famous and considered magical. More likely than not, it was taken by an unknown Saracen foot soldier as a spoil of war. His shield was there, however. He was the only warrior allowed to emboss the metal cover of his shield with Charles's black eagle. Roland's plate armor was also displayed. It evidenced the brutal result of the gaping axe wound of Aelroth, the Saracen giant that was rumored to have struck the final blow that took the great paladin's life. The gash was wide and mortal and eerily resembled the shape of a cross.

The station abutting the wall on the far end was reserved for Richard's father, Ganelon, who once held the honor as one of

Charles's most trusted Peers. There was no armor or weapon to venerate Ganelon's station, and the void ate at Richard every time he was in the room. Ganelon's station remained empty since its construction more than thirty years earlier. The candle in his station was left unlit, never to illuminate the memory of the departed. Ganelon had died at Roncevaux Pass like the other eleven Peers, but not in the field of battle. Ganelon had taken his own life in the cliffs that overlooked the slaughter below.

Ganelon was no friend to Roland, as the two frequently fought over Charles's favor. Ganelon was not the warrior that Roland was. In truth, the only warrior in all of Frankia who could come close to Roland's skill in battle was Oliver whose station rested between the two rivals. Ganelon was known instead as the tactician among the Peers. He was a man who fought with his mind rather than his hands.

He was the Peer who suggested to Charles that the famed Tenth Division take Roncevaux Pass to return home to Frankia rather than make for the longer route to the east passage where the mountains gave way to passable hills. Roland objected to the suggestion and implored Charles to avoid concentrating his men in a ravine. He argued that it would expose Frankia's men to the greater number of Saracen units that could come down from the surrounding cliffs. Charles gave in to Ganelon's overtures as Ganelon falsely proclaimed that his scouts had marked the vanguard of the Saracen army at more than a day's distance. The threat, Ganelon told his king, was far in the distance. Roland told Ganelon in private that once his claim was proven false and Franks died as a result, he would make his rival's dishonesty known to Charles. Ganelon seethed and hatched a plot to bring an end to his rival.

Ganelon bribed a local goat herder to don the clothing of a Saracen herald and approach mighty Roland's tent with an offer that would entice his prideful spirit. The false proposition was from the Saracen leader, Marsile. If Roland was victorious in single combat against the Muslim champion, Grandoyne, then Marsile would withdraw from pursuing the Franks any further and permit the Christian army to return home unmolested. Deep in his own hubris, Roland could not reject such a challenge. He broke from the Frankish ranks to meet Grandoyne farther south, far away from the confinement of the walled pass. Ganelon's expectation was that the oncoming Saracen forces would capture Roland and negotiate his disgraceful return to Frankia. That was what Ganelon sought the most: the embarrassment and disgrace of his greatest rival.

That was not what happened, however. In response to the rumors, the other ten Peers followed Roland back down into the mouth of the valley in support of their brother in combat. The Peers were a family, bound by oath to one another. In the end, all eleven were unceremoniously slaughtered. Aelroth's soldiers swarmed down into the pass, cutting off the Peers from the retreating Franks. With dreadful sorrow, Ganelon watched from an overlooking cliff at what his petty scheming had wrought. The Peers swam in a sea of Saracen steel. The goat herder would recount the story before Charles's feet with tears of agony and repentance. The truth was kept out of the songs that commemorated Roncevaux Pass.

The sound of heavy heels and scraping chain mail drifted its

way into the Peer's room. That didn't catch Germanicus's attention. What drew his immediate curiosity were the voices. Several
men heading into the room were talking loudly in a tongue he
did not know. Germanicus had encountered most all the lands
of the Frankish empire, yet the language brought to his ears was
a mystery. Germanicus and Vaclen looked at each other quiz-
zically, both were intrigued. They then turned their heads to
face the doorway as the men entered. Two men walked confidently into the room and made straight for the long table and
the wine. These were new men. Men Germanicus hadn't seen
before, which could only mean they were the only two Peers he
had never met.

Germanicus and Vaclen had both been Peers for almost five
years. In that period, the Peers had convened seven times, and
of those, there were always at least four empty seats. There were
two Peers who never made a meeting. These were the men of
the marches.

Absence from Peer meetings did not explain their unusual language, however. When he looked upon the men,
Germanicus could only think of them as some fanciful Greek
creatures—half-man, half-beast—except, in this instance, they
weren't half-men and half-beast but rather half-paladin and
half-Saracen. They wore the chain mail and breastplates of
a Frankish officer, but their lower bodies and heads bore the
flowing skirt-covered breeches and wrapped headscarves of
Saracens. Their faces remained covered by their scarves as they
talked. The taller one wore a dark-blue scarf and the shorter one
a yellow scarf. They both wore red skirts with black breeches
underneath, although the shorter man's red cloth seemed

more worn by sun and time. Both men carried dark complexions around their wrinkled eyes. The sun was hard on the men. The men of the marches continued with their conversation as if no one else mattered, shunning courtesy and the custom of the Peers. Germanicus was not the finest symbol of civility, but the way these men owned the room was surprising, and that made Germanicus feel inferior and automatically standoffish.

The men switched to Frankish as they walked over to the table with the wine jugs. By their choice of words, Germanicus assumed they spoke in Frankish not because they cared to be congenial, but rather to let their disdain be picked up by the others in the room. "No goblets," the man in the blue scarf said.

The man in the yellow scarf responded, "They placed them at our seats."

"That makes sense, given this new group," the blue scarf said. "The correct answer stares them in the face, yet they are none too clever to see what is obvious to others." The man with the blue scarf filled his goblet then passed by Germanicus, who refused to cast his stare somewhere else. The blue scarf stopped right beside Germanicus and asked, "Who the fuck are you?"

Germanicus stood slowly as to not give off aggression. He refused to give ground to a man who was roughly the same height and build. "I am a duke of the Frankish Empire and one of the Twelve Peers. If you are also a Peer, as you seem to hold yourself to be, then you will address me proper."

"Very well. Who the fuck are you, my lord duke of Frankia?"

Germanicus found that slightly more comical than insulting and smiled.

"Wait," the blue scarf said. "Your chair is the one with the pig

on it. You must be the Saxon. Used to have a tree as your symbol, but that's gone. The famous oak was made coal for heating
kettles. Your armor bears the emblem of a serpent, the forked
tongue of the devil proudly displayed. Very confusing to make
sense of. I cannot match the flagrant foreign images with your
accent. You must have been educated in Paris."

It was Aachen, but Germanicus nodded just the same and
took a sip from his own full goblet. He hoped the Peer would
pick up on the veiled insult of drinking while others remained
thirsty. "Three things, my brother. First, that is a boar, not a pig.
There is a stark difference in the two, should you find yourself
staring in the eye of a Saxon boar rather than a pig on a farm."
He glared back at the chair with frustration. "I admit, the embroidery is poor. Aachen nuns must be on their backs more than
at their looms."

Blue scarf grunted as yellow scarf retrieved his own goblet
and went to the long table to pour his wine.

"Second, I was a hostage of Charles for eleven years, not a
guest. My immersion into Frankish customs was not a choice for
me." Germanicus paused, waiting for a snide remark.

"And the third?" asked the blue scarf.

"Third? Yes. If either of you had half the sense of a soft-skulled
catamite, you would know who I was without plodding through
the insults—unless, of course, that was your purpose all along."

Yellow scarf finally chimed in. "We have a smart one, Seguin."

Seguin chuckled. "Didn't know they sired those in Saxony."

"You would think not by the way they fight and govern, yet
he did say he was raised in Aachen. Well, a Saxon has made it to
the Twelve Peers."

Germanicus was mildly enjoying himself. Successfully with-standing insults from older Peers was a bit of a rite of passage. For Germanicus, being ignored was the greater slight. "You must do your duty as a Peer with a little more conviction and attend councils when called. I've been a Peer for five years now."

Seguin, the blue scarf, pulled down the wrap from over his upper lip and let it settle below his chin. He was clean-shaven, yet his hair and skin were as dark as that of a Saracen. Seguin took a deep pull from his goblet. "While you have been up north," Seguin said, "plotting rebellion against the emperor with farm-ers and drovers that carry hoes and sickles to battle, I have been slaying as many Muslims as God will permit my cramped hands to kill."

"Saracens?" Germanicus chuckled. "I do not believe you. Yes, perhaps several years ago, but now? Peace has reigned for three years. You would be spitting on the terms of the truce if you did. Clearly the work of the Peers and the oath of your emperor does not interest you."

"I do the work of the Peers every day, Germanicus," Seguin said. "That is who you are, are you not?" Considering the seri-ousness of the eyes that looked upon him, Germanicus thought it was the wrong moment to correct the man regarding his true name. Seguin continued, "Do you think the common man cares for truces on paper? That he is willing to give up his home and farm so easily, Christian or not? That he will not come on a moonless night to open throats of green soldiers sleeping on his land and steal back what was once his?"

Germanicus was uncertain about how to answer. He was suddenly not winning the battle of wits and decided to try his

luck with the yellow scarf. "And you? Do you have the same lei-
surely day to shave yourself as clean as your friend? Can you not
show us your handsome face as well? You two hide yourselves,
dressed like Saracens."

Yellow scarf placed his goblet on the table, keeping his back
to Germanicus. Unlike Seguin, yellow scarf did not simply pull
the veil from over his nose. Instead, he unwrapped the scarf
slowly as he turned to face the room. The unwinding revealed a
separate black scarf underneath. The black scarf was more like
a thin bandage, however, that fit tight over the place where his
right ear would normally show. It then came down across most
of his mouth before disappearing under his left chin. The black
scarf conformed to the man's face, or at least what remained
of it. Germanicus could tell from the contours of the skin-tight
scarf that he had no right ear and part of his cheek and jaw had
been crushed or cut off. The uncovered portion of his left side
wasn't totally free from its own trauma. Down his cheek and
neck ran raised red scars that made it look like he had been
mauled by some great beast.

The yellow scarf closed in and said, "I am afraid our Saracen
friends did the last true shaving I will ever have."

Germanicus wouldn't look the yellow-scarfed man in the face,
focusing instead on the strange man's plated chest. Germanicus
had seen more than his share of wounds before—lost limbs and
scars that carved flesh like rivers through mountains—but there
was something different with this man. His voice, now clear to
Germanicus, matched the queer shape of his face. A serious man.
"I am Brice, and you would be wise to look at me. Look at me!"

Germanicus lifted his chin and obliged.

Brice continued. "I would ask if you know my story, but you most likely do not. I come from nothing, at least nothing that would matter to a Saxon. The men of my family were priests. Priests that were not penitent. Priests that fought for our Lord God until the white bones of their knuckles showed. My family fled Frankia when my grandfather was a boy. Our city was Emporiae. My people fished the sea. Simple lives dedicated to God. The Saracens came from the south like a sea storm. Their terms were simple: convert or die. Not much of a choice."

Brice smiled with a painful grin that was jerked up high along his left cheek. The scars had frozen his face in torqued pain.

"My grandfather fled to Corsica rather than submit. He died on that god forsaken island, waiting with the few left from along the Pyrenees who refused the Muslims." Brice pointed to Seguin. "His people, too. Martel finally came to retake the marches. We won back our towns and villages. Bloody business. Then they came back. Back and forth." Brice moved past Germanicus and refilled his cup. He then sat down, taking his yellow scarf and wrapping his face once again. The pattern on the back of his seat was a simple red cross on a white background.

"We have been killing each other for decades," Brice continued. "The march is now in the hands of Frankia, but the fights still come." He flung his right hand up with a dismissal. "Seguin will tell you. He is the duke of Vasconia. Revel in his greatness! You are a wealthy noble, Vasconia, are you not?"

Seguin shook his head. "If blood and crushed bone could pay for wine and women, I would be Nero reborn."

Brice added, "Aye. In truth, we do not care for truces. The peace for which you speak is for armies, not marauders bent on murder and vengeance. The Saracens will fight until the second coming. Huddled around their campfires and out of range from Christians, they care for peace as much as we do. This is an old hate renewed with each moon."

Seguin took his seat next to Brice, and the two remained silent for a moment. Seguin took over. "We have come to say our farewells to Charles and aid Louis however we can. Louis is who we come to support, not Bernard or these two fine dukes, Richard and Wilfred. It was Louis who came with the forces of Frankia to help scrape the marches free of Saracens. Louis and Oliver cut them down like summer wheat when we were helpless and eating our dogs to keep from perishing. The emir was shocked at Oliver's violence and had to seek terms and prostrate for peace. That was a sight, was it not, Lord Brice?"

Brice answered, "It was. But the peace was set in ink and soldiers cannot read. The Saracens fought on, crossing over hills to kill our men in their sleep. We defend. It has been that way as long as I can recall."

Brice barked to the rest of the room. "We will not abandon Louis as our emperor. Not now! Not ever! We hear the whispers for Bernard. Perhaps he is an even greater warrior than his father. Aye, Pepin was a fine soldier, but he lay dead in some inglorious field north of Venice. Seguin and I made a pledge to Louis and mean to keep it. The marches do not have the gold of Aquitaine or the fine palaces of Burgundy, but it is our men that keep the monsters from the streets of Paris. We are but a few, but we are fierce. Do not cross us, Saxon."

Ogier reentered the room with an elderly monk at his back. Ogier took inventory of the men in the room and nodded to the monk who remained outside the doorway. The meeting of the Peers would begin. The monk closed the door and brought down a thick wooden latch that would lock the room from the outside until the business of the Peers was complete. Ogier walked toward his seat until the noise of the latch caused him to pause and turn around.

The door reopened, and all eyes turned to Einhard standing in the doorway with a wooden box that he held before his belly. Richard announced what was on the mind of every Peer. "Perhaps you are lost, Einhard. The chapel is on the other end of the palace."

Einhard responded, "Yes, thank you, Lord Richard. I have been asked to briefly interrupt this meeting of the Peers on behalf of Louis. It is not unprecedented. Archbishop Turpin attended at the behest of our Lord Charlemagne until he was himself made a Peer."

Wilfred laughed aloud. "You hope to make yourself a Peer, now. Turpin, no less. You do aim high, though your belly rubs so close to the ground. These are troubled times indeed."

"No, Lord Wilfred," Einhard said. "I have no ambition of my own. I only wish to serve our emperor as best as I can."

Wilfred responded, "Then say your peace and leave us. We mean to end this meeting quickly, as the water that floats the empire is now too muddy to see clearly."

Einhard held his breath and lowered his gaze to the floor as he skirted the walls, avoiding the square of chairs in the center of the room. He reached the station at the end of the row that bore no armor or weapons. Einhard gently placed the wooden box on the floor. Einhard looked to Richard and then to the floor. Richard left his chair and cautiously made his way to the last station. Einhard had left the wooden box open, and Richard strained with each forward step to gaze upon the contents. He paused for a moment as he stared into the box and then went to his knees. The room gave Richard silence, and he responded with heavy breaths.

"It is him," Einhard said. "It is Ganelon. Your father. I am sorry his return home has been done in this way, Lord Richard. Emir al-Hakam sent Ganelon's remains with his recent emissary. Our Lord Charles had a standing instruction to return his remains to Aachen. His bones are not to be buried or given rites. He is to stay there in the box since his Peers do not themselves enjoy the comfort of a Christian grave. The emissary tells me he was discovered by the—"

Wilfred interrupted the intrusion to calm his old friend's pain. "Silence!"

Richard sat on the floor and lifted a skull from the box. The room remained painfully silent. The men did their best to look at the walls or the floor out of respect for the moment. It was the first time the old duke had ever looked upon his father. Richard rubbed his fingers over the thick brow and placed his thumbs in the hollow sockets that once held burning blue eyes. Tears fell and blotted the brown skull.

"Hello, Ganelon." Richard trembled and swallowed. His own head felt stuffed with water and pain. "I have carried your shame since I was a boy. It appears I will now be looking on you as I carry the burden further. They say you told Roland to mind the Roncevaux Pass in the promise of some fleeting honor. It was a lie. Your jealousy of Roland made you blind. In the end, it did not matter. You died just the same. Not just you, though—all the others. They will not be with you in this room. You made a pact with the devil. What should you have expected?"

Einhard stared at the aged duke with pity as he writhed on the floor like a crippled beggar. Richard was one of the most powerful men in the empire, but he was floundering on the floor much how the children in the queen's chamber played with their blocks and wooden figures. Brice and Seguin kept their heads bowed low. They detested Ganelon's memory but understood the burden Richard carried. The warriors knew Ganelon as an infamous man, an example among the Peers of what could happen when an oath was compromised. He was the only man despised more along their marches than the Saracens to the south.

When Richard's moment of grieving had ended, he left his father's skull in the wooden box. It was difficult to blame Charles for wishing the dishonorable tribute to his father, even after such a long period of time. When Richard finally took his seat, all eyes in the room focused on the outsider, Einhard. He was aware of the animosity. Even those who favored Louis, like the lords of the marches, were never overtly supportive of the Irishman. Einhard went to the table and made use of the thirteenth goblet by filling it with wine and immediately bringing its contents halfway down. He stayed nervously close to the table rather than approach the Peers.

Einhard spoke fast. "I bring word from Louis. He dispatched a red kite that arrived this afternoon. He has makes for Aachen with all speed. He has ordered that his son, Charles, be wed to the lone daughter of Wilfred of Aquitaine. The wedding is to take place upon Emperor Louis's arrival into the city, which is imminent. Blessings to you, Lord Wilfred. You shall be grandfather to emperors that follow."

There was no excitement in Wilfred's face, so Einhard had to search for courage to complete the rest of his message. "You are to call upon your house to prepare. Five days."

Wilfred rose from his chair. "This cannot be. Basina is betrothed to marry Bernard when she is of age. That was the wish of Emperor Charles."

Richard came to his friend's side. "Do not waste your time, Wilfred, searching for answers from the lips of Einhard. He will only give you half-truths at best. It is all apparent and needs no explanation. Now that our Lord Emperor Charles has passed to heaven, Louis fears the other marriage: the wedding of your gold to Bernard's rightful claims."

Einhard said nothing to Richard's insult, preferring instead to make a mental inventory that he would report to Louis when they next met.

Germanicus joined in with his unsolicited opinion. "Lord Wilfred," Germanicus said, "this could have been remedied by spawning proper male heirs."

Richard instinctively reached for a dagger that was not there. He wanted to plant it in both Germanicus and Einhard. The only difficulty was determining who would go first. "Wilfred's two sons died putting down rebellions from within Aquitaine's own cities, you shameless turd. You should see to your own lame cock!"

Einhard cleared his throat to give the remaining message he had momentarily forgotten. It would not ease the burden within the room. "As you may be aware, the betrothal of one noble house to the heir to the throne of Frankia will invoke the ancient principle of *Primus Inter Pares*. First Among Equals. Upon the wedding of Lord Charles and Lady Basina, the young Prince Charles shall immediately take full possessory rights to the Duchy of Aquitaine without condition of your passing, Lord Wilfred."

Wilfred laughed sarcastically. "*Primus Inter Pares*? Louis invokes a bygone right that would have denied him the very throne he sits on if it were invoked by Bernard's people prior? I do not know whether this is a Greek tragedy or comedy. You will take my lands? My kingdom before I am even in the ground?"

Richard looked at his old friend with pity and thought, *Is that how it ends? As simple as that? Centuries of rule handed down father to son only to be taken away by an absent sovereign who decrees behind the words of a toothless monk?* He was sour with sprouting thoughts of rebellion.

Wilfred's emotions changed from surprise to sorrow and then anger in a few short breaths. Wilfred began to make his way to Einhard, who steadied himself with the table behind him. Richard stood motionless as his friend passed. Wilfred hadn't laid his hands on another man in years, but he was certain he could take Einhard's pathetic life with ease.

Seguin finally stood and intervened. "Stand down, Wilfred. The monk does your emperor's bidding. He is no more responsible than the kite Louis sent to the city. I am mindful to respect your station and rank as Peer and duke, but it has limits."

Wilfred looked Seguin up and down. "You. The two of you have become slaves to Louis. You whores! He sends you coin and troops and you curl up at his feet and beg for more."

Seguin responded, "And what if we did not take his gold and his men, Aquitaine? Would you fill the void?" Seguin scoffed. "If we relied on you to mind the marches, we would all be speaking Arabic or looking for our heads. Speak of what you know. You know nothing of what we do to protect this empire."

Einhard finished by conjuring up the sound of sincerity. "All is not lost, Lord Wilfred. You shall be permitted to retain your status as Peer."

Richard barked aloud and Germanicus silently reveled in his supreme fortune, pretending to be unfazed. He delighted in the misery of others. Richard called on his friend Wilfred to return to his seat.

"Come, Wilfred. Not here. Not now. There are other ways to exercise your grievance." That was a code, one that Einhard could easily decipher.

"I believe there is another matter that remains unsettled." Germanicus pointed to the chair with no embroidery. "Who gets that?" The chair of the twelfth Peer had been empty for half as long as Germanicus and Vaclen were themselves members. There had never been much dispute over the likely successor. Charles had promised a seat to Bernard when he was only a young noble living in Urbino and learning the ways of warfare and strategy. Given the bold move to neutralize Wilfred, the issue of whether to appoint Bernard seemed trivial.

Germanicus saw this issue as another possibility for further calamity. Einhard had collected himself and thought nothing of the question now that the threat on his life appeared to have been thwarted. "Jocelyn," Einhard said, "the count of Argovia. Count Jocelyn shall take on the role of Peer in consideration of his family's many years of faithful service to the empire. That is the wish of Emperor Louis."

The Peers traded puzzled looks and Einhard simply shrugged. Germanicus smiled inside his cup. Like the other peers, he had no idea who Jocelyn was or where in the empire this place called Argovia was located. What he did know was that somewhere outside the palace, Bernard was sharpening his sword. For Germanicus, the trip to Aachen could not have gone any better.

XV

- THE BRANDED BISHOP -

Alexandria was the city where Naji had originally been sent to obtain the relic now lost. It was the busiest port in the Mediterranean, teeming with traders and travelers from throughout the world. The Abbasid Caliphate, which ruled Alexandria and far beyond, had kept a rare but tenuous tolerance for foreign religions. Christians, Jews, and the Shaivas of India were allowed to move within sections of the city and conduct their business, although they did so under severe taxation and the shadow of flippant persecution.

The visitors to centuries-old synagogues and churches practiced their faiths quietly, preferring not to draw attention. The ruling caliphs were wise to realize early on that shunning other religious groups would have catastrophic consequences to the city's fortune. Caravans from the Holy Lands pushed the swollen population to bursting proportions. Ships from throughout Christendom and beyond moored in its port and sailed through the mouth of the Nile into the heart of Africa.

It was Naji's fourth visit to Alexandria. He was sent to meet a man Kasim had long considered a friend. Naji was initially taken aback when Kasim first described the man as a Coptic Christian. Knowing what little he learned of the task up to that moment, Naji had strong doubts that any Christian would accommodate the extreme request of a Muslim. And it was most certainly extreme. Kasim set out his instructions to Naji in a letter.

I am owed a debt. A solemn promise from a man who will not break it. He will not deny you. He owes me his life and more. I saved the one thing he holds most dear in this world from fodder for a pyre. When you give him my letter and he learns that what I ask for is to be placed in the hands of Charles to seal a peace between Muslim and Christian, Córdoban and Frank, he will reluctantly consent.

The man Naji was instructed to find was Yoannis, the bishop of the Coptic Church of Alexandria. Naji had done as ordered. He found the bishop in his church in the Coptic ghetto. Naji delivered Kasim's letter and patiently waited for a response. Yoannis studied the unusual-looking man as he unfolded the letter. While Alexandria was a fascinating city with faces and dress like none other in the world, he had never seen a Muslim man, or anyone else for that matter, with hair like Naji. He did his best not to stare for long and instead focused on the message from his old friend. The letter Kasim had given Naji was not sealed, but it mattered little. The words were not Arabic, and so Naji remained clueless as to what it contained, even though he knew what he had been sent to retrieve.

Contrary to Kasim's assurances, Naji did not find a willing recipient. Yoannis's read the letter several times and paced the isle of his empty church. His pained face told Naji what he feared before he had the chance to speak.

"Thank you, Naji. I know I told Kasim I would grant him whatever request he had of me, but this is . . . It is simply not permissible. It is beyond my power to give your emir what he desires. I know you have traveled far, my friend, and have orders to return with the relic, but this I cannot do. We Copts believe that the crown has powers and that no man may be trusted to possess it. We are its keeper, not its owner. It may please the Emperor Charlemagne to hold the crown of thorns as his own and surely many souls may be in peril, but I am beholden to my own master. I am sorry and I ask you to please send Kasim my deepest regrets. I wish him and his family the best of health."

Naji said nothing in response. He simply offered a nod and left the bishop where he stood. Although he didn't show it, Naji was beyond frustrated and angered. He felt that he had been sent on a fool's errand to obtain an element of the truce with the Franks and had failed. He blamed Kasim, the elite administrator who handled disputes with words and flattery. Naji was not that type of man. There was a time when his hair was like the other Muslims of Alexandria, when his disputes were resolved with violence.

Naji roamed the congested city streets and silently cursed Kasim for his pride. He knew that Kasim would blame him if he returned empty-handed and that, once everything was considered, the emir would heed the whispers of his little cousin and hold Naji accountable. Naji was intent to not let that happen. He had come too far and been trusted with matters too important to his emir for Yoannis to simply deny his request. Kasim had left him no instructions on what to do if the Christian didn't deliver the crown. As he left the ghetto for his ship, Naji vowed that he would return to the church and retrieve what he was tasked to obtain. Kasim's objections to his methods would be dealt with on some other occasion.

Kasim was assigned as the emirate's new emissary to Byzantium seven years earlier. It was the young man's first post. Alexandria was the port Kasim would visit before the last leg to Constantinople, and he would ultimately return via the same route. It was during his first visit to Alexandria that Kasim found Yoannis as a kindred spirit. Yoannis was the youngest bishop to ascend to control of the Coptic Church of Alexandria, a sect of Christianity with many differences from the mother church in Rome. Unlike Rome, the Coptic Church did not benefit from the gifts and protection of European princes. Its very existence was hard and fraught with tribulations. It was an island in the turbulent sea of Islam. The church's relationship with the Abbasid Caliphate was as tenuous as the temperament of the ruling caliph.

Years before Kasim's arrival, Caliph Yazid II ordered all Copts in the city to be marked on their hands and arms with symbols of the cross or the winged lion of Saint Mark. He tore down the iconic symbols of their faith and burned houses of worship throughout the city. Most often, his actions were attempts to fleece the church and its people of gold and silver through further taxes, yet the Copts had always feared that the caliphs would eventually drive them from the land, force them from the last of their ancient buildings, and more importantly destroy their holy relics.

The Coptic Church of Alexandria was one of the oldest churches of Christendom. Where Saint Peter was the first bishop of Rome, the Apostle Mark was the original bishop of Alexandria. What it lacked in majesty the Church of Alexandria more than made up for in its importance to the origins of the faith. Given its ancient ties to Christ himself, the Church of Alexandria held many of the most revered relics in the world. As an apostle, Mark had been a hoarder of iconic symbols related to Jesus. He quietly kept locks of hair from Jesus and Mary, a bowl from the Last Supper, a nail from the crucifixion, and the crown of thorns. The bishop of Alexandria had become a title more in line with the roles of housekeeper and politician than preacher of the gospel. Young Yoannis learned very early in his post that he had to deal with bureaucrats from Rome and foreign scholars seeking to look upon and touch a link to their savior. The collection Mark amassed had to be closely managed and in some circumstances kept hidden from those who wanted more than a gaze at the objects of Christ.

As the bishop of Alexandria, Yoannis's role meant his piety and devotion to the faith would be tested often. The city demanded hard living from all. Disease and taxes were as much a part of Alexandrian life as trips to the water wells. Those who had not submitted to Islam suffered more so. When the *fatwa* was issued by Caliph Al-Mahdi's imams in Baghdad, reinstituting the earlier order that all Christians living under caliphate rule should now be branded as infidels, the young Yoannis was not deterred. Perhaps the decree of the imams would have been reserved for only those Christians of the lower classes. Rather than waiting to see if the local governor's enforcers would come into his church to drag him away, Yoannis walked to the city barracks with his chest bare and his crosier in hand.

Al-Mansur, the governor of Alexandria, took special interest in the bold Christian. "You are the bishop of Alexandria, the beacon of Jesus for all Egypt. Like our ancient lighthouse, you shall be a beacon as well. Your hands and arms will be spared. We will not mark you like a commoner so you can be counted and taxed. We will set fire to your face so all can see the flames from a distance and know you for what you are."

Yoannis was branded with the image of a cross. They burned him on his right cheek. Yoannis screamed but did not retreat when his flesh sizzled into a pale white paste and stuck to the glowing iron. Catching his breath, the bishop then showed the brander his left cheek. Al-Mansur knew the symbolism of his act. He was unimpressed and obliged the upstart bishop with a nod. "Wear them with pride, Christian." The governor showed a satisfied smile.

Kasim first met Yoannis while walking along the island breakwater of the port of Alexandria, where the great Pharos lighthouse stood sentry for the ships of the Mediterranean. The lighthouse dominated the flat city landscape and could be seen from outside the southern boundary of the city even through the windless summer haze. It was a reminder of the city's fabled past. It rose stone by colossal stone at the direction of the Greek Ptolemies. It stood silent witness as the legion of Augustus surrounded Cleopatra's nearby tomb while the queen and her lover Antony took their lives inside.

Men kept the fire lit inside the lighthouse eye like they had for the past thousand years. There was a red brick shack next to the great base of the lighthouse. Carts would enter the shack from the long bridge that attached the island base to the city proper, dumping off piles of wood for storage and protection from the rare rainstorm. What the carts and mules dropped off men carried away. Strong slaves carried bundles up the ramp of the lighthouse and then up unseen spiral staircase that ended at the eye. A long cloud that meandered off into the blue canopy overhead carried away its black smoke like a chimney. Kasim marveled at the process as it played out over and over each day for a millennium. He often wondered at the vast forests of trees that were cut to fuel its fire over the centuries. Kasim sighed and said to himself, "This spectacle will go on for another thousand years."

Then there were the faceless and nameless slaves who had come and gone over the generations. Kasim once followed one of the slaves up the ramp to the entry door, where the stairs climbed around its inside to the top. The steps of the staircase were sandstone, yet through the wear that accumulated over the centuries, hour by hour, the rough surface had become as smooth and as shiny as polished marble. The center of the stairs had grown concave, and looking to the winding top, Kasim assumed that, over the years, the number of slaves who had fallen to their deaths could fill a large village. For all their toil and sweat, all of their years of keeping the fire lit, they only had divots in stone to remind the world that they ever existed. Divots that no one except other slaves would ever see. It was Kasim's nature to think beyond the here and now and think of time and the impact that the past had on the lives of those around him.

It was an unpleasant summer evening as the sun set over the

western shore where land met water. Men walked the breakwater of the port to bask in the precious evening breeze that came
off the sea, yet there was little to be felt that day. It was one of
those days that seemed to drag on slowly. Schools of bait-fish
skimmed the glass waters within the port, and white herons,
satisfied from the day's catch, rose and fell in the slow, pulsing
waves of the Mediterranean opposite the rocks. It was a popular destination for the men of the city who could afford leisure
time. The draw for most was the lighthouse. It was still the envy
of the Mediterranean after so many centuries. Those rare few,
fortunate enough to be free of work, would come to the breakwater after evening prayers and watch the western sky transition from orange to red and then purple. After purple, the beam
of the lighthouse began to dominate the heavens until the following dawn.

Kasim sat on one of the massive stones of the breakwater to
watch the grand ships creeping through the mouth of the port.
Men balanced atop masts as they furled their exotic sails and
screamed in unknown tongues, cautiously navigating around
anchor lines. Kasim wore his thinnest linen tunic and leggings
to soak in as much of the light and salty breeze as possible. The
smells of the sea were a welcome change to the muggy and windowless halls of the Alexandria administrative buildings he frequented. He preferred the smell of rotting seaweed and fish
to the filth of the city, which could be overwhelming at times,
particularly in the summer heat. The Muslims chastised the
Christians for their barbaric indifference toward sanitation, but
Kasim had seen both and found little difference. In his mind,
it was the dry air and scarce rains of Egypt and greater Arabia

that kept the waste and piss of the narrow alleys from festering. Whatever the reason, the evening on the breakwater caused Kasim to long for the openness of his home on Valencia's coast. The air at home was clean and the salt that burned his eyes and lungs was a fond memory. Each time he thought of home, his mind's eye would show him that beach on the coast; his wife and son were there with him.

During his stay in Alexandria, Kasim was charged with the additional task of negotiating port taxes with the current governor of Egypt. Ironically, it was Naji who was originally charged with the task, but he was unsuccessful. It was the hope of the emir that Kasim and his skilled words would prevail where the rough Naji hadn't. The Abbasid Caliphate was the dominant Islamic state of the world and could dictate terms to most of its partners, but the smaller Córdoba Emirate and its lands in Spain was the launching point for trade with the Franks and the rest of western Europe. Kasim would make that fact known to the governor early and often in their talks. He was cautiously hopeful about his ability to negotiate good terms on behalf of his cousin, but the Abbasids were as ruthless in negotiating as they were in war. Kasim found it ironic that it was more difficult to work through common understandings and reach compromises with the neighboring Abbasids than with most Christian nations.

Negotiations had grown fruitless, and Kasim was frustrated. He was already in Alexandria for twice as long as originally planned, and now his crossing from Africa to Spain on his return trip would likely be delayed into the heart of the winter, when the seas could be merciless. Going to the port was a way to take his mind off the daily turmoil he had to endure.

Kasim had come to the breakwater that evening to not only give his mind a reprieve but to also honor a promise. When Kasim was last in his home city of Valencia, he promised his only son, Ayan, that he would place a letter to him in a bottle, and if the boy was good enough—if the son obeyed his mother, minded his prayers, and chores—he would one day find the bottle on the brown sand beach down the hill from his house. "When you find the bottle, I will know. I will see a sign in the evening stars and will journey back home to you and your mother. I promise." It was a foolish notion, but Kasim knew the young boy adored him and would believe it if the father told the child that the sun would one day rise in the west.

When he left home that spring, when the Mediterranean began to calm and his men prepared for his journey east, Kasim gave his wife a bottle with a message corked inside. His son was a dreamer, and Kasim was practical. If all went well in his travels through Alexandria and beyond, the bottle he handed to his wife would be found by Ayan on the beach in the late fall. He now knew that bottle would hold a promise of a return that would be delayed, and that bothered him more. There was something deeper about Kasim's dishonesty that didn't sit well. Absurd as it was, he decided to cast away the message to his son rather than relying on his wife's planned deceit.

Kasim carried a brown glass bottle in his travel satchel. It was a bottle he took from his apartment earlier that morning. The tide would begin to run out of the harbor once the sun had fully set, so Kasim made sure he hurled the bottle with all his strength to keep it from returning into the rocks. He said a short prayer asking Allah to watch over his son and wife. He watched the bottle for only a brief moment and thought of the future, when he could finally bring his son along on his travels. There was so much of the world he wanted to show him. The fading sun gave little light to reflect off the bottle. After a while, he couldn't track it bobbing behind the waves. He had great hopes for its journey.

An unusual sight caught Kasim's attention as he began his long walk to his quarters in the heart of the city. Yoannis was cloaked in a thin tan robe and stood at the foot of the lighthouse ramp. His blond curls were noticeable from afar. He carried a brown sack from which he drew a number of large round bread rolls, handing them out to sitting men. Slung over his shoulder was a massive goat skin that must have weighed down the small man.

Kasim could tell the man was handing the rolls and serving drinks to the firewood slaves. All those walking along the lighthouse were not only free men but those of wealth, apparent in their fine, colorful robes and tunics. The men Kasim approached wore little clothes and had set aside their distinct leather vests that hung over their shoulders to protect their backs from the wood packs. It was still hot, and the men were likely taking a minor reprieve before they started their duties at night, when the need for flames was the greatest.

As Kasim approached on his way along the ramp, he heard a chorus of laughter that seemed out of place considering the misery the slaves carried with them. Kasim was a curious soul and decided to approach the scene. The laughter ceased even before he came close enough for simple conversation. Kasim asked Yoannis, "What is this? Do you own these slaves?"

Yoannis smiled and answered, "I own no man and would

discourage others from doing so." Yoannis didn't turn to ac-knowledge Kasim, preferring instead to keep his smile on the slaves, who had grown nervous at the approach of the Muslim. The blonde man spoke perfect Arabic, which only piqued Kasim's curiosity.

"Why do you feed property that is not yours?" Kasim asked.

"These are God's children. It is my duty to feed them," Yoannis replied.

"Would you feed them, monk, if they were Saracen?"

Yoannis decided to face the curious Muslim. Kasim's eyes were caught in a trance by the red crosses on the man's cheeks, and he immediately knew to whom he spoke.

"Yes," Yoannis said. "Yes, I would. These men are not Christian. Yet they feed the lighthouse, so I feed them." Yoannis spoke to the slaves in Frankish. Yoannis had learned that the men of the woodpile were Saxons who were sold away as a con-sequence of some minor rebellion against the empire. He told the men not to fear the Saracen. He could tell that Kasim was a man of the elite class, based on his dress and well-kept appear-ance, which was a relief. From Yoannis's prior encounters, he knew a soldier would more likely mean trouble. A simple foot soldier could assault the highest-ranking infidel in the region without fear of recourse.

Kasim decided to keep his own knowledge of Frankish to himself in hopes that the bishop would reveal more to the slaves than to him. Yoannis detected that his identity was now known and could either harm or help his cause, depending on Kasim's influence. "They are in good spirits," Yoannis said. "The wine and the bread help."

"You give them wine?" Kasim asked. "They are slaves and this is still caliphate land. They will walk this ramp every day until their last, which may not be that far off. Perhaps you are content to join them."

"Yes and no," Yoannis said. "Their bodies are enslaved, but their minds remain uncaged. They have a love for their gods and a hope for what may come. That is honorable to me and merits a fresh loaf and a draw of wine."

Kasim gave a nod and scratched his beard. He found that the young man spoke like an old soul. The brands on Yoannis's face didn't seem to match the bishop's innocent appearance.

There was nothing hard about Yoannis. But for his crosses, Yoannis's face was delicate and free of the carved lines brought on by the strong African sun. Kasim thought he had the look of some northern man without a beard. His light hair and skin seemed out of place in a tan and brown world.

"You speak Arabic very well, monk. How did you come to know our tongue so well?"

Yoannis disregarded the label of monk. It suited him more than the haughty title of bishop. He had always felt that the appointment was too heavy for his young age. "I was born in Tyre. My father's family were salt merchants from Venice. I learned from my nurse. She was an Arab."

"An Arab slave?" Kasim asked.

Yoannis shook his head and returned his attention to the Saxons. He suspected the Muslim was looking more to cast insults than to subject him to persecution. Yoannis said, "You have an abrasive manner, my friend. What have I done to earn your ire?"

Kasim could only laugh. His understanding of this interesting young man and his connection to Alexandria was becoming clearer with each prod. Venice had been evangelized by Saint Mark during his many travels to spread the faith after the death of Jesus. The Venetians in turn revered the saint. His symbol, the winged lion, became their republic's crest. Its nobles had performed pilgrimages to Alexandria since long before the birth of the Prophet Muhammed. Kasim could only assume that the bishop's family had some link to the saint and disciple of Christ. This link, perhaps, would eventually become apparent.

"So even though you are a monk, the sea is in your blood? Perhaps you can tell me the home of that ship that comes through the breakwater?" He pointed to one of the numerous ships that were casting anchors in preparation for the coming night. "I like to watch the ships come and go. It gives me a strange peace, yet the home of that one eludes me."

Yoannis took a long glare. Perhaps if he answered the Muslim, the man would move along to his destination. "I would guess that it is Cypriot. It is difficult to see its furled banner, but it looks like it flies a crowned red lion. There. You see? It appears to have the Venetian ship style. See, it has the narrow hull, it draws little water, and the tall mast is for the distances across the Mediterranean rather than sailing close to shore. It is Venetian-made. That would be my answer. Cyprus and the greater Peloponnese have been Venetian ports for many generations."

"It seems it is the Venetians who are the conquerors. Perhaps the Muslims should fear your republic over the princes of Europe!"

"Ah!" Yoannis said with a slight chuckle, "You have more sand than water, so your borders are at no risk." Yoannis caught himself briefly, not knowing if he had gone too far. "Please do not communicate that to the governor. He has an appetite for Christian flesh. I would not give him any further cause to make an example of me."

"He has marked both cheeks," Kasim said. "You have no more to brand. You are safe!"

The playfulness in Yoannis wasn't easily extinguished. Kasim's bait was impossible not to take, even if their allegiances didn't align. "I have two more cheeks. I am almost inclined to present them for the next round of branding!" He patted his ass with a free hand and stood on his toes.

"Ha! Well said, monk." Kasim knew he was no monk, and Yoannis knew the Muslim enjoyed the playful jab. The conversation began to flow between the two men. Each was in wonder of the other's travels. Though young, they both found it odd that they had never crossed paths. Yoannis gathered the courage to ask Kasim why he was at the breakwater that night. Kasim shared the tale of his son and the bottle, which spilled into the greater story of his post and the identity of his cousin.

The men talked for some time. The purple canopy that drew men to prayer had faded and was now replaced by the lighthouse's eye of fire. After the bread had been dispensed and the flagon emptied, they left the grateful slaves and walked along the bridge that connected the lighthouse island to the city proper. Yoannis had a slight uneasiness that he masked. He didn't know how either the Muslims of the city or his own Copts would react to him being seen with an Arab from the elite class.

Kasim wanted the young Christian to know he was genuine in his feelings and put his mind at ease. "I feel as though I must tell you that I do not approve of your branding. There are many things of this city that I believe are below the teachings of the Prophet."

Yoannis smiled and said, "I have had my scars for over a year now. All Christians have them. I am the only one that carries it on my face. The rest? It's on their hands or their arms."

"That does not excuse the act. My cousin, Hakam? This would not do."

"Has he not killed thousands of Christians? Did he not wage war on the Franks and the Gascons?"

"In battle, yes," Kasim said. "Princes kill. They collect taxes. They sit in judgment of bickering nobles as comfortably as goat herders. They kill their enemies in battle. Yet I have never known my cousin to degrade an enemy. This is most unbecoming of a Muslim. I tell you this in confidence. If you repeat it, I must deny it."

"I have no reason to call you as witness, Kasim. I am at peace with the scars. They were sore for some time, but the pain has gone. They are now a part of me. I have my own crosses that I bear, if you will."

There was wisdom in the young man's words. Kasim had met Pope Leo III, and he wasn't even a fraction of the man in front of him. "I am pleased I have come to know you, Yoannis. You are unlike any bishop I have met before, and I have met several in my few years of service."

Yoannis flexed a half-grimace and half-smile. "Perhaps that is a sign that I was never meant to be one."

For some reason, Kasim thought the young bishop couldn't be more wrong. He had hoped to meet and talk with the interesting young man again. So long as he remained in Alexandria, the emissary made sure his future visits to the lighthouse were timed with the purple skies and its resting slaves.

What Kasim told Naji was most certainly true. Kasim did save Yoannis's life and the relic he and his Venetian people held in holy reverence. It was during one of Kasim's return voyages home from his affairs as emissary to Byzantium that he performed the act that would end in Yoannis's pledge of a single favor. The exact date was never in question, and both Kasim and Yoannis would remember it for the rest of their lives.

The day was April 25, three years after the two first met. Saint Mark's Day. The modest population of Christians in Alexandria held that day in reverence above all holidays other than Easter Sunday. The Christian ghetto along the eastern bank of the Nile, which was normally subdued throughout the year, exploded with music, dancing, and pageantry. The streets were alive with the sound of drums and the smell of lambs roasting on spits and fish boiling in savory pots of tomatoes and garlic.

The Christians of the city had become brazen in recent years. The governor had not toppled a stone cross or publicly flogged priests in some time. Saint Mark's Day that year involved the opening of wine amphorae in the evening as the celebration and feasting came to an end. Men walked the ghetto streets, secretly sipping from covered wooden cups to mask the sight from caliphate soldiers who patrolled the streets. Yoannis had advised against the open display of rebellion against the governor's strict prohibition, but the people did not listen.

That day, it wasn't the pouring of wine that sparked the out-
rage of the Muslim hosts, turning the holy day into a catastrophe
for Yoannis. Instead, it was the single act of a Christian boy. As
Yoannis would later tell Kasim, the gesture would have caught
little attention had the girl who was the subject of the boy's attention not been Muslim.

According to Yoannis, the Venetians had an ancient tradition among their people that venerated the red rose, which
in turn was prevalent in the Christian ghetto's wall paintings
and carvings. Back in Venice centuries earlier, a common soldier was said to have fallen in love at the sight of a beautiful
nobleman's daughter that he saw passing through the canals on
Saint Mark's Day. In the hope of winning the girl's hand and
her father's approval, the young soldier volunteered to join the
Venetian ranks in Greece against the threat of the Byzantine
army, which was marching to his homeland. The young man
was mortally wounded in battle, but before he died, he managed
to pluck a red flower for the young woman from a nearby rose-
bush. His friend who accompanied him to Greece would eventually return to Venice and deliver the blood-stained rose to the
young woman as a sign of the fallen soldier's undying love. The
friend handed the Venetian girl the rose one year later, on Saint
Mark's Day.

The red roses that flooded the Christian ghetto came from
the flooded plains of southern Egypt, where the people of the
valley venerated the thorned flower since the time when their
ancestors worshipped the sun and used the plant's oil to mend
wounds. Their petals were tossed from second-story windows
and onto the crowd below. Old men placed buds in the hair of

young women. It was a celebration that spilled into the surrounding streets. A Christian boy who was barely older than a
child, but still far from manhood, stepped from the cluster of his
street and approached a local girl who was running her family's
chores. The boy, seeing the girl's simple beauty for what it was,
handed her a red rose and left as quickly as he appeared.

He didn't see her religion; he only saw those big brown eyes
that held a soul a thousand years old. Her father was not far
off and witnessed the event. He chastised his daughter, sent her
home with the back of his hand, and called on the local soldiers.
The simple act of affection blossomed the same as the gifted
rose and spiraled into religious calamity. Soldiers invaded the
ghetto. They beat men and women with the butts of their pikes,
destroyed vegetable stands, and set fires in the hope they would
engulf the whole quarter. Local Muslims followed into the cavity
and incited the soldiers to further violence. The soldiers made
their way through the center of the Christian streets to the ancient church. Their intent was clear. They wanted the main symbol of the outsiders destroyed, and at that moment, they had
their perfect opportunity to avoid blame.

Kasim had been in a nearby meeting with merchants, listening to bickering that seemed to follow him in every port. The elevated noise of the celebration several streets over did not seem
out of sorts to the emissary at first. Then came the screams.

Kasim made no effort to inspect the scene from the nearby
windows. He didn't know the reason for the noise, but he had a
strong suspicion about where it came from. A Coptic cleric broke
through the doors where Kasim had been meeting. He was met
with kicks and punches by the men who showed disdain for the

boy. Kasim called them off. The boy carried a message from Yoannis. It was a plea for Kasim's help, and so he cautiously excused himself. Had this been Córdoba, Kasim's word would carry above all others', save for his cousin's. Here in Alexandria, he risked much in answering the plea, yet friendship compelled him to move forward.

Kasim had no trouble walking through the aftermath of the destruction that led to the simple church chapel. His appearance as a Muslim noble ensured him safe passage. He only had to look for the thickest billow of smoke to know where to go, yet there was little doubt where his path would lead him.

He came upon the modest wooden door to the city's ancient church. The top hinge had been snapped from the stone, causing the old wooden door to delicately hang suspended in the air. Kasim walked behind the altar toward the back of the chapel where stacks of shelves held the church's relics. The shelves had been knocked from their supports and lay piled on the floor with broken clay jars and open wooden boxes scattered about.

Men who had most likely wrecked the shelves were not done handing out destruction. Kasim saw three men bent over with their backs to him. They had tossed off the lid of a decorated wooden coffin placed on a small dais in the center of the back wall. Although he had never entered the church before, Kasim knew the coffin. It was the resting place of Saint Mark the apostle. The men had their hands deep within the coffin, lifting the fragile and dried corpse, which was wrapped in browned tight linen like the pharaohs thousands of years earlier.

"You!" Kasim screamed. "Stop what you are doing! Whatever your anger, it is well quenched. Have you no shame?"

The man that cradled the center of the corpse turned and smiled to Kasim. "I do not know you, but if you value your life, you will go back to wherever you came from."

Kasim growled his response, "If I leave here, it will be to the governor's quarters, and I assure you, before the sun has set, women will be tending to the carvings on your back."

"Fool. We do the governor's bidding."

Kasim could only follow the men who carried the corpse of Saint Mark. He made no effort to dissuade them from their task; it would be pointless and could only end badly. Nor did the men care about his presence. They moved through the narrow streets of the ghetto and into the main market of the city unobstructed. Kasim closed his eyes as he followed at a safe distance and hoped Yoannis still lived. He had no idea what had transpired, but the one thing that was certain was that the lives of the Alexandrian Christians would likely never be the same.

This was bad business, whether Christian or Muslim. The corpse-stealers moved with little effort, and those that crowded the streets gave them deference as they passed. The body of the saint had lightened through the centuries, making the task of the man holding the center obsolete. Kasim wondered if he was simply padding the center to keep the corpse from snapping under its own weight. The crowd of men that had gathered in the center of the market gave way as the corpse of Saint Mark approached. The noise subsided as the path cleared, revealing two men on opposite pans of the scales of power.

Al-Walid, the current governor of Alexandria, was adorned in flowing red and purple cloth. He stood confidently beside Yoannis. The bishop had been beaten and lay naked in the dirt.

Al-Walid took notice of Kasim but paid him no mind. The governor appeared proud and satisfied as he gestured for the men to lay the corpse of Saint Mark on his side opposite Yoannis. A makeshift pyre had been assembled farther in the clearing using wood from some of the older booths of the market. The men dropped Saint Mark with little care or respect for their load. Yoannis looked over at the pyre, unable to lift his head. On his face, dirt mixed with blood, hiding his swollen features.

Kasim wondered if the bishop knew where he was or what was transpiring around him. Yoannis's legs moved, but little else. Al-Walid stepped closer to Yoannis; the toes of his sandals almost touched the bishop's nose. He moved his silk robe from over his knee so he could kneel next to Yoannis. Kasim came in closer to bear witness to an interaction he felt hopeless to stop.

"Bishop," al-Walid said, "for the insult of your people on this day, I shall give you a choice. Choice is what you Christians covet most in this world, is it not? One body shall lie atop this pyre today. It shall be yours or your holy saint. Decide."

Yoannis coughed to clear his throat of blood and phlegm. His breath spawned a small dust cloud. "Mine."

"Yours? That is your wish?" Al-Walid asked.

Yoannis responded, "Mine for my master's. Yes."

"Very well. You two men. Lay this fool upon the wood."

"Shall we open his throat first?" One of al-Walid's men asked.

"No," al-Walid said. "He clearly seeks martyrdom. We will honor his wish." Two of the men who carried Saint Mark grabbed the hands and feet of Yoannis and slung him on top of the wood pyre. Al-Walid stroked his gray and black beard in satisfaction as he turned to the crowd that had formed a cautious semicircle.

Al-Walid addressed the buzzing crowd. "You came to me with your troubles, and I listened to your pleas. This man will pay for the wrongs of his people. He has willingly given his life in payment." Al-Walid gave a nod, and a nearby soldier grabbed the safe end of a log wedged between the bars of a brazier.

Kasim screamed in panic. "Wait! Why do you thirst for this man's death? Why are you intent on destroying a peace that has stood now for more than a century? What is this man's offense?"

Al-Walid gave Kasim a look of irritation. He wanted to strike the Córdoban for inserting himself into matters that were not his people's concern. "A Christian boy has insulted a Muslim girl. The boy approached one of ours with a flower in his hand."

Kasim half-cried and half-laughed. "In the name of Allah, is that all?"

Al-Walid became enraged with Kasim. That was a challenge to his authority that would not stand. "Careful, Córdoban. You are one insult away from witnessing the removal of every Christian head this day, all in payment of your tongue. You have no right to interfere in matters that do not concern you. You press your cousin's authority beyond limits." Al-Walid turned to his torchbearer and gave another nod.

"A choice! A trade!" Kasim screamed. "He trades his life for his saint? I freely give mine for his. I trade my life for that of the bishop!" The crowd murmured in puzzlement and disgust. Kasim blinked and sucked in his breath.

Al-Walid laughed in amusement. "Mansur warned me of you, Córdoban. He said you were a problem, and I see his words were true. He said that your travels have tainted your mind. You see the world as a dreamer. You are not the voice of a king. You defile your own people and offend all Muslims."

Kasim had never thought of himself as a dreamer. That was the title he gave his boy, Ayan. Kasim hadn't thought of his son until that very moment, and he began to doubt the conviction of his offer to trade his life for Yoannis's. He remained silent, and Al-Walid filled the void. Al-Walid had no interest in burning a Muslim, and perhaps that was what Kasim was desperately hoping for. To back down from the challenge, however, would erode al-Walid's own standing among the people of Alexandria.

"Very well," al-Walid shouted. "Your life for his. I will spare you the fire, though. My man Yousef will open your neck for you. I give you a moment to pray."

Kasim was beyond frightened, but he masked his fear through his chin, which he held high. The Muslim soldiers removed Yoannis by rolling him off the pyre. The bishop summoned the strength to bring himself to his knees and look upon Kasim with a smile that caused his split upper lip to flex into two. It was difficult for Kasim to see where any teeth remained. Yoannis turned to Frankish to keep their last moment to themselves.

Yoannis gently said, "I am afraid you have made a poor choice, my friend. These men are intent on ridding the earth of me. This was only a convenient opportunity that you have now spoiled."

Kasim closed his eyes and knew that Yoannis spoke the truth. What had he done but delay what was sure to come? Ayan would now grow to never know his father and only hear the stories of how he belittled himself for a faith that was not his own.

"We met beside stacks of wood," Yoannis said, "did we not?

Withdraw your offer and help me back on top of the wood. Go and live for your son if nothing else."

Kasim looked into Yoannis's eyes and a peace came upon him. Before that moment, only discomfort and uncertainty about the future bothered him. Now, he felt content. "Goodbye, my friend," Kasim said. "Promise me you will live your remaining days with purpose."

Yoannis's tears wet the blood and dirt on his face. He leaned over and felt as if the life of his body was leaving him all the same. As Kasim stood, Al-Walid's man approached with his blade behind his back. Kasim raised his hand to hold him off, and the Córdoban walked over to the pyre. He stepped over the lower-placed logs and moved deep into the wooden bed. He laid himself down, closed his eyes, and gave a nod. The pyre was then lit.

XVI

- THE WATCH -

C harles's body had been moved from the centerpiece of the Palatine Chapel, the large domed octagon along the back of the cathedral, to one of the smaller attached chambers along the south side. The room had been cordoned off with long curtains that reached the arched ceiling. The chamber would be his crypt the following day and the location of his final resting place.

His tomb was a modest sarcophagus, assembled in the center of the space years earlier in preparation for his funeral. Charles didn't want the eternal resting place for his mortal remains to be anything ornate. He feared being ridiculed for vanity. There had to be a sensible balance. The sarcophagus was white marble and gilded with gold around its edges and raised above the stone floor by a series of three steps. The lid was as thick as a wrist and set along the side and covered in a red cloth to keep its inscriptions hidden until the emperor had been sealed underneath.

The covered corpse had been placed on a simple wood slab

alongside the empty sarcophagus. Satchels packed with snow had been filled from piled mounds in the back gardens and lined around Charles's body to preserve him from early smell and rot. The robe of Jesus that had earlier covered his body was removed by monks to keep safe and dry from the packed snow or the hands of observers that wanted to touch the divine. The intent was to cover Charles with the robe before the lid was closed. For the time being, his body and the leather satchels were covered with a thick yellow wool blanket that bore the frightening image of the Carolingian black eagle.

The sun had long since set as members of the family began to gather inside the chamber. An ancient custom was soon to take place. The old ones called the nightlong festivity the "watch". As it was told by the Franks who had family in the eastern forests and hills, farther away from the cities and churches, the watch was a time to say your goodbyes to the departed in a private way, without all of the impersonal ceremony sanctioned by priests. There was another reason behind the watch. Those that were in the process of passing to heaven had to be guarded so that dark spirits did not come to take the departing soul away. It was said that, if everyone at the watch remained awake until the following morning when the body was interred or buried, the soul was sure to find his way to heaven's eternity.

It was for this second reason that the church frowned on the practice of the watch, yet there was little that could be done in the lawless eastern lands. The practice had become less commonplace within the eastern territories in recent decades, which was a major part in why Judith demanded the watch take place. She wanted to put the hand of her Bavarian people into the funeral. Bishop Otto objected, as did Einhard. Alcuin held back his opinion knowing it was pointless to intervene.

There was no better way to remain awake and guard the body of a family member than to do so in the company of kinfolk that were well fed, joyful, and drunk. Women were prohibited from attending the watch for dead men, yet no one objected to Judith's presence. She had acted like Louis's proxy throughout the funeral rites, so there was a good amount of deference afforded to her wishes. The Merovingians of the eastern provinces were the last royals to hold royal watches. Judith had Merovingian blood even though her family roots were in the forests of Bavaria where, until recently, the watch flourished unchecked by the church.

Relatives and close members of the court arrived in the back of the cathedral and huddled in groups. Judith arrived early and sat like a stone as far away from Charles's corpse as the octagon would permit and kept her two wide-eyed boys close by. She wore a long black mourning veil that she pulled tight over her face, covering most of her cheeks so only her eyes and nose could be seen. She gripped a wine goblet that was handed to her, but paid no attention to its contents. For Judith, this was about being seen, not for her, but for her boys.

The watch was familiar to Judith. Her cousin Tassilo, the current duke of Bavaria and Peer, held a watch for their grandfather years earlier. She had been permitted to attend that ceremony and, as a result, knew the watch was an important tool. For lords in the eastern lands of the empire, the watch was more than just a ceremony of celebration and fending off evil spirits, it was the means of deciding succession. Noblemen with claims to provincial thrones used the gathering to make their claim as the next ruler. Judith expected Charles's watch to go on without incident, and if there was any trouble, it would make any would-be challengers step out from the shadows and declare their intentions.

Judith was not blind to the daily smirks nor was she deaf to the constant whispers. She had no misgivings about who and what she was. She didn't have the natural beauty of Regina or Adallind. Nor did she have any of the seductive traits of Louis's consorts he openly praised for all their features and flesh. She could still see the day she was presented to Louis by her father a decade earlier. She remembered Louis's expression when the veil over her face was removed and the lies in Louis' eyes as he feigned approval. That was the most painful moment in her life. She embraced her pain, however; not holding contempt for her husband.

While at first Judith failed to capture Louis's heart, she did in time end up owning all his mind. The two became kindred spirits of a sort. Louis used his wits to root out enemies and Judith plotted to destroy them. She was the eyes and ears of the city while the prince was off performing his duties.

Judith had no tutor in the game of palace politics. She learned from her own experiences, battling against sisters and cousins as a child to eventually make her way to the labyrinth of Aachen's palace where the stakes were the highest. When she wanted motivation, she thought of those courtiers who greeted her with fake smiles when she first arrived in Aachen. They hadn't the conviction to openly confront her. Their cowardice did nothing but stoke her hidden fires in the hope that she would one day descend upon them like an Old Testament angel. It was now her time and she embraced the moment, hoping the sweet joy of victory would live up to her high expectations.

Judith's boys were curious about all the activity in the chamber. It was so different from the solemn church proceedings. Men were loud and bellowed with laughter. They spilled more wine than they drank and spoke with liberal tongues about their emperor, saying things he would otherwise have objected to had he been alive. The boys wanted to touch their grandfather and experience the mystery of death for themselves. Judith kept them close, however, giving them instructions as to how far away they could walk around the room. Both young Louis and Charles were given goblets of wine and told to drink rather than taste. Judith preferred that the boys only pretend to take drinks and keep their wits about them so nothing undignified would occur. She didn't think to do that before the goblets were in their hands and that irked her. Her hope was that the boys would take after her and not be drawn by the goading of older men.

Germanicus had drunk enough to openly scoff at the watch. "They would call us barbarians, yet I do not recall ever drinking with a corpse."

He chose the recipient of the words more wisely than the words themselves. He stood with Ogier, the giant Dane. Ogier was a convert to Christianity, yet Germanicus had always suspected his allegiance to the cross was as much of a farce as his own. Ogier was one of only two foreigners that were ever admitted into the brotherhood of the Twelve Peers. As a convert, his family in the Daneland peninsula northeast of Saxony had forsaken and removed him from access to family wealth. Without silver to bring to the Twelve Peers, Ogier had to distinguish himself like the original Peers: through his ferocity and unquestioned willingness to lead men to certain death. As a newly made Christian, he had to kill more. His own wounds had to be life threatening to matter.

Ogier only stared at Germanicus, unsure how to respond. Germanicus had assumed the Dane would have many of the same reservations he felt as a Saxon. While Saxony was technically a part of the empire and while the Daneland was certainly not, both Germanicus and Ogier's people were held to a different standard.

Germanicus prodded the Dane a little deeper. "Surely you find this unusual. Even though you are now a Christian. You cannot tell me you share the same mind as these men." Germanicus pointed around the room with his goblet, marking men he knew cared little for Danes and the influence of the men of the northern lands.

Ogier felt the only way to rid himself of the smaller man was to give him the answer he wanted, in the hope the child would grow bored and look elsewhere for entertainment. "I do not care for their rituals," Ogier said. "One Christian may find this rite sacred. Another may burn for it. All rests on the opinion of a priest. It means nothing to me." Ogier looked into Germanicus's eyes. "Charles. He means everything to me." The burly Dane was all blonde hair and beard. That only worked to accentuate the seriousness in his stare. "I am lost. Without Charles, I fear we all may be lost."

Ogier had water in his eyes. Germanicus was smart enough

to know when to cease his prodding. The grip of Charles, even in death, was strong.

When Germanicus was Charles's hostage, he was well-kept. He was fed and educated like a prince. As a vassal lord, he was treated with respect, even when other rulers would have punished the subject for fostering rebellion. Germanicus's inherent disdain towards the conquering Franks meant he looked at Charles through a veil. Now, though, there was the revelation that the man he had secretly despised was perhaps his father.

Germanicus left the Dane and walked over to Charles. He looked on his sunken face. He had looked on Charles a thousand times, but he hadn't thought to look upon the corpse's lips and nose as an image of his own. Germanicus thought about all the times Charles had smiled at him or patted the young man on the back. He couldn't recall a single instance where the emperor was critical or judgmental of him. Even as Germanicus once held the emperor hostage in his own lands, Charles offered no threats or curses in retaliation. Charles was more than justified, should he had taken Germanicus' life. In all, Charles had been kinder and more caring than either of his parents. Germanicus wondered whether Charles knew he was his son. What could have been had Germanicus known the truth before it was too late? Germanicus shook his head as he looked down on the man who was now more mystery than enemy. "Nothing," he whispered. Germanicus saw nothing in Charles's face and felt nothing in his own heart.

Germanicus's attention was drawn away as the rumble of the chamber subsided. Bernard entered the room, pushing himself through faceless courtiers who hung near the entrance.

Bernard's face dripped in sweat. His normally well-kept hair was disheveled and matted on one side. Something was caked in the short beard hairs below his mouth. It appeared to be vomit. Germanicus took a seat in the other corner opposite Judith. Germanicus wanted a good view of the show.

Bernard was drawn towards Judith by a pathway cut in the crowd. Judith scrunched her nose at the young man who came to stand before her. "You smell of piss. You are drunk."

"Is this not a watch?" Bernard asked. "I'm supposed to be fucking drunk, am I not aunt?"

"Lest you forget, this is still a chapel. Be mindful of your tongue."

"Did I say something wrong, Aunt Judith?" Bernard smiled. His mouth was wet with wine and spit.

Little Louis came up to his mother's knee, asking her for coins. "Charles!" Bernard shouted. "How tall you have gotten, lad!" Bernard mussed the boy's well parted hair.

"I am Louis. He is Charles." Little Louis pointed to his older brother who was off to the side, standing between Ogier and a man who had to be Bohemian based on dress. The other man was bundled in robes that were laced tight over his chest. Both men towered over young Charles.

Bernard belched in his mouth. "What? Louis. Charles. What difference does it make, you are named for an emperor either way. Good for you, boy!"

Judith tried staring a hole into Bernard, but the man wouldn't give her the luxury of his attention.

Bernard asked little Louis, "Do you know my name, boy?"

The boy shook his head. "Bernard! Like that? Bernard. Do

you know who I am named after?" The boy shook his head again and grabbed at his mother's knee.

"No one," Bernard said. "I have never heard a single fucking song for a man named Bernard. How would you like to have that name as a boy? Get the shit kicked out of you every day in the sparring hall with a name like that." Bernard looked into his cup and took a drink to calm himself. "Although, I must say, it does sharpen your edge a bit. Boys thumping you because of your name. Who you are or, more importantly, who you are not." Bernard squinted at Louis as he worked to hold himself straight. He wanted to be angry at the boy for sitting in the first three seats at the funeral. Little Louis was innocent now, but more likely than not, his young cousin would plot his murder in ten years.

"You asked your mother for coins? You must know that queens do not carry coins. They have servants to carry their purse. What do you want with coins, boy? You are too young for dice and this is hardly the place."

Louis responded, "My cousin Narkus says that, when it is time, my brother and I can place coins on grandfather's eyes. He says it is a tradition of our people and that it will help my grandfather."

"Aye. It's done that way in some of the far-away lands. Not sure why. Does not seem like something that old woman Einhard would approve, but he is not here now, is he?"

The boy shook his head again. "Einhard, you don't like him, do you boy?" Louis looked at his mother then back at Bernard and shook his head with a smile. "Ha! Neither do I!" Bernard shouted. "I knew you and I were kin." Bernard pointed across the room. "Do you see that scruffy looking turd over there with the long white cloak?" The boy nodded for the first time. "His name is Marco. Another funny name, eh? He is an Italian. He is also one of my captains. I know for certain he has silver coins on him because he took five from me this morning. Go up to him and tell him . . . that Lydia demands he give you two coins and tell him Bernard told you so." Bernard nodded to the boy. "Trust me, he will give them to you. Go on." Young Louis looked to his mother who only looked away and the boy took that as a sign of permission to leave aunt and nephew alone again.

Judith scoffed, "I can only assume Lydia is some whore."

Bernard only laughed to himself.

She gave Bernard a stern gaze. "They are no threat to you, you know that. My boys."

Bernard brushed her attempt at sincerity aside. "Aunt, your cup is empty. Let me fill it for you."

Judith raised her hand as if Bernard was a servant. "That . . . is not necessary."

"Of course it is," Bernard said. "We drink our emperor to heaven, eh?" Bernard reached over to a table and grabbed a large jug and poured wine in Judith's cup until it overflowed and then he handed it back to her, sloshing more wine on her dress.

Judith squinted her eyes. "My boys are no threat to you, because Louis will kill you before their balls drop."

Bernard laughed towards the ceiling and shook his head. "Dropped balls? Have your husband's dropped yet? Are these two even his sons or does Oliver do all of Louis's sword work?"

Judith stood and splashed her wine on Bernard's face. Everyone in the room turned and stood silent. Germanicus sat back in his seat, grinning from ear to ear. Bernard frowned and laughed silently as he wiped the wine from his eyes.

"Next time, alert me first. I will open my mouth and we won't waste as much."

"You are no ruler!" Judith shouted.

"Ah! But I am the King of Italy. Should be much more." Bernard pointed over to the emperor's corpse. "He said so and Leo blessed me. Touched me with that same sword."

"You speak treason in front of all these nobles. I can waive my hand and these men around here will throw you into the barracks until my husband arrives and takes your head from your neck."

"Will they? I think not." Bernard stepped into the open space at the center of the room and commanded the attention of all in attendance with his booming voice. "Does anyone *want* to come arrest me for speaking my mind?" There was silence. Bernard threw up his hands and turned a circle to scan the room. "Put better, does anyone here think they *can* arrest me?" Ogier brought his cup to his side and took one step forward. His was the only movement in a frozen room. All eyes turned to the massive Dane who had seen his fair share of violence. Judith smiled in the hope that bloodshed was near.

Bernard's tone lost its levity. "I am drunk and cannot see clearly, but I could still snap your neck before you laid a hand on me. We have fought together. They might not know it, but you do. You stood by me when we were charged to burn Vienna to the ground."

Ogier stood motionless as the young man spoke the truth. He had seen Bernard butcher men indiscriminately with horror and awe. The young noble fought like a Peer of old and was not one to cross. Bernard continued. "You are a good man, Ogier. These nobles here. Him. Those two behind you. They would not piss on your Danish skin if you were on fire. Do not throw your life away for them. It is not worth it."

Bernard turned his back to the Dane knowing the giant would not seize the moment. Ogier's silence infuriated Judith. It showed in her expression. Germanicus raised his eyebrows in admiration at the young man's bravery. This was fine theatre that could only work to the Saxon's advantage.

Judith walked up into Bernard's chest with no show of fear. "You are a brute and even bigger fool. You make empty threats in front of every person that matters, save one. Your threats are just that, words you will not stay present to see through. You will run, won't you? Tonight. You will climb on your horse if you can manage and leave like a coward in the night. We will see if you have the same bravery when you stand before Louis and hear Oliver's warhorse charging from behind him."

Bernard brought his nose down to her nose. "I would cut off Louis's cock and shove it down Oliver's mouth!" There were murmurs of surprise. The young prince had now taken a step too far and he knew it. He scanned the room again for oncoming aggression, but saw none. He made his way towards the entry-way without any fear. There were no guards permitted inside the cathedral and the space that was given as he walked the room told him no one would challenge him that night, surely not after the Dane failed to follow through.

"Tell your husband that I do thank him for bringing me Lombardy. Beaten, not destroyed. They will firm up nice when it comes time to march around the Alps." Judith shook her head and Bernard's words began to clear as if the fog of wine had lifted.

"Oh, yes. I am afraid so. Your husband, in his great wisdom, left the mighty Oliver with only a skeleton of an army to hold and repair Lombardy. He sent the rest outside Verona as a show of strength for his upcoming negotiations with the Venetians. We have been watching from Southern Swabia with great curiosity. I sent word yesterday to have my men moved around into Friuli for provisions. By the time Louis arrives here, poor timing as usual, my men will most likely be dancing through the gates of Pavia. Oliver will be left running all the way to Rome, with his tail between his legs looking for sanctuary. He will find none. That is *my* city."

Judith shook her head again in disbelief and Bernard only grinned in return.

Bernard raised his cup in a toast. "I believe my work here is done."

Germanicus got the suspicion that Bernard had this spectacle planned and flashed a grin to show his amusement. Bernard looked around the room one more time with a satisfied look on his face. Shocked stares looked back at him as he departed. Bernard stopped short of the curtains and turned back into the room. All eyes followed him as he walked over to Charles' body. He knelt to one knee and gently touched his grandfather's hair. Bernard whispered something as he kissed his forehead and stood up.

Bernard grabbed Joyeuse. The magical sword had been placed in Charles' armpit. Bernard pulled the blade a few inches from the scabbard and the room filled with murmurs of fear. It was a real sword. A sharp blade. His grandfather had never let him touch it. It remained displayed high in the emperor's chambers, out of reach of curious little hands. Bernard had always thought it was a toy for show, cased in gold and gaudy jewels. If Ogier or another noble had the nerve to pick up Joyeuse and plant it in Bernard, his story would have come to an inglorious end right there. They did not and Bernard's luck stayed by his side. Only a fool would rob Charlemagne of the symbol of his power. A fool or the next emperor.

Bernard rewarded Judith with a wry smile and then a bow. He held Joyeuse in front of him and said, "Aunt Judith, I beg your leave . . . and I will be taking this with me."

* * *

It was dark and much closer to sunrise than sunset. What little moonlight there was had been hidden behind thick clouds. That was a good thing. Darkness was a much-needed ally. Bernard and his men didn't carry torches. Torchlight could give away their location higher in the hills behind the palace with only sporadic tree cover.

Bernard entered the mouth of the cave complex of the cauldron by walking sideways one slow step at a time. He had to be careful as the ground was rocky and unlevel. He turned around and grunted at his two men that had come with him. They were to stay on the surface. A large crude cross was carved into the side wall of the cauldron's entrance years earlier. It was too dark to see with his eyes, but Bernard knew where it was. He made the sign of the cross then kissed his fingers and touched the base of the carving.

One of his men whispered over to him. "Should you go down there alone? Should you even be here at all? This seems a risk with little reward."

Bernard chuckled lightly. These were good men, but did not understand what Bernard felt. He would risk all for this moment. Bernard responded, "This is probably the only place in Aachen where I neither need nor want you." He had been down there many times as a boy with his grandfather, but never alone and never at night.

"And if soldiers set upon us?" Marco asked.

"Do not worry about me," Bernard said. "Find your way over the cliffs before they come."

Neither Bernard nor his men had weapons other than daggers. They also exchanged armor for cloaks. Not their white cloaks that marked them as soldiers of the kingdom of Italy, but instead dark wool cloaks of peasants. Fighting armed soldiers that likely outnumbered them would have been a foolish exercise. Guile was the more prudent action. Bernard took another step down and looked back. "I do not intend to be down there long. Once I return, we will make our way out of the city."

There was a series of sconces bolted into the walls further below that bid its visitors lower. The light given off wasn't enough to illuminate the rocky ground, so Bernard pressed his hands against the narrow walls to balance himself as his feet searched for solid footing. The rocks became slippery too and he cursed under his breath with each step. As he walked further down, the entry felt like it was narrowing closer onto him. He got the sensation that he was entering the bowels of hell or at least something that was unnatural and unholy. It made him relieved that he kissed the cross at the mouth above. He reminded himself that his grandfather frequented the place, even at night. Despite its dark history, Bernard told himself that there was nothing diabolical about the place, not anymore.

The corridor was long, much longer than he remembered. The moment alone gave Bernard a moment to rethink what had transpired thus far and what was to hopefully follow. He had second thoughts about not only staying in the city, but also going down into the cauldron. Perhaps Marco was right. Aachen wasn't safe anymore.

Bernard had brought some of his own elite corps with him when he entered the city and secretly had the nod from several Peers, but Judith was the unquestionable commander of the city. She roused the palace guards to lock down all gates out of the city and patrol the streets for the rogue prince. Bernard had been expecting her move the moment after he stormed from the watch within the palace chapel. He had willingly taken off the mask of disenchanted grandson to show the face of a traitor. He knew the risks. He had planned for it. He welcomed it.

The corridor came to a merciful end. There was more light at the bottom of the steps where the space opened up into the great cavern. The ground had flattened. Fires from sconces reflected off the churning black water which gave off a low rumble and the sensation that the cauldron was alive. He had a good idea of where the rocks gave way to deep water. If he recalled correctly, the left side of the cave had much more room to maneuver, so he made his way to the brightest sconce along that side.

Bernard had already doffed his hood, but the steam was

becoming uncomfortably cumbersome, so he loosened the strings on his wool cape. A woman's voice echoed from the shadows.

"I have been waiting for you for some time, my prince."

The echo of the cauldron made it impossible for Bernard to discern the woman's location. He just looked out across the water as the steam rose and disappeared. He would talk to the cauldron and wait.

"I have been a little . . . involved," Bernard said. "You know that you are not supposed to be down here alone. It is forbidden to women who are not members of the royal family."

"I have heard!" The woman giggled. "Such senseless rules. I do not care. I am with you now; you will protect me."

Bernard responded playfully, "I am not sure I will be able to protect myself."

"Somehow I believe you could manage. How do you intend to leave the city?" The woman asked.

"I figured I would walk right through the old Roman gates. Will you come with me?" Bernard asked.

There was slight amusement in the woman's response. "No."

"We will move up the side of the main hill just behind here. Thick trees and steep rocks ark the summit. The cliffs are their own wall and require few patrols. We will buy off those we come across or kill them. Horses are waiting on the other side." Bernard scanned the space as his anxiousness grew. "Show me yourself. I want to see you."

Magdeh walked slowly up to Bernard from behind. She was still undetected. "Would you not rather feel me?" She hugged him from behind, grabbing his chest. He was too tall and broad for her hands to grasp each other. Her cheek was firmly planted in the center of his back.

Bernard looked down and saw her bare arms and assumed she was naked. "I had a dream the other night," he said. "You were lying in a field of lavender with white summer flowers in your hair. I did not touch you. I could not, no matter how hard I strained myself." He took her hands in his. "I asked an old monk what it meant and he said you were not meant to be touched. That you were above me. I go to bed wishing that same dream would come back to me again. I want to prove the monk wrong."

He let go of his grip and turned around to see her perfect body in front of him. It wasn't that she was short as much as he towered above all others. He could look her brother Clotho square in the eye. He inspected her through the torchlight and ran his hands over her breasts then pulled her back in. He breathed in her hair and remembered her smell from the last night they had spent together.

It was two summers ago, shortly after her wedding. Germanicus was forced to parade Magdeh around Aachen. Her wedding bed was already cold and the young Bernard was more than eager to fill the void.

Bernard kept his nose planted in her hair hoping her scent would rub off in his beard like it did during that first summer. Her scent must have stayed with him for a full fortnight after they parted. He noticed that her hair was dry although the rest of her body was beaded in droplets of water.

"I never truly cared for this place as a child," Bernard said. "I could never get over the smell. Sulfur to spark fires. Reeks of rotten eggs. I only came here to be with my grandfather."

Magdeh was scratching his back; her cheek was flat to his chest. "Smells like the rest of the country to me. There is no ocean breeze. No salt to clean the air."

Magdeh had kept her hands busy while the two were coupled. She unbuttoned Bernard's jerkin and loosened his breeches. "Come in the water with me. I know you do not have much time."

Bernard wasn't keen on the idea of stripping naked and climbing down into the bubbling water; it would be an inglorious way to die if soldiers came upon him. He kept his reservations to himself. He knew that Magdeh wasn't drawn to a man that worried about trivial consequences. She wanted the prince that walked fearlessly amongst his people and rivals, inviting them to conflict.

Magdeh waded into the water with grace as if she knew the placement of every stone that was hidden in the black underneath. Bernard stood on the ledge with his breeches around his ankles and fought with his boots. Magdeh watched him with a smile and a giggle as she settled into the churning water. She kept her body only half submerged so that her breasts remained out of the water and invited Bernard to come for them. He cursed his right boot until it gave way. Bernard stood tall showing himself to Magdeh. His face and body resembled the marble statues she had seen while walking the halls of the palace; all harmony and sharp lines. The statues missed one element that caught her eye the first time she saw him naked and could not be captured in marble.

For such a young body, Bernard was riddled in scars. His body was a book to her. It told a story of violence and a refusal to let slashes and piercings take his life. Magdeh didn't see them as signs of weakness. They were signs of protest that told of his rejection of death and she could relate. Bernard lowered himself slowly into the water attempting to adjust to the extreme heat of the water. She came to him and began kissing and caressing the scars. Her touch made the heat of the cauldron tolerable.

Magdeh sat him on a stone and straddled his lap. She kissed his mouth and neck while her touch calmly worked him hard below the water. He didn't want her to stop using her hands until she maneuvered him inside her. Bernard slid into her and clutched the sides of her neck to pull her all the way down. He gasped in pleasure and sucked the air from her mouth. He held her breath in his chest, hoping to consume a part of her.

She felt warmer and more mysterious than the first night they were together. Bernard submitted control to Magdeh and she took her time making sure he felt every tightening and loosening of her muscles as she gripped him and kept the cauldron's waters at bay. She kept her rhythm slow and her mouth along the side of his face. Bernard tried grabbing her hips to bring her down on him as far as possible. She pulled his hands free and placed them back on her breast. She wasn't going to let him go so easily. Magdeh kept her pace steady and pulled the back of his hair to force his eyes into hers. The wide muscles along his back began to flex and harden as his body tensed with the onslaught of pleasure. She felt him fill her inside. "You can have this as long as you want," she said to him.

That was what he wanted; more than the crown that had come to consume him. This wasn't the time, however, to test the hurdles that would see his desires realized. Talk of devious husbands or betrothals to little girls would have to wait, and that was only fitting. At that moment, in that place, they were the only two people that mattered.

The night in the cauldron was much different than the first time they made love. That first night was rough and quick. Pulled hair and scratched backs as Bernard took her against the shadowed wall of the palace kitchen. He had to do that quickly before someone found them alone. At that moment, that is all he believed they both wanted anyway. The days that followed would prove different. That early summer night was the first of many during Magdeh's first visit to Aachen.

He knew who she was and didn't care. Night after night, when Germanicus had passed out or was preoccupied with the women he kept in the capital, Bernard would come to her. The servants of the palace where not fully Bernard's to command, but they were certainly not Germanicus's and so they did the young prince's bidding, keeping their eyes to the ground. It became a game at first.

It was fun and intriguing as Bernard and Magdeh pretended to barely know each other in the company of others. Bernard would smile and nod to her as a sign that, later in the night, Magdeh would lay sweating on his chamber bed and he would blow on the little blonde hairs of her lower back. She was pulling him in and he did nothing to fight it.

Bernard hadn't pulled out of Magdeh even though he was now soft. It felt too natural to keep coupled with her. He knew that, if he did, it would start a chain of movements that would eventually lead to him being dressed and out of the cauldron to move pieces on a game board and fight for his claim. At that moment, his future didn't matter. The only thing that did was this strange and alluring woman that made everything else suddenly seem insignificant.

"What does your husband say about what happened at the watch?" Bernard asked.

"Nothing has changed. He will back you. He needs you now that he thinks he has some claim of his own. That bitch mother of his has filled his head with a fantasy that he is Charles's son. He is a fool." That was an absurd idea, even if true, but Bernard didn't feel obliged to voice his thoughts to Magdeh.

"He is a fool . . . and you are beautiful." He kissed her and found the taste of her mouth as inviting as it was the first time they were together.

Bernard had heard stories before he met her. She was a whore. She was a daughter of Lucifer. He didn't believe any of it then and, once she looked in his eyes the first night they came together, he didn't care if any of it was true. His man Marco would remind him that she was a pagan and that would be a problem even if Germanicus was out of the way. His nobles back in Italy would expect a marriage of alliance with a powerful Frankish family, which is what Wilfred's daughter represented. The Italians could be very persuasive. Then there was his mother, Bertra. She would be the toughest sheep to shear once she found out about his senseless choice. These were all knots that would have to be untied at some later date.

"Does Germanicus know you are here?" Bernard asked.

"He calls himself Arminius now."

Bernard chuckled, "Why?"

Magdeh responded, "He says that Arminius is his Saxon name. He has shunned the name given to him by Charles."

Bernard smiled. "He has timed his bravery very well."

Magdeh dug her head underneath Bernard's chin. "I do not wish to talk of him. He is not worth the little time we have together."

"You did not answer my question. Does he know you are here?"

"Here?" Magdeh asked. "I do not know. With you? I would hope not, but he is a cunning man. He schemes with every breath. It is as much in his nature to look for plots as it is to spin them."

"Is that what this is, a plot to punish Germanicus?" Bernard asked.

"If I said that it was, would you come to me again?" It was that way at first. She saw the handsome young king of Italy as a reckless weapon to harm her husband. Then she became fascinated with him. His Italian ways were more refined than the Franks, but he was not soft or womanly, which is what she thought of southern men. His fine clothes and noble disposition did nothing to reduce his manhood in her eyes. She saw him as an equal match to the most feared men from her northern world.

Other than her false marriage, the one aspect that kept Magdeh from completely giving herself over to Bernard was his slavish devotion to his god. He was such a puzzle to her. The man killed with such violence and lack of remorse. He drank with his men until he fell. He cursed without care and he laid with a married pagan woman.

He attacked life with passion and that was what drew her in. She first thought his faith was a rouse. She believed his talk of Jesus and the Church of Rome was as much a performance as the actors who came to Germanicus' court and brought her the Greek tragedies she loved so much. Then she would spy on him in the chapel, spending hours in contemplation. Somehow the man was able to cordon off his faith from his devotion to her, and Magdeh did not think him cynical for doing so.

She quickly took to Bernard out of true affection and desire, but instinctively guarded herself against falling too hard for a man she could never openly love so long as she remained Germanicus' wife. "You are no plot for me," she said. "You know my feelings as well as I know yours. Our eyes tell each other true. Yet we have walls between us that will not fall."

"Germanicus, or whatever he calls himself now?"

Magdeh responded, "He is one. My gods are another."

"If you say my eyes tell the truth, then look at me now." He gently tilted her chin up. "All I know is this: when I am with you those walls do not matter. I will climb over them. Or I will break them down."

"I am yours whenever you will have me. Tomorrow. The next day. For all time if you wish, but that is for you to see through." She wanted him to shout, for Bernard to break down those walls, but that was the wish of the naïve little girl who still prowled the back of her mind. Magdeh knew to shake her mind clear of fairy tales and collected her clothes. "When will I see you again? I am worried."

Bernard smiled. "Do what I ask and the next time we are together I will be placing those white summer flowers in your hair."

HISTORICAL NOTES AND AUTHOR COMMENTARY
AVAILABLE AT:

www.facebook.com/thecrownholder/

or

www.thecrownholderseries.com

Coming in the Spring of 2021:

THE
CROWN HOLDER

- THE DISEASE OF PROPHECY -